THE WARRIOR

& LADY REBEL

Lori,
So happy we are friends. Hope you enjoy my book.
Love,
Terese

Books by

TERESA SMYSER

Heaven Help Us!

The Warrior & Lady Rebel

THE WARRIOR
& LADY REBEL

A Novel

Warrior Bride Series, Book 1

Teresa Smyser

Copyright © 2015 by Teresa Smyser

Cover design by Aaron Smyser

ISBN 978-1519635297

All rights reserved. No part of this publication may be reproduced or transmitted in any form or by any means without written permission of the author. The only exception is brief quotations in printed reviews.

Scripture quotations are from the King James Version of the Bible.

This novel is a work of fiction. Names, characters, places, and incidents are the product of the author's imagination or used fictitiously. Any resemblance to actual events or persons, living or dead, is entirely coincidental.

***Dedicated to:**

Keith, my Warrior husband,
Who battles daily for our Lord and King!
I am blessed to be your Warrior Bride.*

***Acknowledgements:**

Heartfelt appreciation to my family
And friends for all their
Encouragement and support!

To my editor, Joan Orman.

To God, my Friend and
Creator of my imagination.
To Him be the glory!*

Prologue

August 5, 1611

    Lord Nicolas Fairwick couldn't wait to return home. His men and horses needed to recover from their last encounter. Why the king had sent them on such a useless campaign, he couldn't fathom. They gained nothing but lost much. Luckily, Nicolas returned with all of his men, except one. Poor Arnold. Trampled by his own horse when he became unseated during a skirmish. A wasted death. Nicolas shook his head. At least he had been more fortunate than Lord Sherwood and Lord Mathias of neighboring estates, who had lost numerous gallant knights.

    "My Lord, what is up ahead?" Thomas asked.

    Nicolas abruptly jerked back to the present at the sound of his brother's voice. Something white lay on the roadside. He couldn't quite make it out from the distance. "Thomas, take three men and approach with caution. It could well be a trap," Nicolas commanded through a clinched jaw.

    With one simple hand gesture, the rest of his men came to a halt. Each one kept a watchful eye on the nearby landscape ready to do battle if, in fact, it were an ambush. Thomas and the men approached with great care. The closer they came, the more clearly they could see. It was a body lying face down under a tree. The bare feet were slashed and bloodied. The dark hair matted with blood.

    Thomas slowly dismounted as the other three men stood guard. Leaving his horse, he crept closer, his sword at ready. He knelt down beside the body and turned it over. Thomas sucked in a quick breath. A woman! Mud and blood soiled her garment. Looking about, he saw the ground around the body was untouched—no tracks of man or beast. It did not appear to be a trap, so he stood and motioned to Lord Fairwick.

Nicolas rode up to Thomas and halted. Ten of Nicolas's men fanned out in a semi-circle around the body facing outward to be on guard against attack. Nicolas removed his helmet and rested it on his thigh. What he saw made his anger flare. Someone had badly used a woman and left her at his doorstep. Now she was his problem.

"Does she live?" Nicolas asked with irritation.

"She breathes, My Lord," Thomas answered.

Nicolas raked his hand across his dripping wet face as he blew out a snort. "Bring her." He replaced his helmet, nudged his horse, and proceeded down the path toward home.

Each man knew the history behind Lord Fairwick's family. The woman was a bad sign.

1

August 5 present day

"That's it," Elizabeth snapped as she jumped up from the couch, arms flying. After arriving in the states from her mission trip, she had driven straight from the airport to her boyfriend's home. She had wanted to share about her adventure, but he had other ideas.

"Now, honey, don't get mad. Any other girl would be elated if her man wanted to marry her," Jonathan said as he slid his finger down her arm.

Elizabeth jerked her arm away and snatched her purse off the table on the way to the front door. The screen door slammed shut behind her as she jogged down the steps to her convertible. She leaped over the car door and plopped into her seat. She needed to think. After inserting the key, she tossed her purse into the back seat and gunned the engine.

Jonathan followed her out on the front porch and shouted, "I'm not asking you again! Next time, you'll be doing the asking." He banged his hand on the banister as she scratched off without a backward glance.

Chewing on her lip, Elizabeth fumed as she merged onto the interstate toward home. Tired and feeling somewhat jet-lagged, she wondered why he had to bring up marriage when all she wanted to do was relax and share about her recent trip. Jumbled thoughts plagued her as she sped toward her apartment.

Lord, why does he continue to badger me about this marriage thing? How do I know if I'm really in love? Every time he brings it up, I get a sick feeling in the pit of my stomach.

While speeding down the interstate, panic set in. Her chest constricted as though iron bands squeezed tighter and tighter around her. She could hardly get a breath. She needed to get away from him and his persistent question. Drumming her thumbs on the steering wheel, Elizabeth decided to visit her grandparents. Nana and Papaw could always calm her jangled nerves. Their farm was located outside of Lexington, Kentucky, just thirty minutes away. It was a quiet and serene place, a maple tree canopy over the long driveway leading up to their home. The house hid among weeping willow trees. However, one of Elizabeth's favorite aspects of the farm was the barn which housed her sweet horse, Cinnamon. *A peaceful ride along the stream on the back property is exactly what I need.*

Elizabeth had just returned from her mission trip to Guatemala and was seriously considering becoming a short-term missionary. With her love for children, she knew she could have a positive impact on precious kids. *God, each time I think of marriage, I feel confused and my stomach churns enough to make buttermilk. Am I to marry and hope Jonathan will be enthusiastic about mission work or should I follow my heart and leave him behind?* Elizabeth had more questions than answers and didn't have a peace about anything.

Ten minutes later she screeched to a halt in a parking place at her apartment building. She hauled her luggage full of dirty clothes up the stairs to her second floor apartment. Leaving her suitcase right inside the door, Elizabeth hurriedly crammed clean underwear and toiletries into her purse. On the way out to her car she noticed her coffee table overflowing with envelopes and magazines that her neighbor had picked up during her absence.

Without a pause, she ignored the piled up mail and headed toward her car in an attempt to leave her worries behind. With music blaring and her hair blowing wildly in the breeze, Elizabeth headed to Lexington.

In no time at all Elizabeth had reached the exit for the farm. The rest of her drive was a leisure trip on the curvy road that would take her to her oasis. The corn fields looked like an ocean as the stalks swayed in the wind. Elizabeth slowed as she approached the farm and enjoyed the gorgeous flowers lining the road. In the warm breeze, the purple wildflowers nodded their heads at Elizabeth, as if welcoming her home. She stopped midway up the driveway to soak up the tranquil atmosphere as she listened to the birds tweeting high in the trees lining the driveway. That was another reason she loved her convertible; it allowed her to get close to God's nature. As she pulled up to the house, she exhaled a sigh of contentment . . . ah . . . no place like the farm.

She hurried up the stairs, yanked open the screen door and hollered, "Nana, Papaw, where are you?"

Shuffling noises and voices came from the back of the house. Elizabeth skipped through the house noticing how nothing had changed. Furniture and knick-knacks were just as she had left them . . . comforting. She burst into the kitchen. "Hi, ya'll," she cheerfully called out.

Papaw recovered first from her outburst and gave her a powerful hug. "Lizzy," he crooned into her ear, "what a wonderful surprise."

"Heaven sakes, dearest, come here," Nana gushed. After a warm embrace, Nana took Elizabeth's face into her arthritic hands. Studying her eyes, Nana remarked, "You look worn out, darlin'. I've warned you about doing too much."

Lightly taking a hold of Nana's wrists, Elizabeth leaned in and kissed her nose. "Oh, Nana, you always say that. I just needed to visit my two favorite people," she said grinning.

"Sit down, sit down," Papaw insisted. "You need to eat something. You're as skinny as a toothpick."

Elizabeth beamed. She could count on them saying the same thing each time she visited. She relished the familiarity of their words.

"Tell us all about your mission trip," Papaw said as he eased down into the kitchen chair.

"Papaw, is your knee acting up again?"

"It's nothing. I'm just old," he said with a grunt.

Elizabeth tried to catch her grandmother's eye, but Nana quickly turned around to continue making sandwiches. Elizabeth would need to question her grandmother in private. Something wasn't right. She could sense it.

"Get started, girl. I'm not getting any younger," Papaw said, patting her hand.

Elizabeth settled into the chair beside her Papaw. Nana brought their plates over and pulled out a chair as she joined them at the table. They ate lunch and sipped Nana's sweet tea while Elizabeth shared about her trip.

With only two years left of chiropractic school, Elizabeth had taken a break and spent May, June, and July in Guatemala with a mission team from her church. She had helped the doctor administer shots to the native children and treated their parents for various ailments. During the day when there were no patients, she assisted the teams who were telling Bible stories and playing games with the kids. At night the mission teams distributed food to the community and invited the local people to church on Sunday. Her three months flew by as her affection grew for the people. She missed home, but leaving her new friends in Guatemala was heart wrenching for Elizabeth.

After lunch Nana and Papaw retired to their room for a short nap. Elizabeth realized they needed to rest and was happy they didn't change their routine just because she was visiting. Unfortunately, she noticed how slowly they moved around since her last visit. Both of them would need help in the future if they stayed on the farm. Maybe she could get a job in or near Lexington so she could help her grandparents on the weekends. After putting her purse in her usual room, she decided it was a good time to see Cinnamon. Tip-toeing past her grandparents' room, she eased down the stairs into the kitchen. Elizabeth gently closed the back door and made her way to the barn.

Elizabeth stopped just inside the barn door, closed her eyes and let her senses take over. Scents of hay, manure, leather, and horse assaulted her nose. Ah-h-h . . . what a pleasing aroma. Cinnamon put her head over the stall door and nickered in welcome.

Elizabeth ambled over to greet her horse. "Hey, girl. Did you miss me? I certainly have missed you," she cooed while rubbing Cinnamon's velvet nose. She picked up the brush before entering the stall with her usual sugar cube. Cinnamon bumped Elizabeth's hand with her head in affectionate anticipation of what was to follow. Standing very still, Cinnamon swished her tail in contentment. The brushing was therapeutic for Cinnamon as well as Elizabeth.

"Let's get you saddled up and take a ride around the ponderosa. Shall we, girl?"

Elizabeth led her prancing beauty out of the barn and into the bright sunshine. She placed a blanket on Cinnamon's back before lifting up the saddle. After pulling the cinch tight, she adjusted the stirrups as Cinnamon danced around with eagerness. "Come on, girl. I know you're excited about a ride, but let's have some cooperation," Elizabeth laughed. She leaned into Cinnamon and rested her head against Cinnamon's neck. She took one deep breath before mounting—nothing like the familiar smell of horse flesh. Sitting atop her butter-soft saddle felt incredible after being gone so long. "Okay, let's go," Elizabeth spoke as they started out of the yard at a trot.

It was a gorgeous, summer afternoon in Kentucky with cloudless, blue skies. The black-eyed susan and red milkweed lined the babbling stream. As Elizabeth turned her head to gaze at the surroundings, her hair whipped across her chin. Oh, to feel the wind in her face and her horse beneath her. She began to relax as her burdens dripped off like wax from a burning candle.

Thank you, Lord, for this beauty. Your creation is majestic. God, help me enjoy my time here and give me clarity of mind. You know what a mess I am. I wish you would send me a letter with instructions for my life, but I'll be happy if You'll just grant me peace.

Elizabeth rode Cinnamon along the stream and circled back around to the barn after a two hour ride. Both horse and rider were exhilarated from their excursion. Elizabeth spent extra time mucking out the stall and giving her horse fresh hay. Then she gave Cinnamon a bath and a rub down before putting her back in the stall for the night. Elizabeth tended to lose all sense of time when she was with Cinnamon and was surprised at the late hour.

"You enjoy your oats tonight and be ready for me in the morning. Okay, girl?"

Elizabeth strode up to the back door thinking how blessed she was for a Nana and Papaw who kept a room and clothes ready for her. This convenience allowed her to come on the spur of the moment. How thankful she was for loving and considerate grandparents. She was closer to them than to her own parents in Nashville.

Opening the door, two aromas attacked her nose, barbecued beef and . . . men's cologne? Sitting at the table was her cousin, Garrett. *What is he doing here?*

"Hi, Garrett. What a surprise," Elizabeth said deadpan.

"What an enthusiastic greeting," he said sarcastically. "You know, Elizabeth, you're not the only grandchild who wants to spend time with Nana and Papaw."

"Of course, she knows that, Garrett. She's just teasing you," Nana said. Nana's attempt to diffuse the tension between the two of them didn't work for Elizabeth. "Garrett came to help your Papaw make some repairs around the farm. He'll be staying the night, as well, so they can get an early start in the morning."

Elizabeth helped Nana set the table while stewing over the fact that she had to share her grandparents with Garrett. She had been away for three months and wanted them all to herself. She had serious life issues to discuss with them and didn't want Garrett around. Plus, Garrett continually badgered Papaw to sell the farm to him which irritated Elizabeth. In her opinion Garrett was only looking out for himself, not for Nana and Papaw's best interest.

"Okay, you two. Your Nana has cooked up a mess of food, so put your differences aside and let's have a nice dinner," Papaw said sternly.

"Of course, Papaw," Elizabeth said as she kissed the top of his head. She took her seat as Nana began passing the food. Elizabeth's squinted eyes glared at Garrett, who sat across the table from her. Absentmindedly, she put food on her plate while she listened to Papaw tell Garrett about the needed repairs. Garrett was a smooth talker, and she worried about her grandparents' vulnerability. He had better not bring up selling the farm within her hearing, or she would do some physical damage to her selfish cousin.

Elizabeth barely heard the conversation swirling around the table. She was busy trying to figure out Garrett's angle for his visit. She would bet her new nail polish that Garrett had more on his agenda than just helping Papaw. A plan of attack was what she needed.

"Lizzy, are you ill? You've hardly eaten a bite," Nana commented.

"No, Nana. I'm fine. Really. Just a bit tired, I guess."

"First, I noticed how peak-ed you looked, and now you're not eating," Nana said as she stroked Elizabeth's arm.

"Leave her be, mama. She's a big girl," Papaw said.

"Yes, Nana, Papaw's right. Elizabeth's a big girl now. She's probably still recovering from her trip to Guatemala. Right, Elizabeth?" Garrett asked with a smirk only Elizabeth could see.

"Yeah, Garrett. You're right, as usual. I am tired. Nana, I'll save my meal for later. I think I'll turn in early if that's okay with you?"

"Well, certainly, sweetheart. If you're sure you're all right."

"I'm sure." Elizabeth reassured her Nana with a hug. She covered her food, placed it in the refrigerator, and then kissed her grandparents. "Goodnight to all," she added for Nana's benefit. She'd deal with Garrett in the morning.

As Elizabeth trudged up the stairs, she could hear Garrett asking Papaw the best process for growing tomatoes. *Oh, brother . . . Garrett could care less about farming.* He was up to something. He never helped with repairs even when he knew Papaw needed assistance. She figured God must have brought her here to protect her grandparents from Garrett's scheming.

Closing her bedroom door, Elizabeth kicked off her shoes which bounced off the bed post. She only wished Garrett's head had been their target. She rummaged through the dresser drawer looking for some bed clothes . . . ah . . . Nana had one of her own gowns in the dresser for Elizabeth. It was a long sleeved, white, cotton gown that reached the floor. Holding it to her nose, Elizabeth closed her eyes and breathed the smell of fresh air and detergent. The scent triggered joyful childhood memories of time spent on the farm.

While taking a steaming hot shower, she nicked her legs numerous times with a new razor Nana had left for her. Sitting on the edge of the tub, Elizabeth dabbed her deep cuts until they quit bleeding. No need to mess up Nana's gown. She turned out the bathroom light and padded to bed. After turning down the bed, she reached over and switched off the bedside lamp. Snuggled down, she took a deep breath and then slowly released it.

Lord . . . help me. I'm so mad at Garrett; I can hardly be in his presence. Thank You for nudging me to come for a visit. Nana and Papaw need me. Give me the words to say to Garrett tomorrow without upsetting my grandparents. For now, please blank out my mind so I can go to sleep. Thank you for all my blessings. Amen.

Later in the night Elizabeth's eyes popped open to total darkness. Something had startled her awake. With heart pounding and blood rushing through her ears, she didn't move. There it was . . . angry voices. Papaw and Garrett were in an argument! *Bam . . . bam.* Gunshots! She bolted upright at the sound. Frantically trying to untangle herself from the sheets, she heard a scream and another gunshot. In haste, she grabbed her old ball bat she kept under the bed and stumbled toward the door. Jerking the door open, Elizabeth rushed down the hallway toward the back stairway. On bare feet she tiptoed half way down the stairs and paused, listening. Hearing the back door slam, she hurried on toward the kitchen. She hoped to catch Garrett unaware and knock him in the head.

Sneaking up to the doorway, she peeked around the edge. The kitchen was empty. With the bat held at ready, she moved further into the room. Her eyes darted around and noticed the kitchen chair upturned. Blood dripped from the table and pooled on the floor. What had Garrett done with her grandparents? She whirled around and followed blood drops toward the kitchen's back door.

Emerging into the yard, the raging storm slapped her in the face. Rain came down in torrents. Where were Nana and Papaw? In a matter of seconds her drenched hair blocked her view; she couldn't see anyone. She raked her left hand through the matted mess and saw the barn engulfed in flames! Oh no, Cinnamon! As she dashed toward the barn, she came to an abrupt halt when she saw Garrett coming out of the barn. A gun still in his hand, he yanked on Cinnamon's halter. *He's trying to escape on Cinnamon.* Garret looked up when Cinnamon twisted in a circle. *Oh, no! He sees me.*

She was easy pickin's standing in the middle of the yard. With the house too far for Elizabeth to run back, she spun on her heel and sprinted toward the trees before Garrett could get off a shot. She had to get away from him.

"Liz, come back," Garrett yelled. "What's the matter with you? Where are you going?"

The storm was so fierce, she barely heard him. Thunder rolled and lightning flashed, but Elizabeth kept running. If she could make it to her old tree house, she would be safe. Garrett didn't know about her hideaway that Papaw had built especially for her. With a fleeting look backward, she saw Garrett running toward her. Thankfully, Cinnamon had momentarily escaped his hold.

God, help me.

The rain saturated gown weighed her down. She held it up with one hand while running for her life. Rocks and sticks cut into the soft flesh of her feet but nothing was going to stop her. The wet grass caused her to slip; the bat flew out of her hand. Her knee sliced open as she collided with a jagged stone. On shaky legs, she gulped for air as she pushed herself up. Her fear of Garrett was stronger than her pain.

God, help me. Help me!

As she raced through the underbrush, briars tore at her gown . . . grabbing her as fingers from the dark, scratching like fingernails. She felt her flesh tear as she tugged to be free from their grasp. No stopping. Her place of safety was close at hand. Her white gown was a beacon in the night. *Can Garrett still see me?* She dared not pause to look behind. Only a little farther.

Rain pelted her like knife pricks. The storm surrounded her as she sprinted toward her goal. The thunderstorm was like a double-edged sword. It drowned out her pounding footsteps, but it kept her from hearing Garrett's pursuit. There it was! Her rope ladder swayed in the wind. She frantically grabbed for it, but it slipped through her wet hands. One more attempt, and she had a firm hold on it. Her bloody feet slid on the rungs as she struggled to reach the first tree limb. She concentrated on placing one foot after the other until she reached the last rung. Her fingernails dug into the tree as she finally managed to get her stomach over the limb. Her feet struggled to be free of the gown so she could throw her leg over and straddle the limb. Once there, she secured the rope ladder out of sight. The tree house was farther up.

With great determination, Liz climbed to the next limb and grasped it tightly. She couldn't give up. Her life depended on her reaching the safety of the tree house. Thankfully, the tree was in full bloom with the leaves shielding her from Garrett's sight. At last, she reached the tree house high above the ground and crawled to the center of its floor. Tucking her knees under her chin with her arms tightly wrapped around her legs, Liz panted for breath.

God, hide my tree house. Hide me from Garrett. Please don't let Nana and Papaw die. I'll get help as soon as I can escape Garrett. Help me, please, help me!

Elizabeth kept repeating her prayer like a chant. The longer she sat still, the more even her breathing became. As her racing heart began to slow, she felt God's peace cover her shivering body. She could hear Garrett's voice off in the distance, heading away from her. Soon all she heard was the rain and the wind slashing through the night. No sound of Garrett. God had protected her.

Determined to outsmart Garrett, her mind raced with possible solutions—each one discarded as soon as it entered her mind. A circle of blood grew as her injured knee pressed against the white gown. God would provide a way; she was sure of it. She eased down on her side and tucked her feet into her gown forming a human ball. Before she could figure out her strategy, she fell into a fitful sleep.

2

August 5, 1611

Nicolas wasn't sure what he would do with the woman. He hoped she died before reaching the castle, therefore, relieving him of a decision. He didn't need another woman in his castle. His unwed sister was enough to deal with each day. Nicolas was tired, dirty, and disgusted with life. As it began to drizzle, he added miserable to his list of grievances. For all that was holy, God must be punishing him for his sins.

The one hundred men who accompanied Lord Fairwick rode in silence. The woman's condition filtered down the line through whispers. They knew her future was bleak unless she recovered quickly and left the castle . . . or died. Only time would determine her fate.

Nicolas rode in front of his men. He sat erect in his saddle setting a prideful example for his men. They would enter the gates unashamedly. The knights and fighting men under Nicolas's command were the best in the region. They had fought gallantly. Even though none could see any good coming from their campaign, no one had complained. Each time they rode out, it was at great risk to his men and his castle. However, the latest event—finding a woman—could bring a worse kind of disaster, if not to the castle life, to him.

After thirty minutes of travel, Thomas nudged his horse to catch up to his brother. Nicolas cut his eyes over as Thomas approached but made no move to recognize him. Mayhap, if he ignored Thomas, he would stay silent.

"Nick, a word with you?" Thomas asked.

Silence.

"Nick?" he repeated. *Silence.* "You can't ignore me forever."

"What say you?" Nicolas gruffly asked.

"This woman I rescued is heavy. She didn't look big on the ground, but she's dead weight. Since I have a wounded arm, might someone else see to her care?" he pleaded.

"Who would you suggest, Thomas? Who of the men is not weak from hunger and exhausted from our journey? Or injured? Who Thomas?" he asked angrily.

Thomas kept pace with his brother as he contemplated his reply. "You are correct, Lord Brother. When I think of the strongest warrior in our midst, I think of only one. Just one stands out as mighty . . . and strong . . . and vigorous . . . and . . ."

"Cease," Nicolas belted out with frustration. "Hand her over. I will remember your whining ways. The next time we're called into battle, you will be left home watching children." Thomas made the transfer to Nicolas without requiring either of them to dismount. Nicolas was greatly annoyed with the whole situation. Yet, he wrapped the body in his cloak to give her a chance for survival.

Thomas just laughed at his brother's gruffness. He had learned long ago to ignore his middle brother's sharp tongue. He knew Nicolas loved him from the way he had seen to Thomas's care since childhood. Thomas knew women brought out his brother's dark side. One day he would find out the reason for it, but not today.

Thomas dropped back into formation and left his brother to his own gloomy thoughts. Darkness was quickly descending upon them. Thankfully, only a few more miles, and the castle would be in view.

Nicolas glanced down into the woman's face. From what he could see, it was scratched and bloody. Her knotted hair stuck to one side of her face. He didn't know why Thomas couldn't carry her. She was as light as a child. One more peek confirmed his original thought; she wouldn't last the night.

With a hand signal, Braden, his battle commander, was at his side. "Take Hastings and Elwood and fetch Agnes," Nicolas commanded.

Those three men broke rank and rode off toward the village. They realized the seriousness of the injury when Agnes was summoned. She dealt with the critical ones. Many of the men were afraid of Agnes. Some secretly thought she might even be a witch. Of course, Lord Nicolas Fairwick trusted her—so must they.

Nicolas never tired of seeing his castle shining bright in the night. The gatekeeper heralded their arrival. Torches burned all across the parapet to welcome the weary travelers. Lord Fairwick crossed the wooden drawbridge first. He rode to the steps of the keep and turned to wait while his men rode past the gatehouse. All eyes were on him and his bundle. A few gasps quickly fell silent. No one would outwardly question his decision to bring a strange woman into the castle, but there would be much speculation.

"Phillip, have Abigail see that Collette prepares mother's room for our guest," Nicolas said with authority as he tossed Phillip a key he had extracted from the pouch attached to his belt. His older brother hesitated only a moment before he hurried to do Nicolas's bidding.

Watching his men ride through the gates filled Nicolas with great satisfaction. The processional took some time, but it reminded Nicolas that he had returned with all of his men except one—Arnold. Nicolas quickly crossed himself at the remembrance. Once all of the men were safely inside the gates, Nicolas climbed down from his destrier, the woman still in his arms. With long, confident strides, he strode past Angus and Jarvis who were waiting on the top step of the keep to welcome him home. They were too old for battle, but Nicolas kept them busy with other duties. He hoped they wouldn't question him, but he was not so fortunate.

"What have ye in thy arms, My Lord?" Jarvis asked.

"Naught of import, Jarvis."

"But, My Lord, it looks like a woman." Angus tried to peek at her, but Nicolas turned his shoulder and quickened his pace. He was in no mood to listen to those two or anyone else about his guest. Once inside, he strode past the great hall and made for the rooms above.

"Jarvis, be prepared to make ready all Agnes will need," he bellowed over his shoulder. He waited for no reply as he took to the stairs.

After speaking with Abigail, his wife, Phillip had stopped at the top of the stairs in stunned silence. His head swiveled around to see Angus and Jarvis shrugging their boney shoulders in bewilderment. He slowly descended the stairs after Nicolas passed.

"What think you, men?" Phillip asked.

"Trouble," was their only response.

As Abigail turned the key, the door opened on squeaky hinges. Nicolas had ordered the room locked after his father's death, and no one had been in the room for years. Abigail stood watch as Collette scurried to prepare the room adjoined to Nicolas's room. She knocked down multiple cobwebs before adding clean linens to the rope bed. One could access the room only by passing through Lord Fairwick's room. The two rooms had once belonged to his parents many years ago. Abigail shuddered and quickly crossed herself as she remembered Nicolas's and Phillip's father. He had kept their mother, Lady Isolde, a prisoner in her own home. Many times she was locked in her room for inane reasons. Some of the peasants believed the room was haunted by Lady Isolde who was trying to right the wrongs done to her.

"Hurry, Collette," Abigail snapped.

Collette rushed through her tasks to ready the room for the mysterious visitor. Once she was finished, she ran to fetch clean water leaving Abigail alone in the room.

"Is all at ready?" Nicolas asked.

With thoughts of ghosts soaring around in her head, Abigail practically jumped out of her dress at Nicolas's voice. She whipped her head around to see him filling the doorway. All her thoughts about ghosts flew from her mind as she viewed the woman.

"Yea, My Lord," she meekly replied as she curtsied.

"Stop with your act, Abigail. I have no time for it," Nicolas said wearily.

A flash of anger briefly passed across Abigail's face before she masked her emotions. She straightened up, pulled down the linens, and stepped away from the bed and him. He gingerly placed the woman on the bed and backed away.

"You will remain with her until Agnes arrives," he said as he spun around to leave the room.

"But, but . . ."

Nicolas ignored her sputtering and stalked out the door.

"Of all the . . . ," Abigail grumbled. "One day Phillip will take over his rightful place as Lord of this castle," she whispered to no one.

Standing near the bed, Abigail stared at the woman. From what she could see, the fine, white linen gown was muddy with traces of blood, but her feet and head were quite bloody. Abigail picked up a candle and leaned closer. Bending near her, Abigail noticed an unusual ring on her finger. From the jewels in the ring, the woman was someone of consequence. She set the candle down on the table and reached for the woman's hand.

"Abigail, what do ye here?" Agnes croaked coming into the room. She set down the water that Collette had given her when they had met in the hallway.

Abigail jerked back so fast that she stumbled over her own feet and bumped the table. She had enough presence of mind to grab the candle before it toppled onto the woman.

"Up to nay good if ye ask me," Agnes cackled.

"Don't talk to me like that, old woman," Abigail replied angrily. "You forget your place."

"Nay, I know me place. Ye forget yours."

Abigail was furious. She needn't be reminded of her lower position, especially by Agnes. With head held high, Abigail swiftly left the room without offering her help.

"Well, now, m' lady, let's take a look at yer cuts," Agnes droned. She laughed to herself over Abigail's reaction to her. She knew Abigail thought she was a witch. Many people were afraid of her because they didn't understand her healing powers. Their fear kept them away from Agnes which suited her well enough. She liked being alone. It allowed her time to test new herbs. God had gifted her, and she wasn't going to waste time dwelling on ignorant people.

Agnes gently wiped the woman's head and face. The lump on her forehead was alarmingly large. Something or someone had struck her with a hard object. Agnes tenderly probed her head searching for other cuts and bumps. Unfortunately, the woman never stirred—not a good sign.

"M' Lady, I must give ye a name. I can't keep thinking of ye as 'the woman'. Hmm, how about Lady Katherine? From the looks of this here ring, ye're royalty. I wonder if Lord Fairwick noticed it. I dare say, nay." Agnes continued talking to her as she methodically cleaned all the scratches and cuts. She hoped Lady Katherine would hear her voice and respond soon. The longer she went without waking, the less her chance of survival.

"Mmm, mmm, little lady, who beat ye and left ye for dead? Hmm? If only thy tiny, bloody feet could tell old Agnes the story." Agnes tugged the cloak free from under Lady Katherine and then resumed humming to herself as she washed and bandaged the woman's feet. Agnes had applied a cold compress to her face, but only time would heal the bruises and reduce the swelling around her eyes. Lady Katherine never stirred.

"She's in a dreadful state," Agnes commented. She didn't have to turn around to know Nicolas was in the room. She felt his presence.

"Well, I know it. I'm surprised she is still breathing," Nicolas whispered.

"Close the door. I want nary a one hearing us," she said.

Nicolas did as requested. He knew the need of secrecy as well. He came to the foot of the bed and waited.

"Her clothing is of the finest cloth and this ring . . . we must tread carefully with this one. She belongs to someone of import," Agnes remarked.

"Verily, I know it!" Nicolas boomed. Agnes gave him 'the look' and he had the decency to nod his head. "Forgive my loud voice," he sheepishly replied.

He disliked it when Agnes made him feel like a young lad who had misbehaved. He was the Lord of the castle, and she didn't care. Of course, that's what he liked about her, too. She didn't give him preferential treatment. Agnes treated everyone the same—friend or foe.

"I don't need an ill-treated woman in the castle. I could easily be accused of her mistreatment if 'tis some trap," he added crossly. "Unfortunately, my family history precedes me."

Agnes stopped her ministrations and turned to Nicolas. "Ye are not thy father."

"Thankfully, nay. But there are those who would bring me low over this incident and well you know it."

"Ye borrow trouble before it's time. Instead, ye should be pray'n for Lady Katherine's recovery."

"Who? You know this woman?" His voice had gone up a few notches in disbelief.

"Nay, M' Lord, but she needed a name, so I gave her one. I couldn't keep calling her 'the woman'." Turning back to Lady Katherine, Agnes resumed her work.

Thinking there was nothing he could do, Nicolas turned to leave. He was in need of a bath and food.

"Wait. There is something I want ye to see."

Nicolas came to stand beside Agnes as she gingerly removed the blanket from the woman's leg. "Look closely at her leg," Agnes encouraged.

He took the candle and leaned in for a closer look. His stomach quivered when he saw her well defined calf and small ankle. "I see scratches and cuts. What is it you wish for me to notice?" he asked with frustration trying to hide his reaction to her shapely leg.

"She has no hair on her leg. 'Tis smooth as a looking glass," she whispered.

Nicolas wrenched upright and took a step back. "What could have caused it?" he whispered back with wide eyes.

"I know not. A ritual . . . or possibly . . . torture?"

Rubbing his hand over his face, Nicolas said, "Speak of this to no one. I want no gossip traveling through the castle about it." Emotions churning, he strode over and unlocked his mother's trunk. Starring down at her clothes and harp, he took a ragged breath. "Lock the woman's gown and ring in my mother's trunk." He placed the candle and trunk key on the table and wearily left the room closing the door behind him.

Entering his room, he found Brigette standing near the outer portal. He was glad Agnes had insisted he close the door. He loved his sister, but Brigette could be a tale bearer.

"What do you here, little sister? Wanting to help care for our guest?" he asked. Nicolas knew Brigette shied away from anything that resembled work. She was nearly fifteen summers, yet knew nothing about running a household. The fault was his.

"Nay, brother mine. I came to see how she fares," Brigette inquired kindly.

"She does well enough, but . . ." Nicolas let his sentence trail off, for he knew Brigette's mind. She was worried about her place in his affection and its being usurped by another. Nicolas looked up toward the ceiling as if in great thought. He could hear her fidgeting from one foot to another. ". . . if she heals nicely and turns out comely . . . hmm . . . I *am* in need of a wife . . ."

"What?" she screeched. "You wouldn't dare. The king would have your head, and then Phillip and his hateful wife would take over. I couldn't bear it," she said dramatically as she fell into a heap on the floor. "You must send her away and quickly," she cried.

Inwardly, Nicolas cringed at her performance. "I grow weary of your theatrics, Brigette. They do not affect me. I will do what seems best for all. I don't need you to direct my thoughts," he said impatiently. With feet apart and arms crossed, he said, "Get up from the floor and leave me."

Pushing herself off the floor, she flipped her long, blonde hair over her shoulder. "Of course, Nicolas," she sniffed. After wiping her eyes, she asked, "Why is she in Mother's room?"

Leave it to Brigette to get to the heart of everyone's curiosity. "We know nothing about this woman, Brigette. She could be friend or foe. Therefore, she is secure in this room with no way in or out without going past me. I also control who enters the room. Does that satisfy your inquiry?"

"Yea. Thank you, Nicolas." He knew Brigette was trying to smooth over her miscalculation before exiting the room. She needed to stay in his good stead. Her future depended on it.

"Shall I call for your bath?" she asked.

"Yea, thank you," he said absentmindedly. Her fluttering eyes were lost on him as his mind had already shifted to the woman or more importantly to his reaction to the woman. Afraid his father's cruelty would manifest itself in him, Nicolas had forbidden unmarried women to live inside the castle walls. His mother's suffering had left a horrifying impression forever etched in his memory. Now, not only was temptation lying in his mother's bed, but she had ripped open a raw wound in his heart that he thought had scarred over. "God, forgive me, but please take her from this place tonight," he whispered.

3

The room was shrouded in darkness when Nicolas rose for the day. He had slept little, anticipating Agnes' telling him the woman, or rather Lady Katherine, had died. After dressing, he glanced into the adjoining room. Agnes dozed on her pallet beside the bed. He tiptoed toward the bed only to see the covers rise and fall with each breath. Oh . . . she lived.

"She has not stirred," Agnes grunted. "I will alert ye when she dies."

"It is probably for the best, but it will make it most difficult to find her family with nothing much to recommend her," he declared.

"Go, break your fast. I'll stay."

"I will send Colette to see to your needs." With those parting words, he left the room on his way to the great hall. His steps were slow; he wasn't looking forward to the inquisition about the woman or should he say, Lady Katherine.

Descending the stairs, he heard the usual loud talking and rattling of dishes. It was comforting to hear it after the last three months away with the King. However, as he entered the doorway, all eyes turned toward him and talking ceased. It was as quiet as a tomb. His footsteps on the stone floor sounded like a blacksmith's hammer.

He stopped in the middle of the room and slowly turned in a circle with arms outstretched. "Resume your meal. 'Tis only me. Nothing is amiss," he boomed. Mentally shaking his head, he walked up to the dais and sat down between his two brothers, Thomas and Phillip.

Thomas was poised to ask questions when Nicolas held up his hand. Without even looking at Thomas, he said, "Don't ask one question until I have eaten." He then dipped his bread into the porridge and cream. The bite was almost to his lips when he heard Thomas's aggravating voice.

"Yea, Nicolas. Not one question." Turning to Phillip, Thomas asked, "Did you see the woman Nicolas brought to the castle?"

"Out!" Nicolas shouted. "Now!" he added for emphasis. His neck muscles bulged as his face turned red. Nicolas lowered his scowling face and surrounded his bowl with his arms wishing he could make everyone disappear so he could eat in peace.

Thomas scrambled to leave the table but not before giving a hearty slap to Nicolas's back. "I love ye, brother," Thomas whispered in his ear before darting out of reach. Wearing a big grin, Thomas strolled out of the great hall.

"You know he does that to irritate you," Phillip said between bites.

"Yea, but he makes it nigh unto impossible to ignore him."

"I hear he talked you into carrying the wench."

"I'll give him a beating in the lists today for his senseless chatter," Nicolas groused.

Phillip laughed out loud. "Sorry, brother, but your misery is my amusement."

"Get your amusement elsewhere," Nicolas grumbled as cream dripped down his chin.

"On my way, dear brother. I must count the money," he added with a laugh as he moved from the dais. Phillip was in charge of keeping the castle books. Weeks following an unfortunate accident, Phillip had wavered between death and life. When death seemed inevitable, the title of Lord passed to the middle brother, Nicolas. Phillip survived but with great physical limitations.

Unable to sit a horse for any length of time, Phillip remained confined to the castle unless he traveled in a wagon.

Nicolas watched as Phillip limped from the hall. Normally, Nicolas enjoyed bantering with his brothers, but not today. He was tired from battling the King's enemies and disgruntled about his houseguest. It was enough to make his head hurt. He kept his head low as he ate his meal. Finally, most of the people had cleared out of the hall. Peace at last. Then Brigette bounced into the room.

"Oh, Nicolas, I didn't realize you were in here."

Nicolas inwardly groaned; another lie from his sister's lips. He barely lifted his eyes to acknowledge Brigette's presence. "What is it, Brigette, that can't wait until I have eaten my meal?"

"Oh, I don't need anything from you this fine morning. I came to get some bread and cheese to take on my ride."

"Where are you going?" he asked unconcerned.

"Eugene is taking me to see a nest of baby birds down near the beach." Her voice dripped with sweetness.

Jumping to his feet with hands planted on the table, "Not alone," he bellowed.

"Of course, I won't be alone. Eugene will be with me," she said with a huff.

Shaking his head, he continued. "You and Eugene cannot go alone without a chaperone. I have warned you of such impropriety. Colette and Hastings must accompany you."

"You just want to spoil my pleasure. I don't want those people with us," she screamed. "It's just behind the castle on the beach, and Eugene is eighteen. He can defend me," she added with emphasis. With fisted hands on her hips and a scowl on her face, she stood with feet apart.

"Abigail," Nicolas roared. The results of indulging his young sister were glaringly obvious to him. No one else would dare speak to him in that manner. Before Brigette turned to leave, he pinned her with his eyes, "Don't make a move. You are not going with Eugene. You are going to spend the day with Abigail learning household duties. If I am ever to find you a suitable match, you must know these things."

When she saw forcefulness had not worked, she tried her usual tactic—tears. "Please don't make me spend the day with that dreadful woman, please," she cried. "I'll forgo my trip with Eugene, but please don't send for Abigail."

"You will cease this caterwauling. Your insincere tears have no effect on me," he fumed. "I have been remiss in my duty to you and will rectify it today. Abigail!"

Abigail rushed into the room and came to a skidding halt when she saw Brigette. "Yea, My Lord, you called for me?"

"You are to spend the day with Brigette; I want her to begin learning the duties befitting a lady. Report to me her progress at the end of the day. Understood?"

Wringing her hands, he could tell Abigail wanted to come up with an excuse not to work with Brigette. "But, My Lord, I . . ." Abigail sputtered.

"But, Nicolas, please . . ." started Brigette at the same time.

With eyes flashing, he threw up his hands, palms out. "Cease, both of you. That is my final word on the matter."

"Nick, please, don't do this," Brigette persisted as she watched him rush out the door. "Ooo . . . I'm not going to do it," she said through clinched teeth. Spinning on her heel, she stomped from the great hall.

"Brigette, come back here. Lord Nicholas commanded it," Abigail uttered halfheartedly.

* * *

Without moving her head, Elizabeth cracked open her eyes and scanned the surroundings. Nothing looked familiar through her hazy vision. Her heart pounded in her head making it hard to think. The stabbing pain that ran through her body was nearly unbearable. She swung her eyes to the left at the creak of a chair.

"Ah, she awakes," Agnes commented. Slowly rising, Agnes stepped up to the bed. "We thought ye would be dead by now. Ye must come from hearty stock."

Confused, Elizabeth never uttered a word but continued to stare at Agnes. She didn't feel threatened by the old woman. Actually, her throbbing body grabbed her attention when she took a deep breath. "Oh," she moaned as her eyes slid shut.

"Careful, my lady. Ye have grave injuries. Surprised me, ye did, when I saw thy eyes open. A sip of water is what ye need." Agnes poured the water from a nearby pitcher into a crude cup. "Let me raise thy head. It's going to hurt, but ye must have water."

Agnes put her hand under Elizabeth's neck to pour some water into her mouth. Pain shot through Elizabeth's head like an arrow. With eyes closed against the excruciating pain, she bit down on her lip. Most of the water dribbled down her chin, but she received enough to satisfy Agnes. Agnes watched as Elizabeth slipped into unconsciousness. She would need to inform Lord Fairwick of Lady Katherine's surprising development.

"Nick, are you trying to kill me?" Thomas gasped. Nicolas continued to pound away at Thomas during their sword drills. "I asked your forgiveness for my previous comments."

Thomas was no match for his brother. Nicolas had met him in the lists, so he could teach Thomas a lesson. With Thomas eight years younger than he, there was no contest between the two.

Nicolas stood six inches taller than Thomas and outweighed him by four stones. However, Nicolas was relentless in his pursuit.

Hastings stood off to the side awaiting his Lord's notice. Agnes had sent word for Lord Fairwick, and he was to deliver her request. From the corner of his eye, Nicolas became aware of Hastings shuffling from foot to foot. Calling a halt to their practice, Nicolas gave a final shove against Thomas sending him flying into the dirt. Feeling vindicated, Nicolas headed toward Hastings.

"You have word?"

"Yea, My Lord. Agnes requests thy presence."

"Thank you, Hastings."

"Yea, My Lord."

"Braden, train the men," Nicolas commanded.

Nicolas left the lists on his way to the keep. Crossing the bailey, he quickened his pace wanting no one to deter him. Once inside, he ran up the stairs two at a time until he reached the solar. After bolting the door shut, Nicolas laid aside his sword. He took a rag and wiped his face and hands before entering the room to speak with Agnes.

"You have news for me?" Nicolas asked Agnes as he walked in.

"She opened her eyes and drank some water," Agnes reported.

"Did she say her name?"

"Nay. She uttered no words. Her pain was too great."

"What think you?" he asked as he looked at the woman's disfigured face. The swelling and bruises were those of a warrior. *How could anyone survive the beating she must have received?*

Agnes pondered a moment and replied, "She's a fighter. The next few hours will tell the tale, but I think she'll survive."

* * *

Before the sun was up, Elizabeth pried her eyes open and blinked several times. Her tongue stuck to the top of her mouth as she tried to lick her lips. She grimaced as she attempted to lift her arm with no success. After she failed to move even her toes, she felt panicked. *Am I paralyzed?*

"Help," she whispered. "Is anyone here?"

"It's about time," Agnes exclaimed, shuffling across the room. "I had almost given up on ye. Let's try another sip of water." Once again Agnes raised Elizabeth's head enough for some water. She was so thirsty; she choked trying to drink too much. Agnes quickly set the water down. "M' lady, ye mustn't gulp. Let's get ye propped up a bit."

She screamed out in pain when Agnes moved her. Nicolas burst into the room wrapped in a blanket. Elizabeth's head spun with dizziness from the commotion. She quickly closed her eyes to stop the nausea. *Where am I? More importantly, who are these people?*

"What is happening?" Nicolas snapped in a hushed tone. "She probably woke the whole castle with that scream. They will think I am torturing her."

"Calm yourself, m' lord. I must prop her up so she can drink and hopefully, eat. Plus, I need to change her soiled bed." Nicolas's surly manner never fazed Agnes. "Since ye are here, ye might as well help me," Agnes calmly replied.

Elizabeth was mortified. She was positive a bandage-like garment was swaddling her, and she was too weak to prevent them from touching her.

"I think not. I am not suitably clothed," Nicolas stammered out. "Colette is more capable in helping you. I will send for her at once."

"Nay."

That one word stopped Nicolas. Annoyed, he whirled around to face Agnes. It was hard to act lordly with a blanket wrapped around one's body.

Agnes continued preparing the things needed for Lady Katherine's fresh bed. "Ye will need to lift her gently and hold her while I change the bed linens. Colette can't possibly do it." She gave him a pointed look. "I'll wait while ye dress." She dismissed him by turning back to her tasks.

"Please, not him," Elizabeth whimpered.

Agnes looked over her shoulder at Elizabeth. "Don't worry, m' lady, I'll make sure ye are well covered. He'll see nothing," Agnes reassured her. "By-the-by, what would be thy proper name? I've been calling ye Lady Katherine," Agnes said with a toothless smile.

Elizabeth scrunched her face in concentration. *What is my name?* Her head began pounding from the mental effort. "I don't know," she said bewildered. The harder she tried to come up with her name, the more frightened she became. Tears formed in her unblinking eyes.

Agnes smoothed Elizabeth's hair away from the knot on her forehead. "Don't trouble thyself. It will come to ye as ye heal." Her encouragement did nothing to soothe Elizabeth's churning emotions.

When Nicolas entered the room, Elizabeth blinked which allowed her tears to escape. Nicolas froze in place. He knew how to deal with his sister's tears, but this woman was different.

"Stop thy gawking. I need ye to slide thy arms under her legs and back. Then carefully lift her off the bed. Ye must hold her until I am finished changing her bed."

Nicolas watched as Lady Katherine took a shuttering breath and closed her eyes. He wasn't sure if she was in pain or humiliated that he would touch her naked body. Of course, the blanket would protect her from his rough hands but not from the feel of her womanly body next to his.

He gently scooped her up. At first holding her felt awkward; then he cradled her next to his warm body. She tried to stifle a groan but was unsuccessful. Her eyes popped open with pain etched across her pasty white face. Nicolas experienced the first stirrings of protectiveness toward the woman as he peered into her frightened eyes. He knew exactly what to say. "Do not fear, my lady. You are safe." He used the same voice when soothing a horse or a child, and it always worked. When she looked even more distressed, he added, "Agnes is a well-known healer."

Elizabeth's body began trembling uncontrollably. She tensed her muscles in an attempt to stop the quaking but only caused herself more pain. Her whimpering and tears were more than Nicolas could stand. "Hurry, Agnes. She grows weary. I need to put her down," he muttered helplessly. Nicolas was almost as anxious as Elizabeth for the completion of the bed. He shuffled his feet and tried not to look at the woman's face. He felt like a cat in a pond—frantic!

"I'm finished. Ye may . . ."

Before Agnes could finish her sentence, Nicolas hurriedly placed Elizabeth on the bed. When he abruptly removed his arms, her covering shifted. Embarrassed, she started to cry. "I am sorry, my lady. Please forgive my rough handling," he gruffly remarked as he bolted from the room.

Tsk, tsk. "Pay him no mind, Lady Katherine. I'll put things aright." Elizabeth was certain her face could have lit the room without any candles. "Do not feel shame around old Agnes. Ye just lie still while I tend to thy wounds. Once ye feel more like yerself, then ye'll be able to take on Lord Nicolas Fairwick."

4

Five days later.

Leaning against the door frame with arms crossed, Nicolas watched Agnes finish brushing Lady Katherine's hair. Elizabeth could tell he was enthralled with the process. She was dressed in one of his mother's day dresses that Agnes removed from a trunk in the room. Pushing away from the door, Nicolas announced, "I am ready for Lady Katherine." He walked up to the bed and stopped near her.

"She is ready. Ye must carry her to the table. I don't want her walking on the stone steps," Agnes remarked. "Her right foot is not completely healed which could cause her to stumble."

Elizabeth listened to them talk as if she weren't in the room. She was feeling well enough, but his presumption irritated her. No one had asked her if she were ready to leave her room. Swinging her legs off the bed, she looked up at the arrogant man. "I will take my meal in this room," she said firmly. Trying to bolster her confidence, she continued glaring at him.

His eyes traveled from her dangling, bandaged toes that peeped from under her dress up to her face. Staring into her eyes, Nicolas curtly answered, "I think not, Lady Katherine. You have kept yourself hidden from our people long enough. They are anxious to see you."

"My Lord, I don't even know my name or how I came to be near your castle. I'm not ready to face anyone," she stated crossly. She had gone from a confident glare to an insecure scowl. He was an intimidating presence. From the size of his bulging muscles that strained the seams of his clothing, he could wrestle a bear and win. Even so, she wouldn't give in easily.

Ignoring her feeble plea, Nicolas plucked her off the bed. Elizabeth squirmed and pushed, trying to disengage his hold but to no avail. "Stop this selfishness at once," he grunted. Those words had their desired effect. She paused in her struggle and looked up at him.

"Why did you say that?" she fumed.

"You think only of yourself and what you want. Agnes needs a rest from her care of you; yet you want to remain in this room where she is a slave to your every request."

His words made a direct hit. Elizabeth was horrified that he would think such a thing. Her eyes swung around to look closely at Agnes for the first time—really closely. What she saw shamed her. Agnes was a petite, older woman with hunched shoulders. Her tired, weathered face had deep lines fanning out from her eyes and mouth. She looked rather feeble. *Why hadn't I noticed Agnes's frailty before?* "Oh, Agnes, I am sorry for causing you such distress. I never meant to take advantage of your proficient care," she said with heartfelt emotion.

Nicolas glanced at Agnes as they both shared an unspoken word. "Don't worry thyself, Lady Katherine. Lord Nicolas is overly protective of those in his care. I have attended ye out of me own desire. Ye take pleasure in thy midday meal, and don't give it another thought. I will make a trip to me home and gather fresh herbs." While Elizabeth was still in Nicolas's arms, Agnes softly patted her knee. "The walk will do me good. Ye will be safe with Lord Nicolas."

They both watched Agnes shuffle out the door.

As Nicolas shifted her weight in his arms, Elizabeth once again felt panicked. Unanswered questions raced through her mind. Stalling for time, she blurted out, "Before we go, might I ask you a few questions?"

Nicolas tilted his head and studied her face. She figured he wanted to ask her questions, too; so why was he hesitating? His eyes narrowed to mere slits. What was he thinking? She wanted to squirm but instead held her breath wondering what he would do next.

Elizabeth thought he was ignoring her request as he proceeded to walk out the door into his solar. Instead he placed her in one of the chairs flanking the fireplace. He then sat in the chair opposite her and said, "Well, my lady, it seems odd you would wait this long to ask questions." Fidgeting under his direct stare, Elizabeth licked her dry lips and smoothed out her dress. It was hard to appear confident when her feet didn't quite reach the floor. He continued, "I have some questions of my own. So when you have finished, then I will inquire of you. Can I trust you to answer honestly?"

It was all Elizabeth could do not to launch herself at the egotistical man. Did he truly think she would lie? Inwardly seething, she held her tongue and nodded her head affirmatively.

Nicolas leaned back in his chair to await her first question. With the flip of his hand, he indicated for her to begin.

Inwardly, Elizabeth cringed as she watched his hand flip again with an impatience he wore like a cloak. Even though his haughtiness irritated her, he was the one who could give her answers. Taking a fortifying breath, she asked, "First, will you tell me when and where I was found? Then I would like to know what has transpired since you first saw me."

Nicolas had no trouble remembering all the details of her appearance. After he told her about Thomas spotting her on the roadside and her vast injuries, he watched her closely. His eyes bore into hers as if he hoped to see all the answers deep within. Did he think he would discover her true identity simply by glaring? Elizabeth was unaware that her facial expressions were telling a story: thoughtful, confused, and then frightened.

With steepled fingers resting against his chin, he calmly asked, "Have I satisfied your curiosity?"

"Yes . . . for now," she whispered. Elizabeth felt depressed. Nothing he had said jogged her memory. It sounded like a tale about someone else—not her. Her downcast face and slumped shoulders told their own story.

"What is your name and where do you hail from?" he asked.

Elizabeth's eyebrows came together in concentration. Unintentionally, her fingers rubbed across her forehead. It was obvious she was making every effort to remember but couldn't. Then her tortured eyes met his.

"I don't know my name," she faintly replied. "I can't remember anything before I awoke in your castle."

"What if I don't believe you?"

Elizabeth came out of her depressing musings and held him with a penetrating look. She could feel her face heating up as she burned with anger. Leaning forward with a tight grip on the chair, "You think I'm making this up? You think I'm play acting? Are you out of your mind?" she shouted. She forgot about the deep cut on the heel of her right foot and jumped to her feet. A sharp pain shot through her foot and ran up her leg. She screamed out in pain and crumpled to the floor.

Nicolas must have been surprised at her fiery attack since he didn't react quick enough to catch her before she hit the floor. He swiftly knelt down to assist her. She wrapped her arm around his neck as he picked her up. Once he had her back in the chair, he captured her ankle and stretched out her leg. She attempted to snatch her foot from his grasp but to no avail.

"Let's see if you reopened your wound."

Propping her foot on his knee, he tenderly removed the bandage to see the damage. An unfamiliar tingling sensation raced up her leg and landed in her stomach as he held her tiny foot.

For such a brawny man, Elizabeth thought he had a soft touch much like a feather dancing across her arch. She found she liked the feel of his fingers on her foot and ankle. Looking at his bent head, she wondered why there wasn't a wife in the picture. He was handsome, powerfully built, and owned a castle. Of course, it could be his overbearing manner that had the women running in the opposite direction.

"Are you married?" she blurted out.

His hands stilled. Slowly raising his head, he stared into the fireplace mulling over his answer. Following his long pause, he simply said, "Nay." Never looking at her, he finished wrapping her foot and gently released it. When he stood up, his knee cracked. Reaching down, he rubbed it before easing down into his chair.

Elizabeth watched him with confused fascination. *Papaw, is your knee acting up again?* As that thought flashed in her mind, pain exploded in her forehead. "Agh!" she hollered. Her hand immediately went to her face as she swayed in the chair and fell back.

"What is it, Lady Katherine? Is your foot causing you anguish?" Nicolas asked reaching for her. Her eyes rolled back into her head showing only the whites. Grabbing her arms and shaking her, "Lady Katherine, what is amiss?"

Her head flopped back and forth when he shook her. He gripped her chin and lightly slapped her cheeks. "Lady Katherine, stop this at once. Wake up," he demanded.

Groaning, her eyes twitched open. "Wh—at?" she mumbled.

With his face near hers, Nicolas said in a hushed voice, "You had some type of a tremor."

Trying to focus her eyes, she put her hand on his chest and gave a slight shove. "Move back. You're in my space," she mumbled.

Stepping back, Nicolas starred wide-eyed. He acted as if trees had suddenly sprouted from her ears. Elizabeth tried to clear her fuzzy head. With her head bent forward, she briefly rubbed her eyes, and then leaned her head back against the chair. "Whoa, that didn't feel very good."

"What caused your strange reaction?" Nicolas asked.

"Well . . . let me think . . . it was when your knee cracked," she declared.

Rubbing the stubble on his face, he remarked, "My knee had nothing to do with what I just witnessed."

"No, it wasn't your knee, but the memory it provoked. I remembered saying something to my papaw about his knee," she exclaimed as she jerked upright in the chair. Her heart was racing from the excitement of that brief memory. "Maybe this means I'll remember other things soon. Then I'll know where I belong and can get out of your hair," she said with a smile. "At least we know I have a grandfather."

Nicolas wasn't sure how he felt about her recent memory, but he personally knew she had not been in his hair. He would have remembered a woman raking her fingers through his hair. It would have been extremely pleasing. Mentally chastising himself, he tried to focus on her other comment. She was probably right. The sooner she remembered, the sooner he could return her to her family. ". . . tis a good thing, this memory. I will be happy when you are home. I have much to do besides watch over you."

That man could take a pleasant time and shred it like paper. She didn't need to be reminded of the inconvenience she was causing him. He made it apparent at every opportunity. "Have no fear; I'm working on my recovery as fast as I can. I want to leave as much as you want me gone," she said through gritted teeth.

There it was again, her strange speech. Have no fear, indeed. He was afraid of nothing nor anyone. However, he enjoyed their sparring too much for his comfort. As they ogled one another, Nicolas said, "Due to this questioning, we've missed the meal. You may remain here. I will send food to your room."

"Fine," she snapped. She eased out of the chair and hopped on one foot toward her room while holding her dress with both hands. As she heard him rise from his chair, she added without turning, "I don't need your help. Thanks anyway."

"You made a wrong assumption, Lady Katherine. I wasn't going to offer my help." What was the matter with him? He sounded childish even to himself. Running his hand through his hair, he twisted around and left the solar before saying something equally foolish.

* * *

Later in the morning before the noon meal, Nicolas had sent Collette to check on Lady Katherine since Agnes had not returned from the village. His nagging conscious would not leave him alone after his unkind remarks to her when they last spoke.

In her sleep, Elizabeth dreamed of an approaching storm. Leaves whirled around like a funnel while a flock of birds flew and dipped looking for a safe haven. When one bird flew into her shoulder, she jerked awake with a start only to find Collette shaking her shoulder.

"Oh, my lady, you startled me," Collette said as she jumped back from the bed and her hand fluttered at her chest.

Groggily sitting up, Elizabeth's fingers lightly brushed the hair from her face. "I'm sorry, Collette. I was dreaming when you touched my shoulder and thought a bird attacked me. Silly me."

"'Tis only me, Lady Katherine. Lord Fairwick said you had had a rough morning, and I should check on you since Agnes has not returned from the village."

"My foot is still quite tender, but I'm feeling somewhat better after my short nap. Can you assist me to the chair by the window in Lord Fairwick's room? I enjoy watching out the window at the hustle and bustle of the castle folk."

"Surely, Lady Katherine. Let me . . . "

All of a sudden a loud commotion developed in the hallway. Feet pounded up and down the passageway. "Collette, go see what is happening!" Elizabeth said as she sat up on the edge of the bed. Before Collette even made it through the doorway into Nicolas's room, Thomas burst into the room carrying Pierce in his arms.

"Where's Agnes?" Thomas demanded.

"She hasn't returned from the village," Collette quickly replied. "What is amiss?"

Elizabeth had hobbled from her bed into Nicolas's room and was hanging onto the door frame listening to the exchange.

"Henry and Patrick dared Pierce to swallow the egg they found while exploring. We think Pierce has swallowed a grass snake egg. I need to find Agnes immediately."

"A snake egg!" Collette screeched.

Instantly, Elizabeth started barking out orders. She needed herbs, plants, and a clean chamber pot brought to the room at once.

Where the knowledge came from, she didn't know. She was just relieved the remedy was pumping from her brain to her lips.

Thomas stood dumbfounded in the middle of the room with Pierce still in his grasp. "Carefully, set him down in this wooden chair by the window. Make sure you don't jostle him around," Elizabeth said with authority.

"I don't feel good," Pierce whined.

"You shouldn't have eaten anything on a dare," Thomas said disgustedly. "Henry and Patrick are not to be trusted when they plot together."

"Thomas," Elizabeth reprimanded.

Pierce began to cry in earnest. "Am I going to die?"

"Not if I can help it," Elizabeth reassured him. She grabbed and pulled on Thomas's arm so he could help her over to where Pierce sat. Once there, she knelt down in front of him and placed her hand on his knee. "Try to sit very still, and please don't cry. It churns up your stomach. In fact, why don't you tell me what you boys were doing? Okay?"

Momentarily, Pierce's attention changed direction. He quieted down enough to retell the events of the day. While he was recounting all that had happened, Elizabeth mixed water with the herbs and plants that Collette had collected from the kitchen cooks. Silent prayers were on her lips as she worked quickly to produce the remedy Pierce needed. *God, help me. Don't let that snake hatch inside his stomach before I can give him this mixture. Please. Guide me.*

"Now, Pierce, I want you to drink this tonic straight away."

"Will it taste awful?" he whimpered.

"Pinch your nose and you won't taste a thing. Drink up," she encouraged.

Collette stood nearby with her hands folded together in prayer while Thomas huffed with annoyance. Elizabeth held her breath in anticipation. "Collette, the chamber pot, please."

"I don't feel good," Pierce moaned as he clutched his stomach. "I think I might be sick."

Elizabeth was ready with the chamber pot when Pierce heaved up his stomach contents. She watched as the egg propelled out with great force. As soon as it hit the pot, the shell exploded into fragments. All three adults leaned over to see if a baby snake wiggled free but only saw blue shell pieces with what appeared to be a yolk.

"That wasn't a snake egg!" Thomas said with annoyance. "It was a bird egg. Pierce, do you boys not know the difference between a snake egg and a bird egg?" he asked as he slapped his hand against his thigh. Thomas tramped over to the door and abruptly turned back. "You had me believing you were in grave danger!"

"Thomas. Please. Pierce has had a terrifying experience. Do not compound the crisis with your unkind accusations," Elizabeth pleaded when Pierce began to cry again. Still at the feet of Pierce, Elizabeth tried to soothe him as she patted his knee. "It will be all right, Pierce."

"Your parents will hear of this," Thomas said as he left the room.

"Oh dear," Collette breathed.

5

Through the door, Elizabeth could hear Lord Nit-wit fumbling around. She was determined to get out of her room today before he came banging on her door; therefore, she had slept in her dress. Easing out of the bed, she hurriedly used the chamber pot and slid it back under the bed. Elizabeth felt certain she had never used a chamber pot before arriving at the castle. Using a ribbon, she tied her dark hair at the base of her neck letting it fall between her shoulder blades. She hobbled over to the dressing table and splashed water on her face and hands. After drying off, she limped to the door and jerked it open, hoping to startle the bigheaded bum.

Hearing the door bang open, Nicolas wrenched around to see Lady Katherine tottering into his room. With her head held high, her gaze averted, she tried to flounce past him. He reached out, snagged her arm, and held fast. She eventually turned scorching eyes his way.

"Where are you headed so early this morrow, Lady Katherine?" he asked mockingly. Still holding her arm, his eyes traveled over her body.

She had a hard time concentrating with her face inches from his bare chest. Snatching her eyes upward, she said with confidence, "I'm going to break my fast with Thomas. Pray, release me." Even though it tasted strange to Elizabeth, she could spit out their dialect when needed. She had picked it up by listening to Agnes and Colette during her recovery.

"Nay, my lady. I will accompany you this fine morn. You may have a seat near the fireplace while you wait," he said with authority. He left no room for negotiation. Sweeping her off her feet, he deposited her in the chair.

Elizabeth bristled under his direct stare. Furious with his high-handed manner, she held her tongue. This battle wasn't worth her effort. While she simmered, she decided Lady Katherine was not for her. She was going to change her name. No doubt that would aggravate his lordship.

"I no longer will be called Lady Katherine. My new name is Lady Penelope." She wasn't sure why, but she liked that name.

Pausing while buckling on his scabbard, he looked directly at her. "What a preposterous name! You will remain Lady Katherine."

"Nay. You may control my life, but you will not choose my name. It is Lady Penelope," she said with boldness.

Nicolas contemplated her defiant stare. "You are right. I have power over your life while you are basically helpless. I'm a reasonable man," he began while ignoring the rolling of her eyes, "you may change your name if you wish. Is Penelope your given name?" he asked with an arched brow.

Blowing out a snort, "I've told you; I don't know my real name. Believe me; I'll shout it in your ear when I remember it." Elizabeth tended to switch back to the speech that came natural to her when she was angry.

Pinning her to the seat with his eyes, he decreed, "I give you leave to speak your mind when we are in this solar, but you will hold your disrespectful tongue in the presence of others. Is that understood?"

She chewed on her upper lip and squinted her eyes while deliberating over his request. "Does that mean I'm not to speak to you at all outside this room?"

She saw the moment Nicolas picked up on her slight sarcasm. "That is not my meaning, and well you know it." He strode over to the chair and peered down at her. *Uh, oh, I might have pushed him too far.* "I said your disrespectful tongue. If you can be respectful toward me as the Lord of this castle, then you may address me. If not, you might find yourself inhabiting the dungeon."

Feeling uncertain of lord blockhead, she said, "I'm a reasonable woman . . ."

* * *

Her choice of words was not lost on Nicolas. Even in a weakened condition she could hack a man to death with her tongue. She would make a worthy adversary. As she continued to ramble on, he took in her appearance. Today she had a sparkle in her eye like the sun reflecting on water. With the reduction of swelling in her face, she was quite comely. Her hair was neatly tied back, but her dress was rather wrinkled as if she had slept in it. No doubt she was planning something today, but what was the question. He had best keep a sharp eye on her activities since he didn't fully trust her . . . yet.

". . . agreed. Now let's eat. I'm starved." Pushing out of the chair, she lost her balance and grasped his arm. Instinctively, his muscles bunched underneath her hand. "Without a doubt, I had better stay on your good side. These arms could squash me like a bug."

"Starved . . . what an unusual word to use. I know for a fact you are not starved, as you say. Agnes kept you well fed. In addition, I have held your weight in my arms. You are not just bones."

"Obviously, your word choice and mine are different. I'm not sure why," she said thoughtfully, tilting her head. "All I know is words just leap into my mind, and I say them."

"You must have a care, my lady, for some might think you are . . ." He made a quick glance around the room and then whispered, ". . . a witch. And you do not want to be the prey of a witch hunt. It is a horrendous occurrence. You must guard your tongue for your own safety."

"As you say. May we please break the fast? I'm famished."

Inwardly groaning, Nicolas offered her his arm which she gladly accepted. He was considerate of her sore foot as they sauntered down the passageway. Her curiosity attributed to part of the slowness. Her head swiveled as if on a pole. She tried to get a glimpse through every open doorway. She commented on the thick doors which Nicolas explained were mainly for safety but also afforded much needed privacy and warmth.

The floor was made of stones that were uneven in nature. She carefully picked her way so as not to stumble. There were a few scattered burning torches on the walls to light their way. However, much of the walk was in the shadows until they passed the occasional window where light filtered in through filmy glass.

Nicolas took the opportunity to inform her about his castle. His mother's grandfather had been awarded the castle as payment from the King. With its being close to Scotland's border, it was a strategic stronghold. The castle had passed down the family line to her father and then to her husband, Nicolas's father. There were constant repairs to fortify the walls and secure the castle which provided safety for his people. He was confounded when she thought the buttery was where they made butter instead of where the wine was dispersed. Mayhap it was the bump on her head that muddled her recollection. He just hoped she would not have a permanent loss of memory.

At long last they arrived at the great hall and stopped in the doorway. Thomas and Phillip sat at the dais awaiting the meal while several knights were conversing near the fireplace. The majority of the warriors took their meals in the knights' quarters. There were a variety of men and women sitting on benches at long tables.

Elizabeth slowly perused the room. A couple of young boys about eight years old and several young women were preparing the tables with food and drink. There was some sweet smelling blossom crunching under their feet as they scurried about. Each person possessed a small knife to use during the meal. Four large dogs were lying by the fireplace producing an unpleasant odor of wet, dirty dog. Nicolas noticed her unconsciously wrinkle her nose.

Thomas was the first to notice the new arrivals. "Welcome, Lord Nicolas and my lady," Thomas announced with a bow—ever the charmer. "We are so honored to have you break your fast among us." After his declaration, all attention was on Elizabeth.

Nicolas could feel her hand tense on his arm. He reached up, patted her hand, and offered her his first smile before proceeding. "May I present, Lady Penelope."

Nicolas could see the confused expressions on faces as they bowed in her presence. Hopefully, she wouldn't keep that name for long. Even the serving girls had stopped their duties to gaze upon her. Maybe it wasn't the name causing their odd expressions; it could be her face. Thankfully, she hadn't asked to see a mirror, or he would have had to use brute force to get her to the great hall.

"Come, you will join us at the head table," Nicolas murmured. They maintained a slow, steady gait across the floor as each person followed the procession with questioning eyes. The serving wenches snapped out of their bemused stance when Nicolas glared at them.

"I think I must have horns growing out of my head," she remarked. "Even those young boys look shocked."

"Nay, my lady. They are quite dazed at your beauty. You have them bewildered," he said with amusement.

"Humph."

"Come, Lady Penelope. You may sit beside me," Thomas offered, grinning.

Elizabeth settled down between Thomas and Phillip while Nicolas took his place on the other side of Phillip. He didn't want his men to think he was enthralled with the woman. It was best to separate from her.

"We were quite troubled over your welfare, Lady Penelope. You have been sleeping overlong," Thomas commented with emotion.

"Thank you, Thomas, for your concern," she said. Even though Nicolas was not next to her, he was well aware of her every word. If she said the wrong thing, she would be on the receiving end of his displeasure.

"Where are Brigette and Abigail?" Nicolas asked with annoyance. "They know that I require our family to eat meals together."

"Abigail was ill this morn," Phillip answered. "You know Brigette; she does what pleases her. Mayhap she's having one of her peculiar weeks."

Nicolas grumbled to himself. Brigette frequently angered him. Mayhap he would introduce her to Lady Penelope and let her deal with Brigette while she resided at the castle.

"You are looking much improved. I thought you would be dead by now," Thomas said.

Elizabeth giggled at Thomas's blunt remark.

"Thomas," Nicolas roared. "Be mindful of what you say."

"Pray, forgive me, my lady. I meant no disrespect," Thomas replied shamefaced. His youthfulness was apparent when compared to his older brothers. "'Tis I that found you," he boasted as he sat up taller.

"I thank you, Thomas, for your keen eye. I shudder to think what would have become of me if you hadn't taken notice."

Elizabeth stumbled in her conversation as she viewed the food. She picked through what had been placed before her. "Is this oatmeal?" she whispered to Thomas. "It certainly doesn't taste like anything I remember."

"Yes, my lady. It is a cereal made from oats," he whispered back.

"Lady Penelope . . . most unusual," Phillip remarked. "Is that a family name?"

She rotated her head to look directly at Phillip. "I made it up, Phillip," she said with down-turned lips. "I'm having trouble remembering my name or anything else for that matter." Unshed tears pooled in her eyes before she lowered head.

"Pray, forgive me, my lady. It would seem the Fairwick brothers are causing you undue distress."

"'Tis alright. I am recovering and will remember my name soon. But, enough of that. Mayhap one of you wouldn't mind showing me around the castle grounds today. I am in need of some light exercise and sunshine."

"Oh, there is much to see at Fairwick castle. Outside the walls of the keep, the place is bustling with people. What interests you, my lady?" Thomas eagerly asked.

"I am mainly interested in your horses," she beamed.

"Ah. We boast several barns that house our war horses. They are most magnificent." Thomas glowed with pride. "I would be honored to show you around our home."

"Thomas and Phillip have duties to perform, Lady Penelope. I will see to your outdoor activity," Nicolas instructed.

Thomas's face showed his disappointment.

Sighing deeply she replied, "Of course, my lord." Staring at the food, she decided she couldn't choke down another bite. Turning to Thomas she said with a smile, "Thank you, Thomas, for enjoyable conversation." If his red face was an indicator, Nicolas was fairly certain Thomas was smitten.

All three men stood when Elizabeth left the table. As she brushed past Nicolas, she whispered, "I'll await you after I am refreshed." Nicolas noticed how every male in the room followed her exit with their eyes. No doubt, each was fascinated with Lady Penelope. The less they knew about her the better.

"She seems quite tame," Phillip observed.

"Do not be fooled, brother. She is not what she appears," Nicolas sighed.

"I hope we have a chance to find that out for ourselves," Thomas grumbled.

"Thomas, you need to concentrate on your own duties and not bother with Lady Penelope. She will not be here overlong."

Nicolas could tell Thomas was angry with him over Lady Penelope. He didn't need a woman coming between him and Thomas. The brothers had a life together, and it did not include her. After giving his daily instructions to Phillip and Thomas, Nicolas headed out the door to find Lady Penelope. He didn't have to go far. She was standing just outside the great hall talking with Colette.

"Come, my lady. We will take a short stroll around the grounds. Any more than that and Agnes will be most displeased."

* * *

"Did ye see her?"

"She was in the great hall seated between Thomas and Phillip," he whispered.

"What think ye?"

"She still possesses bruises on her face and is favoring her right foot. Me thinks she will be quite comely once she is recovered."

"I do not care about that, ye imbecile."

"What is it ye wish to know?" he asked confused.

"We need to arrange an accident for her."

"Ye mean like falling down some stairs?"

"Nay. There is no guarantee that a fall would kill her. It must be something more accurate and deadly. Let me think on it. Stay close to her and report any other weaknesses ye observe."

"Lord Fairwick is with her most of the time. Also, ye have to go through his chamber to get to her. He will see me."

"Not that close, ye foolish man. Go about yer duties, but keep watch of her whereabouts."

Encircling her waist with his hands, he leaned in for a kiss.

"What are ye about?" she demanded with a quick turn of her head. A mighty shove against his chest produced no results. He was holding tight.

"Ye promised me a kiss," he said as he nuzzled her neck.

"Not until the final act is done. Now release me at once before I cry foul."

"As ye wish, my dove." Backing away, he bowed low so she wouldn't see his angry face. Without looking her way, he quietly left the hallway.

Ugh. How had she missed his foul breath? She would not be giving her kisses to the likes of him. However, she would use him to accomplish the unpleasant deed.

* * *

When Nicolas and Elizabeth walked outside, Hastings was holding a chestnut mare.

"Thy chariot awaits, Lady Penelope," Nicolas announced with the sweep of his arm. "You get to ride while I lead you around the castle grounds. Agnes would be most upset if I allowed you to walk."

Elizabeth carefully approached the horse with her outstretched hand. The mare allowed Elizabeth to pet her nose and neck. "What a magnificent horse," Elizabeth said in awe. "Come, boost me up," she ordered.

No offense was taken by her demand when Nicolas saw how much she appreciated good horse flesh. She stepped into his cupped hands with her left foot and swung her right leg across the bareback horse. Nicolas hurriedly yanked her dress down to cover her exposed legs. "Lady Penelope, 'tis not proper to sit astride. You should sit side saddle. I will walk slowly to keep you from falling," he commented while he held on to her calf.

Cocking her head in concentration, she said, "This feels most natural for me. I believe I might own a horse since I knew exactly what to do." After a few moments of thought, she pronounced, "I will stay astride." Glancing at his hand, "I thank you to remove your hand."

Nicolas snatched his hand free as if scorched. It wasn't often that he was caught with a red face, but Lady Penelope seemed proficient in bringing him to task. With a firm hold on the halter, they embarked on their outing.

The courtyard was teeming with activity. They circled to the right to see the crude blacksmith building. It appeared rickety, but was actually a sturdy structure. It housed the furnace where iron was heated and then shaped into weapons, armor, household objects, and jewelry. The castle blacksmith mainly concentrated on weapons and armor.

"There is Eustace, the finest blacksmith in the region. We are most fortunate to have him," Nicolas said with pride. Nicolas didn't hesitate long enough for Elizabeth to speak to Eustace; instead, she waved a greeting. As the horse plodded along, chickens and children scattered to make a path. The children had grimy faces and tattered clothing; yet, the young ones appeared quite happy and content in their play.

Elizabeth signaled with her legs for the horse to stop, catching Nicolas by surprise. He abruptly turned as she slid to the ground. "What are you about?" he inquired.

"I want to speak to the little ones," she answered off handedly. Kneeling to the ground, she smiled. "Hello. My name is Lady Penelope. Come. I want to be your friend," she suggested with her outstretched hand.

The little girl ducked her head and hid behind one of the boys. The boy that looked to be the oldest boldly stepped forward. "Me name is Henry, named after one of our Kings," he announced with a puffed out chest.

"What an impressive name it is. What about thy friends? I'm sure they have fine names as well."

Pulling the small girl from behind him, Henry said, "This is me baby sister, Merry. She's always taggin' along," he huffed. "These two are Patrick and Pierson. They be twins. I'm the biggest and give the orders."

"Oh, I could see that right off. Ye are a born leader," she said seriously. "I'm new at the castle and wish to make some friends. Would ye be one of my friends?" she asked sweetly.

Scuffing his toe in the dirt, he looked at her thoughtfully. "I think it might be alright. What think ye, Lord Fairwick? Is it acceptable to ye?"

"Well, Henry, Lady Penelope does need a gallant friend."

"I am brave," Henry stated haughtily. After conferring with Patrick and Pierson, he simply said, "It is agreed. All of us will be thy friend."

"I am most blessed to call ye my friends," Lady Penelope said grinning.

After a few moments, Nicolas interrupted their discussion. "Come, Lady Penelope. We must be away," Nicolas insisted. "Henry, you will be in charge of watching over Lady Penelope when she is outside the keep, and I am not about. Can I depend on you?"

"Yea, Lord Fairwick."

Merry started pulling on Henry's ragged sleeve. "Farewell, Lady Penelope," Henry called out as the children ran off to continue their play.

Nicolas was impressed by how Lady Penelope treated the children with respect. Their lowly status hadn't affected her behavior toward them. She gained favor in his eyes from her simple gesture of friendship.

"I adore precious children," she said. While turning toward Nicolas, Elizabeth grabbed both sides of her head and pinched her eyes shut. "Ouch," she exclaimed. While Elizabeth rubbed her forehead, Nicolas took hold of her arm.

"What is it, Lady Penelope? Are you in pain?" Nicolas whispered. He was concerned that she might faint at his feet and didn't want anyone to witness it.

She reached out and grasped his arm as she squinted her eyes at him. "I had another pain shoot across my head when I mentioned the children. Perhaps I'm a mother," she said in confused wonder.

Nicolas chose to ignore that comment. "Your outing has come to a close for today, Lady Penelope." When she didn't argue, he knew he had made the right decision. He wrapped his hands around her waist and hoisted her up on the horse. She remained sideways as he had placed her. Her lack of arguing just confirmed his conclusion; Lady Penelope needed a rest.

6

In the rear of the barn, Thomas sat mending his horse's bridle. He didn't trust anyone else to do it for him. If there was one thing Nicolas demanded, it was proper care of weapons and horse tack. Thomas was thankful that Nicolas had allowed him to train at home. Most young men fostered with another family during their training years, but not Thomas. After their father's death and Phillip's near fatal accident, Nicolas had been determined to keep his family close at hand.

Thomas's head popped up at the sound of a woman's humming. He hoped it was Lady Penelope. Nicolas kept such a close watch on her that Thomas had not been given an opportunity to talk privately with her. With the sun at her back, he couldn't see the face; but he recognized the walk. It was Brigette. She was forever pestering him and causing trouble.

"What do you here, Brigette?" Thomas wasted no time in asking.

"Oh, 'tis you, Thomas. I was searching for Eugene," she casually replied.

Thomas laid aside the bridle and brushed off his hands. "You know you are not to seek him out," he angrily said as he stood to his feet. Thomas pondered if he was annoyed because of what Brigette said or the fact that she wasn't Lady Penelope.

"Not you, too!" she exclaimed. "I'm tired of my brothers telling me whom I can and cannot visit." She flounced down on a bale of hay.

Sitting back down, Thomas resumed his task. He had confidence that if he ignored her long enough, she would find someone else to annoy.

"What think you of that woman?" Brigette nonchalantly asked. Picking at the hay bale, she acted unconcerned as she awaited his answer. Horses nickered, birds chirped, but Thomas uttered no response. "Thomas, I asked you a question."

"I heard you . . . like a fly buzzing my ear."

"Well, what think you?" Brigette was not put off by his attitude. She knew if she persisted, she would get what she wanted. Being the youngest born just before the death of their parents gave Brigette certain leverage with her brothers.

Looking off in the distance, deep in thought, Thomas concluded, "She's gracious . . . well spoken . . . intelligent. I've only talked with her a few times, but I find her quite pleasing." Shifting his focus to Brigette, he saw her frown. She was displeased with his deduction, and he knew what was to follow—a fit.

Jumping to her feet, she exploded. "What's the matter with you? She is wicked and needs to be gone from here. Have you noticed how she manipulates our brother? He doesn't even like women, yet follows her around like a dog in heat. She must have him under some sort of spell."

"Brigette, you must cease this line of speaking before you find yourself at the end of a rod to your backside. You are not above being thrashed if Nicolas gets wind of such speech," Thomas ground out.

Deep in thought, she tapped her finger against her lips, ignoring Thomas. Spinning around, she burst out, "That's it—she's a witch."

"That is enough!" Thomas shouted. Nose to nose with his sister, he persisted, "You will not claim such information as fact. I will not allow it. Nicolas will hear of your false accusation about Lady Penelope. This is serious, Brigette." Thomas spun around to put away his tools. To contain his anger, he kept his back to his sister wanting to avoid her scathing eyes. She had gone too far this time. He would not stand by while she fabricated lies about Lady Penelope.

Brigette realized she might have overstepped some invisible line with Thomas. Thinking fast, she changed her tune. "Wait. I might have misspoken." Thomas's jerky motions slowed, but he didn't turn to face her. "I'm just frustrated at Nicolas's actions around her. He totally ignores me."

Pivoting on his heel, Thomas grabbed both of her arms just above the elbows. "You had best not say another word. Nicolas is your brother. Your childish jealousy is misplaced and unnatural. The problem with you, little sister, is you are spoiled almost beyond redemption."

Brigette twisted free of his grasp. Her arms were stiff at her side with her hands fisted for battle. "How dare you speak to me thus? Nicolas will hear of your harsh treatment of me," she spewed out. "Trust me. You will regret your actions this day." She whirled around and dashed out of the barn.

"I hope you do tell our brother. You will not escape his wrath over this one." His words echoed through an empty barn.

* * *

Elizabeth awoke feeling refreshed after her nap. She was irritated that her stamina was lacking but hopeful she would soon fully recover. What was up with those pains in her head? Sitting on the edge of the bed, Elizabeth contemplated that question. They seemed to strike her when she experienced a flash of memory. It stood to reason that excruciating headaches were in her future if she were ever to remember her past.

Hobbling to the wash stand, she splashed water on her face and dried off with a rag. If she had to make them herself, she was going to replace those coarse towels. She was sure some of her skin rubbed off each time she used one of them. Slipping on her oversized shoes, she headed out of the room.

She glanced up and down the poorly lit passageway and found it to be vacant. Venturing out, she turned left to do some exploring. Right would lead her to the stairway that led downstairs to the great hall. The opposite direction could prove interesting.

Picking her way slowly down the shadowed corridor, she heard voices coming from an open door. Stepping lightly, she stopped after turning the corner. It sounded like Phillip and Abigail. Should she leave the area or make her presence known? As she tried to decide, she heard Phillip moan in pain.

"Send for some steaming water. I need to rest and soak my hip," Phillip grumbled. "The pain is traveling down my left leg again." Another painful groan escaped followed by the rustling of fabric.

"Is there no one in this kingdom who can mend bones?" Abigail exclaimed.

"Don't start again, Abigail. Just do as I requested," he said with irritation. He knew her next words. She never tired of carping over who was lord.

"You should be lord of this castle. Nicolas is impulsive and irresponsible and not fit to rule in your place. If we could find someone to heal your body, you could take your rightful place."

"Cease your complaining. I'm not up for it today."

Elizabeth braced her hand against the cold stone wall as a sharp pain skittered across her head. *Students, pay close attention. I will give detailed instructions on how to diagnose a patient who has a bulging disc and one who has unleveled hips. Many times if you have one, you might well have the other.*

Sliding down the wall, Elizabeth realized she had experienced another memory flash. Sitting on the floor, she felt the pain gradually subsiding; and she regained her focus. Somewhere in her past, she had studied about healing the body. A picture of a class of scholars watching a professor demonstrate a technique on a body was vivid to her. Oh! If only she could remember more of her previous life. One thing was for certain—she could help Phillip.

With renewed vigor, she cautiously stood to her feet. She tittered slightly before her fuzzy head cleared. Elizabeth approached the door that was slightly ajar and knocked. She heard clipped footsteps march toward the door.

Abigail's shocked face came into view. "What do you here?" she rudely asked.

"Hello, Abigail. I was strolling down the hall when I couldn't help but overhear your conversation with Phillip," she kindly replied. Before Abigail could dismiss her, she forged ahead. "I want to offer my services. I have training in healing the bones," she stated.

"You? Ha! You don't even know your name much less how to heal someone. Now go away. Phillip is resting," she growled.

As she attempted to shut the door, Elizabeth stuck her left foot in the way and caught the door with her outstretched hand. "Let's talk to Phillip and let him decide," she grunted as she pushed against the heavy door.

"Abigail. Who is seeking entry?" Phillip muttered crossly.

"'Tis that woman. She says she can help your pain," she scoffed.

"Let her pass. I would be interested to hear her suggestions," he rasped out.

Flushed with anger, Abigail reluctantly allowed her entrance to their private chamber. Elizabeth saw Phillip resting on a divan under the window. His dark hair framed a pale face twisted in agony.

"Come. I would hear your ideas on my distorted body," he grimaced.

Elizabeth dragged a straight-back wooden chair next to him. Abigail took a position at his feet. She could tell Abigail was curious, yet skeptical, about her helping Phillip. From what Elizabeth had heard, many had tried, but failed, leaving him worse from their ministrations.

"Tell me all the details about your pain," Elizabeth encouraged.

Phillip closed his eyes and leaned his head back as he relived the moments that forever changed his vigorous life. With a shaking breath, he launched into his tale. "We were engaged in warfare. Nicolas and I got separated in the mayhem. Usually we warned each other of danger from our backside, but not on this day. Two mounted enemies completely occupied Nicolas. I turned my steed to head toward Nicolas and lend a hand. With my focus on reaching Nicolas, I failed to see the enemy approaching on my right. I raised my shield late but was knocked to the ground. My hip hit a stone. Piercing pain radiated all through my body and caused me to black out. Nicolas later told me that my foot had remained in the stirrup as my horse danced away from the adversary dragging me along. I sustained multiple injuries."

"We thought he was lost to us," Abigail whispered with glistening eyes that gazed at Phillip. "Nicolas brought him home to die. When he regained consciousness, he insisted to name Nicolas his successor. Even if he lived, he knew he would not be able to lead his men into battle or so he said."

"I'm so sorry for the wounds you suffered," Elizabeth tenderly offered. "If you will allow me to examine you, I will be able to determine if I can help you."

"Do as you wish," Phillip said resigned.

"But Phillip . . ." Abigail protested.

With a short jerk of his chin toward his wife, Abigail moved to the chair at the fireplace and plopped down, her arms crossed tightly over her bosom and her lip curled in contempt. It was obvious to Elizabeth; Abigail was not pleased.

"I need you to lie flat on this bed. Don't worry. It will be over as quick as a flash."

Phillip caught Abigail's eye as he wondered about Elizabeth's strange expression.

7

Days turned into weeks for Elizabeth with no solid progress of recovering her memory. Wanting to be helpful, she had tried her hand at sewing and cooking with disastrous results. Even though she remembered sewing up flesh, somehow she managed to increase the hole in Nicolas's socks. She felt as if that were a talent in itself, but Nicolas only growled his displeasure. Her cooking was even worse. She had started a fire in the ovens when she attempted to clean out the built up grease. After the fire, Elizabeth was banned from the kitchen area.

Most frustrating for her was how no one understood the need for cleanliness. She had suggested scalding the tables and utensils after every meal to prevent sickness. Her suggestion was not well received. Her idea of sweeping the floor following all meals was met with total rebellion. Each new proposal she made was hacked into splinters by Nicolas. The only time he was pleased with her was when she was silent and submissive.

Fortunately, for Elizabeth, the Psalms in Nicolas's family Bible had recently been translated into English. As a rule, Elizabeth's days were spent reading from Nicolas's family Bible and trying to avoid the Fairwick family. Nicolas was the worst. He always found a way to humiliate her in front of others. She also realized Brigette would not be a friend. Brigette had recommended that

Elizabeth start walking down the road and see how long it took for someone to claim her. She met with Phillip daily to make adjustments to his spine and hip. He was grateful for her help but usually kept to himself pouring over the castle books. His wife, Abigail, was condescending toward her. Even though Elizabeth was trying to help her husband, Abigail was still skeptical and gave her no leeway. Basically, Abigail was not pleased with her position in the family hierarchy and made everyone around her miserable. Then there was Thomas. He was Elizabeth's champion. She could count on him to come to her defense especially when Nicolas was critical of her. She felt like a prisoner of this dysfunctional family with no possible way of escape.

On one particular day, Elizabeth had remained inside to read from Nicolas's Bible. The Bible was a rare item preserved from his family's past; therefore, he didn't want it removed from his solar. As a result, she had placed it on the chess table near the window, her best source of light. She wasn't sure how she knew about God, but she did. The Bible fell open to Psalm 118. The first verse said *O, give thanks unto the Lord; for He is good: because His mercy endureth forever.* Obviously, God had spared her life for a reason. On down in the chapter she read verse eight: *It is better to trust in the Lord than to put confidence in man.* How true verse eight was for Elizabeth. She certainly didn't trust the men at this castle. As she continued reading, there arose a terrible commotion in the courtyard. She peered outside to see a rider come to a dusty halt near Nicolas. Naturally, Elizabeth couldn't resist listening in on their conversation since the rider was extremely excited and talking loudly.

"My Lord, the King is on his way to your castle," he said breathlessly.

"What?" Nicolas exclaimed.

"I did as ye requested. I kept me ear near the ground for news, and he is most definitely coming to ye."

"What is his purpose?"

"To see ye wed," he shouted. "He said ye was taking too long to get the deed done, and he would find ye a wife. Then he laughed."

"How much time do I have?" Nicolas asked as he began pacing.

"Three, maybe four weeks. He travels with The Queen and her entourage. They be visiting Lord Sherwood and Lord Mathias along the way, also."

Nicolas's agitation was evident by his jerky body language. Elizabeth backed away from the window and eased down into her chair. *Would the King know her family? Could he help her get back home?* As she sat in contemplation, she had no idea her life was about to change drastically.

"Thank you for the warning, my friend. Get some food and drink while Robert cares for your horse."

"Thank ye, Lord Fairwick."

Nicolas saw Hastings headed toward the barn. "Hastings, please send Thomas to me post haste," Nicolas commanded. "I will await him in the war room."

Nicolas strode around the castle and entered the front door of the keep. He marched into the war room and plopped down in his chair. Staring out the window, he began to plan his strategy.

"Brother, I hear you have need of me," Thomas remarked as he sauntered into the war room. "Would it have anything to do with the King's approaching arrival and whispers of a bride?" Thomas dropped into a chair and laughed uncontrollably. "You can't escape your destiny."

"Thomas, cease your womanly outburst. I have an important task for you."

Thomas wiped his eyes with his dirty sleeve before giving Nicolas his attention. "Yea, Lord Nicolas, how may I assist you?" he asked with twinkling eyes.

Nicolas had too much at stake to fight with Thomas. He would get even with Thomas later. "Find seven men and bring them to stand in the passageway outside my solar door. Tell them they will have a private audience with Lady Penelope. When I open the door, they are to act eager and excited to see her. Understood?"

Thomas straightened up in his chair. "That's all that is required?" he asked puzzled.

"Yea, nothing more. They are to remain outside the door until I give them leave."

Baffled by his brother's request, Thomas asked, "What mischief are you about, brother?"

"You are not to question my commands, just carry them out," Nicolas said gruffly.

Thomas shot to his feet and hurried to do his brother's bidding. He didn't want to be on the receiving end of Nicolas's wrath again.

Nicolas quickly left the room and ran up the stairs. He had much to do before the King's arrival. Hopefully, the weather might turn foul enough to slow the King's progress; and no doubt the queen and her ladies would slow him down, too. Stopping outside his door, he took a quick breath and blew it out through his lips. Lady Penelope had an important role to play, so he must proceed with caution.

He opened the door and stepped inside his solar. Seeing her reading the Bible gave him pause. On the verge of backing out of his plan because of his guilty conscience, he pictured the King's niece that had wanted to wed him. She was quite round in form with a mouth full of black teeth. Not to mention that at thirteen summers, she was barely out of the nursery. With renewed determination, Nicolas closed the door.

Elizabeth looked up at the sound of the closing door. "I'm sorry, my lord, I didn't expect you back so soon. I will leave immediately."

"Nay. If you will wait a moment, I have need of your services." Never losing eye contact with Elizabeth, he unbuckled his sword and propped it in the corner.

Elizabeth closed the Bible and demurely placed her hands in her lap. "How may I be of assistance?"

With his hands clasped behind his back, he walked toward her. Stopping within two feet of her, he said, "Lady Penelope, you have been at my castle for one full moon. Is that correct?"

"Yes." She knew he was trying to intimidate her by hovering over her. She stood to her feet which was a tactical error. His close proximity made her weak with anticipation. Even when he insulted her, she couldn't resist his commanding presence. His powerful virility and mesmerizing chocolate eyes snared her as a trap.

"During that time you have tried your hand at cooking and sewing, but with little success. Is that correct?"

He burst her romantic bubble with no effort. How could she forget how fast he could agitate her? "Yes, my lord," she firmly said. "I don't have a good feelin' about this," she mumbled more to herself.

Nicolas knew that she was flustered from her manner of speaking. He didn't want her upset, but he wasn't sure how to avoid it either. "Have you been well fed and clothed during this time?"

"You know the answer to the question. Of course, I have. You have been most hospitable."

"Have I ever asked payment for what you have received?"

"You know the answer to that question, as well. What are you about? Why ask these pointless questions? Just say what you need to say and be done with it."

"Well said, my lady." He walked away from her and then spun around with arms outstretched from his side. "I am in need of a wife and you are the most favorable choice."

Wide-eyed, Elizabeth was rendered immobile. Gazing at his expectant face would have been endearing at another time, but not now. "Are you crazy?" she screeched. "There is no way on God's green earth that I would marry you!"

Of course, Nicolas had expected her negative reaction. Therefore, he had a backup plan. Lowering his arms, he gave her a moment to collect herself before his next strike. She wasted no time in saying her piece.

"Did it ever occur to you that I might already be married? We don't even know my name or my family history. I can't just up and marry you," she continued vehemently. "This has to be the most preposterous idea to pop into your thick head."

He waited while she raged and stomped around the room. He kept silent and her wrath eventually dwindled. He was more interested in the odd words coming out of her mouth . . . fascinating.

"... so, I have to say no, no, and no." After her tirade, she collapsed into a chair, mentally and emotionally spent.

Nicolas eased down in the chair opposite Lady Penelope. "You have made your answer perfectly clear." He leaned forward resting his arms on his legs. He sat quietly a moment staring at his clasped hands. Stretching out, he sat back in his chair and crossed his ankles.

"Lady Penelope, you have an important decision to make." Nicolas paused and gave her a long stare. He watched as she began to squirm under his direct gaze. Rubbing his chin, he continued, "If you are to remain under my protection and consume my provisions, you may either wed me . . . or . . . you may become the castle harlot."

If Elizabeth thought his first proposal was astonishing, this one was utterly beyond belief. He had truly lost his mind to think she would agree to his outrageous scheme. She waited for him to start laughing, but he remained silent. She was livid.

"You cannot be serious."

He rose from his seat and walked to the door. The palm of his hand rested against the door frame. "Your first patrons await you just outside this door."

"I don't believe you," she snapped.

"Come. See for yourself."

Elizabeth bounded out of her chair. She marched toward him with clinched fists, ready to do battle. He stepped aside as she reached for the door handle. "You had better stand back because if I open this door and there are men waiting in the passageway, I'm coming after you," she seethed.

Edging the door open, Elizabeth couldn't believe what she saw. There were seven enthusiastic men smiling at her. They were practically dancing with excitement. Rage boiled inside her, ready to erupt. She slammed the door with such intensity it rocked on its hinges. Nicolas was unprepared for her next action. Whirling around, she launched her body at Nicolas with so much force that they fell to the floor. Her fists pounded his chest, face, and every other body part she could reach. As he wrestled to pin her to the ground, she drew blood with her fingernails. Nicolas tossed her off of him and straddled her. He trapped her hands against the stone floor putting himself nose to nose with Elizabeth. Her chest was heaving from exertion and fury while her eyes scorched him. He rather enjoyed her fiery temper. Any other time, he would have found this arrangement much to his liking.

"How dare you do this unspeakable deed?" she spit out. Elizabeth twisted and bucked trying to dislodge him. Eventually, she stopped fighting his hold for she knew it was pointless. She was no match for his strength. "Get off me, you big baboon. I can't breathe," she panted.

"I know not your meaning, but I don't think it was a flattering remark. If you promise to be civilized, I will release you." He could sense her hesitation and then realized the point at which she was resolved to her fate.

"Fine. Now get off me," she huffed.

Once he let go and rolled off, she sat up. Remaining on the floor, Elizabeth wrapped her arms around her knees and laid her forehead against them. Nicolas settled down next to her but not too close. His cheek was still burning from her assault.

"Why are you doing this?" she murmured into her dress.

"I must wed in haste, and you are my only choice," he bluntly said. "There are no other unwed women in this territory that are suitable to be my bride."

Rotating her head while still resting on her knees, she looked at him. "Why the hurry?"

Shoving to his feet, Nicolas moved to the fireplace. He placed both hands on the mantle and lowered his head. *Sigh.* "The King has asked me to wed since taking Phillip's place as Lord of Fairwick Castle. I have avoided this entanglement for two years, and now the King has threatened to bring me a wife." Pushing away from the mantle, he knelt down on one knee beside Elizabeth. "Therefore, I would prefer you to choose to be my wife rather than become the castle harlot."

Elizabeth sat stone still, but her mind reeled with activity. Her eyes scanned his form. His shoulder length, brown hair framed a strong jaw line. A straight nose nestled between his high cheek bones gave him dignity. Put those features with powerfully built shoulders, arms, and legs . . . a girl could do worse. However, it wasn't his physique that put her off. It was his overbearing, arrogant manner, not to mention the fact that she might already be married.

Nicolas watched her watch him. He was about to demand she marry him or live out her days in the dungeon when she rose to her feet and spoke.

"You are trying to force me into marriage." She defiantly stared. "I have a few terms that must be met before I agree," she dared to say as she stood over him. She figured she might as well go along with his ridiculous request until she could circumvent his plan.

Gazing at her from the floor, he said, "I'm listening, but it doesn't mean I'll agree to your demands."

"Hear me out," she said as she warmed to the idea. Walking around the room and ticking them off on her fingers, she began, "We will keep separate sleeping quarters until I remember who I am. You will not treat me with ill regard in front of others. I get a couple of new dresses and a new pair of shoes that fit. As lady of the castle, I get some authority. You allow me to instruct your sister. And lastly . . ."

"There's more?" he asked incredulously as he rose to his feet.

"And lastly, I get my own horse." Elizabeth stopped pacing and stood erect with arms at her side. She knew she had the upper hand since he was desperate. She just hoped she hadn't left out any crucial details.

Advancing within inches of her, Nicolas ticked off his answer, "You will have numerous new dresses and shoes. As my wife, I will treat you with dignity and honor at all times. I will gladly put Brigette in your capable hands. You will positively have your own horse."

She thought he was going to ignore her other requests when he suggested they sit down to discuss the additional stipulations. He stepped back and allowed her to precede him to the chairs.

Once she was perched on the edge of the chair, he commenced. "I'll gradually introduce the duties you will perform as Lady Fairwick. I wouldn't want you to be overwhelmed with responsibilities. And lastly . . ."

"There's more?" she asked with big blinking eyes.

Once again her sarcasm was not lost on Nicolas. "I will allow you three months sleeping apart. During that time, I will use all of my skills to win your favor. After that amount of time, if you haven't regained your memory, you will be my wife in every way." Pausing, he let her absorb that information before continuing. "We will have many adjustments, but I am willing to compromise within reason. Even though there are advantages to the title of wife, you must remember that I have the final say in matters. Of that, there is no negotiation."

"What if I realize I'm already married?"

"I will release you from this arrangement."

"What if there is a child born to us before I regain my memory of a previous marriage?"

"Then, you may go, but the child will stay with me as my heir."

Gasp! "I could never leave without my child!"

"No one will force you to leave. You may live out your days with me," he said unemotionally.

"Oh, what an impossible mess!" she cried out.

With two steps, he grasped the arms of her chair and leaned toward her. "You worry of things that might never come to pass." With a feather soft touch, he ran his finger down her cheek and across her lips. "Live only for today," he whispered before claiming her lips with his own.

Elizabeth was lost. His warm, moist lips made her head spin. She couldn't think but only experience the lightheadedness of the moment. Chill bumps rushed up and down her spine. He could have asked anything of her, and she would have relented.

Suddenly, a pounding on the door yanked her back to reality. Her eyes flew open. She shoved his face away from her and wiggled out of the chair in a flash. Nicolas grumbled words she had never heard before. He marched to the door and flung it open.

"What is it?" he bellowed. Facing him were seven eager men. He shook his head in disbelief. That woman had him so muddled that he had forgotten the men. "Thy services are no longer needed," he softly spoke. He hoped his words didn't carry over to Lady Penelope. No need reminding her of his previous threat.

The men were terribly disappointed to miss their private audience with the beautiful Lady Penelope. They stomped off grumbling their displeasure. Nicolas leaned his head against the door frame and closed the door once more. The click of the latch was deafening.

Elizabeth's stricken face was all Nicolas saw when he turned. Never leaving his place by the door, he watched her walk on wooden legs toward her room. She didn't look his way or acknowledge him as she disappeared through the opening and closed the door. His guilt made his pulse race in anticipation of what was to follow. Hardening his heart toward her pitiful countenance was the only way to survive his dishonorable act. He worried he might have broken her spirit until he heard her weak voice filtering through the closed portal.

"My name is no longer Penelope."

Smiling to himself, he sauntered over to her door. With his face touching the door, he asked, "Pray, what is your new name, my lady?"

"If I feel like it, I'll tell you on the morrow. Now go away. I'm finished talking to you for the day."

"As you wish, my lady." He was relieved; her fiery temper was still blazing. Nicolas walked to the table, picked up his precious Bible, and locked it back in his trunk. It was a glaring reminder of his shameful behavior. No doubt God was appalled by his thoughts and actions, but his lot was cast. With one last glance at her door, Nicolas attached his sword and strode out of the room.

8

It was late and Nicolas was weary. He didn't realize how mentally taxing it was to scheme against Penelope. A heavy dose of guilt followed each new plot. Her horrified face attacked his conscience. She had been true to her word. She had not spoken to him the rest of the day or evening. It was just as well. Her silence helped block out the atrocities he had planned against her. The Holy Spirit pricked his guilty conscious numerous times during the day, but he disregarded it.

As he entered his room, he noticed her door shut tight. Knowing Penelope, she had probably blocked the door with furniture. Removing his weapons, he rotated his tense shoulders. It would have been nice for someone to rub his taut muscles. Glancing at her closed door, he could picture Penelope being that person . . . *sigh* . . . but not tonight.

He removed his clothing and washed off the daily grime. After his one incident of running naked to her room wrapped in a blanket, he had opted to sleep in his breeches. With his sword nearby, he stretched out on the bed and continued to plot the details of the next few days. He would need to get a special license from the local bishop. He didn't have time for the reading of the banns before the arrival of the king. Then there was the commissioning of Penelope's trousseau. More details swam before his mind's eye until he eventually fell into a restless sleep.

Mother? Father is away on a hunting trip. I watched him leave. It is safe. Oh, my sweet Nicolas. I have missed you sorely. Come, we will play the day away . . .

. . . Hurry, Nicolas. Ye must hide under the bed. 'Tis thy father. Why mother? Why does he keep us apart? There's no time. Ye must hurry under the bed. Promise me ye will hold thy hands over thy ears and not utter a word. Promise me no matter what ye hear, ye will remain silent. Mother, ye are hurting my arm. Hurry! Hurry! He mustn't find ye here. Promise me, not a sound. Twill be our little secret. . . . I promise, Mother.

Startled, Nicolas bolted upright in bed as he reached for his sword. Sweat trickled down his back. His breath came in short bursts. Frantically sweeping the room with his eyes, he realized it was only a dream. Flopping against the pillow, he huffed in frustration. It had been years since he had dreamt of his mother. He laid the blame at Penelope's door. She was the cause of this occurrence. He had sealed his mother's room years ago, and he held the key. Unchaining her door had unlocked long repressed memories of that fateful day.

Jumping out of bed, Nicolas paced around his room trying to dispel the images. His tread was light as he walked to the open window. Gazing at the stars, he wondered if he could have changed the outcome of that day. He had been only seven, but surely . . . shaking his head, he returned to bed; no need to relive what could not be undone.

It was the wee hours of the morning before Nicolas dozed off to sleep again. Images from his childhood floated in and out of his dreams.

Is that reprobate of a son in here? Nay, my lord, 'tis only me. Ye lie, wife. Nay, my husband. Ye will pay for your lies. Please, my lord. . .

Nicolas shot out of the bed like an arrow—his cursed dream was back. Stumbling over to the fireplace, he dropped into the chair. Scrubbing his face with his hands, he realized he should never have allowed that woman into his castle. Embracing her on that unfortunate day had brought him nothing but distress. He had been perfectly content with his life until she entered and twisted his thoughts like a dirty rag. She was the cause of his recurring nightmares. Yet, he was contemplating marrying her. What utter nonsense!

He could hear the early morning sounds as the castle came alive with activity. Nicolas stood and stretched the kinks out of his back and shoulders. There was much to accomplish before the arrival of the king. He washed and dressed before kneeling down at his trunk. Unlocking it, he reached inside to fill his haversack with coin and clothes for his trip. He must remember to get added provisions from the kitchen. The men he had chosen to accompany him would be waiting for him. Gathering his weapons, he placed them beside his sack. There was one last deed to complete prior to leaving.

Stopping in front of her door, Nicolas knocked. *Will she open the door?* Nicolas wondered as he stood thumping on her door. He needed to speak to her before his journey, and time was fleeting. As he raised his hand for a final rap, the door cracked open.

"What is it now?" she asked with agitation. Only her nose was visible, but Nicolas could well picture her unruly hair. He thought her hair silky, but, as of yet, had not tested that theory. Nicolas held back his chuckle—best not to provoke her before dawn.

"A word with you, my lady, before I embark on a journey," he said with authority.

"Can't you just say it through the door?"

"Nay. Please come out . . . or . . . I can come in," he added with humor.

"Oh, good grief! Wait a moment," she hissed.

While he leaned a shoulder against the doorframe with crossed arms, he envisioned her jerking the dress over her head. She was having difficulty based on the grunting and stomping coming through the door. "Do you need aid, my lady?"

"No, you big oaf. I'm done," she proclaimed strutting through the door.

Straightening to his full height, he pointed to the chairs. Elizabeth tramped to the fireplace and slumped in the chair.

Impressing him was no longer an issue for her. She was furious with him for forcing marriage against her will . . . and she was beginning to hate these cursed chairs.

Ignoring her actions, Nicolas calmly walked over and eased into his chair.

"I will be away for five, mayhap six days. During that time, you need not fear, my lady. I have appointed Jarvis and Angus to watch over you. Each time you leave the keep, you will be guarded." He thought his words would comfort her, but instead he saw her anger flare. "Why are you distraught, my lady?"

"Are you afraid of what I might do if left unattended?" she asked with agitation.

"Just the opposite, Lady Penelope. I fear for your safety. We know not your heritage or if you have enemies afoot," he said with concern. "You were beaten and left lifeless on the side of the road. Someone wishes you dead, my lady."

"Oh. I never thought of that." Her face twisted in deep thought. "Do you think I'm in danger?" she asked with wide-eyed alarm.

"I know not but will take precaution just the same. Guards will accompany you each time you step outside the keep. Is that understood?"

"Yes," she answered subdued. "I'll take my babysitters with me wherever I go."

"What an odd word, babysitter. What is its meaning?"

Smiling, she shrugged her shoulders. "I guess it means those who watch over a baby or a child."

"Ah, observing one who is defenseless. I understand. Does that description fit you, Lady Penelope?" he asked with one raised brow.

"No," she sputtered. He could raise her ire with little effort. "You know, you are pleasant to talk to when you aren't insulting me, but it's so rare. Are we done here?"

"For now. Just make sure you heed my words." Nicolas picked up his gear and headed toward the door. Turning and looking directly at her, he wanted to drive home his point. "I need you hale and hearty when I return," he added before softly closing the door.

"Ooo, that man is beyond arrogant." Pushing out of the chair, she walked to the open window. She threw open the shutters and leaned out to see the waiting men. Since the sun had barely peeked out, she heard more than she saw through the early morning fog. Some of the men held torches that would light their way until full sunrise. From her count, there were about twenty-five men awaiting their leader. After a short time, Nicolas mounted his horse while issuing final words to Phillip and Thomas. Just when she thought he would ride off, he turned to glance at the window. His piercing gaze snared her. *Drats. He caught me watching him. That will only inflate his conceited ego.*

Pulling her head into the room, Elizabeth contemplated her bleak future. It was most depressing. She had little control over anything in her life. However, for now, she decided to take advantage of Nicolas's absence and have some fun. She had been a virtual prisoner, but not today. With that happy thought, she did a little dance on the way to her room to prepare for an adventure.

※ ※ ※

"Now is our chance. Nicolas is away and she is unprotected. Surely there will be an opportunity for an accident."

"I will be ever watchful for such an occasion. Do ye have something in mind?"

"She takes the same path from her room each day. Ye could stand in the alcove near the back stairway and give her a hearty shove as she starts down the stairs. She will be caught unaware and, hopefully, tumble to her death."

"I thought ye said she wouldn't die from such a fall?"

"Thou art such a dim-wit. I never said such a thing. Just be ready on the morrow. Ye mustn't miss a chance."

"Doing it on the morrow is a risk. I could be seen."

"Perchance. Ye will need to take measures to safeguard thyself."

"What mean ye?"

Blowing out a loud breath, she realized she had chosen a brainless cur. "Are ye daft? Dress thyself in dark clothing and leave off thy boots. Ye will not be seen nor heard. Take up watch in the wee hours before dawn."

His anger was simmering just under the surface. How dare she call him daft. He would do her bidding for now, and then he would extract payment of his own choosing. She would not gainsay him, or she would regret her decision. Kissing the back of her hand, he said, "As ye wish, my dove." Turning on his heel, he left her alone in the passageway.

"Splendid." Watching him leave, she realized choosing him might have been a blunder. With any luck, she would be rid of him as well. She had much to think about.

* * *

After lacing up her oversized boots, Elizabeth practically skipped out the door toward the front stairway and the great hall. When she came to the junction that connected with another wing of the castle, she paused. Looking down the dimly lit corridor, Elizabeth knew Brigette's room was on that wing. Following a moment of indecision, she ventured toward Brigette's room. Hopefully, she could negotiate some kind of truce with Nicolas's only sister who seemed bent on making Elizabeth's life miserable.

Taking a deep breath, Elizabeth knocked softly on Brigette's door.

"Go away," she yelled. "I want to be left alone."

"'Tis me, Brigette. I thought we could break our fast together," Elizabeth said cheerfully.

"Go away. I hate you . . . you . . . you witch." Hearing Brigette's angry scream, Elizabeth's brows shot to her hairline. *Witch indeed, you little brat.* Fuming, Elizabeth placed her ear on the door and heard moaning. Brigette was a spoiled, hateful girl, but something else was wrong.

"Can I help you?"

"Nay. No one can . . . now leave me," she shrieked.

Elizabeth backed away and headed toward the great hall. She wasn't going to let an odious child ruin her first day of freedom from Nicolas. Once Elizabeth reached the bottom of the stone staircase, she stopped before entering the great hall. Servants scurried about placing food on the long tables and pouring drinks in empty cups. Groups of men were talking while the women corralled children for the meal. Thomas glanced her way while conferring with Phillip.

"Lady Penelope, welcome," Thomas boomed with pleasure. He extended his hand toward her.

Elizabeth strode toward Thomas on the dais. Accepting his helping hand, she smiled. "Goodmorrow, Thomas . . . Phillip, Abigail," she said turning to each one. Addressing Phillip she asked, "May I be so bold as to make a small announcement?"

Looking confused, Phillip asked, "What mean you?"

"I would like to address the men and women gathered here this morning. Don't worry; it's nothing dreadful. It's in regard to my name."

Still baffled, Phillip gave her permission to speak. He was attempting to obtain everyone's attention when Elizabeth blew an earsplitting whistle from her mouth. Astonished faces from around the room turned toward the dais and were equally surprised to see who had gotten their attention.

Elizabeth stood on her chair to be seen by all. Gasps ricocheted around the room when they realized she was the one with the piercing whistle. "Goodmorrow, everyone. Are you having a delightful meal?" She could hear a few mumbled responses. "As many of you know, I'm new to the area. You might also know that I'm having trouble remembering my name or who I am. I have been called Lady Katherine and Lady Penelope simply because I needed a name. Today, I'm going to let all of you help me choose a name that I will retain for an indefinite period of time. Now who would like to be first to suggest a fitting name?" she asked. She rubbed her hands together with enthusiastic anticipation.

The room had gone acutely quiet as Elizabeth fidgeted on her chair. "Alright, who wants to be first?" she asked again. Turning her head, she looked directly at Thomas. "Thomas, how about you? Do you have a favorite name for me?"

Thomas pondered Elizabeth's request. He glanced at Phillip before saying, "I'm partial to Emma. I wanted mother to name our sister Emma," he softly replied before ducking his head.

"Did everyone hear Thomas? He recommends Emma. What about others? What say you?" Elizabeth looked out expectantly into a sea of perplexed faces. Her smile remained in place, but she felt like buzzard meat. She listened to muttering around the tables until at last someone called out Margaret. Then another yelled Anne while someone else shouted Jane. Names were soon echoing around the room uncontrollably as they warmed to the task.

Finally, Phillip stood with raised hands to silence the crowd. "Thank ye for helping select a new name for Lady Penelope. I think she has ample names from which to choose." Twisting toward Elizabeth, he indicated for her to proceed.

"Yes. You have all been most helpful. Now, you will each cast a vote for your favorite name indicated by an upraised hand. Those in favor of Jane, raise your hand."

The men and women were confused with her appeal. They had never participated in such an unusual request and weren't sure how to proceed. Soft murmuring reverberated around the room.

"Come, now. Raise your hand if you want my name to be Jane," Elizabeth instructed again. She demonstrated with her upheld hand.

Finally, two voted for Jane—Ainsley and Jane. Several of the men erupted in laughter aimed at Ainsley who suggested his wife's name, Jane. She was quite round in figure and missing three front teeth. However, she was best known for her jovial behavior.

The men softened the rebuke by calling out, "There can only be one jolly Jane." More laughter followed that statement.

"Thank you, gentlemen, for clarifying the reason for your laughter. Who thinks Margaret is a fine name?"

Seven chose Margaret. Most of them were in one family whose mother was Margaret.

"What about Anne?"

Nine wanted Anne.

"Lastly, who would cast a vote for Emma?" Elizabeth turned and winked at Thomas. When she faced forward, she was astounded that over thirty remaining people raised their hands. Hopping and clapping, she shouted, "Emma it is. I am henceforth Lady Emma. Thank you each for your eager participation." Elizabeth jumped down from her chair and left the dais to greet the men and women who joined in the name selection. She hugged the women and slapped the men on the back to show her pleasure.

"This has been the most exciting meal since Hastings and Collette's wedding," Phillip announced with a laugh.

"I think the whole affair was disgraceful. She stood in her chair and acted shamefully," Abigail exploded. "I can't believe you approve of her actions."

"Don't be so ill-tempered, Abigail. She livened up the morning," Phillip responded.

"I rather enjoyed myself," Thomas added.

"Of course you did, Thomas. You're smitten with her," she spit back.

"Abigail," Phillip snapped. "Hold your tongue."

Abigail promptly rose and stormed out of the hall. No one paid her any mind. The knights and peasants were busy watching Lady Emma. Each of them hoped to get a private greeting from her.

"I know where you should go after the meal," Thomas commented to Phillip as he watched Abigail exit the room.

"Ah, yes, but sometimes the patching up with Abigail is worth the disagreement," Phillip chuckled. "One day you'll know of what I speak."

"Mayhap sooner than you think, brother," Thomas commented while gazing at Elizabeth.

"She's too old for you, Thomas."

Thomas jerked his head around to look at Phillip. "What mean you?"

"Lady Emma. She's not for you. Besides, Nicolas has plans for her."

"Again, what mean you?" Thomas bristled.

"Don't set your sights on Lady Emma. Nicolas would never allow you to wed a woman who has no dowry or helpful alliance to bring to our family. In addition, you have not finished your training nor have you been knighted," he finished.

Each statement was a lethal blow to Thomas. His despondency was palatable. Phillip regretted his bluntness, but didn't want Thomas to have any false hopes.

Thomas finished his meal in silence. Occasionally, he scowled at Phillip but refused to speak to his brother.

When Elizabeth made her way back to her seat, she noticed that Phillip and Thomas were at odds with one another. She tried coaxing a comment from Thomas but without success. When she made eye contact with Phillip, he turned away.

"What's the matter with you men?" she asked in frustration.

"Nothing of concern, Lady Emma," Phillip said.

"You're right. I'm not going to let any of you Fairwicks ruin my happy day." Elizabeth eyed the meat swimming in grease and wisely left it floating. She ate some bread and fruit to appease her hungry stomach. Standing to her feet, she said, "I'll catch you guys later. I'm off for my adventure."

"Catch you guys. . ." Phillip mumbled, "what gibberish."

Thomas looked up at his brother's words to see Phillip shaking his head in bewilderment. With a slight movement, Thomas's eyes watched Elizabeth's swaying hips as she pranced out of the great hall. Jarvis and Angus jumped up and followed after Lady Emma. Mayhap he could relieve one of them of their guard duty today. Phillip couldn't gainsay him if he were protecting Lady Emma. That thought brightened his countenance as he left to complete his responsibilities.

9

Elizabeth's first stop was the carpenter. Once outside, she wrapped her shawl around her shoulders against the cool mist of the morning. Even observing the gray skies couldn't dampen her enthusiasm. Plowing down the stairs, she abruptly stopped and turned to see the wide-eyed stares of Jarvis and Angus. She realized she would need to slow down if they were to keep up.

"Come on, men. Time is wasting." Her wide smile was contagious.

They looked at one another as Angus shrugged his shoulders and muttered, "She's feisty."

"That she is," Jarvis answered with a grin. "Today will be entertaining."

Both men ambled toward her on creaking knees. Elizabeth grimaced as Jarvis winced with each step. Their cracking bones were another reminder of their advanced age. Looping her right arm with Jarvis's arm and her left arm with Angus's, she was ready. "Come, men. Point me toward the carpenter."

"That would be John. He's the best around. Made most of the castle furniture, he did," Jarvis boasted. "He works inside the castle grounds but lives in the village."

"What are ye wishing to have built, Lady Emma?" Angus asked as he withdrew his arm and let it dangle by his side.

"Oh, a little something for the children. It's a surprise."

They turned left and went around the corner of the keep. Men walked the parapet and patrolled the grounds. Each had a sword strapped to his hip, and some had a bow and arrows on their backs.

"Why are there so many guards?" Elizabeth inquired.

"Lord Nicolas takes all precaution when he is away from his home. He increases the guard both here and in the village," Angus stated.

"Does he expect trouble?" she asked with concern.

"Ye must be prepared for all possibilities, My Lady," Jarvis responded.

They continued their stroll toward the building that housed the carpenter while Elizabeth contemplated the dangers of living at the castle. Was her real home any safer? For some reason, she didn't think so.

Many of the peasants stopped in their duties as they watched the trio pass by. They were still quite curious about the woman that Lord Nicolas had taken in and protected.

"Tell me something about yourselves, gentlemen."

Jarvis grinned at Angus when she referred to them as gentlemen. "Not much to tell," Angus muttered.

"We're brothers," Jarvis interjected.

"Twins?" she asked in surprise.

"Nay, my lady. Same father, different mother," Jarvis answered. "I'm the most handsome while Angus is the most skilled."

"Humph," Angus snorted.

"Angus's mother died from cholera not long after giving birth. So our father needed a woman to tend his young son while he was off at war. He clapped eyes on my mother and married her right away. She was with child when our father left to fight with the older Lord Fairwick, Nicolas's grandfather, not two months later. Our father was a knight in service to Lord Fairwick."

Elizabeth was excited. Here were two men who probably knew the story behind Nicolas's father and why Nicolas didn't want unwed women at his castle. Gently probing, she asked, "Then you both knew Lord Nicolas's father?"

"Yay, my lady," Jarvis quickly replied. "We grew up with Lord Anthony Fairwick and had many great adventures serving him when he became Lord of the Castle after his father-in-law's passing. He took Lady Isolde's name."

"Ooo, I would be most interested to hear some of your tales of adventure," Elizabeth all but squeaked.

"Nay," Angus bluntly replied. "We have arrived at the carpenter's shop."

"Oh," she said dejectedly. "Another time, perhaps?"

"Perhaps," Angus said.

Jarvis gave her a wink and a promising smile. The two brothers were nearly inseparable, but she was hoping to get Jarvis alone. He seemed looser of tongue.

Upon reaching their destination, Jarvis and Angus sat on a bench outside the work area while Elizabeth stepped inside to talk with John.

Elizabeth stopped just inside the doorway allowing her eyes to adjust to the dimly lit room. She breathed deeply of freshly cut wood. It was most pleasing to her senses. John barely glanced up to acknowledge her presence as he continued to work.

"Hi, kind sir. My name is Lady Emma and I have need of your services," she sweetly said.

Elizabeth wasn't certain he heard her since he continued to work. Unsure how to proceed, she remained quiet. She definitely didn't want to make him angry by being too forceful. Just when she thought to speak again, he laid down his tools and brushed off his hands.

"What did ye want?" John bluntly asked.

"I'm Lady Emma. . ."

"I heard that part. What did ye want?" John asked again. "I have much to do."

"Oh . . . I'm sorry to disturb your work, but I was hoping to commission something for the local children."

At the mention of the children, John's countenance softened. "Well, come a little closer so I can hear yer request," he rumbled.

If Elizabeth wasn't acquainted with sweet Jarvis, she would think all the men around the castle were gruff like Nicolas.

However, not wanting to miss her opportunity, she moved closer to John's workbench.

"I want a small wagon made for the children."

"Whatever for?" John bellowed.

Not to be put off by his curt manner, Elizabeth forged ahead. "They have so few toys that I thought with a small wagon I could take them for rides around the castle. You know, for fun."

"Fun," he bellowed again. "What nonsense! Do ye have nothing better to do with ye time than to play with wee little ones?"

Red faced, Elizabeth was not to be intimidated. "I guess you have not heard; this is the task assigned to me by Lord Nicolas." There. She had used her best weapon—Nicolas.

Tilting his head to one side and then the other, John calmly said, "Why didn't ye say so in the first place? I didn't realize Lord Nicolas was doing the asking. Of course, I can make one."

He dismissed Elizabeth when he turned back toward his workbench. "It'll be done post haste."

Elizabeth was elated. She didn't bother to correct John's misinterpretation of who was asking for the wagon. He had agreed and that's what mattered most. Right?

Emerging into the sunlight, Elizabeth shaded her eyes with her hand. She found Angus patiently waiting while Jarvis dozed against the building. It was hard for Elizabeth to refer to it as a building since it only had three sides and a roof. She was relatively sure that this was not what she was accustomed to.

Angus nudged Jarvis with his boot. "Get up, Jarvis. Lady Emma is ready."

Jarvis slowly opened his eyes to see Angus and Lady Emma looking at him. He sluggishly rose to his feet, stiff from sitting. "I'm sorry to keep ye waiting, my lady."

Elizabeth was too delighted with her recent conquest to take offense. She had noticed Angus was quick to aggravate his brother which made her feel a little sorry for frail Jarvis. He was such a sweetheart. He reminded her of her grandfather. Would she ever see her papaw again or would she be stuck here the rest of her days? Not wanting to go down that bleak path, she quickly took the men by the arm and headed back toward the keep.

"Shall we go for a walk outside the castle today, gentlemen?"

Angus jerked his arm free from her clasp. "That would be ill-advised, my lady," Angus answered. "Lord Nicolas gave us strict instructions to remain inside the castle walls."

"That's fine, Angus. I don't need an escort to pick wild flowers," she teased as she winked at Jarvis.

"Wha . . . at?" Angus sputtered. "Absolutely not."

"Oh, brother, let her go. She'll stay close by; won't you Lady Emma?" Jarvis added with a return wink as he warmed to the game.

Coming to an abrupt halt, Angus spun to face the pestering pair. "This is unacceptable. Jarvis. You know what Lord Nicolas said, and he's counting on us to carry out his command."

Based on his scowling face, Elizabeth decided she would call a halt to the charade. She didn't want Angus to burst a blood vessel over their teasing. However, before she could say a word, Jarvis erupted in knee-slapping laughter.

"Angus, we are but jesting with you," Jarvis hooted.

Elizabeth thought Jarvis's words would soothe Angus's anger, but they did the opposite. With clamped lips and narrowed eyes, Angus whirled on his heel and stormed off.

"Oh, my. I believe we made him mad," Elizabeth whispered wide-eyed.

Jarvis continued to stare after his brother with a twinkle in his eye. Finally, he had gotten the better of his brother.

"Shall we take a stroll in the garden instead?" Elizabeth sheepishly asked. Curious children began following them as they continued their stroll, each vying for Lady Emma's attention. She was pleased to know the children enjoyed her company. Henry brought up the rear with Patrick, Pierson, and Merry skipping along beside her. Obviously, Nicolas's assignment to protect Elizabeth was taken seriously by Henry.

* * *

"Why are you still inside the castle?" she hissed. "Lady Emma is outside."

"I have been working on a plan and don't need you to tell me what to do. Remember, I'm the one taking all the risk and will be the one to devise her accident," he gruffly replied.

Realizing she was dealing with a dim-wit, she softened her accusations. She didn't need the brainless fool exposing her part in the forthcoming incident. "Please, forgive me. I'm not quite myself," she said quietly as she leaned into his body and placed her delicate hand on his face.

"Of course, my pet," he murmured. Gently removing her hand, he turned it over and kissed her palm. "I'm as anxious to receive my reward as you are to be rid of the witch. Fear not; I will succeed."

"I know you will," she purred. "Then the castle will return to normal, and we can proceed with our plans. The constant worry of being found out is making me quite fretful," she added as she dipped her head for effect.

Placing his finger on her chin, he tenderly lifted her face. "All will be well; you will see. I am as brave as I am cunning and worthy of your affection," he said. Taking both her hands into his, he kissed them once again. "Until we meet again." He gave an exaggerated bow as he backed away, turned on his heel, and left the alcove.

"Good riddance," she whispered when he rounded the corner. What had she been thinking to offer herself to such a disgusting man? She wanted a child, but not with him. He was constantly dirty and smelled of manure. She wiped her hands on her dress with jerky motions to remove the moisture of his slobbery kisses. She shuttered with revulsion. A bath was in order to cleanse away his scent and soak away her uncertainties.

"The gardens will not be as beautiful this time of year, my lady," Jarvis said gazing into the sky. "Spring is when the castle is its most colorful. New grass shoots, trees sprouting their growth, and flowers in full bloom . . . God's exquisite painting," he said wistfully looking down at Elizabeth.

"Jarvis, I didn't realize you were such a poet," she said in awe.

Ducking his head, "Now, my lady, I'm just an old man full of memories. Nothing more."

"Oh, Jarvis, you are too modest. You painted me a breathtaking scene with your words. I call that a poet," she said with sincerity. "I'll be able to envision what the garden will look like come spring. Thank you."

"We will leave ye to yer garden walk, My Lady," Henry said. "Come Merry, Patrick, and Pierson, let's be on our way." All the children skipped off leaving Elizabeth and Jarvis alone.

Elizabeth and Jarvis had arrived at the back of the castle where there were no out buildings, only the quiet, serene gardens. Jarvis stopped and pointed. "Here is the entrance to our gardens. Cedric is the caretaker. He's usually somewhere close by even during the fall season. He says he is preparing the ground for next year," Jarvis said with a chuckle. "He must be correct, for each year the gardens are more beautiful than the last."

"Thank you, Jarvis." As they both observed the dying flowers, she asked, "Care to wander through the paths with me?"

"If it's all the same to you, My Lady, I would rather sit on this bench. The sun feels good on my old bones. You will be safe," he added for assurance.

"Oh, my safety was never in question. I feel quite protected with you close by my side," she added.

Jarvis eased down onto the bench and stretched out his arthritic legs. Rubbing his knee, he said, "I'll be waiting right here for you when you are finished."

Leaning down, she kissed his weathered cheek. "I won't be long," she promised. She didn't remain to see his bright red face wreathed with a smile.

Elizabeth was content to be alone. She had grown weary of having a constant companion even though Jarvis was pleasant company. Now she could think about her future. Meandering through what was left of a once breath-taking garden, she wondered how to alter Nicolas's plans for her. She was not ready for marriage especially to that arrogant man. Humming to herself, she made her way to the rear of the garden near the castle wall.

Looking up she could see several guards patrolling the wall. Their presence made her feel secure. She could say one thing about Nicolas: he was meticulous when it came to safeguarding his property. Contemplating her future as she walked along, she ran her hands over the tops of dried flowers. Upon hearing a scrapping noise, she called out, "Hello . . . Cedric, is that you?" Not receiving an answer, she stopped to listen more carefully. The sound was coming from above. She turned just in time to see a boulder falling toward her. Throwing her arm up for protection deflected the large stone away from a direct hit on her head. However, it struck her arm and the side of her head knocking her to the ground, unconscious.

Jarvis woke suddenly from a short nap. What had awakened him? All was quiet. How long had Lady Emma been in the gardens? Rising from his bench, Jarvis entered the area calling out for her. No answer. She probably was out of hearing range. Further down the path he called again. When he received no answer, he became concerned. Moving as rapidly as he could, Jarvis went through each path and continued to call for Lady Emma. He became more frantic with each step. As he neared the castle wall, he saw her foot sticking out on the path. Walking as quickly as his old knees would allow, he knelt down by her side.

Carefully, Jarvis turned Lady Emma over to see blood oozing from a gash on the side of her head. "Lady Emma," he called. "Wake up!" She did not respond.

Rising to his feet and yelling Cedric's name, Jarvis scurried along the path to Cedric's work area.

Cedric emerged from his hothouse to see Jarvis's panic-stricken eyes. "What is amiss, Jarvis?"

"Come quickly. I need your help. Something has happened to Lady Emma, and she won't respond to my voice." He didn't wait for Cedric to answer, but turned and ran back along the path to Lady Emma.

Seeing Jarvis so upset propelled Cedric into motion. He grabbed some water and a clean cloth and took off after Jarvis.

Upon reaching Jarvis, Cedric noticed Lady Emma lying motionless in his flower bed. "What has happened?" Cedric asked.

"I know not. I left her to walk through the gardens. Now look what has happened. She won't wake up," he frantically replied. "What shall we do?"

"Here, apply some cool water to her face. I'll go fetch Thomas and Phillip. They will know what to do." Cedric bolted out of the gardens calling for Thomas and Phillip as he ran. His frenzied actions brought the castle activity to a halt. Workmen stared after Cedric as he plowed through the courtyard toward the keep. Dashing up the steps, he literally ran into Thomas.

Thomas grabbed Cedric's arms to steady him. "Whoa, Cedric. Slow down. What is the trouble?" Thomas asked with authority.

"It's Lady Emma. She is hurt and unconscious in the garden," he said out of breath.

"Get Phillip and send for Agnes," Thomas commanded as he bounded down the steps toward the back of the castle grounds.

Upon reaching the garden area, Thomas began calling out for Lady Emma.

"Back here," he heard Jarvis faintly cry out. Thomas sprinted toward Jarvis's voice only to find him bent over Lady Emma's lifeless body lying on the ground. He quickly knelt down beside Jarvis and saw the blood on her face and clothes.

"What has happened?" he demanded.

"I'm not sure. She was strolling through the gardens. When she didn't return, I went searching and found her like this."

Thomas glanced at Jarvis. "I thought Nicolas instructed you or Angus to be with her constantly. How was she alone?" he asked angrily.

"'Tis my fault. I told her I would wait on the bench. With guards all around, I thought she was safe," Jarvis replied with regret in his voice.

Thomas had no time to deal with Jarvis. Right now Lady Emma needed his attention. He applied pressure to her wound in hopes of stopping the blood flow. After a brief time, Thomas gently lifted her and began his journey to the keep.

"I'm so sorry. I never thought . . ."

"Cease. Phillip will deal with you about the matter. I have no time to hear it," Thomas abruptly said.

Remorse weighed heavy on Jarvis. He couldn't keep up with Thomas's swift gait. As a result, his pace slowed to a halt. There in the garden, he fell to his knees in anguish. With hands clasped and head bowed to the ground, Jarvis prayed. *Dear God in Heaven, rescue Lady Emma from death. 'Tis my fault for her injury. Punish me for my neglect, but spare her further harm. Please, my Lord and God. In Your son's name I beseech Thee. Amen.*

10

    Nicolas and the men were riding hard. Traveling from Berwick-upon-Tweed to Blyth and back again to get the special license was over one hundred miles. They had averaged twenty-five miles a day over some rough terrain. Plus it had taken two days in the town of Blyth to procure the license. There had been little time for rest. Thundering hooves and jingling harnesses scattered the birds into the air. Talking was kept at a minimum so they could hear approaching riders. Even though fatigue was heavy on their shoulders, each man kept alert to possible danger.

    Approaching darkness would force them to stop for the night. Nicolas gave a hand signal to slow his group to a trot. "Up ahead is some forest at the base of the Cheviot Hills. What think you, Hastings? Should we stop for the night or keep riding?"

    "The men will do what you command, my lord."

    "I know that, Hastings. I'm asking your opinion."

    "The horses could stand a rest, and the men would be grateful for fresh food."

They continued to ride in silence until they reached the secluded spot among the trees. The weary men dismounted to set up camp. Six men went to hunt game, and six spread out around the perimeter to guard their camp while the remainder tended to the horses and started small cooking fires. The base of the hill at their backs provided safety and protection from the elements.

It wasn't long before they sat around the fires eating roasted bird and rabbit. Nicolas had brought along some of his most seasoned warriors. They were accustomed to traveling fast with quick stops and little rest. However, tonight was a welcomed change.

Sitting on a tree stump at the outskirts of the camp, Nicolas listened to his men talk quietly among themselves. He gazed around the group and was thankful for such honorable and loyal warriors in his service. He didn't doubt that any one of them would give his life to save him or his family. God had truly blessed him.

"More drink, My Lord?" Hastings asked bringing Nicolas out of his musings.

"Yes, thank you."

Hastings poured cool water into the crude cup and turned to leave.

Looking into his cup, Nicolas casually asked Hastings, "Do you think I have lost my wits?"

Hastings stopped and slowly turned back to face Nicolas. "My lord?"

Rising to his feet, "'Tis nothing . . . just questioning my own sanity," he said. After a big gulp, he tossed the remainder of his water to the ground and clapped Hastings on the shoulder. "Don't mind me. Just the rambling of a very tired warrior."

Hastings thought for a moment and then said, "You are doing what you feel is best. No one can fault you for that."

"Ahh, Hastings, thank you. You're a good man. Go, attend to your duties. I'm going to get some rest."

"Yes, my lord." Hastings reluctantly left his lord alone. Nicolas was unsure of his latest decision, and none of his men felt confident even to offer him their opinion on the matter. Sometimes it was a curse to be the leader.

The men finished eating and snuffed out the fires before settling down for the night. The guards changed out every couple of hours to allow each man adequate rest. Nicolas slept lightly. He was trained to hear unusual sounds in the night. *Ch-o-mp . . . ch-o-mp . . . stomp.* The sound of the horses was music to his ears. Suddenly, the stillness of the night shattered. Nicolas bolted upright at the crashing through the forest. He was not necessarily worried that it was an enemy. An enemy would be soundless. It had to be one of his young guards who obviously needed more training in stealth. However, as a precaution, his men watched the forest with their swords at ready.

Bursting through the trees was Walter.

"Walter," Nicolas hissed, "what are you about? You were loud enough to alert our neighbors in Scotland, you clumsy oaf!"

Wheezing for breath, Walter sputtered out, "They are here." *Gasp.*

"Who is here?" Nicolas demanded.

Gasp. "Our neighbors from Scotland." *Gasp.*

That was enough to get the men scrambling. Chainmail was quickly donned, swords strapped on, horses readied. Nicolas grabbed Walter by the shirt, "What mean you?"

By now Walter had regained some breath and was talking rapidly to explain what he had seen. "There were thirty-five mounted Scotsmen crossing the border into England. They were heavily armed."

"Reivers!" someone whispered.

"Hastings, Henry, Peter, and Edmund, come," Nicolas ordered. Nicolas pulled his commanders together to plan an attack. He was not going to allow the Reivers to wreak havoc at his backdoor. While they strategized, the rest of the men and guards were putting soft cloth over their horses' hooves. Since they were outnumbered, the element of surprise would benefit their cause. In a matter of minutes, the company of men was ready to strike.

Nicolas and his warriors easily picked up the trail in the moonlight. The reivers were being careless thinking they were alone in the area—talking and laughing as they road down the hill. This was one time Nicolas was relieved he had brought twenty-five of his best fighting men. Many times he traveled with less than five men for speed. As he rode, Nicolas became angry. It was supposed to be a time of peace between Scotland and England, yet here were some ruffians out to cause mischief. More than likely, they would steal cattle. However, some raiders ravaged homes and took hostages . . . but not tonight.

The reivers came upon a field of cattle. They slowly surrounded the livestock and began herding them together. Nicolas waited until the Scots circled out around the cattle before stepping out of the shadows to confront the invaders.

"Those don't belong to you," Nicolas calmly said while casually leaning on his saddle. From the outside, Nicolas exuded a relaxed posture; however, his insides were as taut as a bow—ready for battle.

The raider's heads snapped up at the sound of Nicolas's voice to see three mounted men blocking their way. *Swoosh.* Claymores slid from their leather sheaths with lightning speed.

"Well, nou laddie, hoo might ye be?" the leader drawled out unfazed. His men were poised and ready to attack Nicolas. They were thirty-five men against only three. Outrageous odds.

"I'm Lord Nicolas Fairwick of Berwick-upon-Tweed. Who might you be?" Nicolas repeated back the man's words.

"Sairy, *My Lord,*" he said with distain, "but ye'll not gie me name."

"And you'll not be getting those cattle," Nicolas responded sternly.

"Ah, ha," he laughed aloud. "Who weel stop us? Ye three? A think not." His men joined in with the jest unaware that Nicolas's warriors surrounded them. Cattle stamped and mooed their displeasure.

"As I said, you will not be taking those cattle. You and your men can surrender now, or we will be forced to persuade you to change your mind," Nicolas continued.

"Weel, thenk ye for thit option, but nae. If ye'll remove ye scrawny seilves, me men hae work tanicht. Ye can gae straecht back whaur ye are frae—Bu-r-rwich-Upon-Twea. Dinna fash yerself weeth me work and we'll let ye live." The leader was very pleased with his remarks as he looked to his men for approval.

"No."

The Scottish leader became furious with Nicolas's one word. He needed to get those cattle across the border before morning dawned, and Nicolas was standing in his way. It was time to remove the obstacle. Raising his sword high above his head, he gave a battle cry that split the night air.

At the same moment, the remainder of Nicolas's men stepped from hiding—arrows drawn for flight and aimed at the leader.

"McDougal, leuk aboot. Wee ar surrounded," one of his men blurted fearfully. The raiders were distracted as chaos erupted around them. Twenty-three mounted warriors appeared out of the darkness which spooked the cattle. The livestock began stamping, bumping, and brawling. The raiders whipped their heads around comprehending their dilemma.

"That's correct. You are surrounded with the first arrow aimed at you, McDougal," Nicolas shouted above the clamor. He paused and let that sink in before continuing. "Now, I say again, surrender."

"Nae," McDougal yelled as he charged toward Nicolas. Four arrows released immediately with two hitting their mark. One struck his side the other through his neck. McDougal went down in the midst of the cattle. Nicolas charged forward to clear away the cattle while at the same time raiders rushed forward in hopes to save McDougal and to kill Nicolas. More arrows rapidly discharged to fell four more Scotsmen. Clashing swords and screams of death rang through the air. Nicolas blocked a sword with his shield while swinging his sword through the middle of his enemy. The man fell forward on his pony and tried to steer away from Nicolas, but several cows jostled his pony as they frantically ran from the melee. The man fell to his death under sharp hooves. Nicolas glanced around and was relieved to see his men had the upper hand in the battle.

Charging to assist Hastings, Nicolas saw several trampled men on the ground. The Scotsmen were arrogant and foolish this night and were paying a high price for their rebellious ways. Tonight Nicolas would send a strong message back to Scotland that England would not tolerate their raids especially during peaceful times. Living on the border of England and Scotland, Nicolas had fought many skirmishes over cattle and looting of homes. Hopefully, this would be one of the last ones.

Catching the reivers unaware had definitely worked to their advantage. Within a short time Nicolas's men had killed or captured the Scotsmen. The cattle had scattered leaving only dead bodies sprawled on the ground. Those taken captive were corralled in the middle of Nicolas's warriors.

Nicolas rode up to the prisoners and counted. Only seven out of thirty-five. What a waste.

"Are you all from the clan McDougal?" Nicolas asked.

Looking at him with anger and contempt, no one answered.

Edmund put his sword to the neck of a young man. "If you want to live, you had best answer Lord Fairwick," he gritted out. The man shook from fright as Edmund held fast. Would the lad act foolishly by remaining silent?

Edmund had the boy's face tilted so he could see into Nicolas's eyes. Nicolas saw fear battling with courage. When Edmund nicked the boys neck, fear won out.

"Ay," he weakly replied.

"Since you have answered me, you shall live. Peter, bring me a horse for the boy," Nicolas commanded. With his attention once again on the boy, he said, "I'm sending you back to your people. You are to tell them what happened this night. If the Laird of Clan McDougal wants to claim the rest of these rebels, he will find them down the road at the Castle of Lord Kerr, the owner of these cattle."

"Nae," many of them shouted. "Juist kill us nou," they pleaded. "Thaur is no aurnor in being a hoostage in this cursed England," some roared.

"Honor!" Nicolas belted out. "You have no honor. You are a disgrace to your country and to the McDougal clan. I wouldn't be surprised if your kin leave you in the Kerr dungeon to rot."

One of the reivers tried to break free and escape, but Hastings struck him with the hilt of his sword and knocked him out.

"Tie him up, Hastings, and put him on the back of one of those ponies. The rest of you misfits will walk to your destination," Nicolas barked. "Let's get going. We've wasted enough time with this adventure. It's about two miles to the Kerr holding and I want to be on the road home by sunrise."

"Edmund, look over our wounded and see if all are travel worthy."

"What about their wounded, Lord?" Edmund inquired.

"Don't squander away your time on them unless they are critical. The rest of you men prepare for our journey to Kerr Castle."

"Ye arn't goin ta juist leave our dead, ar ye?"

"Your clan can claim them or the vultures can have them. They are not my concern. You each gave up your right to an honorable burial when you crossed the border with ill intent," Nicolas snapped.

Nicolas looked over the gruff reivers. "If any of you slow our progress without due cause, you will be struck down." Glaring at them in the eyes, Nicolas shouted, "Onward."

Once Edmund had tended to Lord Fairwick's wounded, he brought up the rear of the procession. Thankfully, none of their men had been seriously injured nor killed. He had gone to the men lying on the ground to see if any lived, but no. From what he had seen, they had appeared very young. Edmund prayed for their souls after one final glimpse at their lifeless bodies. Border raids were a messy business and not one he hoped to confront again anytime soon.

11

Bang, bang, bang... "Brigette, open this door immediately. 'Tis your turn to watch over Lady Emma and relieve Abigail," Phillip said sternly.

Shuffling over to the closed door, Brigette whined, "Phillip, I don't feel well. Can't Collette do it?"

"No! Get dressed straight away. I'll escort you to her room," Phillip said with irritation. "Don't make me wait overlong." Phillip grew weary of his sister's selfishness. She did what she wanted, when she wanted and never offered to help anyone. Phillip would make sure Nicolas heard of her recent antics when he returned. Something needed to be done before she was ruined for marriage—spoiled beyond redemption.

"Agh," she screamed out. "You'll regret this, Phillip," she muttered.

After much huffing and stomping about, Brigette finally emerged. "You can't make me like her," she ground out as she flounced past Phillip. Stunned, Phillip watched her retreating back and wondered where they had gone so wrong in raising their sister. Nicolas couldn't return fast enough.

Phillip watched Brigette stomp down the hallway until she turned the corner and was out of his sight. She obviously wanted to make her point clear about her displeasure; he only hoped her actions hurt her feet. It seemed Brigette wanted to be anywhere than near Lady Emma which puzzled Phillip. He caught up with his sister to see her parade directly through the door without knocking, her back rigid and nose in the air. With a deep sigh, Phillip leaned against the wall and waited for Abigail. This was one time he was relieved Nicolas was lord of the castle . . . women!

"Take your leave, Abigail," Brigette barked. Phillip cringed, but didn't interfere. He knew her condescending tone of voice would make Abigail livid. Those two got along about as well as Scotsmen and Englishmen.

"How dare you talk to me in that manner?" Abigail said with disdain. Rising to her feet, she pierced Brigette with squinting eyes. "You certainly don't give me orders, little sister." Brigette hated the reminder that under no circumstances would she rule at the castle. Since Nicolas had not married, Abigail oversaw the castle meals and guests. If the brothers could find someone to take her, Brigette would be married off—the sooner the better was Phillip's thinking.

* * *

Brigette ignored Abigail as Brigette stood by the door tamping her foot. All she wanted to do was curl up and sleep. She was dying and no one knew it. Brigette certainly didn't tell Abigail for fear Abigail would taunt her to her dying breath.

"Remember, dear sister," Abigail sneered, "you are to check on Lady Emma and see to her needs. Lord Nicolas will be furious when he finds out she came to harm. Don't heap coals on your head by mistreating her." Abigail left the room before Brigette could think of a nasty retort.

"You horrible woman," Brigette let fly as she shut the door that led to the hallway.

"Not well done, Brigette," Elizabeth softly said.

Surprised, Brigette spun around to see Lady Emma grasping the door between the two rooms. She was shaking from the effort to stand and was as white as flour except for the side of her head. It was purple and black. "Lady Emma, you shouldn't be out of bed."

Brigette hurried over to Lady Emma and took her by the arm. "Let me help you back to bed before you fall on your pretty face," Brigette ground out. She was not happy she had to help the woman much less touch her. Elizabeth leaned heavily on Brigette's arm as they both staggered to the bed.

"You are too weak to be out of bed."

"That's why I'm so feeble. I need to get some exercise instead of staying in bed day after day."

"Listen, I don't feel well myself, and it will be helpful if you will just stay in the bed today," Brigette said. Brigette tucked Lady Emma into bed and started to leave when Lady Emma grabbed her hand.

"Thank you, Brigette," she whispered.

All Brigette could do was nod her head. She didn't want to have any feelings for the woman, especially pity. Pity could lead to caring. She pulled her hand free and quietly left the room leaving the door ajar.

* * *

Elizabeth let out a sigh. Befriending Brigette was not going to be easy. She would think on that while doing some in-the-bed exercises, starting with leg lifts. Lying in bed was making her weak, yet both Phillip and Thomas were adamant about it. She knew they feared what Nicolas was going to say when he returned from his journey. Therefore, she needed to improve, hoping to lessen Nicolas's outburst that was sure to come. As she completed her fourth leg lift, she heard a moan coming from Nicolas's room. *What is wrong with Brigette?* After listening to Brigette's incessant moaning during six more exercises, Elizabeth gingerly got to her feet. She was amazed at how much stronger she felt after a few minutes of movement. Still feeling fragile, Elizabeth cautiously made her way to the open door to take a peep. There she saw Brigette curled up in the chair by the fireplace holding her stomach and whimpering.

Grasping furniture as she went, Elizabeth padded over, squatted down and placed her hand on Brigette's knee. "What's wrong, Brigette?"

"Nothing," Brigette said while pushing away Elizabeth's hand. "Leave me alone."

"Brigette, you are sitting here curled up and groaning every other breath. Obviously, there is something hurting you. Please tell me. I might be able to help."

Humph. "You can't even help yourself. Look at you, injured and feeble," Brigette scoffed. "Just leave me be."

Elizabeth eased down to sit upon the floor at Brigette's feet. Brooding Brigette wasn't going anywhere. "You might not know this, but I am a healer like Agnes. I have been able to help Phillip with his hip. Did you know that?" When Brigette failed to answer, she continued. "I have studied much about the human body. Will you not trust me? If it's beyond my experience, I can call for Agnes."

"No, don't call for her," she vehemently replied. "No one can help me," she cried, "for I'm most certainly dying."

Taken aback, Elizabeth paused a moment before responding. "What makes you think you are dying?"

Sniff . . . sniff

"Tell me," Elizabeth encouraged.

"Very well. I suppose I should tell someone before my final breath," Brigette said with her head in her hands.

Elizabeth had to smile at Brigette's performance even though it was obviously staged for effect. An actress, Brigette was not.

"Many months ago I awoke with a cramping stomach. I thought it was something I had eaten to cause my sour belly. However, it lasted several days even though I ate very little. Then the worst happened . . . I began to bleed. It was a small amount at first, and later it got worse." *Sniff.* "Just when I thought I would be dead in a matter of days, all pain and bleeding stopped. Naturally, I hoped it was gone forever until weeks later it returned again. This pattern has repeated itself numerous times. So you see, it must be God punishing me for my sins—a slow death," she said as her head rolled to one side. Once her tale was completed, she began to cry in earnest.

Elizabeth let out a sigh of relief. Thankfully, Brigette wasn't dying. Lightly touching Brigette's knee, Elizabeth smiled and said, "You are not dying."

Brigette's weeping was so loud, she didn't comprehend what Lady Emma had said.

"Look at me, Brigette."

Opening her eyes, Brigette turned her head and frowned down at Lady Emma. "Wha-t?"

"You are not dying. I know this for a fact. Your body is preparing to nurture a baby one day. It happens to all women. Has no one told you about this?" she asked incredibly.

Sitting up straighter, Brigette scrubbed the tears from her eyes. She had just heard the first encouraging words since her predicament began. "I'm not dying?" she asked bewildered.

"No. Actually, you are a healthy woman preparing for your marriage days. Has Abigail never told you of this happening?" Elizabeth asked.

Narrowing her eyes, Brigette glanced toward the door. "No," she spit out. "She is a mean woman." Gazing back at Elizabeth with her frown in place, "I hate her."

Elizabeth ignored that last comment and rose to her feet. "Come. I have a remedy for those stomach cramps." She carefully headed toward her room without taking notice if Brigette followed. More than likely Brigette would want freedom from her misery, so Elizabeth expected Brigette would accept her help whether she liked Elizabeth or not.

When Brigette arrived in Emma's room, she hesitated only a moment before asking, "What are you doing?"

"I'm heating a brick. Take your shoes off and climb into my bed," she said. "You can remove your dress, as well, if you like."

Shrugging her shoulders, Brigette proceeded to remove her shoes. Elizabeth glanced around. "The heat will work best if you take off your dress and keep on your shift."

After slipping off her shoes, Brigette untied the front of her dress and pulled it off. She sat on the edge of the bed to remove her stockings. When her bare feet touched the cold floor, she swiftly climbed in the bed and pulled a blanket up to her nose.

Once Brigette was in the bed, Elizabeth brought over a heated brick wrapped in a cloth. Pulling back the blanket, she placed the small brick on Brigette's stomach and covered her back up. "Now rest. I'll replace the brick when it cools. In the meantime, I'll mix up some herbs for the pain."

Brigette watched Lady Emma mix herbs in a dish. She closed her eyes. "The heat is quite soothing on my aching stomach. I just hope my brothers don't come to check on you and find me in your bed instead. That could prove most unpleasant."

Elizabeth just shook her head as she crumbled mint in the mixture to make it more palatable. Shuffling back to the bedside, she lightly touched Brigette's shoulder. "Here. Drink this. It will begin to ease your pain after a few minutes."

Brigette raised up on her elbow and took the cup. *Sniff.* "It doesn't smell too tasty," she said with a wrinkled nose.

Giving the cup a nudge, Elizabeth said, "Pinch your nose, and then drink it down quickly. You will be pleased with the outcome."

Brigette held her nose and eyed Elizabeth before gulping it down. "Ech, that was vile. Are you trying to poison me?"

"Brigette, you really must stop your theatrics. It's not becoming to a young lady. Most men do not like it," she added. Taking the empty cup, Elizabeth tenderly brushed Brigette's golden hair from her brown eyes that were so much like Nicolas's. "You are very beautiful, Brigette," she softly spoke. "One day, when you are older, some man will see the remarkable woman God created just for him."

Brigette suddenly grew still and stared into Elizabeth's eyes. "I can't remember the last time another woman touched me in this manner . . . it is pleasing. I feel warmth spiraling through my body." She sleepily gazed back at Elizabeth. "Think you I am beautiful, truly?" she asked wistfully.

"Yes. Now get some rest. I'll be in Nicolas's room if you need me."

Brigette snuggled down under the covers and let out a sigh of contentment. Elizabeth stood there for a moment thankful for her breakthrough with Brigette. Hopefully, she would have more opportunities to mentor Brigette.

Father, thank You for this special time I've had with Brigette. Please allow our relationship to grow into a friendship. She can be a sweet girl when she's not play acting for attention. Help me to bring out the Godly young woman hidden behind her pretense. Amen. Oh . . . I guess I should also ask for Nicolas's safe return. While I'm asking, can You please, please let me regain my memory? Amen.

Leaving the door ajar, Elizabeth dragged the blanket off Nicolas's bed on her way to the wing back chair. The activities over the past little bit had drained her of all energy. She stoked the fire before dropping into the chair. With the blanket barely tucked around her, she, too, dozed off—both women unaware of the skirmish that was to come.

12

After six days of hard travel, Nicolas and his men rode into view of the castle. Torches blazing in the night sky were a welcomed sight. Mulling over his trip, Nicolas realized he had accomplished his main task of securing a marriage license plus thwarted raiders from wreaking havoc on Lord Kerr's lands. Taking care of the raiders had been a delay he had not planned upon, but, all in all, a successful mission.

"Hastings, lead the men home," Nicolas instructed as he pulled up his horse. "I'll bring up the rear." Nicolas remembered the last time he had returned from an assignment—he had brought home a woman. Now weeks later, he was planning to marry the woman. Verily, he must be mad.

Watching his men ride by, Nicolas once again wondered if he were being too hasty in his decision about wedding the mysterious woman. Maybe the messenger had been incorrect about King James declaring that Nicolas take a wife. Perhaps the King wasn't bringing his niece to wed him at all. He shook his head to dispel the image of a child bride. No . . . he had to take action to preserve his sanity. Waiting to see what the King would do could be disastrous.

"'Tis good to be home, is it not, My Lord?" Peter asked riding alongside Nicolas.

"Yes, Peter, the castle is a magnificent picture. Hopefully, we can remain until next spring without any more unwanted adventures."

"Ah, a long winter with me wife would be a pleasure. By next year, I'm sure to have a son," he said grinning wildly.

Returning his grin, Nicolas didn't make further comment. Would he also have a son by next year? Not likely. First, he must wed, and then work to win the Lady's favor. That undertaking could take much time. She was not easily swayed. Ah, but he was up for the challenge.

Clomp . . . clomp . . . clatter. Hearing the hooves rattle across the draw bridge was a sweet melody. Cheers arose as he and Peter entered the courtyard, and the portcullis dropped in place for the night. Guards and families filled the area ready to greet their returning husbands, sons, and brothers. Thomas and Phillip were awaiting Nicolas on the top step of the keep. They did not look pleased. What could possibly have happened in six days? Probably something to do with Brigette. She was constantly tormenting her brothers.

Men led the horses off to the stables where the horses received royal treatment. Every man knew that in battle you were only as good as your horse. Therefore, great care was given to the steeds with a rub down and plenty of extra care.

Nicolas trudged up the steps in no hurry to hear complaints from Thomas and Phillip. Usually, Thomas was jovial even in the toughest times. Brigette must have really been in rare form to cause his frown.

Slapping his brothers on their backs, Nicolas commented. "You two look like the world is ending tonight. What has you both so sour?"

"To the war room," Phillip said. No pleasantries were exchanged. This did not bode well. The Fairwick's only used the war room for war strategizing or giving or receiving unpleasant reports. Not quite the homecoming Nicolas had hoped to receive. After removing his sword and other weapons, he plopped into the nearest chair. "What has you two in such foul humors?"

When they both started to speak at once, Nicolas held up his hand. "One at a time."

"I will start. 'Tis my story to tell," Thomas began.

"Thomas, 'tis not a story, but a dreadful event," Phillip sputtered out.

Nicolas sat up a little straighter. Phillip was visibly upset. "Give me the whole of it, at once," Nicolas boomed.

"Lady Emma went . . ." he started when Nicolas held up his hand again.

"Who is Lady Emma?" he asked.

"Your Lady. She changed her name again while you were gone. Please, don't interrupt again. 'Tis urgent I get it told," Thomas erupted.

Nicolas had not seen his two brothers in such a state. Naturally, a woman was involved in the mess. "Get on with it then."

"Lady Emma took a walk on the castle grounds with Angus and Jarvis. Angus and Jarvis had a tiff and parted ways leaving only Jarvis to guard Lady Emma. Anyway, they walked to the gardens after a stop at the carpenter's. Jarvis let Lady Emma enter the gardens alone while he waited on a bench. When she didn't return, he went looking for her. That's when he found her lying on the ground near the rear castle wall. She had been struck by a large stone."

Thomas took a breath which gave Nicolas an opening to speak.

Nicolas jumped to his feet looking fiercely at his brothers. "Does she live?" he roared.

"Yes, Nicolas. Calm yourself," Phillip interjected as Nicolas bolted from the room taking the stairs two at a time. He needed to see her for himself. Running down the passageway, he threw open the door to his chambers. There sat Brigette and Lady Emma at the chess board.

"Nicolas," Brigette squealed. "You're finally home." She jumped up to run to him when a hand restrained her. Jerking her head around, Lady Emma gazed into her eyes.

Smiling. "Properly, please," was all Elizabeth said.

Brigette quickly composed herself. She made a low curtsy to her brother and smiled at him. "Welcome home, Nicolas."

Unfortunately, Nicolas had eyes for only one.

Brigette reacted poorly when Nicolas failed to recognize her. Her head swiveled from Nicolas to Lady Emma and back again with daggers shooting from her eyes. With her dress still clutched in her hands, she dashed past Nicolas as a sob escaped her. Four days of Emma's working with Brigette shot down as a delicate bird in flight. Reparation would have to come at a later time, for now it was time to deal with Nicolas.

A soft sigh trickled out. "Not well done, My Lord. Your sister gave you a proper greeting, yet you ignored her."

"She will recover," he said absentmindedly. From his position just inside the door, Lady Emma looked healthy. He strode to where she was sitting and took her chin in his hand. Gently applying pressure, he turned her face so he could see the left side. His eyes grew wide at what he saw. The left side of her face was black, yellow, and purple with the dark color circling her left eye.

Elizabeth delicately removed his hand and rose from her seat. "I am fine . . . truly. I will explain all to you after you've eaten and had your bath," she said with resignation.

Rubbing his hand over his dirty, unshaven face, Nicolas stepped back from her. He knew his smell was horrific, but he needed to see that she was well. "I'm sorry if I have offended you, my lady. 'Twas not my intent," he replied.

"You have not offended me. I simply know that you are hungry after such a long journey and would feel more relaxed after a hot bath. It soothes tired muscles. That's all. I will see to your needs."

Taking hold of her arm as she attempted to walk past him, he said, "No. You remain here. I will return when I am more presentable." After he released her arm, he crossed his arms and took an authoritative stance. "What have you done to Brigette?"

"As I said, I'll tell you all when you return," she said with a smile. "Much has transpired since you left. Some things good and some things not so good."

They stood only a hand width apart staring into each other's eyes. His crisscrossed arms almost touched her face. Not to be intimidated by his size or posture, she held her own and didn't back away.

"Very well. I will return shortly. Be prepared to share past events." Nicolas flung his arms down and turned on his heel exiting the room. Elizabeth blew out her breath through her lips. The initial confrontation was over.

* * *

The hour was late when Nicolas finally made his way back to his room. Phillip and Thomas had continued to fill his ears with the happenings of the castle all during his meal and bath. They had been worse than two harping women. Usually Phillip was content to stay busy with the castle books, but something had shifted while he had been away. Nicolas wasn't sure he liked the protectiveness of Thomas and Phillip over Lady Emma. Surely after a night's rest in his own bed, the issues would seem less daunting.

Jarvis and Angus stood guard at his door when he came up the stairs. "You two may leave now. I will have a word with you on the morrow."

"Yes, My Lord," they said in unison. He watched as they lumbered away with hanging heads. He almost felt sorry for the two old warriors, but their actions had almost cost Lady Emma her life. Therefore, he would hold them accountable for their deeds despite their advanced age.

Pushing open the door, he found Lady Emma dozing by the fire. He closed and bolted the door before taking a seat in the opposite chair. He removed his boots and stretched out his legs toward the roaring fire. Lady Emma had been right. His hot bath had relaxed his aching body. The warmth from the fire was soothing as well. His lids began to droop as he watched Lady Emma sleep. Her mouth moved on occasion as air puffed from her rosebud lips. It relieved him to know that she now felt safe enough to sleep like a babe—no cares or worries.

From what his brothers had told him, Lady Emma had suffered greatly these last few days. She had been unconscious for two days, Agnes unsure if she would recover. After waking, her mind had been befuddled. Thankfully, her dizziness had receded along with the debilitating headaches. Now all that remained was the outward evidence of her accident.

There had been a search of the gardens, but no clues surfaced. Cedric had thought a loose stone had fallen out of the wall. However, upon inspection, that had not been the case. Someone had deliberately hurled a stone at Lady Emma. Questions haunted him—who would do such a thing? But the more disturbing question was why?

Looking at her now, she appeared as an innocent kitten curled by the fire. Who was she, really? Was she in trouble? Had she made enemies who would not stop until she was dead? In all honesty, did she know her true identity, but chose to keep it hidden? All the questions kept swirling around in his mind with no outlet. One thing was for certain, he was no closer to solving the mystery than when he first found her.

Nicolas awoke with a jerk. *Puff... puff... smack... smack.* Lady Emma was snoring lightly and smacking her lips. Her loud snort woke her up as well.

Squirming around, Elizabeth pried open her eyes to see Nicolas looking at her. With the back of her hand, she wiped the drool from her mouth. Drowsily she asked, "Did I fall asleep?"

Grinning, he said, "Yes, my lady. You have been resting."

"Did I snore?"

"More like a snort," he answered straight-faced.

Even though her cheeks tinged pink, she seemed unflustered by his response. Straightening up in the chair, she said, "Well, let's get this inquisition over. I suppose you want to hear about my accident."

"Yes."

"I doubt if my version could be as entertaining as Thomas's version. He tends to exaggerate the facts with great animation," she said fondly.

"That is the very reason I would hear the truth from your lips," he said as his eyes narrowed in on her moist lips. He noticed that when she had them pursed they resembled a small bow. Nicolas already knew they tasted sweet as new wine. Maybe he would get the opportunity to savor them again in the near future, he thought keenly.

"I was taking a walk with Jarvis."

"Why wasn't Angus with you?"

"He left before we got to the gardens."

"Stop trying to protect him. I know he and Jarvis had an argument. I will deal with them and their part in this debacle later. Now continue."

He watched her brows draw into a frown. She was being protective of the two brothers which any other time would be an admirable quality . . . but not now.

She leaned forward in her chair. "I'm not going to continue unless you promise to deal gently with them," she stated.

"That is none of your concern. I demand that you tell all as it happened. Remember, I am Lord here, and you are to obey me." Nicolas was agitated. He didn't need anyone to tell him how to discipline his men particularly a woman.

Her scowl deepened as she looked at him through squinted eyes. The purple and black surrounding her left eye was almost painful to look at.

"Carry on," he said with a flourish of his hand, unperturbed at her outburst.

"Fine, but I'm doing it under protest," she said flopping back against the chair. With a huff, Elizabeth launched into her tale.

Unfortunately, Nicolas's mind wandered as she retold what he had heard from his brothers. He hated to admit to himself, but he admired this woman. She was strong in character, yet knew the right time to yield. She could be a formidable foe, but he hoped her to be his powerful ally. Even though bruised from her mishap, she was still a beautiful woman. Her eyes sparkled like sun shimmering on a pond. Those legs . . . ah . . . those legs neatly tucked under her blanket were as shapely as those of a swift gazelle. Their loveliness burned into his mind's eye after the first night. He had experienced her strength, yet her movements' exuded elegance.

". . . so I left Jarvis sitting on the bench at the entrance of the gardens. I meandered aimlessly through the paths until I found myself at the backside of the gardens near the castle wall. That's when I heard a scrapping noise. I called out thinking it might be Cedric, but I didn't receive a response. When I heard it a second time, it sounded as if it were coming from above me. At that time, I turned, glanced up and saw a huge rock hurling toward me. I flung up my arm to protect my face, and that's the last thing I remember until I awoke in bed."

Nicolas had leaned forward resting his arms on his knees hoping to stay engaged while he listened. Hearing the story again only confirmed his first suspicion, someone wanted Lady Emma dead. But who?

"You saw no one?" he asked incredibly.

"No one at that moment. However, I had seen a few guards earlier. They were walking along the wall looking outward. You know . . . guarding the castle against bad guys."

Nicolas knew there were fewer guards in the rear of the castle overlooking the cliff to the sea. He had questioned the ones on guard that day and was convinced they were innocent of any wrong doing. That left him with a most unpleasant conclusion. The assassin was someone they all knew and trusted . . . a most dangerous combination.

Elizabeth watched as Nicolas clasped and unclasped his hands dangling between his knees. He was giving her words great consideration and concentration. As his emotions played across his face, it was obvious when he had reached a conclusion.

"What do you think?" she asked concerned. "Do you know who might want me dead?"

Pushing forward, Nicolas rose from his seat. He walked across the room and smacked his hands on either side of the window. *Should I tell her my suspicion?*

Placing both hands on the arm of her chair, Elizabeth peeped around the chair. "Well?" she persisted.

Dropping his hands, he turned to face her. "I know not who tried to kill you . . . but I feel certain it was someone I know and trust."

"Why do you say that?"

"I have questioned all the men who were on guard duty that day, as well as the men at the castle entrance. No one entered or left the castle that was unknown to them. That means," he said as he pounded his fist into his open palm, "it has to be someone already within the castle that works or lives here."

He was livid! He or his brother Phillip had handpicked the ones working at the castle. That meant they had a traitor living among them—one that must be stopped. He would have to take great precaution to safeguard Lady Emma, his betrothed. No one got the better of the Fairwick brothers.

Elizabeth slowly rose from her chair to face Nicolas. Hugging her arms around her waist, she asked, "What should I do?"

Seeing her anxious expression softened Nicolas's demeanor. Within three strides he was before her. His hands wrapped loosely around her upper arms. "Have no worries, My Lady," he began as he tenderly pulled her into his embrace. "I will see to your protection. No harm will befall you," he murmured close to her ear.

He could feel her tense body relax in his arms as he rubbed circles on her back. Nicolas might be enraged that one of his own would betray his trust; however, there was one positive outcome— Lady Emma was certainly more amiable toward him. That was one benefit he would enjoy for the moment. Tomorrow was soon enough to find the traitor.

13

Standing on the steps outside the keep, Nicolas gave new instructions to Thomas. "Thomas, I want you to follow Lady Emma from a distance. Be mounted and fully armed with sword and crossbow. I have instructed Angus and Jarvis to stay by her side at all times. However, due to the recent events, I will be at ease knowing you are close at hand."

"Shouldn't Angus or Jarvis be punished for their lack of protection?" Thomas asked in frustration. "Let one of them stay behind. No harm will befall her if I am by her side," he boasted throwing his shoulders back.

Nicolas knew of Thomas's fascination with Lady Emma and was taking a risk appointing Thomas as her guardian just for a day. Hopefully, Thomas would not disappoint him for Nicolas had much to do to prepare for his wedding day, as well as find a traitor among them.

"This is their punishment, Thomas. Angus resents looking after Lady Emma when she plays with the children. He says it's below a warrior's rank. Jarvis is loaded down with guilt and wishes absolution from her care. But I know you, Thomas. If I permit you near her personhood, you will succumb to her charms hindering your ability to spot the enemy. Now, stop questioning my directives," he demanded as he popped Thomas on the back of the head. "You are showing your immaturity as a warrior by challenging my authority."

Nicolas saw Thomas's flaming glare and was thankful Thomas had the presence of mind to keep his mouth shut. Thomas detested Nicolas's treating him like a child even when Nicolas was accurate. Hopefully, Thomas would prove his worth and be a most perfect protector of Lady Emma today. Nicolas's focus shifted to Lady Emma in the courtyard. Her face glowed as children gathered around her anticipating the promised adventure.

"What will we do, m' lady?" Merry squealed as she danced around Elizabeth's skirt.

"Oh, Merry, 'twill be a most grand day," she said as she gazed into their expectant faces. "Come. Lord Nicolas promised we could journey outside the castle walls today. I have plans for the hill not far from the gates. Is everyone ready?"

"Yea. Come, let's go," Henry yelled as he took off at a run toward the gate. Pierson and Patrick were not far behind. Merry and her friend, Gwendolyn, held hands and skipped after the boys, giggling and laughing.

"Angus and Jarvis, are you all set for our great adventure?" Elizabeth asked.

Jarvis offered a wide smile to Lady Emma while Angus wore his usual frown. She ignored Angus and laced arms with both men before setting a leisure pace toward the gate.

"What a glorious day to enjoy God's creation," Elizabeth remarked as she looked heavenward. She was so thankful for the clear day. Usually, there were rain clouds present, but not today. Elizabeth felt God had provided her with a special day to treasure after her brush with death, and she wasn't going to waste a minute.

"Wait for us at the drawbridge," she called out to the children.

"Trying to get those children to follow orders is like trying to corral wild horses," Jarvis said, shaking his head.

The threesome watched as the children ran circles around the guards at the castle entrance. Dust clouds swirled around each child. Elizabeth snatched her arms free and forcefully clapped her hands to get their attention. Her shawl slipped to the ground as she marched toward her flock of chicks.

Upon hearing the loud clap, each child came to a skidding halt and glanced around to see what was amiss. After reaching the children, Elizabeth knelt down in the dirt to eyeball her dusty brood.

"Now, children, before we embark on this grand adventure, there are a few rules you must follow; or you will be left behind," she stated firmly. "First, you will not stray far from my side. Second, you must obey immediately if I give a command—no questions asked. Do you understand?" she asked, gazing into wide-eyed stares.

"Yea, m'lady," Merry meekly replied as Gwendolyn stood immovable from fright.

"Yea, m'lady," Patrick and Pierson answered in unison.

"Why are ye giving the orders?" Henry challenged. "And how far is too far?"

Elizabeth was not surprised at Henry's resistance. She realized Henry thought he was in control since Nicolas had given him the task of looking after her. She needed to set him straight using her best argument—Nicolas.

"Lord Nicolas told me I was the commander of this outing since 'twas my idea," she said as she straightened to her full height. She had to admit it did sound rather childish even to her. Nevertheless, it worked. Henry just shrugged his shoulders and turned and smacked Patrick on the back before both boys took off running around Angus. Observing Angus's perturbed expression, Elizabeth hid her smile behind her hand while her eyes danced with merriment. Jarvis placed the shawl around Lady Emma's shoulders as he regarded his brother's discomfort.

Nicolas watched with fascination as Lady Emma gathered her flock together. He didn't hear what she said but was impressed that she obviously had Henry won over. The boy was stubborn and brazen when it came to his seven-year-old abilities. If trained properly, Henry would become a spirited warrior. Shaking his head, Nicolas turned and went inside to talk with Collette about Lady Emma's wedding trousseau. Once that was underway, he would move on to his more important duty—finding her attempted assassin.

* * *

"Race you across the drawbridge," Elizabeth yelled as she took off running. The boys were quick to take the challenge while the girls skipped along holding hands once again. All was right in their world.

Jarvis and Angus brought up the rear, with Thomas not far behind. The guards on the wall peeked down with curiosity. They seldom witnessed such a scene, children frolicking with adults joining in just for pure pleasure. Once the group had cleared the drawbridge, the sentry resumed their patrol. Even during times of peace, there was always the possibility of danger.

"Whoa, boy," Thomas soothingly said to his horse. "I know you want to run, but we have an important task to perform this day," he added as he pulled back on the reigns to keep a proper distance from Lady Emma. His duty was to watch for danger, and he planned to see it through no matter how intriguing she was to watch.

"Where we headed?" Merry asked after she caught up with the others.

"Not far," Elizabeth said. "From the castle wall, I saw a perfect spot about a half mile down the road. It's an ideal grassy hill for what I have planned."

"What will we do there?" Gwendolyn whispered.

Smiling into Gwendolyn's questioning eyes, she said, "A grand adventure." Witnessing Gwendolyn's bashfulness each day tore at Elizabeth's heart. She hoped her time spent with Gwendolyn would bring the girl out of her shyness. She was a precious little girl that needed a boost in her self-esteem, and Elizabeth planned to do just that.

"Ooh, did ya hear that, Merry? A grand adventure," she repeated.

The ragtag group continued walking and skipping along until they reached the "perfect spot" Lady Emma had mentioned. It was a grassy hill that ended on a flat area fifteen feet lower. The leveled off space was about twelve feet wide before a steep drop-off that fell toward the rushing stream. The stream was one of the water sources for the castle. It was approximately ten feet across with depths up to five feet.

"What will we do here?" Henry asked in disappointment. "It's just grass."

"Oh, it's much more than that, Henry. I see an excellent place for our special races," Elizabeth concluded. "Here's what we'll do. Gwendolyn, Jarvis, and I will go down to the bottom of the hill and stand in the middle of the flat area five feet apart where we will judge the winner."

"What?" the twins said in unison.

"Be patient, boys. I'm not finished. Merry will stand here and start the races," she added as she looked at Merry. "It's a very important task." Turning back toward the boys, she said, "On her mark, you three boys will drop into a roll and see who gets to the finish line first without running into your opponent."

"Aww, that's easy," boasted Henry. "I'm sure to win every time. I'm the oldest."

"Being the oldest doesn't necessarily mean you'll be the winner. It has to do with speed and accuracy. Remember, you can't roll crooked or you'll bump into one of your opponents. Plus, anyone going beyond the judges will be disqualified."

"What? Dis . . . dis . . .quafeed? Why?" Henry demanded with hands on his hips.

Henry probably didn't even know what disqualified meant, but his body language told her he knew it wasn't good. If Elizabeth didn't know better, she would believe Henry came from Nicolas's loins. They had similar mannerisms and tone—both exhibiting a commanding presence. "Because there is a drop off that leads to the stream. I don't want anyone rolling down that hill for fear you wouldn't be able to stop before reaching the water. Can you swim?" she asked Henry.

"Of course, I can," he bragged. Throwing his thumb out toward Patrick, he said, "But 'e can't swim."

Patrick ducked his head from embarrassment. "Me da will show me when I'm older," he murmured.

"'Tis alright, Patrick," Elizabeth soothed. "I've made the rules and expect each of you to obey. No one will be deemed a winner if he doesn't follow the rules. Any further questions?"

It took a moment, but finally all agreed to her terms—no rolling past the judges. The judges went to their places and waited for the three boys to spread out and get ready for the first contest. Angus and Merry stayed at the top of the hill with Thomas close by looking on.

"Everyone ready?" Elizabeth yelled out from her position down the hill.

"Yay, yay," Henry called down. "Let's git started."

Merry held her hand up in the air and looked at each boy. "Go!" she yelled as she dropped her arm. The boys quickly dropped to the ground and began rolling down the hill. Pierson went crooked and headed in the wrong direction while Henry and Patrick were gaining speed toward the finish line. Merry waved her arms and yelled encouraging words to both of the boys as she hopped up and down with excitement. Gwendolyn squealed with delight as Patrick headed toward her feet. *Kawam!* Gwendolyn crashed down on top of Patrick as he collided with her legs. He had won the first round by an arm.

"Patrick wins our first challenge," Elizabeth shouted.

Henry jumped up and stomped over to Elizabeth. "I was the winner," he proclaimed with fists at his side.

"No, you weren't," Elizabeth corrected him. She squatted down in front of his rigid body. "Henry, it is not well done of a warrior to question the outcome of a competition. You must win with dignity, as well as lose with dignity. Lord Nicolas would expect nothing less from his men." She waited while he mulled over her words. "Now run back up the hill and try again," she said smiling.

Patrick laughed as he started up the hill. "Did ye see Pierson? He was all over the place. Come on 'enry, we'll show him how it's done." Patrick's easy-going attitude won Henry over. Soon they were all laughing as they trudged up the hill.

Henry won three times and Pierson won two times with Patrick winning only the first contest. When Elizabeth said it would be their last time, Patrick was determined to win at all costs. As soon as Merry gave the signal, Patrick stretched out straight as an arrow which allowed him to gain speed quickly. However, he veered away from the group on his descent and tumbled over the next hill, plunging toward the rushing stream.

Elizabeth turned and ran to grab Patrick as he went by but was too late. Knowing that he couldn't swim, she watched in horror as he soared toward the water unable to stop. A sharp pain flickered across her head causing her to stagger and fall to one knee. She shook her head to dispel the fuzzy vision.

Elizabeth lurched to her feet with mere seconds left to divert the disaster unfolding before her. "Bradley, stop at once. The water is too deep. You will drown if you don't stop!" she screamed.

Elizabeth was barely able to keep her focus as she barreled down the hill leaving her shoes behind. With each step she frantically tore at her skirt. She needed to alleviate extra weight in case she had to jump into the water. After one more yank, she stepped out of her skirt without missing a step. Next went her shirt leaving only her chemise and bloomers.

Angus and Jarvis took off after Lady Emma, but were too slow to catch up. Henry and Pierson were unaware of any trouble until they came to a stop on the grassy plain. As they waited for their swirling heads to clear, they heard yelling. When they realized what the commotion was about, they promptly jumped up and ran toward the stream. Thomas had been watching the surrounding area when his attention was jerked back to the group by the screams of Merry and Gwendolyn. After a swift kick, his horse plunged down the steep slope slinging mud behind him.

"Bradley, you must obey me. Stop, I say," Elizabeth yelled.
Splash!
"No!" she cried panting for air. Seconds later she reached the edge of the stream and saw his head surface. Without hesitation, she jumped in the icy water. She gasped for air when her head came out of the frigid water. Immediately, she pumped her legs and swam toward his little body as it bobbed up and down in the flowing water.

Twice Elizabeth reached for him but missed. The current was swiftly carrying him downstream and away from her. She must reach him. Her arms grew weary from the struggle against the water as she put all her strength into kicking harder. Water rushed over her head and nearly blinded her as she made another attempt to grab him. Thankfully, she was able to snag his pants. She began to pull him toward her while she treaded water. The current was strong, but Elizabeth was determined they would not drown today. Once she had his head above the water, Elizabeth struggled back to the shoreline. Thomas had been racing along the water's edge and was there to pull them both to safety.

Elizabeth dropped onto her knees next to Patrick. She shivered as she turned Patrick onto his back to check his breathing. Water dripped from her stringy hair onto Patrick's face, yet he didn't move.

"I don't think he's breathing," Thomas exclaimed as he bounded to his feet.

By now everyone in their group had reached Patrick and Elizabeth. The girls were crying as they held on to one another. Henry and Pierson were white faced as they stared wide-eyed at Patrick. Jarvis could barely control Thomas's steed as it pranced around with agitation.

"Hold that horse still, Jarvis, before he tramples young Patrick," Angus roared. Jarvis quickly moved the horse up the hill away from the children all the while keeping his eyes on the scary scene.

Elizabeth tilted Patrick's head, opened his mouth and began to blow her breath into his body. Her cold, blue lips could barely feel Patrick's mouth.

"Come on, Bradley, breathe," she gasped pressing on his chest. "You're not going to die on me this time."

Thomas danced from foot to foot and glanced at Angus. "Who's she talking about and what's she doing to Patrick?"

"I don't know. . . I think she's confused. You better stop her before she kills him," he added after seeing her push on Patrick's chest.

Before Thomas could act on Angus's idea, Patrick began to cough. Elizabeth rolled him to his side as Patrick coughed up water. After emptying his stomach, Patrick began to cry. When he realized Patrick was alive and crying, Thomas knelt down to offer assistance.

Elizabeth sat back on her haunches gazing at the young boy. The pain in her head had returned with a vengeance not to mention the burning in her shoulders and back. "Take Bradley home. His mother will know what to do," she said. Pierson rushed in, fell on Patrick and hugged him so hard that Patrick cried harder.

"Stop that, Pierson," Thomas demanded. "Move away from him. I need to get him to the castle. Angus, you and Jarvis stay here with the children and Lady Emma. I'll take Patrick and get some help." With Patrick in his arms, Thomas quickly mounted his horse and disappeared over the ridge toward the castle.

Once the initial danger had passed, Elizabeth gave in to the pain. One moment she was watching Thomas ride away; and the next moment, she slumped to the ground unconscious.

Henry ran to her side and touched her face. "Is she dead?" With that question, the girls began to cry in earnest.

"Merry and Gwendolyn, stop that caterwauling immediately," Angus barked. "Run and get Lady Emma's clothing. We need to get her warm as soon as possible."

The loud weeping faded as the girls scampered off to gather the clothing. The remainder of the group hovered over Elizabeth wringing their hands.

"What's the matter with 'er? Why was she calling 'im Bradley?" Henry demanded.

"I imagine she was a little confused from the shock of the cold water and her fear for Patrick. She'll be fine," Angus attempted to reassure them. "We need to keep her warm while we wait for help to arrive."

After Jarvis covered her torso with his outer tunic, he knelt beside Elizabeth and began to pat her hand gently. Henry sat down and did the same with her other hand. Soon the girls rushed in with her skirt and blouse. Angus tucked Elizabeth's clothes around her cold, still body. Merry and Gwendolyn continued to cry, yet no one uttered another word.

14

"Rider approaching," the sentry called out. Word quickly spread through the guards to the people in the courtyard. One man hollered at Lord Fairwick to inform him the rider was Thomas, and he was riding hard.

Nicolas dashed toward the gate just as Thomas bounded across the drawbridge. He jerked his horse to a stop and slid off with young Patrick in his arms.

"Take Patrick to his mother. He fell in the stream and needs to warm his body," Thomas said to Hastings as he placed Patrick in his arms. Then he turned to his brother, "Get your horse and come swiftly. Lady Emma is in need."

That's all Nicolas needed to hear before promptly taking action. He jumped on a nearby saddled horse and headed out behind Thomas. He knew Thomas would give him the details as they rode. Nicolas didn't have to hear the whole story to understand the grave situation. What would he find? Would Lady Emma survive? Would she take a chill and never recover? Not liking the direction of his mind, he quickly captured his thoughts and didn't allow himself to dwell on possible outcomes; instead, he concentrated on the thundering hooves as they barreled onward.

When they arrived on the scene, Nicolas was alarmed at what he saw. Clothes covered Lady Emma's outstretched body. The girls were huddled at her head, rocking back and forth as they cried. With ashen faces looking at Lady Emma, Jarvis and Henry each held her hand while Pierson whimpered behind a tree. However, that wasn't the most disturbing sight. It was Angus. He knelt at the water's edge, facing the water with his head bowed as if in prayer. If he were praying for Lady Emma's soul, it did not bode well. Angus never prayed for anyone.

As Nicolas leapt off his horse, everyone scrambled out of his way. Jarvis grabbed the horse's bridle to keep him at ready for Lord Nicolas.

"Is she going to die?" Henry asked.

Nicolas scooped up Lady Emma. "Of course not!" he boomed. "She but needs her rest after such a harrowing ordeal."

"Thomas, get Agnes," Nicolas said as he strode toward his horse. He placed his foot in the stirrup and mounted with Lady Emma snug in his embrace. He made sure she was carefully wrapped in her clothing before kicking the steed into a gallop.

"Jarvis, see that the children make it safely back to the castle," Thomas ordered. He mounted in seconds and raced toward the village.

* * *

The three brothers gathered in Nicolas's room while Agnes tended to Lady Emma. Thomas paced between the door and the fireplace where Phillip sat staring at the flames. Nicolas stood rigid by the window leaning his head against his fisted hand. While Lady Emma struggled to survive as she lay in his mother's bed, long suppressed memories flooded his thoughts.

Woman, is that boy in here?

No, my husband. I would not go against ye're wishes. Slap! *Do not lie to me, ye miserable woman. Ye will pay dearly for ye're untruths.* Slap!

Please stop, My Lord. Please.

Remove thy clothes and get in that bed.

Please, don't do this despicable thing.

Do as I say!

Nicolas shuttered at the remembrance. His father had beaten his mother and done unspeakable things to her that day along with a castle harlot named Eleanor. Nicolas had felt helpless as he listened to the horrors happening just above his hiding place. Even now, he knew if he had made his presence known, it would have meant certain death for his mother and probably him as well. Nicolas rubbed the small scar on his palm, a constant reminder of how his nails had dug deep into his hand while he hid under the bed. At the present, his stomach churned at the memory.

Thankfully, Nicolas wrenched from his dark remembrances when Agnes emerged.

Thomas whipped around with wide-eyed anticipation while Phillip jumped to his feet. Nicolas, however, remained stock-still across the room, expecting the worse.

"She's resting peacefully. I can do nothing more for her. Ye must wait . . . and . . . hope," Agnes said matter-of-factly. "I will return shortly." She didn't remain for a reply but shuffled out the door.

Phillip eased down in the chair with a frown between his brows.

"That's it?" Thomas exclaimed with disbelief.

"Thomas, this is the way of life. You must learn these things," Nicolas said expressionless.

"There must be more we can do!"

"'Tis in God's hands," Phillip added shaking his head.

"If she survives, I'll need to have the ceremony straight away before another unfortunate accident befalls her," Nicolas stated.

Thomas strode over to Nicolas and grabbed his arm. "How can you be so emotionless?" he asked through clinched teeth. "You act as if she is worthless . . . of no more value than . . . than . . . a weed."

Nicolas removed his arm from the window and let it fall to his side as he slowly turned to face Thomas. He tolerated Thomas's outburst because he knew Thomas felt responsible for the near drowning. He was young and inexperienced with handling distressing situations; therefore, Nicolas would be lenient with Thomas's disrespect.

"What would you have me do? Stomp around the room, yelling and cursing at God for this injustice. Would that change the outcome?" he asked with a penetrating stare.

Nicolas watched as Thomas blinked back his tears. Nicolas couldn't bear the anguish he saw in his younger brother's eyes. "Come, Thomas, let us not quarrel." Wrapping his arm around Thomas's rigid shoulders, he steered him toward the door. "Go tell Collette we need some food brought to my room. 'Twill help pass the time."

With his head hanging low, Thomas opened the door to leave the room. He stumbled over Jarvis and Angus, who were once again positioned outside the door of Nicolas's solar. No doubt, both suffered intense guilt.

"He is young," Phillip said once Thomas was gone.

"Don't I know it. 'Tis the only reason he left here on his own two feet," Nicolas remarked. "Thankfully, he has yet to be hardened by life's atrocities."

"He's also quite smitten with Lady Emma," Phillip added.

"That I know as well, brother. Thomas has much to discover. Life is not all we dream it to be," he said in a distant voice. "Mayhap I have protected him too much."

"Nay. I'm glad Thomas did not have to witness the carnage that we saw by his age."

The brothers fell silent as they withdrew into their own thoughts. Phillip remained by the fireside while Nicolas gazed into the night sky . . . searching for what, he knew not. He resorted to praying for Lady Emma to keep his mind occupied and far from the horrible day that changed his young life forever.

Soon Thomas burst into the room with a spring in his step and a smile on his face.

"I know Lady Emma will recover," he announced with surety.

Nicolas turned to glare at him. "And how do you know such a fact?" he asked stone faced.

With sparkling, expressive eyes, Thomas launched into his explanation. "I saw her do things today that were magical. She brought young Patrick back to life when I know he was not breathing—most assuredly dead. After much thought, I've decided she must be a fairy or a spiritual being sent from God to help us," he exclaimed as he strutted toward Nicolas.

Nicolas was stunned at Thomas's ridiculous logic. "Thomas, don't make such a judgment," Nicolas ground out in a loud whisper.

"Why not? . . . 'tis a reasonable deduction," Thomas said in defense. "You don't always know the answers," he yelled as he smacked his hand against the chair.

Nicolas grabbed Thomas and had him in a headlock. "You will have the peasants up in arms and ready to burn her at the stake for witchcraft," he said as Thomas struggled against the hold. Just when the two brothers were about to come to blows over the issue, a small voice filtered into the room.

"Stop it."

Three heads snapped around to see Lady Emma wavering in the doorway. With Nicolas and Thomas locked together, Phillip was the first to come to his senses. He shot out of his chair and was by her side before Nicolas and Thomas released their hold on each another. Shuffling feet echoed through the silent room as Phillip guided her to a chair.

Thomas yanked out of Nicolas's hold and stumbled toward Lady Emma. Nicolas took in her pale appearance and wondered again if she would survive the night. Realizing only God had control over the outcome, he walked to stand by the hearth—close to her chair.

She looked at three expectant faces hovering over her. "Please sit down," she rasped out. "Looking up makes me dizzy."

Thomas immediately knelt at her feet, his anger at Nicolas clearly forgotten. With arms crossed, Nicolas leaned against the hearth, leaving the chair for Phillip. Nicolas spoke first. "You shouldn't be out of bed, Emma. You have suffered much today."

Before she could respond, Thomas said, "I knew you would survive. You're an enchanted fairy, aren't you?"

Nicolas kicked Thomas's leg. "Thomas!"

"Please, stop this quarrelling. It makes my head hurt," she said rubbing her forehead. "To answer your question, no, Thomas, I'm not a fairy or an enchanted anything. If you will cease this squabbling, I will try to answer your questions about today," she declared.

Before Nicolas could form a thought in his head, Thomas blurted out, "Why did you keep calling Patrick by the name of Bradley?"

Surprised by his question, Elizabeth closed her eyes in thought. Bradley . . . Bradley, where had she heard that name before? Placing her finger between her brows, she pressed hard as if that would rouse her memory. Suddenly, her eyes snapped open. "I remember! I remember another fact about my past," she said. Her eyes focused on the fire as if the flames held the answer.

"I was a young girl, about nine, playing with other children near a pond. Some of the older kids jumped in the water and were teasing my friend Bradley about not being able to swim. Unfortunately, I took up for Bradley by yelling back at those mocking him which made his disgrace complete." Tears welled up in her eyes as she continued.

"I begged him not to do it, but to my horror, he jumped in anyway. His whole body submerged with only his outstretched hands flailing above the water. Running to the water's edge, I screamed for one of the older boys to help him, but they were laughing too hard to hear me. Sadly, I didn't have strong swimming skills and was afraid I might go under, too." Taking a shuttering breath, she said, "He drowned." Silent tears rolled down her cheeks as she closed her eyes as if to shut out the painful sight.

The crackling fire was all that broke the silence as the three men sat motionless. Each dealt with the information in their own way. Rubbing the back of his neck, Nicolas could identify with her agony. He had witnessed the death of children from falling accidents to horrible diseases—their silent faces still vivid to him. Burying a child was a dreadful task. It forever left a terrible mark on one's memory.

Elizabeth brought them out of their musings when she said, "Since I took the children on the outing, I was the one responsible for their safety. Therefore, I was going to save Patrick from drowning or die trying."

"But, Lady Emma, Patrick stopped breathing; he did die," Thomas blurted out. Rising to his feet, he threw his arms wide and said, "Then I saw you bring him back to life with a kiss."

Nicolas flung his arms down as he pushed away from the hearth. "Thomas, that is preposterous. Only God can bring someone to life after death," Nicolas said as he strode to the window. "You have to be mistaken." After a slight pause, he whipped around and marched over to stand behind Phillip's seat. "Isn't it so, Lady Emma?" he demanded.

His knuckles turned white as he gripped the chair awaiting her reply. Thomas ceased his fidgeting while Phillip leaned forward in anticipation of what she would say.

"Well, actually, Thomas is partially right."

"What!" Nicolas and Phillip said simultaneously.

"Even though I'm not sure who I am, I do know I have knowledge in healing," she rushed to say. "I was confident if I blew air into his body and massaged his heart that he had a chance of recovery. What I did for Patrick came natural to me." She glanced up at the ceiling with her eyes dancing back and forth. "It was as if I had done it before," she said thoughtfully. When Nicolas thought she was finished speaking, she swung her eyes back to them. "However, as Nicolas said, God is the One who brought him back to life. God just used me as an instrument."

"You're an angel," Thomas whispered wide-eyed.

Elizabeth hid her smile when Nicolas popped Thomas on the back of the head for his last comment. She knew Nicolas would never go along with that . . . an angel indeed. If not an angel or a fairy or any other spiritual being, who was she? She twisted her robe with agitation at the question that plagued her daily thoughts.

Nicolas had heard enough for one night. He didn't need her to fill Thomas's head with any more nonsense. "Enough," he barked. "We have overtaxed Emma with our questions. She needs her rest. Come, I will assist you to your bed," he said. As his eyes met hers, she held him captive, as if they were alone in the room.

Phillip cleared his throat which broke the spell. "I hope you rest well and make a speedy recovery, my lady," he said as he stood and bowed low. "Come, Thomas, we need to find our own beds. Tis been a trying day for all." He gave a slight tug to Thomas's sleeve to make his point clear.

Nicolas watched as his brothers left the room. When he looked back at Emma, he noticed she rubbed her robe back and forth between her fingers. Taking her actions as a sign she was overtired, Nicolas said, "Come, Lady Emma, I will assist you to your room." Nicolas gently scooped her out of the chair. Once she was settled in his arms but before he had taken a step, their eyes locked together.

She grabbed his shirt as her eyes filled with tears. "Patrick could have drowned today. I could have drowned today! What was I thinking?" she cried out as she twisted his shirt even tighter. "What's the matter with me? I've almost died numerous times, and now someone near me almost died." She loosened her hold on his shirt when she realized her tight grip. "I'm a danger," she said as if it were a matter of fact.

As Nicolas gazed into her watery eyes, he knew she needed more than rest. She needed reassurance. With her still firm in his arms, he sat down in the chair. He didn't say a word but held her close. She all but melted into his embrace as he caressed her neck and back while he waited for her to speak. It was a tranquil time as they sat close to the fire in peaceful silence. He could easily get used to the way she felt as her face cuddled under his neck. It was pleasant.

Nicolas knew immediately when she fell asleep. Her body went limp and a sigh escaped her parted lips. Not wanting to disturb her, he carefully readjusted her weight and then proceeded to prop his feet on the foot stool. He dared a peep at her face. Thomas was right; she looked angelic.

15

"Please, be still, m' lady. I must lace up the back," Collette grunted.

Elizabeth stood fuming. Nicolas had allowed her only two days to recover from her near drowning and then demanded marriage. Since arriving at the castle it seemed most of her days included recuperating from life-threatening encounters leaving her no time to figure a way out of this marriage fiasco.

"Oh, ye are such a beautiful bride," Collette said giddy with excitement. "Did ye know that Lord Nicolas had yer dress made by a skilled seamstress in the neighboring town? Yes, he did," Collette continued. "Nothing but the best for his new bride."

Elizabeth was biting her tongue to keep from saying what was on her mind. If she could only get her hands around his neck for persisting with this hare-brained idea . . . Ooo what she would do! However, it helped listening to Collette's mindless chatter. Distraction was good.

"I heard him say he picked the blue satin as a symbol of yer purity. Of course, he didn't know how the color would add to yer beauty. The lace overlay of the bodice takes me breath, it does. It's not often I see such finery."

"Are you almost finished?" Elizabeth snapped. She hated to be short with Collette, but she had heard enough about how beautiful she was on this wonderful day. Poppycock! It could prove to be the worst day of her life.

"Yea, m' lady . . . just need to finish yer hair."

"I thought we were leaving my hair down," she huffed.

"Yea, but ye must have these fresh flowers woven into yer loose hair," she said. "'Tis tradition. Lord Nicolas won't be able to see anyone else when he gets a glimpse of ye," Collette gushed. Collette pulled the sides of Elizabeth's hair up to the crown and secured it with pins. After tugging out a few curls to frame her face, she then took great care in pinning the flowers all through Elizabeth's wavy hair. When Collette seemed satisfied with her work, she gently turned Elizabeth toward the small looking glass propped on the chair.

Elizabeth sucked in a quick breath as she gazed in the mirror. She *was* stunning. Colorful flower petals crowned her head with soft curls framing her face giving her an innocent look. The jeweled belt around her waist drew her eye down the long, wide sleeves with their points near touching the floor. A contrasting navy blue silk lined each sleeve. Her satin slippers peeped from under the full skirt. As her eyes traveled up to the sparkling pendant around her neck, reality hit. This was no fairy tale wedding; she was a dressed up puppet participating in a farce. The locket felt more like a slave collar—heavy and constricting—rather than a piece of beautiful jewelry.

Releasing a deep sigh, Elizabeth murmured, "Well, let's get this show on the road."

"What did ye say, m' lady?" Collette asked frowning.

"Where do I go from here?"

"Oh. We wait for Hastings to come for ye. He will escort ye to the front steps where he will hand ye over to Lord Nicolas . . ."

Collette couldn't have picked more appropriate words. Handed over indeed . . . handed over to her executioner, Lord Swollenhead, Elizabeth thought.

". . . then together ye will go to the village chapel," she said clapping her hands with delight. "His sister, Brigette, along with his brother, Phillip, will be waiting on the chapel steps. All of the castle folk and villagers have been invited to attend this blessed day. Everyone is excited to witness Lord Fairwick's wedding day and to see . . ." Collette quickly snapped her mouth shut and hurriedly turned to clean up the room.

"And see what?" Elizabeth asked. She watched as Collette avoided eye contact. "And see what, Collette?"

Slowly, Collette straightened. With tight clasped hands and downcast eyes, she whispered, "To see the mysterious woman Lord Fairwick is to wed." Lifting her eyes to meet Elizabeth's, "They are but curious and mean no harm, m' lady."

Thoughtful for a moment, Elizabeth allowed a slow smile to emerge. "I'm not offended, Collette. I would do the same thing. In fact, I would probably arrive early to get a front row view."

A wide grin broke across Collette's face as a sigh escaped her lips. She followed Lady Emma to the open window and once again took up her chatter. "Oh, my, look outside. Even the rain has stopped for yer special day." Collette patted Elizabeth's arm before returning to straighten the room.

Elizabeth watched birds in the near-by tree flutter about with no concern for the morrow. They somehow knew that God would take care of their needs. *Lord, if you care about the birds of the air, do You care about me . . . about this offense being committed against me? Will You swoop down and rescue me from this predicament?* "Save me, Lord, save me," she whispered.

* * *

On the front steps, Nicolas paced to and fro. Had he lost all sense? Like the waves of the sea, his stomach pitched and rolled. He was about to wed a stranger. But what choice did he have . . . Lady Emma or possibly the king's niece? He shuttered with the thought of the king's niece. He must finish the deed before the king arrived or possibly be saddled with a child for all eternity.

Thomas stood at the bottom of the castle steps holding the two horses. He watched his brother walk back and forth. "Stop pacing," Thomas declared. "Collette said you would scuff your boots if you paced. I wonder how she knew what you would do."

Nicolas stopped and looked down at his attire. Collette had worked tirelessly to complete his outfit. She wanted it to match Lady Emma's dress that had arrived from the seamstress only two days past. The light blue tunic had slashed sleeves with navy blue inserts to coincide with those of his lady. The dark trousers were carefully tucked into his gleaming black knee boots. *What is causing them to sparkle and shine?*

Glancing around, he noticed the courtyard was shadowed by the clouds except for one ray of sunlight. Looking heavenward at the gray clouds, Nicolas saw a sunbeam streaming through the clouds which illuminated the horses and bounced off his boots—a heavenly sight. Grateful the rain had ceased, he wondered if the sunshine was a sign from God. Perhaps God was pleased with his decision to marry Lady Emma. His intended bride certainly wasn't overjoyed. She had yelled her displeasure at him once again this morning before stomping into her room to prepare for the day. Either way, knowing that Lady Emma was beyond angry with him, he was thankful rain would not add to her foul mood.

Looking at the horse he had handpicked for Emma, he hoped she would be delighted and forget her anger toward him. Having a horse to call her own had been one of her demands. Therefore, he had searched diligently for a fine specimen to present as a surprise on their wedding day. It couldn't hurt to start the day off on good footing to help soften her opinion of him.

"Here she comes," Thomas announced as Lady Emma stepped out of the castle.

Thomas's pronouncement brought Nicolas out of his musings; he twisted around to see her—breathtaking! Her shining hair was wreathed with flowers and her face framed with curls. However, what caught his eye next was the sun glinting off the silver threads running through her gown as her hips swayed with each step. The twinkling reflection made him think of their night to come. Would she be a wife in every way or would she carry through with her threat to deny him? Only time would tell.

"You look most beautiful today, my lady," Nicolas said as he tenderly took her hand and bowed low while placing a warm kiss on her palm. She shivered in response—from delight or revulsion, he wasn't sure. When he straightened, he saw her eyes fixed on the horse. Releasing her hand, he gestured toward the white palfrey. "Does she meet with your approval?"

Without taking her eyes off the horse, Elizabeth gathered her dress in her hands and walked slowly down the steps. She stopped at the bottom before speaking. "She is magnificent! Is she truly mine?" she asked, never taking her eyes from the horse.

Nicolas came up behind her and leaned close to her ear. "Yes," he whispered.

Elizabeth quivered as his warm breath traveled down her neck. However, she didn't allow his nearness to distract her from the prize before her. "What is her name?" she asked breathlessly.

"You have the privilege of naming her since she is yours. Do you have any thoughts?" Nicolas asked.

"I will decide later after some consideration. For now, boost me up," she said looking over her shoulder at Nicolas.

Without hesitation, Nicolas encircled Elizabeth's waist and hoisted her into the saddle. "She is to your liking?"

"Yes. Absolutely," she said with a smile. "She is most resplendent in all her finery. But 'tis the only thing I approve of about this day," she added with one brow raised.

Leave it to Emma to be forthright about the situation. Nicolas had had no doubt she would mention her displeasure in some way, and she had not disappointed him.

With a silly grin on his face, Thomas handed her the reins, bowed, and backed away from the horses. He went to join the five knights waiting to escort them to the church. Nicolas mounted his black steed and turned to give Lady Emma her instructions. Before he could utter his next words, she gave one more scathing remark.

"'Tis most fitting you are riding the black horse representing evil, and I am on the white horse symbolizing good. Would you agree, Lord Fairwick?"

Nicolas forced himself to relax his clinched jaw before he broke a tooth. She was not going to ruin his day with her acid tongue. "Oh, my lady, you cut me deeply. Shall we put aside our differences of opinion and try to enjoy all the festivities planned for this day? The castle folk and villagers have gone to great trouble to make your day special. I hope you will not disappoint them," he said by way of a warning.

"Unlike you, I would not dream of hurting anyone because of my own selfish desires."

Nicolas chose to ignore her last taunt. He would not be drawn into a verbal altercation just before their wedding ceremony. Instead, he put on a smile, nudged the horses forward, and began telling her about the upcoming ceremony and what to expect. He was thankful she followed his lead without further ado.

"The wedding ceremony will be conducted on the church steps by Father Bryan, the local priest. I will give the rings to the priest, and he will bless them before we exchange rings . . ."

Elizabeth interrupted him by saying, "I don't have a ring to exchange with you."

"I have taken care of this matter. Everything needed is already at the church . . . except the two of us, of course."

"Oh, I see . . . you've left nothing to chance."

"Perceptive, Lady Emma. I am a man who takes care of details. Have no fear; I will see to all your needs as my wife, as well. Even though you are going into this union with some hesitancy, I believe you will find it much to your liking if you will but allow us a chance." Before she could make any response, he continued.

"Once we have exchanged our rings, the priest will pray a blessing over us. We will enter the church as husband and wife where we will kneel at the altar. Father Bryan will pray again, and then we will celebrate mass by taking communion together. The only other people inside the church will be Phillip, Abigail, Thomas, and my sister, Brigette."

"I suppose now is a good time to let you know that I have changed my name again. It is Isabelle," she announced with a quick glance his way.

"What!" Nicolas exploded. He brought his horse to a halt and grabbed the halter of Elizabeth's horse. "Why have you done such a thing right before our ceremony? Are you trying to see if I will murder you before we are wed?" he seethed.

Elizabeth sat ramrod straight looking directly ahead when she spoke. "No. Emma just didn't seem to fit me. For some reason Isabelle is better . . . I'm not sure why, nor can I explain it. It's just a feeling I have here," she said as she placed her hand over her heart. She tipped her chin downward and angled her face toward Nicolas after her declaration. She looked ready to do battle.

He signaled for Thomas to come to him.

"Yes, Lord Fairwick, how might I assist you?" Thomas asked as he wiggled his eyebrows at Elizabeth.

Nicolas leaned close and whispered in Thomas's ear at which time Thomas bolted toward the village. Nicolas straightened on his horse, released the halter, and set out toward the church. Elizabeth's horse followed without any direction from her.

Elizabeth realized Nicolas was very angry with her this time. His rigid posture spoke of his annoyance. As they rode along in silence, Elizabeth could see people lining the road up ahead. She momentarily forgot her irritation over the forced marriage and asked, "What are those people doing?"

"They want to see the beautiful bride that has ensnared my heart. Since I have taken three years to marry, they think this marriage is birthed from our great love for one another. Otherwise, why else would I hasten to the altar when no other young maiden has piqued my interest?" He slowed his horse and looked directly at his future wife. "Do not give them reason to think otherwise. It would not bode well for either of us if they suspect anything but a love match. That kind of news could reach my enemies, as well as the King, and things could go poorly for you."

"How so?" she asked with brows drawn together.

"I can explain at another time. Now is time for us to rejoice and make merry."

Elizabeth recognized that she didn't understand these people, nor did she understand the lord of the castle. They all seemed foreign to her. She decided that until she could find a way out of her present mess, she would indeed take pleasure in the day. With all the mishaps that plagued her, who knew, she might not survive another week. On that dreary thought, she was determined to treasure the occasion.

When they approached the edge of the village, a minstrel played a lively tune and began to walk in front of the horses. Nicolas was pleased when Lady Isabelle smiled and waved to the people lining the road. The peasants cheered and clapped as the two horses walked by.

The bride and groom were a striking pair dressed in their wedding finery. It wasn't often the peasants witnessed such pageantry. Blue silk blankets under the polished saddles brightly arrayed each horse. Bells adorned their bridles that jingled with each step. The knights were magnificent as they carried their shining weapons decorated with colorful ribbons. The whole procession was one of grandeur and beauty that would be talked about for years to come. Finally, the Lord of the castle was getting married.

16

In just a short time, they were before the priest. Elizabeth took in her surroundings with wonder. The family stood on the lower chapel steps while the masses gathered closely around the wedding party. Abigail stood next to Phillip wearing her usual scowl. Brigette stood next to Thomas looking absolutely beautiful with her beaming smile. Nicolas took hold of Elizabeth's hands once she passed her bouquet to Brigette. After the priest welcomed all to the blessed event and prayed for them, she heard Nicolas repeat the wedding vows to her. She felt panicky. This couldn't be happening. It had to be a dream. The sounds around her had faded into the background as she watched his lips move with each word.

"I, Nicolas, take thee, Isabelle, to be my wedded wife, to have and to hold, from this day forward, for better, for worse, for richer, for poorer, in sickness, and in health, til death do us part, if the Holy Church will ordain it. And thereto, I plight thee my troth."

His eyes held her bound like a tight rope—immovable. Her eyes blinked once when he completed the vows. Nicolas then signaled with his head for her to repeat the vows to him. She tried to moisten her lips, but her tongue stuck to the roof of her mouth. Elizabeth's eyes grew large as Nicolas's penetrating stare stabbed her to the bone. No doubt her jittery body could be felt by Nicolas as she observed the stiffening of his shoulders. She hoped she could refrain from losing her breakfast on his boots.

"I, Isabelle," she squeaked, "take thee, Nicolas." She stopped. Her mouth was open but nothing else came out. She shot a quick glance toward the priest who was patiently waiting. He nodded his head and gave her a smile of encouragement. Elizabeth coughed a couple of times and cleared her throat. When she looked back toward Nicolas, his narrowed eyes were enough to spur her on.

She turned to the priest and asked, "May I begin again?" Her question brought snickers from the crowd.

"Of course, my child," Father Bryan replied gently.

Elizabeth decided there was no escaping this charade and that she might as well get it over with. She rapidly whispered her vows to Nicolas but refused to look at him. She kept her eyes on his chest even though he squeezed her hands to get her attention. He might force her to marry him, but not coerce her to look him in the eyes while doing it.

In no time at all, Father Bryan blessed and prayed over the rings before the exchange, and then escorted them into the church for communion. True to Nicolas's word, only the immediate family went inside for that part of the ceremony. The church was deadly quiet as they proceeded toward the altar. The swish of her dress and the staccato of Nicolas's boots bounced off the walls like hail pellets. They knelt at the altar for more praying and blessings over them. Elizabeth didn't think she had ever received communion where the priest placed it on her tongue. It seemed foreign to her. She found it quite disturbing to receive communion and blessings from the priest for a sham of a wedding. Did Nicolas mean his vows . . . did she? *God, forgive me for what I have done this day in Your Holy presence. Please don't zap me for being a fake. Rescue me; I beg of You.*

Nicolas released a loud sigh when they stood to exit the church. He obviously was relieved that she hadn't run out screaming and waving her hands like a crazy woman. He winked when she peered up at him. He wore a silly grin as his eyes twinkled back at her.

"It is done," he said. "Now we greet the people. Come, wife," he said as he pulled her along toward the door. She had to take two steps to each one of his long strides. He burst through the closed doors holding her hand high in the air. The people cheered and clapped while they chanted, "Kiss her, kiss her."

Nicolas turned to her as he lowered their arms. He pulled her forward against his chest which compelled her to look up or have her face squashed against his tunic. "They want a kiss. Will you allow it, my wife?"

Elizabeth was surprised at his request but most appreciative of him asking her first before taking what was rightfully his. As she looked into his eyes, she was reminded of what a handsome devil he was when he wasn't aggravating her with his arrogant behavior. If she weren't careful to guard her heart, she could easily be captivated by his magnetism and grow to love him. The danger would be if he didn't love her in return. She must fight against falling victim to his irresistible, boyish mannerisms. Peering at him now, he seemed almost bashful as he gazed into her eyes. How could she say no to that vulnerable face?

"Yes," she softly replied.

Nicolas bent down to accommodate her smaller stature. The closer he got, the faster her heart beat. When his warm, moist lips touched her dry lips, she was lost in the moment. A tingling sensation traveled up and down her spine while her stomach flipped. She clutched his tunic to steady herself. When he lifted his head from their kiss, she dreamingly opened her eyes and honed in on his lips. Instead of pushing him further away, she placed her hands on either side of his face and tugged him back down for more. She forgot all about the bystanders as she relished their intimacy. He enveloped her with strong arms that wrapped around her waist and pulled her tighter against his chest. For the first time since arriving at the castle, she felt cherished and safe. He deepened their kiss as if not wanting it to end.

All too soon they were both tugged back to the reality as the group roared with laughter and made coarse remarks. Nicolas broke their kiss and peered at her with a crooked grin. "That was a most pleasing first kiss, Lady Isabelle. I look forward to future kisses from you and what might follow those kisses."

His statement was like a splash of cold water in her face. She stepped back from his arms and blew out a huff. "Don't hold your breath," she murmured.

Nicolas either didn't hear her or didn't understand what she meant for he just offered a big smile and took her into his arms. "Come, wife, we ride together back to the castle. Thomas will see to your horse."

Elizabeth took pleasure snuggled in Nicolas's embrace. His muscular arm anchored her to his chest while he waved with the other and guided the horse with his strong legs. There was no danger of falling with him at her back. Being so close to him, she sniffed the fresh scent of soap and his unique manly smell. Quite pleasing. She rested her left hand on his arm which was around her waist and waved to the people with her right hand. People danced around the wedding entourage waving handkerchiefs. Their shouts of encouragement were near deafening. It all seemed so surreal to Elizabeth until Nicolas spoke into her ear.

"I took great delight in our wedding kiss, my wife," he murmured. "It was such a welcome surprise. I hope it will be repeated."

Elizabeth stiffened slightly at his words. She didn't know what had come over her. One minute she was fuming at the forced marriage, the next she was a shameless hussy kissing her husband with abandon. *I must truly be losing my mind.*

"What say you, wife?" he asked as he nuzzled her neck.

All the loud merrymaking ceased to exist for Elizabeth as a shiver ran across her neck. She couldn't admit how irresistible her good-looking husband was to her. It would afford him too much leverage with her heart. More importantly, when had she stopped seeing him as her captor and begun seeing him as a romantic interest? Were her thoughts betraying another's love for her? Oh, how all of these questions were such a nuisance to consider. She still didn't remember who she was or if she were already married; yet, here she was entertaining dreamy images of her and Nicolas. *God, what am I to do with these feelings? Am I being unfaithful to another? "Trust in the Lord with all thine heart; and lean not unto thine own understanding. In all thy ways acknowledge Him and He shall direct thy paths."*

Elizabeth took a moment to ponder the special verse the Lord had brought to her mind. One thing was for sure, until the Lord saw fit to reveal her true identity or remove her from her current predicament, she would be a faithful wife while protecting her heart. Nicolas already had great sway over her even though she knew he didn't love her. What would happen to her if she actually fell in love with Nicolas? She quivered at the thought.

"You haven't answered my question, lady wife," Nicolas rumbled softly.

"Kisses, yes. Beyond that, no," she said with finality.

"Ah, what a sweet beginning. I anxiously await the night."

His breath stirred the curl by her ear making her tremble. *Lord, help me survive this day and what is to follow.*

Upon reaching the castle, Elizabeth took note of all the trestles set up in the courtyard. "Are we to celebrate outside?" she asked.

"No. This is for the peasants. Our great hall is not large enough to accommodate all of the well-wishers, so their merry making will be under the stars tonight. That way no one will feel left out of the festivities. We will enjoy our entertainment inside if that meets with your approval."

"Oh, of course. I was just curious."

Nicolas stopped his horse with his legs and slid to the ground. He left one hand on his wife's leg as he gazed into her eyes. "Are you ready, wife?"

Blowing the curl off her forehead, she looked at her surroundings. The courtyard was full of men and women bustling about preparing for the feast. She peered down at her husband and said, "Let the games begin."

He tenderly lifted her out of the saddle and held her firmly against his body. She had to strain her neck to look into his eyes. "All will be well, wife. You will see. Fear me not; I can be the most gentle of men." He once again touched her lips with his own and ended with a kiss to the tip of her nose. Taking her hand, he positioned it on top of his arm and escorted her up the steps into the keep.

Elizabeth's heart was racing after their interchange making it hard to breathe. First she was hot and then cold which left her hands clammy. She was certain he could feel her trembling as he led her along. *What must he think of me? He must know that I lose all sense of my surroundings when he kisses me. Oh, my . . . troubling.*

The great hall was brimming with guests. Many were their own folk, but some were from neighboring castles. The lords and ladies were dressed in such finery that she had not seen since awakening at Fairwick Castle. The women's dresses had plunging necklines that bordered on indecent with jewels and lace enhancing their bosoms. Elizabeth felt her face grow warm from embarrassment. She cut her eyes toward Nicolas to see his reaction to their immodest attire, but he hadn't even noticed. He was receiving well wishes from the men as they slapped each other on the back. She wondered how the men kept from being knocked to the floor. Then Nicolas turned his eyes on her. They were full of tenderness and something else. But what, she wasn't sure.

"Come, Lady Isabelle." He drew her up on the dais and turned to all the guests. It didn't take long for everyone to quiet down as they awaited Lord Fairwick's announcement. "May I present my lovely, new bride, Lady Isabelle Emma Fairwick." He then kissed the top of her hand. He peered up into her eyes before he turned it over and proceeded to kiss her palm, as well. He winked and then straightened to his full height never losing eye contact. Such an intimate display of affection.

The room erupted into applause, whistles, and shouting. It was obvious, all approved of the marriage of Lord Nicolas Fairwick and Lady Isabelle Emma Fairwick. Instead of being irritated that he put Emma in her name, she thought him quite clever. Now no one would question the change in her name at the wedding. She gave him a salute with her hand before sitting in the throne chair at the head table.

She sat to the right of Nicolas with Thomas and Brigette on her right. Phillip and Abigail were seated to the left of Nicolas.

Phillip, Thomas, and Brigette laughed and smiled as they enjoyed the festivities while Abigail wore her usual sour expression. They each had a clear view of the entire hall as servants brought trays of food to the tables. The serving girls were dressed in their best, as well as the young boys decked out in shirts and jackets. The food kept coming: goose, venison, wild boar, peacocks complete with feathers, potatoes, carrots, ale, cider and more. The tables seemed to strain under the weight of it all. Elizabeth did notice there was only one chalice between her and Nicolas—filled to the brim with ale.

Turning to her husband she asked, "Where's my water?"

Without even looking her way, he responded. "We will share the wedding cup . . . 'tis tradition."

Elizabeth looked at the cup with wide-eyed apprehension. Somehow she knew she didn't drink ale or spiced cider. Her preference was always water. Maybe she could get some water if she asked sweetly.

She placed her hand upon Nicolas's hand. That definitely got his attention. He quickly turned toward her with one raised eyebrow.

"Yes, wife?"

"I am most happy to share the wedding cup with you, but may I please have some water, too?" she asked while smiling.

He waited so long to answer she thought he was going to deny her simple request. He turned his hand over to clasp her hand as he cocked his head to the side. "Of course. I hope to be able to grant many of your requests in the future. Will you be able to do the same?" he asked with penetrating eyes.

Her eyes widened ever so slightly, then narrowed. Two could play his game. She hesitated several seconds before answering. "I might, within reason, of course."

He threw back his head and burst out laughing. Then he motioned for a serving girl to come forward. "It would seem our marriage will be quite interesting, wife."

"Oh, you don't know the half of it," she murmured.

It was an out of body experience for Elizabeth as she watched the festivities. People were actually celebrating her wedding.

Women were flirting with men who might or might not be their husbands. Men were making obscene gestures as they became inebriated. Obviously, some of them had started drinking before the wedding took place. Tankards crashed against tables in good humor as the guests talked and laughed. All were in such high spirits.

Musicians played soft music from the balcony as everyone enjoyed their meal. Elizabeth found she couldn't eat the peacock. It made a beautiful presentation on the tables, but eating the meat was out of the question. She did find, however, the venison and vegetables quite tasty. As she cleansed her fingers in the bowl of rose water, she looked around in wonderment. Was all this truly for her? If so, why did she feel like a spider suspended from her web watching a play with elaborately dressed actors?

Hours passed quickly while Elizabeth enjoyed the food and musicians. The merriment of the guests was almost contagious. Looking at the happy scene one would never guess the turmoil brewing inside her.

"Your wedding was so wonderful," Brigette gushed. "I hope Nicolas will allow mine to be so grand."

Elizabeth was startled back to the present. She smiled at Brigette with gladness in her heart. It had not been that long ago when Brigette had wanted her gone from the castle. The spiteful words Brigette had directed toward Elizabeth had been like daggers to the soul. Now there was a peace between them that had been forged through Elizabeth's patience and perseverance with Brigette. "You will have a magnificent wedding if I have any say about it," Elizabeth reassured her.

Thomas leaned around Brigette to address Elizabeth. "She won't have much of a wedding day if she doesn't start obeying Nicolas," Thomas bluntly stated while waving a drumstick.

"Oh, Thomas, you do love to stir things up," Elizabeth said. "Please be kind to your sister. It is my special day and I want no squabbling between the two of you." Elizabeth suddenly felt motherly toward the two siblings. Could saying the words "I do" immediately change a person?

She noticed that Brigette stuck her tongue out at Thomas when she thought Elizabeth couldn't see. Thomas retaliated by grabbing said tongue and pulling it before quickly releasing it when Brigette tried to bite him. Elizabeth giggled at the sight.

"What is so amusing, my wife?" Nicolas asked.

"Your sister and brother are entertaining me with their outward expressions of affection for one another."

"Oh?" He bent forward and glared at the two. "Do not create a disturbance on my wedding day or both of you will be excused before the dancing."

Elizabeth knew she needed to diffuse the situation before it got out of control. How embarrassing to have a family quarrel for all to hear. With a feather light touch to Nicolas's hand, Elizabeth turned his attention to her. She gave him an affectionate smile. "Husband, did you not say there would be dancing?"

Nicolas quickly changed his focus to Elizabeth. She could tell her "come hither" smile had worked. He looked absolutely confused. *Well now I know how to bumfuzzle my husband.*

With a flick of his wrist, the tables vanished to make ready the dance floor. The serving girls and lads made quick work of moving aside the candelabras and sweeping the floor. Benches lined the walls for seating.

When Nicolas rested back against his chair, Elizabeth noticed that Abigail still picked at her food. "Abigail is the food not to your liking?" she asked. She saw Abigail tense immediately. Phillip took hold of Abigail's hand and placed his other hand upon her back.

Slowly she turned her head toward Elizabeth and said, "I'm not feeling well today."

"Oh. I'm sorry."

"Come, I will escort you to our rooms," Phillip sweetly said. Still holding her hand, he drew her up and placed her hand through the crook of his arm. He turned to Nicolas and said, "If you will excuse us. I will return shortly."

Nicolas's eyes shifted from one to the other. "Of course, brother. Do as you wish."

Abigail hesitated and then spoke to Nicolas and Elizabeth. She nodded at each as she said, "Many blessings on your marriage."

They both watched as Phillip led Abigail out of the hall. Nicolas let out a low growl. "Is she ever going to be happy? Her disagreeable countenance is most bothersome."

Thankfully, at that time the jugglers came into the room to perform before the dancing started. They skillfully handled fruit, balls, and knives. When they brought out flaming sticks, Elizabeth unconsciously grabbed Nicolas's arm. "Oh, my. This looks dangerous," she whispered. "If they miss, they could burn the place down!"

Nicolas patted her hand. "Don't worry, wife. All will be well; you'll see. I have hired these men before and know them to be quite accomplished in their trade. In addition, there are buckets of water just out of sight. A precaution."

Much to Elizabeth's relief, the jugglers didn't drop a flame and executed their drills perfectly. They even incorporated acrobatics into their routine which was most impressive. When they finished, the men bowed and waved at the crowd. One performer stepped forward, and with a sweeping bow he presented Elizabeth with a lace scarf. "May you have peace and happiness in your marriage, Lady Isabelle." When she stood and accepted the gift, her husband also stood to his feet. Elizabeth's smile faded from her face as she slowly sank down to her chair wondering what her husband was about to do. He was most unpredictable.

Nicolas held his hands up, palms outward, to silence the crowd. As the room of guests quieted, he raised his drink. "I want to offer a toast to my lovely new bride." Peering into her upturned face, he said, "You honored me this day when you became my wife. God truly blessed my home when He dropped you into my life . . . ."

Well, this certainly is a pleasant surprise, she thought.

". . . Now, may we be fruitful and multiply with many sons."

The crowd went wild. They erupted into applause and stomped their feet. The sound was deafening. Several intoxicated men shouted lewd comments which only added to Elizabeth's embarrassment. She felt the heat move up her neck into her face. It would not be wise to cause an upheaval during the wedding feast;

but when she could get Nicolas alone, she was going to yank that wicked tongue out of his mouth.

"Oh, what a delightful speech," Brigette said. Her eyes shone bright with awe as she gazed at her brother.

Elizabeth knew delightful wasn't the appropriate word to describe the scene. She was mortified in front of their guests. Half of the people present swayed and staggered as they tried to stomp their feet. A few even fell to the ground which caused a loud uproar of laughter. And then there was Nicolas, quite proud of his little talk . . . standing proud as a stallion. With narrowed eyes penetrating her husband's profile, Elizabeth was contemplating her next move when Nicolas grabbed her hand.

"Come, wife. We shall start the dancing." Before stepping off the dais, Nicolas looked up at the musicians and gave a quick nod of his head. They immediately began playing much to Elizabeth's annoyance. In her estimation, the evening had been flowing nicely until Nicolas had irritated her with his speech. Now she had to endure dancing with him in front of all the guests. The only thing in her favor was how most of the crowd were drunk and probably wouldn't remember much about the night.

As Nicolas held her in his arms, yet again Elizabeth was forced to look up or have her nose flattened into his chest. When her eyes met his, she saw something akin to tenderness. He tightened his grip on her waist and turned on his boyish smile. With each spin around the dance floor, Elizabeth's determination to remain mad at Nicolas weakened. She dissolved into his embrace and was transported to another place . . . just the two of them. The room and its occupants disappeared as they swirled around the room gazing at one another—she, mesmerized by his dark brown eyes. All too soon the melody ended and the enchanted spell was broken. Once again she was very aware that all eyes were on them.

Elizabeth moved to extract herself from Nicolas's embrace, but he held fast. "One moment, my lovely wife." Facing the people, Nicolas and Elizabeth were standing in the archway that led to the hallway off the great hall. With his arm sweeping the room, he addressed the guests. "Please avail yourselves to the dance floor while my bride and I take this opportunity to speak with our guests," he boomed.

Nicolas ushered his wife around the room thanking the neighbors for attending their wedding feast. They barely spoke with each couple as they circled the room. When they came near the head table, Nicolas leaned close to Thomas and issued some orders concerning the guard for the night. He obviously didn't want Brigette or anyone else to hear his word based on his conduct. Elizabeth heard bits of the conversation only because she was wedged against his side. Once he finished, he pasted on his smile and commenced strutting around the second half of the room.

Would this ever end? It seemed each woman they approached had a more revealing dress than the last. Elizabeth watched to see if Nicolas gawked at the plunging necklines, but was pleased to note he barely acknowledged the female presence, but instead shook hands with the men and proceeded on. *I guess that's one redeeming quality of my new husband—he is oblivious to other women.*

At long last their excursion was over. Before Elizabeth even had time to make a comment, Nicolas swept her up in his arms and made a dash for the stairs that led to the second floor. He didn't slow when he reached the stairs but took them two at a time while still carrying her. She had grabbed his neck with her arm to keep balanced, but stared in shocked horror.

"What are you doing?" she gasped as she took her free hand and pushed against his chest.

"No time to talk. You can thank me later. We must hurry," he huffed out with each step.

Elizabeth peered over Nicolas's shoulder to see a horde of boisterous men and a few women following not far behind. When Nicolas reached the second floor landing, he took off at a run toward his room down the main hallway. Elizabeth clung to Nicolas in horror as she watched the crowd of yelling people start running as well—toward them.

"What are those crazy drunkards doing?" she squeaked out just as he launched through the open door to their suite of rooms.

Nicolas dropped Elizabeth to her feet before he spun around, slammed the door shut and dropped the bar across it. "Whew! That was close."

In the middle of the room Elizabeth stood trembling. She had wrapped one arm around her waist and the other lay across her chest as if for protection. "Wha . . . at was that all about?" she stammered.

Nicolas leaned his back against the closed door while the crowd banged on the door and yelled suggestive words about the couple. He gave a silly grin as he pushed away from the door and made a move toward his wife. She immediately took a few steps away from him. When the backs of her knees hit the chest at the foot of the bed, she sank down to sit upon the chest with one arm wrapped around the bed post.

Nicolas was surprised that his new wife didn't understand about the tradition. He could tell she was utterly shocked at what had just transpired. Her breaths were quick and short. He decided to tread lightly where Lady Isabelle was concerned. He didn't want to frighten her.

He decided to use his horse-gentling voice with her. "'Tis alright. There is nothing of which to be afraid. They will soon leave us in peace. Thomas will see to it. Are you not familiar with the bridal tradition where the guests escort the new couple to their room?"

"No. If that is the tradition, why were you running, and why did you feel the need to carry me?" she asked with bewilderment. "And why are they still so rowdy outside our door?"

Nicolas edged toward the hearth chairs and angled one of them toward his wife as she continued to sit at the foot of the bed. He eased down into the chair without making any sudden moves that might cause her to panic.

"I was protecting your sensibility."

"My sensibility? What are you talking about?" she asked.

Nicolas could tell she was beginning to calm down from the excitement. She breathed more normally and the wildness in her eyes had diminished. "The tradition is for them not only to escort us to our rooms, but to strip us of our clothes and throw us into the bed together. I didn't imagine you would want to be undressed in front of a throng of witnesses."

Her hand rapidly went to her throat as her face glowed red from embarrassment. "Uh . . . no. You are correct. I had no idea about this ritual. Thank you for sparing me that humiliation," she said as she shook her head in disbelief.

The rumble from the hallway dissipated as the people ambled back down the hallway toward the staircase. They left a deafening silence in their wake. The popping of the fireplace sounded loud to Nicolas's ears. *Now what should I say to Isabelle? She looks like a frightened rabbit caught in a snare.*

"Did you find the meal and entertainment to your liking?" Nicolas asked his new wife.

She blinked several times as if coming out of a stupor. "Oh . . . uh . . . yes . . . it was quite delicious. I was, however, surprised at the peacock display. They are such magnificent birds; I can't imagine killing and eating them. Nevertheless, I do appreciate the effort that went into making this an exceptional day. From the splendor of the horses all the way to the jugglers, it was a magnificent day."

With each sentence she spoke, Nicolas saw his wife relax. Her hands rested in her lap as she tilted her head in consideration of his question. She made a lovely picture perched on the chest. The tight curls that once framed her face had wilted giving her a little girl appearance—one of innocence. He could see the fatigue in her eyes that were usually bright with adventure.

"Well, Lady Isabelle, this has been a most eventful day. I believe we should take our rest for the night. What say you?" Nicolas asked. Immediately, he noticed her shoulders tensed. *Now why did my words make her anxious?*

Elizabeth stood to her feet. "You are correct. I am quite weary after the day's activities. Might I call for Collette to assist me in removing my dress?"

Nicolas observed her rigid posture and knew she was fearful of what he might do next. He sat very still in his chair as he watched her squirm under his direct stare. "There is no need to call for Collette, I will assist you," he calmly replied.

Her hands remained at her sides as she gripped her dress. "You said you would not touch me once we were married," she hurriedly said.

Rising from his chair, he slowly strolled over to stand within an arm's length of his bride. "No. I said I would not demand we consummate our marriage until you were ready. I will, however, use everything in my power to hurry your decision," he said while smiling.

"Never mind. I will get the dress off myself," she blurted as she side-stepped him and went to her bedroom door.

Nicolas stood motionless as he watched her attempt to unlatch her door.

Whirling around, she demanded, "Why is this door locked?"

"Now that our marriage vows have been exchanged, there is no need for you to go into that room."

"But what about my belongings?"

"Look around you, Isabelle. Do you not see your possessions in this room?"

Elizabeth made a quick inspection of the room and found he had moved her personal items to his room. Her dresses hung on hooks on the other side of the bed with her shoes lined along the wall under the garments. Even her divan stood under the window.

He watched her chest heave with each new breath. She was definitely agitated at him, but he didn't care. She was his wife and lady of the castle. Now was the best time to get her accustomed to her new role which included sleeping in his bed.

"Come, my lady, let me aid you with your dress."

"No . . . um . . . not yet . . . uh . . . not until you give me the full story."

"The full story?" he asked with a tilt of his head.

"Yes. There are secrets attached to the room I slept in, and I want to know them if I am to remain in here with you. You owe me some type of explanation," she insisted.

Nicolas could feel his ire rising. She certainly had put a damper on his ideas for the night. He didn't have to tell her the horrid story behind his mother's room. He stomped over to the window and threw open the shutters. Leaning his hands against the window ledge, he breathed deeply of the night air. Hopefully, the cold air would cool his anger of the reminder about the dreadful events that surrounded that room.

Nicolas's knuckles grew white from his grasp of the casement. His thoughts ran rampant as he vacillated between withholding the information and telling all. Would it dishonor his mother if all were revealed? If his wife knew the story, would she be sickened by his cowardly act that fateful night? She might be forever lost to him if she knew the truth? With the night already ruined for him, he decided to divulge his secret that had scarred him forevermore. Maybe he could finally get some peace if he spoke the words out loud. "Sit down, and I will tell all," he said reluctantly.

17

Elizabeth kept her eyes on her husband's rigid back as she gradually made her way to one of the chairs by the fireplace. If the tone in the room hadn't been so serious, she would have laughed. It never failed; she received bad news in those chairs, and she felt certain tonight would be no different.

Nicolas released his grip on the window ledge and trudged toward his chair. He walked as if rocks weighed down his boots. Elizabeth noticed his face was void of emotion. She watched as he plopped down and released his breath with one long huff. He rubbed his forehead and closed his eyes momentarily before focusing on the flames that sputtered and hissed.

"My father was an evil man," he began. "My mother was a saint for putting up with him all those years. I can't remember one time when he was pleasant or kind to her. It was an arranged marriage, one I'm sure she regretted."

Elizabeth could tell the topic was difficult for Nicolas by the way he jumped around in the telling of the story. She wished he had started at the beginning but decided to remain quiet and let him gather his thoughts. A queasy unrest began in her stomach which she was certain would not dissipate any time soon. If she felt this way, Nicolas had to be in agony over the tale.

"Phillip was the oldest, then me, and Thomas. Phillip was being groomed to take our father's place as lord of the castle, so that left me and Thomas to play and fend for ourselves. My father would not allow us to visit our mother, whom he kept locked in that room. She was seldom allowed outside of these two rooms unless my father was hunting and the maids let her out. Even with the atrocities done to her, she was always sweet and loving toward her children."

A brief smile crossed his face before it disappeared into a frown. "I was her favorite child. As soon as my father would leave to go hunting, I would run to her room pulling the maid behind me . . . her keys clinking together. On this particular day, father had taken his two hawks on his hunting expedition. I knew he would be gone all day and possibly overnight. As a six- year-old lad, I could hardly contain my excitement of spending hours with my mother—all to myself. Thomas was still in nappies, cared for by a wet nurse. Mother seldom got to see him since that hussy pretended Thomas was her own child and not mother's," he spit out.

Elizabeth sucked in a quick breathe at his words. She tried to hide the noise by coughing when Nicolas's head jerked around to look at her. That's when she saw the surprised look in his eyes. *Did he forget I was in the room?* Oh, how she wished she had not reopened the raw wound he carried with him. If only she had thought of another way to forestall getting ready for bed, the night would not be shrouded with such grief and torment.

Nicolas rubbed his eyes before continuing with his tale. "Anyway, we were playing a game in her room when I heard my father's angry voice floating down the hallway. There was no time for me to leave the room without my father seeing me. My mother was too afraid that my father would kill me if he saw me exit from their adjoined rooms through his door. So she hid me under her bed and had the maid quickly lock the door. It would not seem unusual for a maid to be cleaning my father's room when he was out hunting, so the maid was safe."

"I was such a coward. I should never have left my mother to face him alone," he belted out as he jumped up to pace the room.

Elizabeth watched him repeatedly pound his fist into his other hand. A tear slipped down her face as she pictured a frightened little boy trembling under his mother's bed . . . afraid for her and . . . afraid for himself. Oh, what a dreadful a scene.

"Oh, Nicolas," she murmured.

He continued on as if she hadn't even spoken. "Lord Fairwick was angry because his horse had gone lame, and he had to return home for another horse. He had to take his anger out on someone, so my mother was the target. After unlocking her door, he stomped into her room and immediately accused her of having me in the room. There was no reason he should have known that unless one of the servants had told him."

Nicolas had gone to rubbing his head and neck as he paced from the window to the door and back again. Elizabeth was certain he would soon draw blood from the way he attacked his neck. She was glad there were no weapons in his hands. Her eyes darted around the room and saw his sword propped up by the bed along with several daggers on the night stand. Thankfully, they were not in his line of sight.

Soon Nicolas returned to his chair as if exhausted from his journey around the room. She was certain the retelling was taking an emotional toll on him as well as a physical one.

"I remained under the bed with my fingers in my ears, but I could still hear every strike . . . slap   . . . and punch that landed on my mother's body," he all but whispered. Tears leaked out of his eyes as he leaned his head against the chair and looked at the ceiling. It was if he were visualizing the sight again.

"My mother had made me promise not to reveal myself no matter what I heard or saw from my position under the bed. If there was one thing that pleased my mother, it was obedience. I wanted her to be proud of me, so I stayed silent while my father nearly beat her to death as he raped her . . . sounds . . . like a wounded animal caught in a trap   . . . sounds I never want to hear repeated."

Nicolas leveled his head and looked at his wife. "When my father was done, he left to go hunting. After almost killing his wife with his hands, he left to go hunting!" he bellowed. Scrubbing his face as if to erase his fury, Nicolas resumed the account in a quiet, yet raspy voice.

"I crept out of my hiding place to see the results of Lord Fairwick's brutality. My mother was so badly abused that I would not have recognized her if I weren't certain it was she . . . blood covered her face and arms. The violence that day has haunted me all the days of my life. It left a gaping wound in my heart that was far worse than being run through by a sword." He took several deep breaths as if to get control of his emotions. "Brigette was conceived that day. Under no circumstance was my mother permitted to hold her baby girl. Of course, my mother was never the same after that beating anyway. All that was left of her was a frail carcass of the woman I knew as my mother. She died soon after giving birth to Brigette."

He got up and added several logs to the fire, but not before Elizabeth saw tears rolling down his cheeks. She wasn't sure how to proceed with him tonight. She had forced his hand on revealing the hideous truth about his father and the sickening results of a man gone crazy. Now what? Would Nicolas be like his father? Heaven help her if that became true. As she contemplated her own questions, she didn't realize she was twisting her dress into a knot.

"Put your mind at ease, Lady Isabelle. I am not my father even though on many occasions I wanted to slit his throat while he slept. If it were not for Angus and Jarvis, I probably would have committed that sin. Thankfully, my father died less than a year after my mother's burial. I think he contracted a disease from sleeping with numerous harlots; at least that's what I heard repeated around the castle. Of course, I was only seven at the time and had no idea what it meant; I just knew his death was from a disease that ate away his flesh. It was an excruciating demise, and I was glad of it."

Elizabeth sat in silence with her eyes fixed on the dancing flames as she absorbed all that his words meant. Her new husband had lived a life full of guilt that ate at his very soul while harboring bitterness because he couldn't forgive. Of course, Elizabeth wasn't sure how she could forgive such a heinous act against a loved one. *Oh, God, Almighty, give me wisdom. How can I help*

Nicolas recover from this deep-rooted offense? He is in a cavernous pit that he has been unable to claw out of after all these years. Give me words that will comfort and aid my husband's recovery. Is this the reason You have brought me here—to help him? If so, I will need Your direct intervention. Help me, God!

When she looked at Nicolas, she found his eyes locked on hers. "Have I frightened you, Isabelle?" he asked. "Remember, you are the one who wanted the answers to the bolted door. Now you know all the wickedness surrounding that room, and why I do not wish for it to remain open."

Elizabeth loosened the tight hold on her dress and rubbed her hands over the wrinkles. "No. No, you have not frightened me. The story is quite shocking . . . and . . . upsetting to me. I never like to hear of someone's being mistreated for any reason, especially a woman with no defense against a husband whose word is law." Elizabeth licked her dry lips and saw Nicolas's eyes follow her tongue which briefly distracted her. Was he remembering their shared wedding kiss?

"Do you see my father in me?" he asked gruffly.

Elizabeth didn't hesitate. "You are nothing like the man you described. He was a depraved man full of evil intent." As she gazed into her husband's vulnerable face, she knew she had to clarify what she actually saw in him. "Even though you didn't want me in your castle, you were generous with your provisions. I have never lacked for food, clothing, shelter, or protection." She hinted at a smile when she said, "We won't count the attempts on my life. Those you couldn't control." She watched him scowl at her comment. "As I've observed you interact with your men, you have been honorable and fair in your dealings with them. I also find no fault in your care of others. You are a man of integrity who is well respected by almost everyone here."

"Almost everyone?" he asked on a snort.

"Now, Nicolas, you know there is no way one man can be liked by all in his domain. Even Jesus was not adored by everyone."

He sucked in a sharp breath as he crossed himself. "You dare to bring Jesus into our conversation? It isn't appropriate to talk of our Lord in that way," he said in a hushed voice.

Her smile widened as he squirmed in his seat. She felt a different tactic was in order. "Do you think God has a plan for every man?" she asked.

His brows drew together as he tilted his head in thought. "Hmm . . . I really hadn't thought about it. What is your reason for this direction of questioning?"

"Based on the study of scripture in the Holy Book, I believe that God has a plan for each of His followers."

"My mother was a follower of our Lord Jesus Christ." Nicolas thought for a moment before his face became a mask of anger. "You mean to say that you think God planned for my mother to be beaten by my father?" he growled.

"Absolutely not!" Elizabeth exclaimed. "You're jumping ahead of me. Please, allow me to finish." She held her breath in anticipation as she observed his telling behavior.

Nicolas leaned forward resting his arms on his thighs with his hands clasped tightly between his legs. He stared at his fisted hands for several moments before responding. Without looking up he said, "You may continue, but do not disparage the memory of my mother."

Elizabeth decided not to react to what he said. She most definitely had not meant to cause him additional grief, but God had impressed her with an insight she wanted to share with Nicolas in hopes to lessen his grief. "Do you remember the account of Adam and Eve in the Garden of Eden?"

With the change in the direction of the conversation, his shoulders visibly relaxed. "Of course. Most everyone has heard that story," he said. He straightened and leaned against the back of the chair. He must have forgiven her his perceived insult toward his mother since his hands rested in his lap.

"God's first couple had a good thing going in that garden until Eve yielded to the serpent's temptation and bit the fruit. Naturally, not wanting to be alone in her fruit-tasting extravaganza, she invited her husband to partake. Immediately, sin entered the world never to depart until Jesus returns. With that one event, evil came on the scene and man has not been the same since."

"I know the story well. What does it have to do with God's having a plan for every man's life?"

"With that one act of disobedience, all future men are born sinners in need of a savior. Some will accept God's free gift of salvation and others will reject His gift of salvation. All through the history of the Bible we see examples of how God uses imperfect, sinful people to accomplish His goals. So in your case, from what you've shared with me, here is what God has impressed on me about your family. Your father was a man who probably rejected God's gift shown by his conduct toward your mother. In other words, his behavior was full of evil and wickedness. He trampled those around him who he felt were weaker than he. A true man of God would be more like Jesus. His actions would mimic those of Christ, such as: loving kindness, gentleness, humbleness, meekness, faithfulness, and self-control, to name a few. From what you tell me, your father exhibited none of those characteristics of Christ."

"These things about my father I know full well. You have shared nothing that I did not already know. Again I ask you, what does this have to do with God's plan for each man?"

"Oh, Nicolas. You are an impatient man, to be sure. This is not a quick explanation. Please, if you will but wait, I will get to the point."

"As you wish. I will attempt to be patient. Carry on," he added with a flick of his hand.

Elizabeth decided she needed to hurry along before he totally shut her out. "You are the man you are today partly because of your father." She heard Nicolas's quick intake of breath and immediately held her palm out toward him. "Since he was so vile and brutal in his treatment of your mother, you became just the opposite. You endeavor to treat women with kindness and protectiveness as the weaker vessel. You earned your men's respect, not out of fear, but because you treat *them* with respect and with justice. Phillip was groomed to be lord of the castle, but God knew you would be the ultimate ruler of this realm. Therefore, every man and woman who crossed your path during your lifetime helped shape you into the great leader you are today. A perfect leader? No. An impressive leader? Yes."

He sat still with his eyes locked on hers as he soaked in all that she had said. Before long, he rose from his chair and walked over to the window. After gazing into the night sky, he turned and sat on the ledge facing Elizabeth. "I do not see how my mother's fate fits into God's plan. She was a wonderful woman, yet she suffered greatly. I would be most angry at God if He planned her demise."

"God did not plan her demise, as you put it. Remember, God created the perfect, sinless world until Adam and Eve messed it up. Now Satan reigns over this earth devouring all who will follow him. Regrettably, man uses God's gift of free will to rebel against God and pursue Satan's course. These corrupt men and women wreak havoc and destroy those in their path. Unfortunately, your mother was a victim of a cruel man. Even though your mother played an important role in your life with her tenderness and love that she expressed to you during the short time you were together, she was in the path of the destroyer. She had accomplished what God needed her to do and God rescued her from your vicious father by taking her to heaven to live with Him for all eternity. God didn't cause her death—He saved her!"

Nicolas's jaw flexed several times as he clenched his teeth. Elizabeth had seen him do that previously and knew he was mulling over what she had said. Would her words free him from his childhood guilt? Her eyes followed him as he rose from his perch to pace the room once again. However, this time his feet did not stomp the floor, nor did his fist pound his hand. No, this time he walked in soft contemplation—hands clasped behind his back and head down. Back and forth he went as if she weren't even in the room. Suddenly, he stopped.

"We need to prepare for our rest. You will sleep in my bed, but you may have a pillow between us to protect your virtue. Fear not; I will not force my attentions on you for I am weary of body and mind." As an afterthought, he said, "Come, I will loosen the ties of your dress."

Startled by his abrupt change in their conversation, she unfolded her legs from underneath her and stood to her feet.

Actually, she did feel safe in Nicolas's presence since the somber mood in the room had engulfed them both. He posed no threat to her tonight, but what of the nights to follow? No need to borrow trouble from tomorrow; she would deal with each night when they came.

As she presented her back to Nicolas, her own fatigue washed over her as if she had been dunked in a pond. Her limbs became like limp, wet grass ready to lie down at the water's edge. The heat from his closeness was a blanket to her exposed skin as a shiver ran down her spine when his finger grazed her back.

"It would seem my touch has an effect on you. Whether welcoming or not, I suppose I will have to wait to find out." After the last ribbon was unlaced, he removed his hands and stepped away.

Elizabeth looked over her shoulder to see him close the shutters to the window and then sit on the edge of the massive bed to remove his boots. She remained near the fireplace, unsure of what to do next. Her bare skin cooled with each moment she hesitated. He removed his shirt and crawled into bed with his pants still on. That was a relief. Holding her dress against her chest, she tiptoed around to the far side of the bed where her clothes hung on pegs. There on her side of the bed was an ornate white night gown spread across the bed covers. With her free hand she felt of the material—silk. Such a luxurious gown . . . Collette was right . . . he had spared no expense for her, his new bride.

Hiding behind the bed drapes, Elizabeth's wedding dress slid down her body while she quickly donned her night gown before the dress had time to hit the floor. She peeped around the curtain to see Nicolas's silhouette against the reflection of the glowing fire—he was lying on his left side facing away from her. His light snoring gave her a sense of safety. She tried to climb into the bed gently but ended up falling and rolling toward the center of the soft mattress. Her limbs went flying in all directions as she tried to keep from touching Nicolas while her gown tangled around her legs.

"You could never sneak up on your enemy," he said deadpan.

Her head whipped around at the sound of his voice. "I'm sorry I disturbed you. The bed was higher up than I anticipated," she whispered.

"Hopefully, this will not be a nightly occurrence."

"No. I will get a footstool to use." She rose up on her elbow, jerked her gown from around her feet and plopped back down. Then she realized the need to draw the bed curtain to shield her side form the draft filtering in through the shutters. She crawled to the bed's edge and jerked on the curtain until it had completely enclosed her side of the bed. It took her a few minutes to arrange her blankets for warmth and to keep any wandering hands at bay. After much wiggling and twisting, Elizabeth finally settled down and was still.

"Do you have your nest made?" Nicolas asked.

She could hear the smile in his voice. It was good to know she hadn't married an ogre. "Yes. I believe I have completed my nesting ritual."

"Goodnight, Isabelle," he sighed.

How did he make her name sound so provocative? A delicious shiver raced down her back all the way to her toes. Oh my, she was in trouble. "Goodnight, Nicolas."

18

Nicolas wasn't so sure that having Lady Isabelle in his bed was a good idea. When he had first devised his plan of getting her into his bed, it had seemed like an excellent idea; but now after a near sleepless night, he wasn't so sure. Her fidgeting had lasted for what seemed like hours, and then just her nearness had kept him awake until the wee hours of the morning. Now he was weary. As he prepared for the day, his new wife slept as a babe. He had glanced at her several times expecting her to awaken, but she had remained buried under a mound of blankets. Maybe if she had fewer covers, she would need him for warmth—now that sounded like a delightful scheme.

Nicolas took the flat of his sword and popped his wife on her backside. "Awaken, wife. It is time to break our fast." After purposefully cutting his hand, he smeared blood on the sheets before he returned his sword to the scabbard and left the room.

As Nicolas sat in his chair at the high table, he noticed everyone kept their distance from him. They knew he was a bear to contend with when he was tired, so each servant gave him a wide birth. They probably suspected he and his wife had been enjoying each other most of the night, but they were sorely mistaken. He might be a newly wedded man, but he remained celibate. Let them think what they would; at least it kept the probing questions silent.

Phillip entered the room and immediately came toward Nicolas. With a hearty slap on Nicolas's back, Phillip asked, "How do ye fare this fine morning? Did ye find marriage to your liking?" He didn't even wait for a reply before gulping down a couple of bites from his bowl of gruel.

Nicolas had to bite his tongue not to lash out at his brother for being insensitive. He was not about to divulge the little secret of being married in name only. With any luck, his state of affairs would make a change for the better. "I will adjust," he mumbled.

Phillip nearly choked on his meal. Turning his head toward Nicolas, he sputtered, "You will adjust? You do make me laugh, brother. I find the marriage bed such a delight."

"Cease with this line of conversation about you and Abigail. I do not wish to have those images in my head. And do not bring it up in front of Isabelle," he grumbled.

"Ah, here comes your lovely bride as we speak. She looks no worse for wear," Phillip couldn't help but add.

Nicolas punched his brother in his side causing Phillip to spill his drink down his shirt. Before Phillip had a chance to retaliate, Elizabeth had reached the table. "Goodmorrow, gentlemen," she said.

Nicolas looked directly at his wife and thought she looked a bit sheepish as she made her way to her chair. He noticed she wouldn't make eye contact with him; maybe she was uncomfortable after their unusual first night together. "Lady Wife, did you sleep well," he asked with a devilish smile.

Elizabeth turned toward him with wide eyes. She quickly masked her surprise at his question by dropping her gaze at the food. "Yes, husband, I slept well."

"Aren't you going to ask me how I slept?" Nicolas asked.

Phillip had leaned forward to look at Lady Isabelle as the conversation took a fascinating path. He seemed most interested in her response. He placed his hand against Nicolas's chest to push him backward, therefore, clearing his line of sight.

Elizabeth poked at her food and took a drink of water as she stalled in answering the question. "Nicolas, you have embarrassed your new bride. She is shy this morning," Phillip said.

Quietly, she said, "I'm a dreadful bed buddy. I took forever to situate my blankets and get comfortable. Then not long after that I needed to go down the hall for a brief moment and Nicolas wouldn't let me go alone."

Nicolas huffed loudly. "Yes, Isabelle. I was unfamiliar with the numerous visitors sleeping in the hallway who could have accosted you." Turning to Phillip he said, "So I held a torch to light her way and walked with her. She stopped suddenly at the end of the hallway near the door to the garderobe which caused me to bump into her back. She fell against the door frame and struck her head. Once back in our room, I had to apply a cool compress to her face so there wouldn't be a big knot on her head. I couldn't afford wild accusations stemming from our first night together."

During the whole tale, Phillip just smiled broadly. When Nicolas took a breath from his story Phillip said, "welcome to marriage. 'Tis a wonderful affair."

Nicolas watched his wife's face turn apple red as she ducked her head and studied her food. He could tell she needed rescuing, so he said, "Isabelle, I would be most pleased if you would agree to accompany me on a ride today."

Her head jerked up to look at Nicolas with eyes that glowed with excitement. "Truly? I would be honored to go for a ride across your . . . or um . . . our kingdom," she said breathlessly.

Nicolas noticed she had not delayed claiming a kinship to his realm. He, however, had no concern for it—she was only a woman with few actual privileges. Did women rule in her homeland? He knew not; but, here, he was the ultimate ruler and judge. "I will have Robert prepare our horses, unless you want to ride pillion with me?" he asked in jest.

"Oh, no. I wish to ride my new horse. She is so magnificent; I want to see if her ride compares to her beauty since her walk to the church doesn't count as an actual ride."

"Very well. Once you have finished your meal, meet me on the castle steps. I will see that all is ready for the day." Nicolas excused himself, and strode out the door giving orders as he walked.

***

Elizabeth hurried through her meal as she reflected on her good fortune. She would get to ride her fabulous horse with her handsome husband as her escort. A quiver shook her body.

"Lady Isabelle, it would appear you are eager to be in your husband's company," Phillip said.

"We-ll, I am thrilled at the thought of the wind in my face as I race my fine horse along the green grass of the pastureland."

"Ahh, I see. Maybe you will best my brother today," Phillip said with a smile. "Have you thought of a name for your horse?"

"Actually, no . . . I haven't had time to give it much thought. I'm afraid my mind has been preoccupied with other matters."

"Of course. Hopefully, at the end of your outing today, you will have many pleasant memories to store away. Now, if you will excuse me, I must check on Abigail." Phillip pushed back his chair to rise when Elizabeth placed her hand on his arm.

"Is Abigail unwell?" she asked with a frown between her brows.

"Well . . . it is the strangest thing. One moment she is fine and the next she feels queasy. The mornings are her worst time. Just the smell of food makes her stomach flip in rebellion. I hesitate to bring Agnes to our rooms, for she and Abigail do not fare well together. Would you . . . possibly come to our room this evening . . . and . . . um . . . maybe examine her to see if you could determine what ails her?" he asked sheepishly.

Phillip's discomfort with the subject was clear on his crimson face. Elizabeth wasn't surprised at his shyness on the topic, but for some reason the subject did not embarrass her. It must be because of her past medical training she had remembered. This line of talking felt familiar to her. "I will be happy to come tonight. What time would be best?"

"Since Abigail is so self-conscious about her predicament, I think it best to come once all in the castle have retired for the evening . . . if that suits you," he added, "and can we keep this quiet? Abigail is persnickety about these issues."

"Of course. I will see you tonight." Just as she whispered her response to Phillip, she looked up to see Nicolas standing in the archway. He held her cloak at his side but it was the scowl on his face that grabbed her attention. Without a backward glance toward Phillip, Elizabeth quickly stood and hurried over to her husband.

"I came to see what had detained you from our outing. Phillip?" he rumbled.

"Oh, how thoughtful of you to fetch my cloak," she cooed. She turned so he could lay her cloak across her shoulders and then fasten the clasp. As she linked her arm through Nicolas's stiff arm, Elizabeth spun him around to head out the door. "Phillip just had a question, and I was attempting to answer it," she said sweetly. "Come, let's go," she said as she gazed into his flashing eyes. "I think I will best you today in a race. What think you of that, dear husband?"

Her change in the subject had its desired effect on Nicolas. He strolled outside with Elizabeth on his arm as if he didn't have a castle to run, men to train, or possible enemies afoot. *At least he's pretending to forget what he just witnessed. Oh, bother, I hope he's not jealous over my talking to Phillip. Proud men can be such a nuisance.*

The majesty of a fine horse never ceased to take her breath away. Standing on the castle steps, Elizabeth gazed at two fine specimens—her white horse and Nicolas's black horse. Robert held the reins to Nicolas's prancing steed while Eugene held her docile mare. As Elizabeth's eyes traveled over her mare, she noticed Eugene watched her intently. What was he about? His glare bore into her eyes and made her uncomfortable. Had she offended him at some point? Before that thought had time to take root, Nicolas spoke softly in her ear.

"A splendid horse for a beautiful lady." His warm breath tickled her cheek.

Chills danced down her spine. *Oh, my.* She could feel heat travel from the pit of her stomach all the way to the roots of her hair. Her fine-looking husband could flip her stomach with one simple statement. Elizabeth knew if she turned her head slightly, her lips would touch his. Afraid she would succumb to her own temptation to kiss her husband, Elizabeth squashed that idea. Without taking her gaze from her horse, she said, "Thank you, kind sir."

"Come, I will help you mount up," he said.

Nicolas led her down the steps to her horse and paused with his hands around her waist. "I look forward to our time alone together today." He then lifted her effortlessly into the saddle. Taking the reins from Eugene, Nicolas handed them to his wife. Just as she reached for them, Nicolas grabbed her hand and planted a kiss first on her hand and then on her palm.

Elizabeth was held mesmerized by the touch of his fiery lips. A tingle skittered up her arm. All conscious thought took flight as she watched him adjust her skirt to cover her legs. His burning touch on her knee made her lightheaded. How would she survive the day when a simple kiss on the hand had her woozy with excitement and dreaming of tight embraces? Nicolas just grinned as if he understood her predicament.

Fluidly, he mounted his horse, and off they trotted through the castle gate and across the drawbridge. It was soon apparent to Elizabeth their protectors were not to be left behind. The guards were just beyond the drawbridge awaiting the duo. Elizabeth decided not to let the numerous guards dampen her day with Nicolas. She was determined to ignore their presence and take pleasure in her surroundings. The sunshiny, crisp day was awaiting her exploration and enjoyment.

Nicolas left the main road that led to the village and cut across his domain. Elizabeth noticed the fields had turned brown in preparation for the winter weather soon to follow. The crunch of the ground reminded her of roasting nuts crackling in an open fire. When they came to an open plain area, Elizabeth decided to see what her mare was capable of doing. She gave her a swift kick and burst forth leaving Nicolas behind—or so she thought.

In mere seconds Nicolas was beside Elizabeth with his head low to the horse's neck. He obviously was up for the challenge of a race with his wife. He kept pace with her with little effort.

"I will race you to that tree stump in the distance," Elizabeth yelled. She didn't wait for his acknowledgement, but kicked her horse and never looked back.

Galloping to catch his wife, Nicolas reached for the reins to her horse; but Elizabeth veered away and left him with her laughter ringing in his ears. "Stop, Isabelle," Nicolas shouted.

At that command, Elizabeth turned her head to see Nicolas bearing down on her with a determined face. *Is he mad because I'm winning?*

"Stop, immediately," Nicolas shouted again as he came alongside her. Instead of seizing the reins, he grabbed her around the waist and pulled her into his lap. Without a rider, her horse made a sharp turn and headed in the opposite direction kicking up its heels in agitation. Gradually, Nicolas brought his horse to a stop.

"Isabelle, did you not hear me call to you?"

With rigid shoulders, she twisted around and came face to face with mutinous eyes. "Yes, of course I did. Those in the grave heard you; however, before I could bring my horse to a halt, you jerked me off and into your lap which was totally unnecessary," she blurted.

"You were in grave danger," he growled. "There is a steep drop off on the other side of that stump. I didn't want to risk missing the reins again, so I did what I thought was best."

They both sat motionless on his horse while puffs of breath swirled around their heads. Both of them silently stewed in their aggravation with each another. As the seriousness of the situation began to take hold in her mind, Elizabeth's stiff body gave way as she sagged against her husband. "I could have been killed?" she asked.

"Probably by a broken neck," he said quietly. Nicolas blew out a slow breath before adding, "I regret if my actions angered you, but your life is worth more to me than your feelings."

Elizabeth let the ramifications of that statement swim around in her mind for a moment. "Oh . . . I see," she said crossly. She attempted to draw away from his chest, but he was having none of it. He cuddled her tight. As a tear slipped down her cheek, Nicolas reached up and wiped it away with his finger.

"I think not, Isabelle. Your perception is not mine. You believe that your value to me is only for my gain, but that is not true. These past months you have become dear to me in ways I don't even understand," he whispered. "So allow the breeze to blow away your tears, and let us carry on with our day together."

The creak of the saddle and the buzzing of insects were the only sounds circling around the tranquil setting. *Sniff* Was Nicolas truly glad he had chosen her as a wife? *Sniff* Should that please her? Oh, good heavens, it was too beautiful a day to waste time on such heavy thoughts. Wiping her nose and then flipping her hair over her shoulder, she said, "Alright. But only if I get to ride Midnight."

Even though he still held her close, Nicolas leaned back with a frown and peered down into her resigned face. "Who is Midnight?"

She raised her chin in annoyance at his tone. "That's the name of my new horse," she said.

Nicolas's head fell backwards as deep laughter erupted and echoed across the open field. "You named your solid white horse Midnight? Incredible!" he laughed again.

"Well . . . I wanted her to stand out." She sniffed one last time and tried to wiggle out of his embrace.

"She will definitely stand out just as you will dazzle those who cross your path." Elizabeth perked up at the compliment. "Look at me, Isabelle, and hear me well," he said. "You may ride Midnight, but no more racing between us. I need you to stay close by my side since you do not know the dangers that lurk hidden from sight."

"Oh, all right," she said with pouted lips. "I will agree with you on this point. I guess there's no need for me to endanger myself when I already have someone who wants me dead. Right?" she asked flippantly.

Nicolas reared back. "I sup—pose," he sputtered out. "Isabelle, you never cease to startle me with the direction your mind flows. My life with you shall be most fascinating." He lifted his hand to signal his men. Within seconds Midnight was in view.

Elizabeth peeked around her husband's wide shoulders to see guards surrounding them. She had completely forgotten that she and Nicolas weren't alone. "I'm ready; please lower me down," she said. When he didn't readily reply, she looked up at the same time he bent forward. *Oh, my. I believe he is going to kiss me! I should not allow it . . . but, I do want it. I'm just a shameless woman torn between wanting my husband's attention, yet wondering if there could be another love in my life.* Her heart doubled in time as her thoughts fluttered about while she awaited Nicolas. When their lips touched, she was lost. She became lightheaded and disoriented. Her head banged against his chest when he drew back.

"It would seem my kiss has caused you to swoon, dear wife," Nicolas chuckled as he raised her chin.

Let him think what he wanted, but Elizabeth knew she had just experienced a slight memory jolt. She could remember a kiss by someone in her past, but his face and name remained closed to her. She briefly closed her eyes and gulped in several quick breaths before placing her hands flat on Nicolas's chest. Gazing into his eyes, she asked, "Will you take me to the tree where you found me?" She hoped her kiss would carry some weight in his decision to appease her curiosity.

Nicolas didn't even blink as he studied her face. Elizabeth remained motionless while she waited but honed in on the customary tic in his jaw that appeared each time he was frustrated. Would he refuse her request? She certainly hoped not. Elizabeth needed answers and felt sure the tree would initiate some remembrance.

He broke eye contact and looked at the surrounding trees. "It could place my men in possible danger. It is near the border of Scotland," he said as he turned back to her.

She couldn't keep her face impasse any longer; it crumbled. "Oh . . . I see. I thought we were at peace with one another. Naturally, I wouldn't want anyone to be put in danger because of me. I'll get down now," she murmured. Nicolas didn't try to stop her this time; she managed to slide down the side of his horse and reach the ground without falling.

"Wait."

With her anguished eyes boring into his, he gave way. "I'll take you, but only for a short time. And when I say it's time to go, you will obey immediately. Understood?"

A smile broke from her lips as she placed her hand on his boot. "Thank you."

"Mount up, my lady, and we'll be away."

19

Nicolas steered the group back toward the road and headed northwest from the castle. Elizabeth managed to take in some of the breathtaking landscape even though Nicolas had set a quick pace. It was probably because of the dark clouds that had begun to form overhead. Hopefully, the storm would hold off long enough for her to see the place where they had found her.

After what felt like an hour's ride, Nicolas slowed to a walk and nodded his head which signaled his men to fan out to provide protection. Elizabeth stayed quiet, not wanting to draw attention to their group in case there were sentinels near the border area. Of course, the jingle of the bridles was so loud that the sound caused the birds to take flight. The flap of their wings made a thunderous ruckus.

"There is the tree," Nicolas said as he pointed to a large oak at her right. "Thomas spotted you lying at its base with your head toward Fairwick Castle and your feet positioned toward Scotland. You may take a brief moment to study the tree," he said in a low voice.

"Thank you," Elizabeth whispered. She dismounted from Midnight, held up her skirt, and carefully picked her way to the foot of the tree. With eyes closed, Elizabeth placed both hands flat against the tree trunk and waited . . . for what, she was unsure. Nothing happened. She stood unmoving and continued to wait for a revelation, but nothing came to her. Opening her eyes, she removed her hands and walked around the base of the tree—searching for clues to her past. Still nothing. *"Oh, God in heaven, please, please reveal my past to me! I'm begging You. Please tell me my name!"* She moaned as she placed her forehead against the bark.

Nicolas could stand it no longer; he jumped off his horse and came up behind her. Lightly taking hold of her slumped shoulders, he murmured, "Isabelle, I'm sorry this has not provided you with answers, but we must be away from here before the border guard comes to question our presence. Animosity still abounds, and it would not end well for either side."

She turned around, and her anguished eyes pierced his heart. "Of course, you are right," she said. "I don't wish for a confrontation with a Scotsman." Over her shoulder she took one final look at the tree as she trudged beside her husband back to Midnight. Nicolas tenderly picked her up and placed her in the saddle.

Before Nicolas had time to mount, his own guard returned and said, "They are headed this way, my lord."

When Nicolas looked at Elizabeth, her eyes covered half her face. There was one way to erase her fear. With a devilish smile, he said, "Shall we race toward home, wife?"

Elizabeth quickly recovered from her fright and with twinkling eyes, she said, "By all means, husband."

Nicolas and Elizabeth bolted down the road. Their guards even joined in the jocular atmosphere as the wind carried their laughter. No Scotsman would catch the merry band of travelers today.

Once they were deep onto Nicolas's land, the group slowed their pace. The wind whipped around them as additional black clouds formed in the sky. Nicolas turned in his saddle to discern the seriousness of the approaching storm. "It would seem we might be caught in a rainstorm. I know of a cave near the seashore if you are game for an adventure," he called to Elizabeth with a mischievous grin.

Elizabeth scanned the faces of their guard to gage their reaction to Nicolas's idea; and based on their cheerful faces, it appeared they were ready for the escapade. Two large splashes hit her in the face; but what was a bit of rain when she was in the pleasant company of her brawny, handsome spouse who would protect her with his life? A beaming smile spread across her face as her eyes twinkled with delight. "Lead on, O mighty husband." She quickly threw her hand over her mouth as a giggle erupted.

That statement got the men into an uproar. "Mighty husband, indeed," one of them shouted as the others laughed and hooted with pleasure. Nicolas raised one brow at his wife while he watched red creep from her neck to her ears. Without another word, Nicolas kneed his horse and headed southeast at a trot. From the swirling of the dark clouds and the approaching thunder, they would all be drenched soon if they didn't get to cover. The cave was closer than the safety of the castle, hence the best choice.

Nicolas just pointed toward a hidden trail since the howling wind made it nigh on impossible to hear. The embankment was steep, but he knew his wife was on a sure-footed horse and that she was an accomplished rider. Large drops of rain fell just as they rode out on the sand.

"This way," Nicolas shouted. At that moment, Elizabeth looked at him with frightened eyes. She had observed the ominous sky, as well. *Do they have tornados in this part of the world?* she wondered. To the naked eye, it looked as if they were headed toward a solid rock with a deadly storm behind them when Nicolas pulled back hanging vines to reveal the entrance to the cave. Several guards entered ahead of their lady to make sure no harm would befall her when she rode inside.

The opening was big enough for them to enter only two at a time; but once inside, the cave opened into a large room with a high pinnacle. There was plenty of space for the riders as well as the horses. After their horses were secured in the back of the room, the men who went in first began to build a fire with the wood and kindling that was located in a pit in the center of the cave. There was a slight opening directly above the fire pit to allow the smoke to escape. Elizabeth shuddered from the dampness of her clothes and was relieved to see the beginnings of a fire.

Elizabeth kicked her foot out of the right stirrup just as Nicolas came to help her down. "Here, Isabelle, let me assist you." He lightly gripped her waist and slowly lowered her to the ground. He felt the coldness of her skin as their bodies collided with one another. He met startled eyes when she gazed up at him, eyes full of awareness. She seemed as affected by their brief contact as he was. "Come over to the fire. It will be warmer soon," he said.

"Thank you. It is quite co-old, isn't it?" she stammered as she wrapped her cape around her body for warmth.

Nicolas was amused at her inconsequential conversation. *So my touch has her addled. Good!* Nicolas guided her to stand before the fire, and he moved in close to stand at her back. His body heat would help insulate her from the cold draft whirling around them as it sneaked in through the cave entrance.

"This is used by seamen when they are delayed by bad weather such as we are today. It's a courtesy to leave fresh wood and kindling for the next unfortunate souls who are stranded for a time."

"Like a code of honor?" she asked through chattering teeth.

"Yes . . . I suppose . . . like a code of honor." He wrapped his arms around her with his chest flush against her back. "Let me share my warmth with you, wife."

"Ahh, that feels nice. How is it men are always hot and women are cold?" she innocently asked.

Nicolas noticed several of his men turn toward him and grin at her question. He just hoped none of them offered to express their manly opinion on the subject. They could be quite crude when they talked about the way of a man with a woman. "It would seem that God made us different so we can complement one another. Would you agree?" he asked.

Her head moved from side to side as she thought about his question. "Yes. I think I would agree with you." She leaned her head against his chest and gave a soft sigh. "God is so wise; He knew exactly what we would need to live in harmony."

Nicolas was enjoying the feel of his wife's body close to his; but from the way she was sagging against him, he knew she needed some rest. His men had brought over a large piece of drift wood for them to sit upon. It was kept inside the cave for just such a time as this.

"Let us sit for a while, Isabelle. We can bring out the provisions that cook prepared for our outing today. Hopefully, the storm will blow out to sea by the time we are refreshed."

Before he moved, she turned in his arms and whispered, "Is there enough food for the men as well?"

When he gazed down at her upturned face, her wide innocent eyes mesmerized him as all thought flew from his mind. Her delicate hands felt like butterflies on his chest while whiffs of rose petals assaulted his nose when her hair swept across his chin. As soon as his men chuckled, he was jolted out of his trance. "I'm sorry. Wh-what did you say?" His eyes still locked with hers, Nicolas felt heat race up his neck and blow out the top of his head. He suddenly stepped back from her embrace causing her to stumble forward. Instinct made him reach out to prevent her from falling on her face.

A frown formed between her eyes. "What's the matter? Did I say something wrong?"

Nicolas knew his actions had hurt her feelings. The hurt showed on her face. Ignoring her last question, he answered her previous one. "Never fear. Cook always packs a bountiful meal to be shared by all in the traveling party. The men will take turns guarding the entrance and eating. Come. Let us sit while we partake of this tasty fare." His answer seemed to mollify her for the time being.

They ate in virtual silence with each lost in his or her own thoughts until Elizabeth found some berries and cream. She took what appeared to be a blackberry and dipped it in the rich cream. "Mmm," she moaned with eyes closed. "This is delicious. Here, try one," she said as she dipped another one and offered it to Nicolas.

Instead of taking it from her hand, Nicolas pulled her hand to his mouth and allowed her to feed him the succulent fruit. His lips closed over her delicate fingers as he took the berry into his mouth.

He watched as some juice ran down her outstretched arm, and then . . . his eyes met hers. It was if they were being woven together as a tapestry—one stitch at a time. Both were aware of the intimacy of the act. Nicolas didn't want to break the spell, but knew it was not the time for such a pursuit. Even though their outward display was not overtly affectionate, Nicolas was very aware of his men.

Standing up abruptly, Nicolas said, "Thank you, Isabelle. That was delicious; however, I find I need to stretch. Will you join me at the cave opening to watch the storm?"

Elizabeth was so lost in the moment that she didn't realize the abrupt change in Nicolas. "Yes, of course. I do like to keep a pulse on storms. I don't think I like them very much, but I'm not sure why," she said with a tip of her head. She took Nicolas's hand and permitted him to draw her to her feet. Once he let go of her hand, she dusted off the back of her skirt and then her hands. They walked around the log and over to the entryway. The guards walked several paces outside the cave allowing the two some privacy.

Nicolas drew back the hanging vines and leaned against the wall holding the vines in place. Crossing his feet at his ankles, he gazed out at the turbulent sea. "Now is not a pleasant time to be at sea."

Elizabeth stood near his side and shuttered. "Absolutely not. If the sea were cream, it would be making butter," she remarked. "Watch how the waves crash into the shoreline. If I were superstitious, I would think God is angry at us the way He is churning up the depths of the sea. Of course, I don't believe in such."

"No. 'Tis the way of His creation, though . . . with the cycle of weather, I mean."

"What is the name of the sea that is so violent this day?" she asked.

"You are looking at the North Sea."

"The North Sea . . . I'm not familiar with that sea. I wonder why I'm not."

"Do not vex yourself for lacking knowledge about the geography of our land. You will learn it soon enough."

"Well, I do know that it has gotten colder since we left this morning."

"I should have warned you. It won't be long before winter is upon us with great force. Therefore, our mornings begin cool with temperatures rising during the day, and then they drop drastically as the sun sets. Since women are colder by nature, or so you tell me, then you will need to dress accordingly." Nicolas stepped away from the wall and drew her into his arms. "Of course, when I am nearby, you will be warm," he said as he nuzzled her neck and inhaled deeply. Her hair smelled like a young rose full of fragrance which pleased his senses.

Nicolas was pleasantly surprised when she didn't stiffen at his actions. He took that as permission to stay nestled together until the rain subsided. So far his endeavor to woo his wife was proceeding nicely. Years ago Phillip had tried to introduce Nicolas to women by providing a mature woman for him when he was but fourteen years old. Nicolas had been revolted at that attempted fiasco by his brother. He had run from the woman, disgusted with her and Phillip. His brother never again tried to force a woman on Nicolas.

As Nicolas held his wife's body close to his own, he realized he would never do anything to harm her. He found the more time he spent in her presence, the more cherished she became to him. *How did my father ever justify his cruelty to my mother? I think only of providing protection when I'm with Isabelle; and, well, hopefully knowing her more intimately.*

"Ooph," Elizabeth breathed out when Nicolas squeezed too tightly. "Nicolas, please loosen your hold," she puffed out.

Nicolas immediately released his wife. "Forgive me, Isabelle. My mind was wandering," he stammered. "Did I hurt you?"

Elizabeth turned to face him. "No, I'm unharmed. But you must have been thinking about war or something just as deadly by the way you suddenly crushed my stomach." She smiled and said, "You should know that it takes more than a forceful embrace to put this girl down."

Frowning at her, he said, "Again, my apologies. I hope you realize I would never knowingly harm you."

"Of course, I know that, you big oaf," she said as she playfully shoved his chest. "Come on, I think the rain has stopped." Elizabeth lifted her skirt and darted out of the cave before Nicolas had a chance to recover from their encounter.

Mumbling to himself, he strode after her. *She is going to get herself killed by charging forward unaware of her surroundings.* Not once did she stop to check the beach before she hiked to the water's edge. Nicolas and his men scrambled to catch up to Elizabeth while they scanned the beach for danger.

When Nicolas reached her side, she was at the water's edge with her arms outstretched on either side of her. "Isabelle, you charged out of that cave without a thought to possible danger," he fumed.

Lowering her arms, she ignored his flare up and said, "Isn't God's world glorious? He sends the rain to refresh the earth just as He sends people to enrich my life." She turned and looked pointedly at Nicolas. "God is my ultimate protector, Nicolas, but He has allowed you to help with the job," she said sweetly. "I guess He knew I would need a keeper here on earth. And yes, you are one of those who has enriched my life . . . so far."

Taken aback by her declaration, Nicolas was momentarily speechless. During the companionable silence, the splash from the waves and an occasional seagull were the only sounds. *She believes I enrich her life. Humph. Of course, I do. It is good she is aware of it. But is there another who has loved and protected her? Do I love her?* She interrupted his wondering before he had time to pick apart those questions.

"There are times when I feel like the sand—shifting. No control. No stability. I have no past and an uncertain future. It's most unsettling at times." She looked up to see Nicolas watching her intently. Not wanting to ruin their day, she decided to reserve the serious talk for another time. "Listen to me, I'm being a Debbie-downer. Enough of that melancholy mumbo-jumbo. Come on. Let's go home," she announced. She grabbed up her dress and swiftly headed back toward the horses not waiting for Nicolas to respond.

Mumbo what? Rooted to his spot, Nicolas just shook his head as he stared at her retreating back. His wife had effectively spun a web around his heart; he realized he wanted her to be his—unreservedly, with no thoughts of her past intruding on their intimate moments. He wanted to be the one in her thoughts and the one she turned to for protection and love. As he reached his horse, his wife was mounted and waiting for him. When had she started giving the orders? More importantly, when had he started following her dictates?

20

Nicolas's eyes followed his wife while she readied for bed. Her movements were graceful and soothing. It always brought a smile to his face when she hid behind the curtains to change into her bed clothes. With the rustling of her dress, he imagined her every move which only fueled his growing passion to know her intimately. Every time she emerged from her hiding place, there was a brush in her hand.

She went through the same ritual each evening—she perched on a stool near the window and brushed her flowing hair until the ends crackled. After several strokes, she would hang her head upside down with her hair dangling over her face. Did she realize the tantalizing picture she painted for him with each stroke of the brush? Was she aware that he ached to hold her in his arms and kiss her with abandonment? He closed his eyes with an inward moan. How long would he have to endure being so close to her, yet unable to touch her as he dreamed about?

"You're awfully quiet this evening. Is something wrong?" she asked. With her head still hanging over her lap, she parted her hair and peeped out at Nicolas.

The question snatched his wandering mind back to the present as his eyes popped open. Caught unaware, he said the first thing that came to his mind.

"No. there is nothing wrong. I am thinking of tomorrow's plans."

His answer came out strangled and made him sound like a halfwit even to himself. Her words had provoked an unsettling stirring in the pit of his stomach. Indeed there was something wrong with him! He desired his wife to be his and his alone . . . forever! Scrubbing his hand across his face, he wondered when had he allowed this acute desire for his wife to grab him with such a stranglehold! Angry with himself for permitting his emotions to rule his head, he abruptly stood and marched toward the bed.

"I'm turning in for the evening. I have much to do on the morrow," he said harshly. From her quick indrawn breath, he knew his remark had offended. He didn't mean to be a brute, but he couldn't stop himself. Memories of why he never tolerated unwed ladies in his castle doused him in the face and cooled his ardor. Life had been more tolerable when he didn't have a wife, and he shouldn't forget that reality.

"Oh," she whispered. "All right. I will be along once I've made my trip to the necessary."

Still unable to control his temper, he growled, "I don't understand why you won't use the chamber pot like everyone else."

"Because I don't want to, Lord Nasty!" she hurled back.

Nicolas almost grinned at the "Lord Nasty" remark, but not quite. He could hear her jerky motions as she clunked the stool in the corner and as her brush landed with a "plop" in the chair. "At least take a torch to light your way," he mumbled. He just couldn't bring himself to be pleasant to her since she was the one who had triggered his unwanted thoughts of love and tenderness.

"Fine," she ground out.

The crashing of the door was his signal that she was gone. *What's the matter with me? I'm as twisted as a braided hemp rope.* After a few deep breaths, Nicolas realized he should have escorted his wife down the passageway. There hadn't been a recent attempt on her life; but until he caught the predator, she was still in danger. Rising from the bed, he pulled on his stockings, but not his boots. He opened the door and gazed toward the end of the hallway. Her torch hung on the wall outside the privy door, so he knew she had made it safely. He leaned against his door and waited. No harm would befall her as long as he watched.

Finally, the door opened, and she came out. What she did next surprised Nicolas. She turned her head in all directions as if to scout out the area. When it appeared she was satisfied all was clear, she headed down the other passageway instead of coming directly back to their room. *What is she about?* Nicolas pushed away from the doorway and darted after her to see where she was going. His stocking feet awarded him the secrecy he needed. Just as he rounded the corner, he noticed the edge of her gown disappear through the portal to Phillip's room. *What the devil?*

Nicolas eased back around the corner and plastered himself against the wall. The longer he contemplated her strange actions, the more clearly he understood. He had never felt such fury as was coursing through his body. Blood oozed from under his clenched fists as his body burned with rage. He banged his head against the stone wall hoping to make sense from what he had just witnessed, but he could only arrive at one conclusion. His wife had no interest in her new husband because she was giving her favors to his brother!

As he made his way back toward his room, Nicolas's mind was a storm of thoughts—whirling out of control. *Why would Phillip do this to me? Do I mean so little to my brother that he would betray me in this way? The problem surely lies at Isabelle's door. She is behind all of it! I should never have trusted a stranger. I'm no more than a dim-witted fool by allowing my feelings for Isabelle to blind me to her true nature.*

Nicolas stomped into his room and paced to and fro trying to solve his latest dilemma. How should he punish Isabelle for the calamity that seemed to be unfolding between them? He could not and would not permit her to escape unscathed from her actions. Without realizing how hard he was tugging on his hair, he suddenly winced in pain. Shaking his head, he went and splashed water in his face, hoping to douse his fiery temper. Not wanting Isabelle to realize he knew about her secret rendezvous, he pulled off his stockings and climbed back into bed. Still seething with pent-up emotions, Nicolas vowed to exact retribution on his wife.

* * *

"You're recovering nicely, Phillip. I think we can reduce your adjustments to twice a week instead of every day. How do you feel with the progress you've made so far?"

"It has truly been a miracle what you have accomplished. I never thought I would see the day when I could actually walk without excruciating pain. Even Abigail can see the difference in me. Can't you, my dove?"

Elizabeth could tell Abigail wasn't pleased with Phillip's question as she fidgeted with her apron before responding. Abigail had never quite warmed up to Elizabeth even though Elizabeth had been with the family for months. Thinking she would eventually regain her memory and leave, Elizabeth had never pressed the issue with Abigail.

"Yes, Phillip. You seem in less pain, and that's what's most important to me," Abigail all but mumbled.

Abigail's less than complimentary answer didn't faze Elizabeth. She was more interested in seeing Phillip restored to health than in receiving accolades. "Well, I had best return to my room before Nicolas comes looking for me. He makes it harder and harder for me to sneak away to treat you. When are you going to reveal the 'new you' to your brother, Phillip?"

"I had hoped either to dance into the great hall one morning or join Nicolas on a ride around our property. I'm waiting for the right time to surprise him," Phillip said with a broad smile.

"I hope it will be soon. I think he grows suspicious of my wanderings," Elizabeth said. Acknowledging Phillip and then Abigail, she said, "I'm off. May you both sleep the sleep of a babe." On those parting words, Elizabeth let herself out, retrieved her torch, and made her way down the long passageway.

Once reaching their door, she placed the torch in the receptacle on the outside wall before opening their bedroom door.

When Elizabeth entered their shared room, she noticed Nicolas was lying still. She couldn't tell if he was asleep, but decided not to make any undue noise. The blaze from the fireplace lit the room enough to keep her from stumbling over a chair or stubbing her toe on the bedpost. As she eased under the covers, Nicolas let out a loud snort and flipped over without waking. Pleased that she had not awaked the sleeping giant, Elizabeth snuggled down with no idea of the mayhem that awaited her on the morrow.

21

When Elizabeth woke, she found Nicolas had already left for the day. She must have been quite worn out from the previous day's excursion and her late night helping Phillip not to hear Nicolas fasten on his sword. Each morning when he slid it into the scabbard, it made a swooshing sound that would wake her. But not today. Stretching her arms above her head, she smiled at the thought of her husband. Remembering their intimate moments from yesterday warmed her body from the inside out. She felt as giddy as a young girl with her first kitten. Maybe if she hurried, she could get to breakfast while Nicolas was still eating.

Stopping at the entry into the great hall, Elizabeth gazed around at the bustling activity. The young boys and girls were scurrying about serving the tables with food and drink. The hum of chatter was a comforting sound to Elizabeth's ears. She realized she was falling in love with the castle folk and their unassuming ways. The idea of living with these people at the castle no longer was a dreaded thought to her but a satisfying reverie.

Releasing a deep breath, Elizabeth turned her attention to the dais. Just seeing Nicolas made her insides flitter as if a feather tickled her stomach. After their warm embraces and shared kisses yesterday, Nicolas looked quite irresistible this morning. She smoothed her hands down her dress as she made her way toward her husband. *Is this love?* Elizabeth's steps faltered when that question shot through her mind. Since God had left her in this place, He must have had an excellent reason. Maybe, just maybe, she was to love her husband and bring about healing in his heart. As that idea ricocheted around in her head, she felt at peace about her purpose in life—no longer fearful of the future, but expectant.

"Good morning, fine warriors of Fairwick castle," Elizabeth said to Nicolas, Phillip, and Thomas. As she slid her hand across Nicolas's shoulders on the way to her chair, she felt his muscles flinch as if she had struck him. Elizabeth snatched her hand away so as not to cause undue pain. "Are you in pain this morning?" she whispered to Nicolas.

"No," he snarled with his focus straight ahead.

Elizabeth was perplexed by his crankiness. Once again trying to diffuse his ill temper, she placed her hand on his arm to gain his attention. However, before she could utter a word, he jerked his arm away from her touch. This action left her rattled and hurt. What had she done to cause his displeasure? Not wanting to draw attention to his foul humor, Elizabeth reached for a cup of water, but her shaking hand knocked it over.

"Can you do nothing right?" he bellowed as he turned angry eyes upon her. The conversation in the hall ceased to exist as all eyes turned to the dais.

Elizabeth went from hurt to enraged in a single heartbeat. With slow, deliberate moves, Elizabeth stood to her feet. "Yes . . . yes, I can do something right," she said as her eyes bore into his. With lightning speed, she stabbed her eating knife between the fingers of his sword hand barely missing his middle finger. Only for a brief moment did she enjoy the startled look on his face before she left the hall. Her rigid back was the only thing that held her upright when all she wanted to do was run screaming from the crowded room. She didn't stop, but continued on outside the keep.

Elizabeth's arms swung wildly at her side as she tramped her way to the barn and to her horse, Midnight. The moment she stepped inside the barn doors, the sweet smell of hay and horse began to calm her frazzled nerves. Not wanting anyone to catch up with her, Elizabeth put on the bridle and mounted bareback from a stool. She eased Midnight out the door and took off at a fast trot right through the castle gates and across the drawbridge. Once free from the castle, she kicked Midnight into a gallop wanting to put a good distance between her and her soon-to-follow guards, Angus and Jarvis.

With no destination in mind, Elizabeth continued on the road which was safer for Midnight—less concealed holes to avoid. Still unable to make sense of Nicolas's outburst, her eyes flooded with tears as she replayed his angry words. She urged Midnight faster as if distance could erase the disturbing scene from her memory. Horse and rider flew past the villagers working in the fields who were unaware of the trouble brewing between their lord and their lady.

Unconscious of the passage of time, Elizabeth noticed Midnight had worked up quite a lather. Not wanting to cause injury to her horse, Elizabeth gradually slowed her to a clipped walk. For the first time, she looked around at her surroundings and nothing looked familiar. Of course, she had rarely ventured far from the castle, so it was no wonder the area looked foreign to her. She pulled Midnight to a stop and whipped her head from side to side looking for a recognizable landmark in her surroundings. Nothing. She took comfort in the fact that the sun was shining bright . . . well, at the moment anyway. How far had she come? Was she at the edge of their property or worse; was she near the border? Looking behind her, she saw that the road curved out of sight; but looking forward, she saw a slight incline that topped out a quarter of a mile up.

Elizabeth decided to ride up the hill and take a breather on the boulder up ahead. Midnight could rest while Elizabeth waited on her guards to show up. Without a doubt, Angus and Jarvis would eventually find her since she had not veered off the road. Surely they would be along shortly.

She sidled up to the boulder and slid off Midnight while keeping hold of the reins. From this vantage point, she could see a good distance in both directions. From her sitting position, it would be easy for Angus and Jarvis to see her perched atop the bolder.

Midnight began eating grass around the rock oblivious to the turmoil inside her owner.

The tears on Elizabeth's face had long since blown away or dried until she allowed herself to rethink the incident at breakfast. Fresh tears began to fall, plowing a path through the road dust on her cheeks. *God, I thought You wanted me to love Nicolas. My heart is engaged beyond my control.* With her face in her hands, she permitted her tears to flow freely. Her shoulders shook from her unchecked sobs. *What am I to do now, God? What?*

"Ar' ye hurt?"

Elizabeth snatched her hands away from her face as a scream erupted from her lips. The ruckus prompted Midnight to jerk free from her hold and trot a few paces away into the forest. The reins tugged on Elizabeth's arm causing her to lose her balance and slide off the rock onto her knees. There at her bleary-eyed level stood a little boy. A filthy little boy. "Wha--t?"

"Ar' ye hurt?"

"No . . . uh . . . no," she sputtered. Rising to her feet with her right hand over her heart, she felt for the rock with her left hand and leaned against it for support. "You scared me half to death."

"A'm sairy. Me name is William. Whit's yer name?"

Nicolas's words washed up just in time to prevent a disaster. *My enemies could use you as leverage against me if you are taken as a hostage.* "My name is . . . um . . . today my name is Penelope." She dared not give her true name since she felt certain she was in Scotland—enemy territory.

Cocking his head from side to side, he asked, "Why ar' ye here, crying?"

"Oh, that. I'm having a pity party." Elizabeth attempted to scrub away her tears with the heels of her hand.

"A whit? A party by yerself?" he asked through squinted eyes.

"Oh, never mind. I'm hot, tired, and quite thirsty, though."

"Haur. I hae water in me pouch." William unhooked a water bag from the sash around his waist. He uncorked the top and polished off the opening with his grimy hand before passing it to Elizabeth.

Elizabeth didn't want to offend William even though she wanted to wipe off the mouthpiece with her dress. Instead, she took a tentative sip while William watched with wide eyes. "By the way, what are you doing out here by yourself?" Elizabeth asked.

"A've been playin' doun at the poond. Tis me favorite place. But A'm glad ye came along. Do ye like little boys?"

It took her a moment to understand his question due to his strong brogue. "Yes, I love little boys and little girls. In fact, I've done quite a bit of playing with little boys lately."

"Hae ye nou?"

"Yes, I have," she said with a grin.

"That's guid. That's reel guid. Me thinks ye shood come home with me."

Hidden in the forest, he watched his son interact with a beautiful lass. Who was she, and why was she so far from home alone? With her accent, she definitely wasn't Scottish. She didn't seem a threat to William, but Daniel kept his eyes scanning the area just in case she had others with her. As a precaution, his men had spread out to search for guards belonging to the woman.

Standing to her feet, Daniel saw the woman hold out her hand to William who eagerly accepted. *Ah must teach him to be cautious and naut so trusting of a stranger—even if the stranger is a bonnie lass.*

"Come, William. There is a storm brewing and we need to find shelter. Do you have any ideas?" As soon as the words left her lips, a snapped twig caused her to spin around and gasp. There sat Daniel on his black war horse wearing his kilt. She immediately shoved William behind her back as if to shield him from danger.

Seeing her action pleased Daniel, yet he showed no emotion on his face. "Weel, lass, ye seem to hae something that belongs to me."

As the woman began to take quick shallow breaths, Daniel noticed her rapid heartbeat in her throat. She straightened her back and put on a mask of determination before demanding, "Who are you and what do you want?"

She certainly had gumption standing up to him with no mode of defense when he could easily slay her with one swipe of his sword. William squirmed until he finally poked his head around her dress. She had a death grip on William's arm preventing him from getting free. All he could do was peep up at Daniel and say, "Hi, Papa."

The woman looked down at William and repeated, "Papa?" Loosening her grip on William's arm, she took hold of his hand and turned back toward Daniel.

"Mount up, wee William."

Once the lovely, forest nymph released William's hand, he scampered off into the woods to retrieve his horse. While he was gone, the woman marched up to Daniel with her hands on her hips and eyes flashing. Looking directly at Daniel, she exploded.

"What do you mean allowing your son to play at a pond by himself?

Daniel opened his mouth to respond to her preposterous accusation, but she continued without taking a breath. Daniel tuned out her tirade and instead made an adjustment in his original assessment of her. She was definitely exquisite to gaze upon, but she was not serene as he first thought. The woman in front of him was a ferocious mother bear protecting her cub. Here stood a woman placing herself between an unknown child and what she perceived to be danger. Impressive.

". . . and not to mention, he is filthy and in need of a bath."

Daniel watched her heave a deep breath and then blow her hair out of her eyes as if exasperated. *Very nice.* His mind whirled with possibilities. She would do nicely for what he had in mind.

* * *

Elizabeth heard a horse approach; hoping it was Angus or Jarvis, she was surprised to see seven mounted men surrounding her with all of them wearing frowns and . . . skirts?

"Penelope, these ar' me father's men, but ye can ride with me," William offered.

"I think not, young William. She will ride pillion with me," Daniel said.

With her arm outstretched and palm facing outward toward William's father, Elizabeth said, "Oh, no thank you. I must be on my way back home riding my own horse. She's grazing in the forest. My husband and his men will be along shortly. Don't worry about me. I'll be fine."

Shaking his head, no, Daniel continued to walk his horse toward her, as did the other warriors until they encircled her. Daniel held his hand down to her and said, "Come."

"Ye must do what me father says. Dinna anger 'im."

Elizabeth whipped her head around to see William looking at her with anxious eyes. Not wanting to upset William, she smiled at him. "It's alright, William, your father is not mad at me. He understands women have to think through each dangerous situation and weigh the options. He would expect no less from me. Right?" she asked as she turned back to Daniel.

"Come," he bellowed. "Douglass will bring yer horse."

Eight horses and eight pair of naked legs were close enough to touch and smell. Whew! With no viable options popping into her mind, Elizabeth relented. "Since it is growing dark with the approaching storm clouds, it would appear that my best course might be to come home with you, William. Thank you for inviting me." Elizabeth stepped up to Daniel and grasped his outstretched hand. Once she placed her foot on top of his boot, his large, firm hand jerked her up in front of him.

Not sure of Daniel's temperament, Elizabeth decided to treat him with kindness until she could come up with a plan of escape. Her previous harsh words about the care of his son might have put him in a foul mood. So a compliment was in order. Hm, what to say?

"Your strong, powerful horse is impressive. He didn't even flinch when you added my weight." All she received in response was a grunt from Daniel. *Oh, dear. I'll have to do better than that lame comment. Think! Think!*

With only a hand signal, the company of men took off at a brisk pace. She twisted around to see about William, but Daniel blocked her view.

"The boy is safe."

Elizabeth jumped at his unexpected words. "Oh. I wasn't the least bit worried."

"Liar," he scoffed. "Ye might want to ken that I sent yer men back to yer husband with a message from me."

Elizabeth's eyes flew to Daniel's face. "You didn't hurt them, did you?"

Daniel's eyes bore into hers. "Nae."

Swiveling her head back around, she tried to act unconcerned. "What kind of message?"

"Dinna fash yerself. For nou, ye will be me guest." He tightened his hold on her and looked straight ahead. Conversation had ended.

Elizabeth realized she had muddled the day after storming out of the castle in a rage. Why did she continue to let her temper rule her head? Crossing swords with Nicolas never ended well for her. Today she was caught in a web of her own making and needed to devise a strategy of escape, but was too weary to think. Daniel's massive, warm chest was the perfect place to rest her head. Why not? As a married woman, she felt a wee bit guilty, but decided to worry about that later. Sleep now. Escape tomorrow.

When her body went limp against Daniel, he knew she was asleep. At least she was wise enough to know when she had been bested. He had forgotten how excitable a woman was over non-essential things. William, for instance. Everyone knows boys rarely bathe especially when winter approaches. Women . . . he had missed how they could turn the mundane into an adventure. Yes, life would not be dull with this one around.

He was certain his bonnie captive belonged to Nicolas, his old friend, who resided across the border from Daniel's beloved Scotland. What good fortune when she rode onto his land; he was going to keep her. He had triumphed over his nemesis for the last time. With that joyful thought, Daniel smiled for the first time in years.

* * *

Elizabeth squirmed as she began to awaken. When her eyes fluttered open, she was sheathed in total darkness that had overtaken the riders while enroute to Daniel's castle. Overhead was a blanket of dark, storm clouds. As she rubbed her eyes, she ignored the fact that her elbow had caught Daniel on the chin. Dancing flames drew her attention. "What is on fire?" she exclaimed as she leaned forward.

"Noothing. 'Tis the castle awaiting ma arrival. Nou cease yer movement. Horse dae nae like it."

Total dread settled over Elizabeth. What would become of her? Possible dungeon time? Were Daniel and Nicolas enemies for sure? Her hands twisted in knots as questions flew around in her head. She wished she had stayed awake to watch which direction they rode or if they made any turns. Oh, dear . . . how was she to find her way home now? Nicolas would not come for her. He was probably rejoicing that she was gone. Unshed tears gathered in her eyes, blurring the light cast off by the castle torches. Even though Nicolas was an unpredictable ogre to live with at times, his castle had begun to feel like home. Would she ever see it again?

Instead, Daniel's castle loomed up ahead. She tried deep breaths to calm her frazzled nerves so she wouldn't swoon at the sight of his warriors lining the battlements. They were fully armed and were screaming like banshees. She had landed in a rattlers' nest!

When Daniel and his men clamored over the drawbridge, an enormous cheer went up. Elizabeth tensed and whipped her head from side to side taking in the warriors in kilts and war paint. The great cry lasted until every rider was safely inside the castle gates. Elizabeth's quick breaths and hammering heart had caused her to get light-headed. She snatched her head around at the rattling chains to see the portcullis bang to the ground. The ground reverberated from the force. Elizabeth realized the danger of her situation and promptly fainted.

Once again Daniel tightened his hold when he felt her body go limp. His men had scared her with their shouts of support for their returning Laird and the prize he had brought home. This little English woman had a lot to learn about Scottish ways. It was a good thing he was a patient man.

22

Angus and Jarvis were out of breath when they came hastening into the great hall without Lady Isabelle. Angus stood erect and unmoving in front of Nicolas while Jarvis eased down on a bench. "My Lord," Jarvis wheezed, "we have lost your lady!"

Nicolas was not overly concerned about his wife. She had a way of turning up after she had gotten into a mess of one kind or another. Jarvis was usually emotional when it came to his wife so his reaction couldn't be trusted. On the other hand, Angus's drawn face was something to consider.

"Tell me the whole of it," Nicolas sighed. "What has she done now?"

"As you remember, My Lord, we followed Lady Isabelle out of the hall; but when we reached the courtyard, she came bursting forth from the barn on her horse. Bareback!" Jarvis hesitated while his words settled on the crowd that had gathered to hear the news. Nicolas began to tap his fingers on the table while he waited. Jarvis was too dramatic for Nicolas's taste. The more Jarvis aged, the slower he was to relay a story. Nicolas rotated his hand toward Jarvis to get on with the telling.

"Anyway, she had a good head start on me and Angus. We had to saddle our horses because we're too old to ride bareback." Jarvis paused as he gulped down some ale that a servant had plopped down next to him as if to fortify himself to tell the rest of the tale.

If Nicolas waited for Jarvis to finish his account, darkness would be upon them. "Where is my wife, Jarvis?" he yelled.

"She rode all the way to Scotland and was captured by your enemy, Laird Daniel McKinnon!"

A hush settled over those in the room like a mist.

He leaned forward, "What did you say?" Nicolas pushed out through gritted teeth.

"He has the story aright, My Lord," Angus added.

All eyes now focused on Lord Fairwick to see what he would do. Women clinched their aprons while men held tight to their tankards. The women flinched when he burst out with laughter. "Oh. This is too good to be true. Daniel with my wife inside his castle grounds?" Nicolas gave a belly role of laughter. "I'm going to let him keep her for a few days before I fetch her. He will probably bring her home post haste and beg me to take her off his hands. I didn't realize until now; I've had the best defense against that aggravating man living right under my roof!"

His people failed to see the humor in the situation, especially his brother Phillip, whose face and neck had turned deep red. Phillip moved further into the room, sidestepped Angus to have a clear view of Nicolas. With clinched fists, Phillip demanded, "How can you be so flippant with your wife's life?"

Nicolas sobered at once. He was already jealous of the camaraderie Phillip had with his wife and seeing him jump to her defense only angered him more. He rose slowly to his feet and came around the table and stepped down to the floor. "What's the matter, Phillip? Are you missing my wife?" Nicolas sneered. At that moment, Nicolas didn't care that his question brought dishonor to his brother's character. So be it.

Phillip charged at Nicolas with full speed using his head like a battering ram. His reaction caught Nicolas off balance. The force took them both to the ground with Phillip on top. Phillip had diligently been doing his exercises Elizabeth had prescribed and was able to hold his own with Nicolas for a brief time. He landed some well-placed punches before Nicolas flipped them both and jumped to his feet hovering over Phillip, who lay on his back.

Nicolas wiped his bloody nose and lip with his sleeve. "I will not fight you, Phillip, and you well know it."

"Why? Because I'm a cripple?" Phillip threw off the hand Nicolas offered to assist him to his feet. Instead, Phillip pulled himself upright. He gave Nicolas a fiery glare before walking stiff-backed out the door.

"No, because you're my brother," Nicolas said to no one in particular. He stared into the empty archway where Phillip had exited and wondered how Phillip had been able to fight him and still walk out of the room without a limp. Shaking his head in wonderment, he glanced around the room and could read the disappointment in the people's eyes. He didn't need their judgment to feel the full measure of guilt from hurting the one man who loved him unconditionally. This was his wife's fault! Her presence had disrupted the closeness he shared with his brothers. Maybe he would leave her with the McKinnon. Looking at the horrified faces gazing back at him was reason enough to bring her back—his people loved Lady Isabelle.

"Stop worrying. I'll go get her," he hollered. His grumpy attitude sent the people running out of the hall except for Angus and Jarvis.

"We're sorry, my lord, that we couldn't defend your lady. She was too far ahead of us and encircled by warriors on horseback by the time we rounded the bend in the road," Angus said, wagging his lowered head.

Walking up to the two older men, Nicolas slapped them on the back. "Don't worry, men. The McKinnon will not harm her. By now he knows she belongs to me."

"I'm not worried about him harming her, Lord Nicolas. I'm worried about him keeping her." With those parting words, Angus and Jarvis shuffled out of the hall leaving Nicolas alone.

Remembering the ill treatment he had directed toward his wife since their marriage caused Nicolas to pause. Guilt pricked his conscience. The mixture of hurt and anger on her face from their morning altercation came back to haunt him. Uneasiness snaked through his gut. What if she decided to stay in Scotland?

Nicolas dropped into the chair flanking the fireplace and threw his leg over the arm. His thoughts wandered to his wife, Lady Isabelle. Well, it was Lady Isabelle when she left that morning. His wife—a woman who could set his head spinning with a smile. When she turned on the charm, he was rendered daft. At those moments, all he could think about was devouring her with kisses and dreaming of more. The strategy she had used to entrap his heart was worthy of a seasoned warrior. Scrubbing his face with both hands, Nicolas made a decision. He would make things right with Phillip, and together they would come up with a plan to rescue his wife.

His bones creaked as he stood from the chair. Stretching his hands high above his head, Nicolas heaved a sigh. "Daniel, get ready to be undone for I am coming for my wife." Nicolas took the stairs two at a time eager to speak with Phillip. He never liked to be at odds with either of his brothers. It didn't set well on his stomach. Down the long hallway he went, turned the corner and heard heated words coming from Phillip's room.

"Why do you continue to cower under his arrogant rule when you should be the lord of this castle?" Abigail fumed.

"Now, Abby, you know he only took over because we all thought my death was close at hand," Phillip answered.

Nicolas halted outside Phillip's door and eavesdropped on their conversation. Abigail resumed her tirade.

"That was over two years ago. I loathe admitting it; but with Isabelle's help, you grow stronger every day. Your limp is hardly noticeable. I daresay her healing powers are the best kept secret of this castle unless you include your brother's blindness."

"Lower your voice, Abby. Isabelle doesn't want her gifts made known. She's afraid the peasants will think her a witch if they find out. Plus, she hasn't revealed it to Nicolas yet. She's waiting for me to make public my progress."

"Humph! Nicolas cares only for himself and increasing his holdings. He cares naught for anyone else much less his wife."

"Hush, Abigail! There will be no more disparaging words against my brother."

"Why do you always defend him? You know he thinks you're in love with his wife, don't you? It sickens me the way he treats you. He doesn't even care enough for you or his wife to find out what's really happening when she comes to your room."

"Abigail! Enough," Phillip hissed. "Stop your ranting, or at the very least, close the door. What if someone heard you . . . or worse . . . what if Nicolas heard you?"

BAM! Thunk! The door closed and the security bar dropped in place.

Nicolas stood frozen in the shadows. What did Abigail mean with all her ramblings? Isabelle a healer? And what about her accusations directed toward him—arrogant, selfish, and uncaring? Was he all those things she accused him of being? Massaging his chest, he acknowledged that Abigail's harsh words had found their mark, piercing deep into his heart. He should have heeded his mother's warning. One never hears anything good about oneself when eavesdropping.

Nicolas stumbled to his room, shaken by what he had heard. He shut the door and walked on wooden legs to the window and threw open the shutters to stare at his holdings. His holdings? It all should have gone to Phillip, the eldest; yet, no one thought Phillip would survive his grave injuries. Nicolas didn't even want to be Lord, but had taken over at what he thought was Phillip's dying request.

Gripping the window seal, he sighed deeply. What to do now? He walked to the middle of the room and looked about. He missed his wife, her clumsiness included. Was she clumsy because she feared him? Was he such a monster that she was afraid to tell him she was a healer? If so . . . he had become his father! He groaned in agony at that revelation. Burying his face in his hands, he wept. He wept for all he had lost because of his father: his childhood innocence, his carefree attitude, his zest for life and worst of all . . . his mother. His father had killed his mother as if he had run her through with a sword.

Nicolas sank to the floor on his knees and sobbed. The great warrior and leader of his men reduced into a babbling babe. The image of his mother caused such an acute pain that it crippled him. Nicolas remained on the cold, stone floor until the ache in his knees caused him to dry his eyes. During that time, darkness had crept in and besieged him with the glow from the fireplace his only light. When he stared into those dying embers, he knew what action he needed to take to save his wife . . . and his soul. First, he would reconcile with his beloved brother, the man he admired and needed. Then he would liberate Isabelle and bring her home to stay—forever.

* * *

Elizabeth's eyes fluttered open. She lay perfectly still, allowing her eyes to roam her surroundings. The bed she lay in was a plush, four poster bed decorated with ornate coverings. The bed curtains were tied to each bed post allowing the sun to shine upon her. Glancing down the length of her body, she was relieved to see all of her clothes intact minus her shoes, not to mention how thankful she was to be in a lavish room instead of the dungeon.

She propped herself up on her elbows to get a better look-see of the room. To her left was a dresser with a small looking-glass attached. Along that same wall was a closed door she assumed led to the hallway. Directly in front of her was a stone fireplace that sported a blazing fire which warmed the room. To her right were two narrow windows with a trunk on the floor between them. Not a bad dwelling for a prisoner.

Swinging her legs off the bed, she slowly stood up facing the dresser. On it sat a pitcher of water and a wash bowl. Her main focus was to locate a chamber pot. Bending down, she peered under the bed and spied her deliverance. After making use of the porcelain pan, she shoved it back out of sight. Taking the pitcher, she poured water in the bowl to wash up. She dipped her hands in the cool water and splashed some on her face. She lifted a small towel to pat dry. Now, to face her captor.

Before Elizabeth had a chance to try the door, it was pushed open from the outside. In walked Laird McKinnon without even checking to see if she was presentable. Men!

"I hope you slept well, Lady Penelope."

"I must have. I don't remember anything after we rode into the castle. How did I get in here?"

"I took care of your needs with the assistance of Edna."

"Thank you very much, kind sir. I appreciate your hospitality. If I might trouble you for a little something to eat and drink before heading on my way, I would be most grateful." Back in the recesses of her memory, she heard the words 'never show fear.' Elizabeth cradled her clasped hands and stood erect with a serene smile plastered on her face.

"I have come to escort you to our great hall, but first," clapping his hands, "I have fresh clothing for you to wear." In hurried two young serving girls with several dresses and an assortment of shoes that they promptly displayed on the floor.

"Not sure of what would be to your liking, I have provided many choices. The lasses will assist you while I await you in the hallway." Daniel abruptly left the room, closing the door as he left.

"But mine are fine," she said to the closed door. The serving girls giggled as they unlaced Elizabeth's dress and pulled it over her head. Her stomach growled and reminded her she had eaten nothing yesterday—Nicolas's fault for sure. Her uncontrolled anger had landed her in the arms of her husband's enemy—literally. She felt as if she were being dressed and stuffed for the main course. The bodice had a deep plunge showing too much of her chest. *Oh my, what a mess.*

The women pulled her hair back with a red ribbon. Smiling broadly, they seemed pleased with the outcome of their work. They parted ways giving Elizabeth access to the once-again open door. *Who opened that door?* There against the wall with his arms crossed over his chest and his feet crossed at the ankle was the laird of the castle. Muscles bulged straining his clothing. She had to admit, he was a dashing figure in that skirt.

Pushing away from the wall, Daniel scrutinized her from top to bottom and gave a nod of approval. He met her at the threshold.

"You fill out the dress very nicely. Come, let us break the fast," he said as he extended his hand toward her.

After smoothing her hands down the front of her dress, Elizabeth stood with her arms hanging by her side. She cocked her head and asked, "Why is it that you speak like an Englishman now when earlier you spoke as a Scotsman?"

"All in due time, my dear. All in due time. You will find I am a man of numerous talents. Come." His outstretched hand beckoned her to take it.

Hesitantly, she stepped into the hallway and placed her hand in his firm grip. Daniel's eyes bore into hers as if he were measuring her worth or maybe her trustworthiness. What did he plan to do with her? Would he act the gentleman now only to turn evil later? She felt his eyes on her as they strolled toward the great hall. She kept her face averted so he couldn't observe her apprehension. Not being able to discern his intentions left her feeling off balance. Oh, why had she ridden so far from home? Pride. Nothing but foolish pride.

Daniel had drawn her hand through his arm and slowed his pace. He patted and rubbed her hand as they sauntered on. "You're thoughts, my lady?"

Elizabeth flinched at his question. "Oh . . . um . . . just wool gathering." She could hardly think with all the rubbing, patting, and stroking he was doing to her hand.

When she was not forthcoming with information, Daniel asked, "How did you find your accommodations?"

Glad she could be honest with her answer, she said, "The bed slept great. I slept like the dead." Then glancing his way, she commented, "Maybe you drugged me so I wouldn't be any trouble to you."

Daniel stopped in the middle of the hallway. "You wound me with your accusations," he said with a hand over his heart. "Is that how Nicolas deals with you?" he asked with one brow raised.

She jerked her hand from his hold. "Of course not! Nicolas would never resort to such controlling behavior!" she exclaimed.

"Then why would you think it of me? We Scotsmen are not the barbarians you English are taught to believe." His lips tightened into a grim expression.

She didn't want to anger Laird McKinnon since her escape might depend on his consent. "Shall we choose a trivial topic to discuss? Something less controversial?" she asked with pleading eyes.

Daniel faced forward and strode down the hall. Elizabeth had to run to catch up with him. *Oh, my. This is not going well. Come on girl, what's non-threatening? William!* "Where is young William this fine morning?" she blurted out.

Instantly, his expression relaxed and his pace slowed at the mention of his son. "Ah, my son is up at the first rooster crow. He is most assuredly out causing a stir among my men or pestering the women as they wash, or possibly plotting some wicked event to make my hair turn gray. He excels in the latter."

Laughing, Elizabeth once again slipped her hand through the crook of his arm. "What a delightful young man he is. I love children of all ages and hope to have some of my own one day," she said wistfully.

"How long have you and Lord Fairwick been wed?"

"Only a short time," she said.

"You might already carry the next heir."

"Oh, no. That's not possible," she blurted out without thinking just as they entered the great hall. *Great. Now he knows I'm married to Nicolas!* When Daniel looked at her with a grin, she felt the heat rise up her neck into her face. "We should not be discussing such a delicate matter," she hissed and promptly turned her head away only to be greeted by the stares of his people.

* * *

Daniel was delighted. If Penelope was not presently breeding, then he could take her for his own with a free conscience. He would steal her away from Nicolas, make her his wife, and have a mother for William. What sweet revenge against Nicolas for all the times Nicolas had beaten Daniel in archery, tournaments . . . and . . . with the women. Now Daniel would be the victorious one!

The eyes of the peasants followed his progress as he and Elizabeth walked into the room. The on-lookers were intrigued. Daniel placed her beside him at the head table—a position of importance and remained standing to introduce her.

With his hand raised for silence, Daniel said, "Meit and welcum, the bonnie, Lady Penelope."

The men crashed their tankards on the table and stomped their feet while yelling. The wild roar of the people caused Elizabeth to tip sideways in her chair from fright. She quickly righted herself to keep from total humiliation. Daniel watched as her blush spread to the tips of her ears. Yes, she would be a pleasing addition to his castle. Smiling for the second time in twenty-four hours, Daniel was ready to begin his assault on Lady Penelope's sensibilities to win her for his own.

Before the cock crowed, Nicolas had bathed, dressed and gone straight to Phillip's room. He knew Phillip's progress would be slow in the morning due to his stiffness after a night's sleep. Another reason Phillip refused to take his rightful place as Lord of the castle—he could not react quickly if needed. Taking a fortifying breath, Nicolas knocked on Phillip's door. "Open up, 'tis Nicolas."

It seemed that Abigail took her time before cracking the door open. "What do you here at this early hour?" she spit out.

"Abigail!" Phillip bellowed from within. "Cease this attitude. You're beginning to sound like a fisherman's wife. Now open the door."

The door jerked open and revealed an unhappy sister-in-law. Her frown would have brought lesser men to their knees in repentance, but not Nicolas. He was accustomed to her crankiness. "'Tis alright. I have come to beg you both for your forgiveness for my ill treatment of you. My eyes have been unlocked to see my arrogant ways, and I am here to right our relationship."

With her hand still holding the door, Abigail stood rooted to the spot. Her eyes were round with disbelief as her lips opened and shut like a fish catching bugs. Phillip put his hand on his wife's shoulder. "Abigail, stop your gawking. You look ridiculous. Come in, brother mine. Say what is on your heart," Phillip urged.

Nicolas closed and bolted the door. He didn't want to run the risk of their being interrupted by a maid or overheard. Nicolas planned on apologizing to Phillip in public since their altercation had been quite public, but for now, more was at stake than simple forgiveness—they needed to talk of war!

23

After breaking their fast, Daniel and Elizabeth strolled around the castle grounds as Daniel pointed out the best aspects of his holdings. She tried to act interested, but was wondering why they hadn't come across his stables. He directed them toward another gate within the castle walls. It was a maze of trees, bushes, and dying flowers. Elizabeth could tell the gardens had once been beautiful but were past their blooming time. Winter was not far off, but his vegetables were still sprouting with healthy plant life. Off to one side were a group of trees with an elegantly carved wooden bench underneath. The limbs hung over the bench providing widespread shade to enjoy on a sweltering day.

"This looks vaguely like an English garden," Elizabeth remarked.

"Yes. It was my mother's pride and joy. She designed it and picked every seed planted in the garden. She was English and my father was a Scottish Laird."

"Ah. So that explains it."

"Explains what?"

"How you speak with a heavy Scottish brogue and then can switch to near perfect English." Removing her arm from his, Elizabeth sauntered over to the bench and sat down. Daniel remained where he was and watched her fluff out her skirt while gazing around the garden. "What do you hope to gain by showing me your castle grounds?" Elizabeth asked him with a pointed look.

"Why, Lady Penelope, you have such a devious little mind. I'm proud of my home and enjoy sharing it with a lovely woman. It's not every day one such as you rides through my gates. So, will you allow me to boast today with no ulterior motives?"

Could she be wrong in her assessment of Daniel and his purpose? Was he as innocent as he claimed, or would he try to use her against her own husband in some way? Tilting her head one way and then another, Elizabeth decided to change the direction of the conversation. "My name is no longer Lady Penelope, but Lady Marion or Mary for short," she announced.

With hands on his hips and sporting a screwed up face, Daniel asked, "Why?"

"'Tis a long story, but if you want to hear it . . ."

"I have nothing better to do. Please, enlighten me," he said, relaxing his stance.

"Ha, nothing better to do," she mumbled. "I'll make it short. I hit my head and can't remember my name. Therefore, I try on different names to see if any of them feel like a fit—rattle my memory. There you have it," she said with finality as she leaned back with her hands holding onto the bench.

Daniel stood quiet for a moment before bursting out with laughter. Elizabeth scrunched her face in disapproval and confusion. "Why are you laughing? It is a sad tale, yet you make light of it."

"Oh . . . please forgive me," he said as he wiped tears from his eyes. "I'm not laughing at your terrible circumstance, but at the merry chase you must put Nicolas through each day, a scene I would like to observe secretly."

More than a little put out with his attitude, Elizabeth rose from the bench and put fisted hands on her hips. "Are you friend or foe?"

Daniel's smile froze on his lips. He, too, straightened to his full height and paused as he bore into her eyes. His direct stare made Elizabeth squirm and wish she hadn't ask the question. With a shrug of his shoulder, he asked, "Well, Lady Marion, shall I continue in my boasting? I have saved the best for last."

Realizing he wouldn't be forthcoming with an answer, Elizabeth decided to take his olive branch with a change in the subject again. All the dancing around topics was causing her head to spin. "What might that be Laird McKinnon?"

"My stables, of course. You will be impressed with the prize that is hidden within," he said as he wiggled his eye brows. When she did nothing but squint her eyes at him, he said, "Come. You can judge for yourself."

Elizabeth kept telling herself she would not be impressed. This Laird was a braggart, and she didn't like it. He was trying too hard to amaze her. Why? When they turned a corner, her eyes grew wide with admiration. The stable buildings alone were quite elaborate; she could only imagine what magnificent horses were housed inside.

"Would you like to see what awaits you inside?" he coaxed.

Her gaze took in the intricacy of the woodwork of the stable doors, absolutely breathtaking in design. "Yes. Yes, I would," she all but whispered.

Daniel swung open the double doors with a flourish. He then took her hand and pulled her into the darkened interior. Once inside, they paused a moment to allow their eyes to adjust to the dim light before proceeding to the first stall. Noise rang from the tack room at the end of the stable. "Sounds like Finley is making repairs on our tackle."

Elizabeth peered into the first stall to see a beautiful chestnut mare with a blazing white bolt on her forehead. The horse pranced around her stall as if to show off for her laird. After her grand display, she paraded over to the half-door and nudged Daniel's shoulder. "She seems to be expecting something from you," Elizabeth said.

"Yes. I usually have an apple or carrot to offer, but not today, little lady," Daniel said to the horse as he petted her velvety nose.

Elizabeth reached up to pet the horse, but jerked back when the horse neighed loudly at her. The chestnut backed away and pawed at the ground while she threw her head up and down in agitation. Elizabeth was startled at the response when only moments before the mare had been docile.

"Don't ever reach your hand toward one of my horses without asking me first. They are friendly with me, but are trained for battle, not for pets," Daniel said in anger.

"You could have warned me in advance. It's only natural I'm drawn to such a beauty that had not shown any previous aggressive behavior. I'm not a novice around horses," Elizabeth said with a harsh voice. "It would seem that you were so intent on boasting that you failed to give adequate instructions when we first entered."

With neck veins bulging, Daniel's face grew red. He drew in a deep breath and let it hiss out between his lips. He glanced away from her face for a moment; but when he turned back to her, he had once again gained control of his anger. "Please forgive me, Lady Marion, for not properly instructing you. I am most thankful you came to no harm. Come. Let me show you my favorite among the stables if you are still agreeable to it."

Elizabeth stood unmoving looking into his eyes trying to read his disposition. He appeared contrite and sorry. She would have to take him at his word until he proved otherwise. "Lead on, O mighty laird," she said with the flourish of her hand and sweeping bow.

Daniel gave her a slow grin and pulled her outstretched arm through the crook of his arm. "I keep my prize stallion in the last stall away from the other horses. He is slightly high strung."

"Only slightly?" she added on a laugh.

They continued down the center of the stable with Elizabeth's head swiveling from side to side to glimpse the other horses. She made a mental comparison of his horses to those of Nicolas. In her opinion, Nicolas had the finer horses. The bottom of her dress made a swishing sound as it dragged through the straw and dirt adding to the music she loved hearing—chomps, stamps, snorts, and neighing of her favorite animals. The smell of the hay, horses, leather, and even the manure was a pleasing aroma to Elizabeth—comforting.

"Where's my horse?" Elizabeth asked with her brows drawn into a frown.

"She has been placed in another stable away from my war horses. Do not fret; she is safe and well cared for," Daniel said. "I realize you rode in on my horse, but I don't think you were able to appreciate his abilities since you fell asleep once you were in my arms," Daniel said seductively.

"Not well done of you to mention that incident, laird. I had experienced an exasperating morning and was not at my best." Elizabeth pulled loose from Daniel's hold and walked to the stall housing William's horse. "May I pet William's horse?" she asked with her eyes focused on the horse.

"Yes, of course. She is our most gentle in the barn." Daniel's chest puffed out. "I have been training William since he was barely out of nappies so Rosalyn was a perfect choice for his first horse. She is 15 hands high with a smooth gate to accommodate her young rider," he proudly recited. "She is allowed to stay with the war horses so she can be near her mother."

Rubbing the silky nose of Rosalyn was soothing to Elizabeth after the on-and-off-again flirting from Daniel. Even though she and Nicolas were at odds with one another, Elizabeth was a one-man woman and knew a playful attraction could be dangerous. As she stood stroking Rosalyn, the heat from Daniel was cooking her insides. It was time to move. Pronto!

Stepping away from Daniel, Elizabeth started walking toward the back of the barn. The longer she was near Daniel, the easier it was to forget she was a prisoner, not a guest. Needing a distraction, she asked, "What have you named your horse?"

He glanced sideways at her before leaning back and laughing out loud. She stopped mid-step and pivoted to face him. "I see no humor in my question," she exclaimed with her nose in the air. He was laughing at her expense, and she didn't like it. It made her feel like a brainless young girl. How dare he?

There she stood with a rigid body and fire spewing from her eyes. Daniel reined in his mirth with difficulty and said, "Please forgive my outburst, Lady Marion. I'm not sure what Nicolas does, but we Scotsmen never name our war horses. They are warriors like us, not pets. If I'm in need of him during a battle, I simply refer to him as Horse," he finished with a grin behind his hand.

"Well, that is where you are wrong, Laird McKinnon. You have actually named him after all—horse—which is a ridiculous name." She threw back her shoulders and flounced off.

Daniel shook his head as he watched her retreating back. She was full of fire and determination which excited him . . . he would have her for his own!

24

Early the next morning, Phillip sat rubbing his chin deep in thought. He and Nicolas had met in the war room to discuss their battle plans. Nicolas had devised a plan to free his wife, and now Phillip would analyze it for any pitfalls. The brothers had found that working together on war strategies produced the best results.

"Do you think your wife will understand her role in this rescue?" Phillip asked skeptically.

"I have no doubt. She is a clever one, my wife," Nicolas answered proudly.

Phillip had to smile at his brother's complete turnaround toward Lady Isabelle. He couldn't wait to see how their lives would unfold in the future after she was home where she belonged.

"Do you think you should take Agnes along?" Phillip asked.

"No need. I am thoroughly versed in this new kind of war tactic, thanks to my lady," he said with a grin.

That was another thing Phillip noticed about his brother since he had wed Lady Isabelle; he smiled easily. "I will secure the castle while you are away and make ready for your triumphant return."

With a serious face, Nicolas said, "Phillip, I will gladly turn the castle over to you when you feel physically ready. You have made great strides in your recovery with my lady's healing approach and rightfully should be the lord of the castle."

Phillip studied Nicolas for only a few seconds before his serious response. "No, Nicolas. Even if I became strong in every way, the answer would still be no. The people have come to trust your leadership and respect your decisions. It would be pointless to change roles because we both know that you would make . . . a terrible steward!" Phillip dodged the playful punch that Nicolas threw his way.

"Brother, you have taken a near death experience and fought your way back to a normal life with little complaint along the way. Your positive outlook on life amazes me and makes me yearn to be more like you even though I have tried before and failed. Father always wanted you to succeed him and wished me to the devil," Nicolas solemnly said. "I wanted to make sure you have no regrets and were pleased with your decision keeping me as the lord."

"Yes, brother mine, I am content. As for our father, give him no more thought; because I assure you, I do not. What he wanted has no weight in our decisions today. We are men full grown and wise in our own right. Therefore, we will continue on as we have since my accident never mentioning our positions again. Agreed?"

"Phillip, it is good what you say. Once Lady Isabelle returns home, with your help, we will work on restoring our family to oneness. I have allowed our relatives to splinter and go in their own directions, but no more. After that is accomplished, I will make every effort to find Brigette a worthy husband before she is too spoiled and not worth having. Any input you have to offer on that matter will be welcomed."

Phillip just shook his head. "Hopefully, we aren't too late." Both brothers laughed as they left the room to put their plan into action.

※ ※ ※

While walking in the garden with William by her side asking questions, Elizabeth suddenly felt the ground shake. Unaware of what was happening, Elizabeth grabbed William's hand and ran toward the castle. As they rounded a corner toward the front of the castle keep, she saw the men at arms rushing about as if preparing for battle. Shouts echoed all around the courtyard as warriors scrambled to the walls with their weapons. The portcullis lowered. Elizabeth had released William's hand as she turned in circles watching the frenzy of activity, yet understanding none of it.

"William, to the keep," his father commanded. "Lady Marion, come with me," Daniel ordered. William dragged his feet as he went up the steps to the keep. He stopped just inside the doors and turned to watch the frantic commotion. Daniel yanked Elizabeth along behind him, shouting orders to his men as they made their way to the outer wall stairs.

"Stop. You are hurting me," Elizabeth spit out. She attempted to tug free but he had a firm grasp on her wrist. "You are going to pull my arm out of its socket," Elizabeth fumed.

"I think not. You are made of stronger stuff," Daniel said. He persisted in hauling her up to the paramount.

"What is going on? What caused the earth to shake? Why are you taking me to the top of the wall? Why are your men preparing for battle?" Elizabeth fired out. She tripped on the last step and would have fallen to her knees, but Daniel's firm hold yanked her upward into his arms.

Daniel's eyes roamed her face and form. He smiled and said, "All in due time, Lady Marion, all in due time." The breath from each word swept across her cheek sending a shiver down her back. "Come and see what the disturbance is about."

Elizabeth peered over the wall and gasped. Surrounding the castle were hundreds of warriors dressed in full battle armor with Nicolas sitting on his mighty stallion in front of his men. "Oh my," Elizabeth wheezed. Her trembling hand touched her lips. "It's Nicolas," she whispered.

"Yes, Lady Marion, it is Lord Fairwick, my old friend," he said gruffly.

Elizabeth stared in wonder at the impressive display in front of her eyes and was momentarily touched that her husband had come for her. Of course, he had taken his sweet time and left her fearing for her future. For all he knew, she could have been rotting away in the dungeon. She was miffed, but glad to see him nonetheless. Nicolas was such a handsome, strong man whose very presence demanded her attention.

"Lord Fairwick," Daniel shouted, "ar ye loust?"

Nicolas's laughter boomeranged around the castle. "No, my friend," he yelled back.

"Ar ye makin a hoose call then?"

"You might say that. I have come to collect what belongs to me . . . my wife." His stallion nodded his head as if to agree. The jingle of the bridle rang out in the stillness of the moment.

"Weel, nou, thon is interesting. It seems a bonnie lass wandered haur a few deis hence. Cood she possibly be yer misplaced wife, auld frien?" Daniel taunted. Daniel's men burst out with laughter which spurred Daniel in his heckling. "A've found her mooth ta be verra tasty. She weel mak a fine mither to young William, so A've decided ta keep her fer me awn."

"What!" Elizabeth screeched. "You wouldn't dare," she said with indignation. Daniel ignored her as he waited for Nicolas's reply.

Nicolas didn't flinch at Daniel's insinuations, but they left him boiling on the inside. He noticed the dress she wore had a plunging neckline. If Daniel had taken liberties with his wife, he was a dead man. However, instead of carrying on with their verbal battle, Nicolas turned his attention toward his wife. He removed his helmet and looked intently at her. "As I said, I have come for what is mine. Wife!" he bellowed.

"Yes, husband," she hollered back.

"Be prepared to leave this keep in two days."

"Ye surely jest. Louk around ye man. The castle is weel fortified and ye noo we kin haud oot fer a lang time or at least until I tire of yer lady wife."

Nicolas ignored Daniel and repeated, "As I said, I will return for you in two days. And wife . . . remember . . . don't over indulge on your favorite drink for I want you to be able to sit your horse without assistance," he added for extra emphasis. He certainly hoped she understood his hidden message or their plan would not succeed.

Elizabeth's eyes grew wide with astonishment. How dare he imply she was a drunkard in front of everyone? Her fisted hands stayed hidden in the folds of her dress; yet if she weren't careful, fire would spew forth from her lips.

"Did you hear me, wife? Only a sip."

Trembling from her pent up anger, she started to hurl back an insult, but stopped with her mouth open. Her neck stiffened, and she clamped her lips tight. She knew what he was implying! Oh my, this was not good.

"Wife?"

Regaining her composure, her hands gripped the top of the castle wall. "Ha, husband, maybe I'll change my favorite repast; but rest assured, whatever I indulge in, I will drink my fill."

Daniel and his men broke out in a fit of laughter. Elizabeth could see her answer stirred her husband's ire by the pull of his mouth. She felt somewhat vindicated from worrying whether he would leave her here to languish away. Without giving Nicolas a chance to remark, she looked straight into his dark eyes and said, "I will be ready."

From the corner of her eye, she had seen that Daniel had watched the interplay between her and Nicolas. Hopefully, he wouldn't figure out their secret before she had a chance to escape.

"Don't get any brave ideas, Lady Marion. You will stay at my side for the next two days to insure your safety," he said with a smirk.

After Elizabeth's parting words, Nicolas gave the signal for his men to withdraw. Tipping his head toward Elizabeth he said, "Until then, Lady Wife, have a care." He gave a final glare and pointed his sword at Daniel's chest. "Two days, Daniel, and I will have you under my boot." With a thundering roar, Nicolas and his men disappeared from view.

"Come, Lady Marion, preparations must be made. Your husband is planning an attack, but I will be ready."

Trailing behind Daniel, Elizabeth made her way to the castle doors asking questions the entire time. "Were you and Nicolas childhood friends? Did you grow up together as secret friends since Nicolas was from England and you from Scotland? Did you really mean you planned to keep me or was that just to stir my husband's anger?" All of her questions bounced off Daniel's back as he marched through the castle courtyard issuing orders and catching William, who had not remained in the keep, by the hand.

"William, you and Lady Marion will be spending a few days in my chambers."

Jumping with excitement, William asked, "Can we play with your chess set, Father? May we look at your childhood weapons? Will you be there to tell some stories?" Daniel hushed William's questions with a simple touch to William's lips.

"We will talk later. Go gather items needed if you were camping under the stars with my men. I will even erect a special tent for you and Lady Marion." Daniel smiled into his son's upturned face.

William scampered off to do his father's bidding. Daniel turned toward Elizabeth and gave her instructions. "You will remain with William until this siege is over—safely locked in my solar. Have no fear, for no harm will come to you if you obey my orders."

"Of course, no harm will come to me. My husband's men are sworn to protect me. You are the one who should be concerned, for Nicolas will not relent until he has won the day."

Daniel grabbed Elizabeth's upper arm and with his face close to hers said, "Do not lecture me, Lady Marion, for I know Nicolas well and taught him much of what he knows about warfare. I will be victorious and win the prize."

"The prize, as you call it, is not worth what your people will endure," she said through tight lips.

Loosening his hold on her, he softly replied, "That's where you are wrong, my lady. Do not underestimate yourself; you are worth more than rubies or gold."

She could only shake her head in denial at Daniel's folly, for he knew not what was about to take place.

"I will send an armed guard to accompany you while you get the necessary provisions for you and William to be sustained for several days." As she opened her mouth to reply, he stroked her mouth with his thumb. "Do not gainsay me on this . . . I insist."

Jerking her face away from his inappropriate advance, Elizabeth pulled away and took off toward her room. His laughter carried after her down the passageway, taunting her. *Did I invite his touch with my actions? Is my stomach a fluttery mess because I enjoyed the stroke of his finger? Or am I just a jittery jumble because my husband wants me?* Elizabeth didn't have time to dissect her feelings; she had a job to do and not much time to accomplish it.

Elizabeth made sure she had several buckets of water for drinking and bathing. Daniel questioned her need for so much water when she told him that she and William would at least be clean prisoners. Daniel had reassured her that she was not a prisoner but a valued guest.

William scurried back and forth between his room and his father's solar bringing an armful of toys, books, blankets, and special keepsakes. It was all a grand adventure for him to be locked in the room with Lady Marion. She noticed his gleeful expression each time he passed her in the doorway, yet she was saddened to know the outcome at the end of the two days. It would be far from happy. Her job was to do her best to protect William from witnessing the horror of war—a war that was totally unnecessary.

The first night passed uneventfully. Elizabeth read books to William until her voice went hoarse, and then they played chess. She was amazed at how he grasped such a difficult and challenging game at the tender age of five. Of course, she knew nothing about his mother; but his father was an intelligent man. She supposed the apple didn't fall far from the tree.

William and Elizabeth were engaged in their second game of chess when she heard heavy footsteps approaching the door. There was mumbling on the other side of the door as Daniel talked with the guard. The door creaked open to reveal Daniel carrying a tray of food. William gave his father a brief nod before focusing back on the chess board. William's king and queen were in trouble; therefore, he had no time to talk with his father. Elizabeth had won the first game; and by the way William frowned over the pieces, he didn't want to lose again.

"Good even', Lady Marion and William. How goes the battle on the chess board, son?"

Without taking his eyes off the board, William said, "A'm surrounded, Papa. Can ye help me?"

Daniel set the food on a stool and ruffled William's hair. "Sairy, William. Ye must decide yer plan of attack or retreat based on what ye deem best for all concerned."

William looked up with forlorn eyes into his father's face. "A'm afraid Ah have no option but defeat, Papa, and Ah hate to lose."

Daniel took William's place at the board and sat William in his lap. "Weel William, 'tis much like life. Ye execute yer best strategy; and when ye lose, ye must learn from yer mistakes and try nae to repeat them in the future. Juist leave it far now. Ah wish us to eat together," Daniel urged.

Elizabeth wondered if Daniel would feel the same way about defeat after tomorrow. Would he learn from his mistake of being overly confident? She hoped William remained untouched by what was in store for the people at the castle. Oh, how she dreaded tomorrow.

"Come, Lady Marion. Join us as we share this fine fare."

25

"All is ready, my lord," Albert whispered.

"No one detected you?" Nicolas whispered back.

"No, Lord Fairwick. I'm as swift as a cat, but as quiet as a mouse," he boasted with a toothless grin.

Nicolas returned his grin with one of his own. The look Nicolas would see on Daniel's face the next time he approached the castle to claim his wife would be worth the trouble Daniel had caused. Nicolas rubbed his hands together and then grabbed Albert around the neck as they scurried back to camp. Peeking out on occasion, the moon hid behind the clouds, giving them good cover.

Once they had joined up with their own men who had accompanied them on the excursion, Albert said, "This is most excitin', Lord Fairwick. I have never been privy to this kind of fighting; I think I like it." Albert was referring to his pouring a mixture of herbs into the well water inside Daniel's castle walls. Daniel had been quite smug when he had boasted as a young boy to Nicolas about their water source being untouchable by the enemy. Daniel's father had dug a well in the center of the courtyard to supply them with endless fresh water that could sustain them during a siege. Now that precious water was going to make them ill. His wife's concoction of herbs was unknown to

Nicolas's childhood friend, now turned enemy. Revenge never felt so satisfying.

"What do we do now, my lord?" Albert asked.

"Stay alert and wait, my friend . . . just wait. Did I mention you will be rewarded for your heroism in implementing our plan?"

"I'm not sure what imple . . . impleme . . . well, what that word means, but I do understand reward," Albert said with a sparkle in his eyes. "Me mission 'twas easy once you told me about the secret gate. Most of the laird's men were looking out toward the road in the front of the castle. I was but a shadow dressed in all black. Did I mention they had left the cover off the well? It made me job as simple as rolling out of me bed," Albert laughed.

"Get some well-earned rest. You have done a job worthy of a full night's sleep without guard duty," Nicolas said as he gave Albert a hearty smack on his shoulder.

"Thank ye, my lord," Albert said as he grabbed a hunk of cheese and bread on his way to his blanket.

Nicolas strode out into the rode with his hands on his hips. He wanted Daniel to see him as he gazed at the glow coming from the castle torches. Had he made the potion strong enough to make them sick or would it take down Daniel's warriors? Either way, he would soon have his lady wife, and they would start afresh with one another. *I pray our lives will be better.*

* * *

"Well, lassie, it would seem your husband has changed his mind. There has been no activity during the night and none this day. It is nigh on to even' time," Daniel casually mentioned as he watched out the window.

"If you recall, Laird McKinnon, he said he would be back in two days. I wouldn't let my guard down just yet," she said as she continued to brush her hair in front of the roaring fire.

Daniel walked up behind her and with a feather-like touch stroked her hair. "As I have said before, do not lesson me on warfare, Lady Marion."

Elizabeth immediately jumped up and whirled around to face him. "Don't touch me in that manner," she said with a jittery voice.

Letting his hand fall to his side, Daniel stood rooted to the spot, transfixed by her beauty. "How did Nicolas ever let you go? He was an idiot not to see what he had before him."

"You know nothing about us and shouldn't make accusations about something you don't understand," she spat back.

Without moving a muscle, Daniel raised a brow over her outburst. "You seem too quick to defend your marriage. Why is that, do you suppose?" he asked as he stared into her wide expressive eyes.

Elizabeth broke the stare by walking to the windows and throwing them wide open. She could see the small fires in the distance and knew Nicolas had not given up. "I am not defending my marriage, for I have no need to do so." Whipping around so she could observe his response, she went on, "You, on the other hand, are not my husband and should honor the sacred vows of marriage by ceasing your assault on my sensibilities. I have no desire to be unfaithful to my husband and will fight you with every breath I breathe if you try to force me in anyway."

Still standing near the chair she had vacated, Daniel stayed thoughtful for such a long time that Elizabeth was afraid he was planning such an attack on her person. Her eyes darted around the room for any type of weapon to use against him since he stood between her and the door to freedom.

A slow smile spread across his face. "Calm yourself, woman. I have no intention of forcing myself on you or any other woman for that matter. In fact, I'm usually fending off the ladies that come in my presence. Some even say I am quite handsome," he said as he puffed out his chest.

"Oh, good grief; give me a break," she said as she rolled her eyes. "You are so full of it," she huffed out.

"Give me a break . . . full of what?"

Elizabeth kept right on talking, ignoring his question. "Stop trying to convince me of why you are such a good catch. I'm married to Lord Fairwick and quite content with my life. So leave . . . me . . . alone!" she said as she stamped her foot for emphasis.

* * *

Good catch? She was uttering such nonsense. Daniel began to have his first misgivings of choosing her for William's next mother. Was she touched in the head? Was this why Nicolas didn't have a care for her safety? Was she Nicolas's new weapon to use against him?

Backing toward the door, Daniel made a quick glance at his sleeping son, unsure if he should leave him alone with her. Her eyes followed his to William and then swung back toward Daniel.

"William is safe in my care. I would never harm him or cause him any distress. He has not reached the age of manhood where I would want to pinch his head off as I have felt toward you at times," she said with a sweet smile.

That statement stopped him in his tracks. "Pinch my head off?" he asked as he scratched his head. "My lady, you have said some very strange things since I walked into this room tonight."

"Oh, stop fretting. Those are just some family sayings you wouldn't understand."

Daniel was about to make a scathing comment when his guard yelled for his attention. Before he could respond, Elizabeth said, "So it begins."

Not waiting to see what she meant, he turned quickly and barked, "Shut and lock this door." He exited the room only to smack into a frantic guard. "Laird, come quickly," he blurted out.

Daniel could hear footsteps running to and fro through the castle as he made his way down the winding staircase. The stench of sickness was thick in the air. If Nicolas had poisoned his people, Daniel would torture Nicolas until he begged for mercy, yet Daniel would not relent.

Running outside, Daniel met more of the same. Guards, warriors, women, and children, were all moaning and hurrying to privacy to empty their stomachs. *Aurgh!* Daniel hollered long and loud. Nicolas had somehow poisoned his people without his knowledge. How had he accomplished the feat?

Turning to his man at arms, he bellowed, "Is there anyone that is not sick?"

"Not many, my laird," he weakly replied before turning green and running around the corner of the castle.

Daniel slowly turned in circles watching everyone inside the castle gates hustling to relieve their sick stomachs. A fire started in his belly and worked its way into his face. His hand pounded the hilt of his sword still strapped to his side. Someone would pay for this atrocity! He took off running back into the keep and up the staircase to his solar. The open door meant she had not followed his explicit demand. He burst through the doorway where he found William sleeping peacefully and Lady Marion humming softly to herself as she sat before the fire. She had known . . . !

"What do you know of this illness your husband has inflicted on my people?" he demanded through gritted teeth. He approached her with clinched fists at his side. It took all his training as an honorable man not to grab her by the hair and jerk her up.

She continued to stare into the fire. "I told you not to underestimate my husband."

Daniel grabbed her arm and yanked her out of the chair to face him. "You will tell me how to counteract this sickness immediately if you value your life," he threatened.

Standing nose to nose with a fierce laird, Elizabeth calmly replied, "I can't answer when I don't know what he did." Daniel squeezed her arms so tight that she cried out in pain waking William.

William raised up on one elbow and rubbed his eyes. "Papa, dinna 'urt Marion?"

Daniel shoved Elizabeth behind him and turned toward William. "Go back to sleep, my son. I am just asking Lady Marion to help me with a very important task and in my haste for an answer, I accidentally squeezed her arm."

"Alright, Papa. Ah loue her and dinna like it when she cries, be mair careful," he whispered as he lay back down on his pallet.

When Daniel heard William breathe deeply, he grabbed Elizabeth's wrist and dragged her into the hallway. He reached behind her to shut the door when he realized the guard was missing. As he whirled around to confront Elizabeth, he became light-headed and felt queasy. Holding onto the wall for support, he again demanded, "What must I do to help my people?"

"I must know exactly what mixture he used in order to give you an accurate antidote."

"Is it a sickness unto death and will William be affected?" He needed quick answers before he passed out or lost his meal. "Quickly, quickly," he said in a strained voice.

"William is safe if he drinks only what I have in his room. No one should die unless Nicolas used something I know nothing about," she hurriedly added.

Daniel barely heard her as he staggered to the privy to empty his stomach. He heard Elizabeth outside the privy door; hopefully she would assist him to his room when he finished. If all his men felt as wretched as he did, they were all open game for Nicolas. He opened the door holding his head with one hand and grasping the wall with the other. Elizabeth put her arm around his waist and gripped his belt for added support as he stumbled toward his chambers.

"*Ach* . . . I'm going to kill Nicolas!"

Elizabeth helped him into his room and over to the bed before his knees collapsed forcing him face forward onto his bed. She unbuckled his sword belt and put it aside. Next, she pulled off his boots. As she swung his feet and legs around onto the bed, he rolled over and grabbed her arm. "I am surely going to die," he moaned.

Elizabeth masked her grin with a cough and with a somber voice said, "No laird, you will not die this day or in the near future from this malady. However, you must release me and let me do what I can to ease your troubles."

Once he released her wrist, his arm plunked onto the bed with a thud. Elizabeth hustled about the chamber getting wet cloths, a bowl, fresh drinking water, and pulled the chamber pot close to the bedside. She didn't plan on sticking around for him to recover, but would see that he had everything he might need to pass the night.

With closed eyes, he grimaced when he said, "I suppose you will run back to your husband and leave me here to die."

"Yes. I will leave you here; but not to die, I promise you. And, yes, I will return to my husband's side where I belong." She eased down on the bedside near his hip and said, "Daniel, you are a good man who can provide a woman with many fine things and a life of luxury; but I am not that person. You have treated me well, and I will not soon forget it. Have no fear; it will become my mission to find you a suitable wife who will compliment your personality and character, not to mention, will be an excellent mother for sweet William."

"Oh, no. Please don't," he groaned.

With soft laughter, she added, "See. You have a funny sense of humor that needs a mate who will appreciate your efforts. I will not rest until my undertaking is completed."

"Oh-h, just go away and leave me to my misery," he murmured.

"You are so dramatic. You should have been a girl," she giggled.

"Heaven preserve me," he lamented.

"Listen well, Laird McKinnon, and don't interrupt until you've heard the whole of it. I have a plan where no one will be harmed, other than being sick a few days. And once you've recovered, you can go back to being the fierce laird of your clan minus one woman." He listened to her harebrained plan of escape which no one would be able to stop. As she rattled on about her idea, he came to realize Nicolas had sent her to be Daniel's undoing. Nicolas knew he would not be able to resist such a bonny lass. All he could do now was clinch his jaw and hope the ailment would soon pass. Daniel would make Nicolas pay for his latest crusade against him.

Midway through the night, Elizabeth changed her name to Florence, as she scurried about the castle trying to nurse the sick. She wasn't sure why that name popped into her mind, but decided to keep it. She also moved William into the adjoining room, well away from his father and her nocturnal activities. During the night she mixed up a strong brew of herbs for the ill ones to help settle their stomachs and put them in a deep sleep. Naturally, she didn't explain the whole of her remedy for she wanted no opposition when she left the castle. Wanting Daniel to sleep well into the day, she administered a healthy dose to him before dawn.

"Drink this down and you will feel better soon," she crooned.

"What is it?" he managed to ask.

"Some soothing herbs for your upset stomach." Trying to distract him, she added, "I should tell you, I have changed my name during the night to Florence."

"Whatever for?" he moaned pathetically. "I liked Marion."

"I'm not sure why; but for some reason it seemed to suit this particular situation. Who knows, maybe it's my real name." She raised his head so he wouldn't lose a drop of her concoction."

"Eewwee! This stuff is foul. Are you trying to inflict the final blow?"

"Oh, quit being a baby. Take it like a man. You'll feel better for it," she scolded.

"Humph! No one has ever called me a babe and lived."

Elizabeth ignored him and went about tidying up the room. She expected him to get drowsy soon.

"Stop movin' round the 'oom so fath," he slurred. "I thee too of ye. Wha' did ye pu' in me drin'?"

"A little of this and a little of that to make you recover; so, stop questioning my nursing abilities.

"Yer wha'?" he asked as his eyes drooped shut.

Elizabeth stood unmoving and listened to Daniel's breathing. It grew steadier and slower which indicated to her he would soon be totally out. Good! She went to check on William. He had slept soundly during the whole evening. It was no wonder. The little guy had played hard and long all day. Now he was granted the sleep of babes, for sure. The fire in the hearth cast a glow on his angelic face. Thankfully, he had remained untouched by the tainted water. Reaching down, she brushed his hair from his brow. Oh, how she would miss him. He so ensnared her heart that it ached to think of leaving him, but leave him she must. She didn't belong here no matter how much he wished it. This aching and tightness in her chest would not be so breathtaking if she didn't have to use William to help her escape. Unfortunately, it was her only plan.

Elizabeth lightly shook William's shoulder. He rolled onto his back and began rubbing his eyes. Peering up at her, he asked, "Whit is it, Marion?"

Oh well, she would have to go back to Marion for young William. She placed her finger to her lips. "Shh. We must whisper. Your father and his men are sick, so we mustn't disturb them. I'm in need of your help. Can you wake up enough to help me, William?"

"Aye," he yawned. He pushed off his blanket and began pulling on his boots. "Whit are ye aboot?" he whispered as he stood to his feet. His little hand took hers which caused the knife to twist in her heart.

She lightly squeezed his hand. "We're going on a great adventure."

"Is papa coming?" he asked as they came into Daniel's room.

"No. I'm afraid you're father is too ill."

Tugging on her hand, he questioned her logic. "Shouldn't we stay haur in case he needs our help?"

"Don't worry. I gave your father some healing herbs that will help him rest and feel better when he awakens. He would be proud of your helping me." She only hoped she was telling the truth. "We're going to help his men; I have a plan."

He followed her with the blind trust of a child. They left the room and made their way down the stairs and out the door before he tugged her to a stop. "Ah dinna think we should go ootside. It's verra dark and Ah dinna see any of papa's men aboot," he said quietly as he looked around.

Kneeling down in front of William, Elizabeth reassured him. "Don't be frightened. You know your father's men are guarding the castle even when we can't see them. I also have a knife to protect you from harm." She gave him a hug and rubbed his back until she felt his tense muscles relax. With his arms around her neck, she picked him up and continued creeping toward the garden.

While staying deep in the shadows Elizabeth said, "William, I need you to direct me toward the postern gate." His small finger pointed in the direction of the back of the garden. Good, she knew that area. "Soon dawn will appear, and we'll be able to see."

Hugging her neck tight, William said in her ear, "Ah loue ye, ma lady." He then kissed her cheek.

She stopped and returned his kiss. "I love you, too, William." Tears gathered in her eyes. She hated using him in her get-a-way scheme, but the thought of finding him the perfect mother somewhat eased her pain.

They made their way through the gardens until William found the postern gate which was well behind the castle—far from prying eyes. Elizabeth set William down. "Hold onto my skirt while I do a search." She felt his small hand scrunch her skirt as his body leaned into her leg. Sweeping aside the hanging vines, Elizabeth found the gate. She unlatched it and pushed it open in stages. Each movement caused a slight screeching noise. Thankfully, there wasn't a guard to be seen anywhere. Sneaking away was a noisy business.

"Ah've never gone oot this gate," William said.

"Isn't it fun to go exploring?" Elizabeth muttered.

"Yea, 'tis great fun!" he whispered loudly as his little boots fidgeted in place.

Elizabeth knelt down on her knees so they were at eye level. "This is where you must be brave, young William." When he would have interrupted, she placed her finger on his lips. His wide eyes and cherub face were almost her undoing. "You will not be going with me. I have an important duty that only you can perform. You must return to your father with an urgent message from me. I have written down the cure for their illness, and it should be given straight away. Can I count on you to carry out this vital mission?"

Tears gathered in his eyes as he backed up one step. "Why ar ye leaving me? Ye said ye loued me. Ah want ye to be me mither." Stiffened shoulders replaced his earlier exuberance.

Each word cut her deeper than the first. She took hold of his tiny hand and said, "I'm so very sorry, William. I *do* love you, but I cannot stay. I belong to another. But . . . I won't relent until I find you the perfect mother. You have my word." Her own tears trickled down her face as she gave him a trembling smile. "Will you trust me?"

He came into her waiting arms while they both cried for what would not be. After a short while, William pulled away and stood like a miniature soldier. "Ah'm ready to do me mission."

Elizabeth reached inside her cape and brought out a crumpled piece of parchment. "Here is your assignment. Can I count on you to be swift?"

"Yea, me lady. Ah will not disappoint ye."

"Oh, my sweet William. You could never disappoint me."

She went out the gate and turned back. William looked so tiny in the shadow of the gate. His small voice reached her. "Weel ye veesit me?"

"You can count on it. Now, off with you." She waited until he had turned and run from the garden. Elizabeth felt relief as she scampered into the woods surrounding the castle. The sun had begun to peep though the morning mist which helped light her path. Any guard worth his price would easily hear her traipsing through the forest as she stomped along. Elizabeth didn't want to startle Nicolas's men and have them accidentally shoot her with an arrow. That would be a terrible ending to her ordeal.

It wasn't long before she heard a rustling and then the word, halt. "Is that you, Robert?" Elizabeth asked.

"Lady Isabelle?"

"Yes.'Tis me." She blew out a breath before coming face-to-face with Nicolas's man, Robert.

26

Today was the day. Nicolas and his men would storm the castle of Laird Daniel McKinnon and retrieve his bride. He certainly hoped he would have an opportunity to confront Daniel. How dare Daniel steal Isabelle and then jeer at Nicolas perched high upon his castle wall! Oh, yes, Daniel would rue the day he interfered with Nicolas.

Nicolas paced back and forth from the woods to the road. The morning fog clung tightly to the ground and made visibility nearly impossible, but for how long? Nicolas rubbed the back of his neck as he contemplated riding under the cover of the misty fog which would risk injury to his horses and men, or waiting until the fog burned off giving them and their enemies clear vision. He longed for the day when Phillip would accompany him on his battles—if nothing else, at least to give him council.

At the sound of a broken twig, Nicolas spun around. There she stood. "Isabelle," he mouthed. With the early morning sunrise behind her, there was a misty glow surrounding her body. The hood had fallen away from her head leaving her unbound hair blowing gently in the breeze. She was a vision of beauty—a sweet distraction. Her slight movement drew his eyes to her tightly clinched hands next to her stomach. Oh, no! Was she ill? Had she drunk the tainted water?

Nicolas made a straight line to his wife and stopped within a hand's breadth. With tight fists down by his side, Nicolas asked, "Are you ill?"

She spoke only one word, "No." Her upturned face showed traces of tears. What had happened to cause her such distress? Had The McKinnon mistreated her or was she unhappy to return to Nicolas? Mentally shaking his head, Nicolas was determined to make a fresh start and having doubts about her actions was an unfavorable beginning. "Are you hurt, then?"

"No."

Nicolas relaxed his stance at her answer. However, when she was not forthcoming with anything but one word answers, he changed his approach. "I am pleased that you are well and unharmed." Before he could utter another word, she burst forth into fresh tears.

"I had to leave Midnight," she cried.

Ah. Now he understood her red eyes and tear stained cheeks. Nicolas pulled her into his arms and was thankful when she melted into his embrace. Her anguish was almost tangible as he held her close while she sobbed. "I will get her back for you. Do not fret," Nicolas assured his wife.

Elizabeth reared back from the tight embrace. "Oh, no! Do not think about going into that castle. Daniel will kill you for sure," she exploded.

Nicolas went rigid at the mention of Daniel's name. "You call him Daniel?"

"Yes," she sniffed. "It's a long story, but he asked me to call him Daniel. Since I was at his mercy, I didn't want to rile his fury over such a small issue."

Her answer pacified Nicolas for the moment. He needed to get the full tale, but now was not the time. Isabelle was free, and they needed to be away before some of Daniel's men rode in pursuit. "Come, wife. You will ride pillion with me as we did on our wedding day."

Nicolas tramped toward his camp of men pulling Elizabeth by the hand while he barked orders for withdrawal. When he stopped near his horse, Elizabeth ran into his back. Nicolas whipped around to catch her before she tumbled to the ground. Once again he drew her into the circle of his arms. With her upturned nose looking like a cherry, Nicolas bent and gave it a tender kiss. He took his thumbs and wiped away a few stray tears under her puffy eyes. "Cease this waterfall. I will get your beloved Midnight back for you. Trust me, Isabelle."

Sniff. With hope in her eyes, she said, "I want to believe."

"That is a start, lady wife. I will take it. Now, let's be away from this distasteful country." Nicolas tossed Elizabeth into the saddle. He settled his helmet in place and climbed on behind his wife. She squirmed about to find a more comfortable seat when she realized Nicolas was in his chainmail.

She twisted her head around to have a closer look at her husband. "You wore your chainmail to rescue me?"

Nicolas halted his movements to look directly at his wife. "Yes, Isabelle. All of us were prepared to invade the castle with force, if need be, just for you."

Her open lips formed an 'O' but no sound emerged. Nicolas decided those parted lips needed to be shut, so he gave her a kiss that left her speechless. The saints be preserved . . . he had found a way to silence his wife . . . a kiss. As he mentally stored that information for future use, he took up the reins and headed toward home. The fog had lifted enough to assure them of safe travel, but provided sufficient cover from Laird McKinnon's men. They set out at a brisk pace in military formation with Nicolas leading the way.

* * *

Elizabeth rested against Nicolas's chest and let out a deep sigh. She had finally escaped and landed right where she wanted to be—in her husband's arms. The thought surprised her when she remembered their parting words which had been full of anger and hurt. That early morning argument seemed so distant; Elizabeth couldn't even remember what had started the quarrel. Maybe her forgetfulness was a good thing. Somewhere in the back of her memory she could hear the words *forgive and forget* which was exactly what she planned to do provided Nicolas didn't resurrect the past.

Inhaling deeply, Elizabeth was soothed by her husband's aroma which was a cross between an earthy smell and his leather jerkin. Both scents brought her peace and comfort. Could she find contentment and fulfillment living with Nicolas as his wife? All of her previous worries about her past seemed hazy. Not as important. And no wonder. The most recent days she had vacillated between a warrior woman and a cowering child. One moment she had felt strong and in control of her situation and the next second she had feared for her life. What if Daniel had succeeded and had kept her a prisoner? A shudder wracked her body at the thought of the war that would have occurred.

Nicolas leaned close to her ear. "Are you cold, Isabelle?"

"No, I am fine." She snuggled deeper into Nicolas's cloak as she relished the way he said her name. His voice was warm and almost seductive . . . or was that her fanciful imagination? She could easily get used to the harmony they shared at this place and time. But would it last? She prayed so.

Once they were miles across the border into England, Nicolas removed his helmet and attached it to the saddle with a leather strap. "Ah. Now I can breathe deeply of your fragrant hair," he said as he touched his nose to her head and then came around to nuzzle her neck.

A giggle escaped Elizabeth's lips as she squirmed in the saddle. "That tickles," she said while maneuvering her neck for easier access. With all her wiggling around, she almost lost her balance. "Aye," she squealed when Nicolas tightened his grip around her.

"This has been a most pleasing romantic interlude, but I think it best we cease this activity until we are safely inside our castle. Once there, we can resume our play. Yes?" he whispered in her ear.

Chills that started in her head, traveled to her toes with warmth pooling in her stomach. Nicolas's advances were a delightful surprise. After being held captive for days and not knowing what would happen to her, this was a welcome change. The way Nicolas acted gave her a glimpse of a hopeful future together.

    The sun had risen higher in the sky casting a brilliant glow through the slight mist that remained. Relaxed, Elizabeth's eyes began to droop as the landscape blurred in front of her. She felt safe and secure with Nicolas and his warriors at her back. A bit of a rest would be refreshing after her sleepless night. Elizabeth drifted into an enjoyable dream where love, hugs, and kisses abounded.

* * *

    Hooves thundered across the wooden drawbridge as Nicolas and his men arrived home. Startled, Elizabeth awoke to the roar of castle folk who lined the catwalk and the courtyard. Someone even played the trumpet to herald their victorious return. She glanced around at hundreds of smiling faces as some reached out to touch her leg when they rode past.

    Once Nicolas and Elizabeth were in the center of the courtyard, Nicolas turned his prancing horse around in circles for all to see them. "It would seem our people have missed you, my lady." Nicolas grabbed her hand and raised it high in the air which sent the people into a chanting frenzy—Isabelle, Isabelle, Isabelle.

    Elizabeth's happiness bubbled up from inside forcing out laughter and stopping with a broad smile. Giddy with excitement, she had to admit to herself that she belonged here . . . with these people . . . with Nicolas. As they continued to spin around, she saw Thomas, Brigette, Phillip, and even Abigail, who seemed pleased to see her. They all shouted greetings to her. She was thankful God had preserved her.

    Thank You, God for Your protection. I think I have found my home at last. I doubted Your wisdom of plopping me at Fairwick Castle, but now I am contented to stay here the rest of my days. Even if You never reveal my true identity to me, I will be at peace.

Right when Elizabeth was getting dizzy from the sea of faces spinning around, Nicolas brought them to a halt. He slid to the ground and reached for her. With her hands on his shoulders, Nicolas lowered her down and brought her up against his chest. "Now we will show our solidarity and our renewed pledge to one another." Before his words had time to register with Elizabeth, he took her mouth in a passionate kiss for all to witness.

Whoa! Her world tilted. It amazed Elizabeth how the change in her attitude toward Nicolas made their shared kiss that much more fervent. There was a buzzing in her ears as her heart drummed a fast rhythm. She broke the heated kiss and gasped for air to keep from bursting into flames. There stood Nicolas with a silly grin of satisfaction on his face. All of a sudden the roar of the people hit her full force. They were not alone. "Ugh," she groaned as she hid her face in his jerkin.

"Come, wife, I will rescue you once more. We have given them what they needed." He lifted her in his arms. The clapping and cheering mob parted as he made his way toward the keep.

"Lady Isabelle, are you well?" Thomas asked as he ran to catch them.

"Yes, thank you for asking, Thomas," Elizabeth yelled. She craned her neck to see Thomas, only to find him swallowed by the crowd.

"Welcome home, my lady," Jarvis called.

"'Tis good to see you, Lady Isabelle," Angus added.

There stood Jarvis and Angus in their usual spot on the top step of the keep. Their forlorn faces pricked Elizabeth's conscience. She owed them an apology. She knew guarding her probably made their lives miserable. Bless them. They were such darlings to put up with her waywardness and still be sweet and forgiving toward her. "It's good to see you, gentlemen," she said over Nicolas's shoulder.

Their first stop was the war room where Elizabeth assisted Nicolas in removing his chainmail. She wondered how the men could do anything wearing such heavy armor. It took all her strength just to tug it over his head. Once that was completed,

Nicolas quickly donned his shirt and pulled her toward the great hall.

When they arrived in the great hall, the room was buzzing with activity. White cloths embellished the tables along with an abundance of food. Nicolas placed her on her feet but captured her hand in his. With a sweeping arm, Nicolas said, "A victory celebration to welcome home the lady of the castle. What think you?"

Stunned. It was the only word to describe how Elizabeth was feeling. She found it hard to believe that so many loved her and took joy in her return. It hadn't been that long ago that someone had tried to kill her right here at this castle. Was that person still around? Elizabeth allowed her eyes to roam the room but only saw vibrant smiles of welcome. "Overwhelmed," she finally whispered.

She tripped along behind Nicolas as he strode to the dais. All through the room words of welcome, cheer, and encouragement boomeranged around. Once Nicolas and Elizabeth were at their places of honor, Nicolas hushed the crowd with a raised hand. "Greetings, family and friends of Fairwick castle. Today we celebrate the triumphant return of Lady Isabelle, who has returned to us whole and unharmed."

"Praise be to God," someone shouted.

"Where's the priest?" Nicolas asked as his head scanned the room.

"There he is."

The priest stepped forward from near the fireplace and came to stand before Lord Fairwick and his wife.

"Please, Friar, offer up a blessing on this event and thanksgiving for the safe return of Lady Isabelle," Nicolas said.

Elizabeth heard the friar begin his prayer, but before she could capture her thoughts, her mind began to wander. Inside she was shaking from excitement and a bit of astonishment. She could not have imagined how receptive the people would be of her return. There was no doubt they loved and respected Lord Nicolas, but she had defied him at every turn; yet, they still held her in high regard.

Oh, Lord. Again I thank You for these people. Their response is greater than I ever envisioned. You have provided for me over and beyond what I could have done for myself. Thank You.

"Amen," pronounced the friar.

"Let us begin," Nicolas boomed.

Thomas, Brigette, Phillip, and Abigail emerged from the crowd to take their places next to Nicolas and Elizabeth. They all seemed to talk at once—firing questions about Elizabeth's ordeal. What had happened? Was she harmed? Did The McKinnon put her into the dungeon? How had she escaped without Nicolas's help? On and on they went. She could barely draw breath to answer one question before another one followed until Nicolas put a halt to their inquiry.

"Leave her be. Can't you see she is beyond exhaustion and needs nourishment?" As usual, Nicolas had the last say at the table. Thomas frowned and Brigette pouted. Oh, what a wonderful homecoming Elizabeth thought. Everyone acted in typical family custom, and she adored them for it. At long last, she was home!

27

The celebration carried on most of the day. At one point, Nicolas saved Elizabeth from the mirage of questions and well wishes by suggesting a ride in the countryside. She was eager to go until she remembered that Midnight remained captive. Her feet began to drag on the way to the stables.

Nicolas stopped in the middle of the courtyard and turned to his wife. "Wife, you must trust me. I will retrieve your precious Midnight."

"How did you know what I was thinking?"

"I am more attuned to your emotions. I will not underestimate you again, my fair lady. When I think how you could have injured my sword hand with that knife . . . let's just say I have learned a valuable lesson. Never to take you for granted again." He gentled his remark with a grin and his palm to her cheek.

"You're different," she said through squinted eyes.

"I'm glad you noticed. There is much for us to discuss; but for now, let's enjoy a ride along the beach. Shall we?"

She gave a tentative smile and said, "Lead on, O mighty husband."

Nicolas insisted she ride with him. He suggested they could talk along the way. Of course, Elizabeth was only too happy to comply with that request since she would be held close by her husband. She liked the new Nicolas and looked forward to what was to come.

The time was midway between dinner and the evening meal. The sun was warm on their backs, yet the wind had a bite to it. Elizabeth decided to straddle Nicolas's horse so he would consent to riding faster than a trot. She wanted to feel the wind smacking her face to remind her she was alive and well. "Faster," she urged.

Nicolas obliged her request by hunching low and kicking his horse into a run. He nestled his face next to Elizabeth's ear. "I like the way you think, Isabelle."

The horse's hooves barely touched down as the ground disappeared under them. Elizabeth didn't need to turn around to know their guard was close at hand. Their protectors would scan the area and make sure all was safe for them to proceed which allowed Nicolas and Elizabeth the freedom of adventure.

It took only a few minutes to reach the path to the beach, but the ride had been exhilarating. The path was almost hidden from sight with overhanging trees and brush. Nicolas slowed his horse to a walk before venturing down the rocky slope. Leftover rain dropped on them each time they bumped against a leaf or a branch. Thankfully, Nicolas's horse was sure-footed on the loose rocks. His stallion was a rare find among war horses. Just the thought about his horse caused Elizabeth a shooting pain in the chest. *Midnight, oh sweet Midnight.* Fighting back tears, she was determined not to let her depression over Midnight mar their time together.

They burst out of the underbrush to a beautiful sight. The sun shimmered on the water as waves crashed onto the sand. After riding into the middle of the sandy beach, Nicolas stopped his horse. "'Tis a glorious sight. Look yonder," he said as he pointed. ". . . a rainbow, hovering over that rock formation. See it?" With his face next to Elizabeth's, his breath tickled her cheek.

"Oh, yes, breathtaking. God's promise shining forth."

Nicolas's arms were securely wrapped around Elizabeth, snuggled tight as a horseshoe to a hoof. Neither seemed to want to move and break the enchanted spell that encompassed them. Seagulls called from above and some swooped down to catch fish.

After a few moments of enjoying the scenery, Elizabeth asked, "Can we walk along the shoreline?"

"As you wish," Nicolas said. He hopped out of the saddle and waited for Elizabeth to swing her leg around. Then he grasped her waist and dragged her up against him. With a finger wrapped around one of her curls, he said, "I like it when your hair is disheveled. It is most becoming."

With eyes locked together, Elizabeth could feel the blush rising in her neck. She knew the men could see what Nicolas was doing, but hoped they didn't hear his remark. Would she ever get used to so many eyes watching their intimate moments? Dipping her chin, she sidestepped Nicolas. "Come on," she said as she took off running toward the water.

When she arrived at the water's edge, she sat down in the sand and removed her shoes. Even though the water would be frigid, she wanted to feel the water and sand in her toes. She glanced back to see Nicolas watching from a distance. He had not moved from his spot.

Elizabeth stood and eased up to the water. In spite of the first chilly wave that took her breath away, she didn't move. Instead, she looked out at the horizon and enjoyed God's handiwork. *Oh, how majestic is Your world, God.* With outstretched arms and closed eyes, she spun around in circles, laughing and giggling when she fell to her knees.

Nicolas was close at hand when she went down. His warm hand engulfed her small cold one as he helped her to her feet. They stood apart facing each other with their hands still linked. "When you began turning in circles, I thought Thomas was right . . . you were a sprite that was about to disappear from my view. But alas, I still have you."

"Yes, you still have me," she whispered. Not moving but turning her head toward the water, she said, "I used to feel like those waves. Tossed to and fro with no place to settle. No place to call home. No family known to me."

"And now . . ." Nicolas tugged her into the circle of his arms. ". . . you have me. I will be your family. And with God's help, your protector and your champion," he said tenderly.

"Oh, Nicolas. Will we be able to live in harmony and not strangle one another?" she asked with a crooked smile.

Nicolas rumbled with laugher. "'Twill be an adventure, for sure." After giving her a feathery kiss on her cheek, Nicolas leaned down to snatch her shoes while holding fast to her hand. "Your walk awaits."

The two walked hand in hand with Elizabeth's feet splashing through the water's edge. The sound of lapping waves, chirping birds, and buzzing bugs was a tranquil scene that was meant to be captured on canvas. At one point, Elizabeth bent down, scooped up a handful of water and splattered Nicolas in the face. Momentarily stunned, he released her hand which allowed her to sprint further down the beach. She didn't get far before Nicolas grabbed her around the waist and spun her around in circles until she begged for mercy. Nicolas's boisterous laughter couldn't drown out Elizabeth's high-pitched squeals of delight as the wind snatched them from their lips.

Nicolas set her on her feet but kept her back to his chest. She was once again facing the sea. Holding her in place, he said, "Like those seagulls, you may freely soar but know that you have a nest for safe landing. My prayer is that our castle will always provide a safe haven for you as well as the children we will have together." He gently turned her around to face him. Gazing into her eyes pooled with unshed tears, he added, "This is our new beginning. No more secrets between us. In time, I am confident we will grow to love and respect one another the way God planned marriage to be." Her lips opened to reply, but Nicolas sealed his declaration with a mind twisting kiss, stopping her from further comment.

When Nicolas broke their embrace, Elizabeth gulped in some much needed air. *Whew. My husband sure can leave me breathless from his kisses. I could get used to those.* On that happy thought, she looked to see her shoes and stockings floating out to sea. "Oh, no. Look."

"Let them go," Nicolas said. "It will allow me a good reason to carry you around." On that statement, he hoisted her over his shoulder and gave her bottom an affectionate pat as he strolled toward his horse. All the while, Elizabeth shouted for release as she pounded his back.

So much for a new start, Neanderthal man. Even while Elizabeth's up-side-down head bobbed around, she wore a smile of contentment on her face.

* * *

All eyes turned to Nicolas when he came into the keep cradling his barefoot wife. He marched past the curious on-lookers and headed straight up the stairs. "We are not to be disturbed," he called out for all to hear.

Elizabeth melted into his shoulder from humiliation. Once they arrived on the second floor, she drew back and asked, "Why did you say that? Now the people are going to think we are going to our room for an intimate evening. How embarrassing! That's not what you meant, is it?" she asked with trembling lips.

Nicolas didn't stop until they reached their room where he kicked the door shut with his foot. He felt his wife's body go rigid in his arms and saw the fear in her face. His dream of sharing the marital bed crashed like a broken pitcher. After the time they had spent on the beach, he had envisioned a magnificent ending to their day. One shared in the big four poster bed. Heaving a deep sigh, he was resigned that until she was more comfortable with the idea, he would have to tread lightly around the issue of intimacy.

Walking over to a chair, he sat down with Elizabeth still in his arms. Once she seemed comfortable in his lap, he said, "You have been away for nigh onto a week. We need time alone to discuss your ordeal. I need to hear the whole of it, and I don't want everyone in the castle being privy to the information." When her body relaxed and her frown replaced with a smile, he knew his words had the desired effect on Isabelle. But when her eyes cut toward the bed, he knew there was more work to be done.

With one finger, Nicolas put a stray lock of hair behind her ear. "Yes, I had hoped to share the bed with you tonight; however, when we come together as man and wife, you will be a willing partner. I will not pressure you in any way. . . I give you my word."

"Thank you," she whispered. She took his face between her hands and brushed her lips across his. "You are a good man, Nicolas."

From that tentative kiss, Nicolas was on fire. He needed to get away from her before he burst into flames. "Let me send for food to be brought to our room, and then I'll hear your tale." After rising to his feet, Nicolas placed Elizabeth in the chair he had just vacated. "You may wish to freshen up while I go see about our food," he said right before his hasty exit.

* * *

Elizabeth's head swam with emotions. It was hard to process all that had transpired over the last week. One morning she had been mad enough to sever Nicolas's head from his shoulders with a sword and in the afternoon that anger had turned to fear when confronted by Laird McKinnon. Daniel had caused her to question her relationship with Nicolas and tried to convince her she was better off in Scotland with him. While being held captive, there had been no rest as her emotions swung like a pendulum. Whew! Just thinking it through was taxing.

She rose from her seat and walked over to the window. Throwing open the shutters, Elizabeth propped her shoulder against the wall and gazed into the twilight sky. The busyness of the castle was coming to an end for the day. Below her window, she could see men who had finished their work and were returning to their families in the village. A slight breeze stirred her hair as it slid across her cheek. Reaching up, she untied the ribbon and massaged her tight scalp. *Ahh, that feels good.* Too much thinking had tensed her whole body.

God, is Nicolas part of Your plan for my life? Is he to be my protector? If I'm to be his wife and stay here the rest of my days, I pray You will fill me with Your peace. Amen.

After praying, Elizabeth stood silent and waited to hear from God. Stars twinkled and appeared to nod in her direction. All of a sudden, the door banged open. Throwing her hand over her heart, Elizabeth spun around to see two men bringing in a tub.

"Whar do ye want this, m' lady?"

"Oh, my. You frightened me," she said with a shaky voice. Elizabeth realized she had never seen the two men standing only steps away. One looked sinister with his dirt streaked face and blackened teeth. "Um . . . how about through that door, there," she said and pointed toward the open doorway connecting the two rooms. She was thankful to see Nicolas had unlocked her old room. Elizabeth moved to stand near the fireplace where she could easily grab the poker if she needed to club one of the men if they chose to attack her.

After depositing the tub in the adjoining room, she heard them laying a fire in the fireplace. The two men walked out the door and into the passageway without even looking her way. Good gracious, her imagination was running wild. She needed to calm down her jittery self. Elizabeth heaved a sigh of relief and a nervous giggle escaped. No sooner had she placed a hand over her trembling lips, when a single file of five women came through the door. Every one of them carried two pails of steaming water which they proceeded to dump into the tub.

Elizabeth stood wide-eyed as she watched each woman curtsy to her before leaving the room. The last one shut the door on her way out. Mentally shaking her head, Elizabeth managed to squeak out a thank you as the door closed. Her new-found husband must have arranged this luxury for her. He was a definite charmer when he put his mind to it. She planned to take advantage of the lavish indulgence Nicolas had provided.

As if in a trance, Elizabeth left a trail of her dress and over tunic behind as she stepped out of them on her way to the tub. When she entered the room, steam hovered above the tub that sat beside a roaring fire. The scent of lavender filled the room. Standing with her backside to the fireplace, she removed her chemise and bloomers. Grasping the side of the large tub, Elizabeth sank into delicious bliss. She held her breath as she submerged her head. While floating under the water, she felt the tension drain from her body.

When she could hold her breath no longer, Elizabeth shot up out of the water with a gasp. Water sloshed over the side and splashed onto the rug. She peered over the edge to see what kind of a mess she had made; there within her reach was a cloth and a bar of lavender soap. Nicolas was treating her like royalty. Just the thought of him sent a tingle down her spine.

Time escaped her as she savored her bath. The room had grown dark and shadows danced around the room in the firelight. In fact, she hadn't heard anyone in the other room since tumbling into her euphoria. Looking down, she noticed her fingers had wrinkled and the water had grown tepid. Standing up, she stepped out of the tub and wrapped a large towel around her body tucking in the corners. Another small towel was there to wrap around her hair. She padded over and dropped into the fireside chair.

As Elizabeth scanned the room, memories of her first days in the castle rushed through her mind. Scared, anxious, and panicky were a few words that described her earlier emotions. Through those harrowing days, she had managed to remember bits of her past. There was a papaw in her life, and she was a healer of some kind. Other than that, her past was sketchy at best. For some reason, God had kept her name and total memory recall from surfacing. Why?

Even as she contemplated why God had plunged her into this mysterious place, she realized it no longer mattered as much to her. God would reveal all to her in His timing. Meanwhile, she recognized her outlook on life had changed. Nicolas's family had grown dear to her heart, as well as the castle folk. The outpouring of the love and approval she experienced today had been remarkable. She no longer felt like an outsider, but considered herself one of them—accepted. Still, if she were honest with herself, she knew the real reason for her drastic transformation . . . Nicolas. His attentiveness and heart-felt affection today had turned her head like a well-greased wheel. A warm flush overtook her body at the thought of her handsome husband.

Unsettled by her fanciful thoughts, Elizabeth flipped her hair over her head and fingered through it. It wouldn't take long for her hair to dry in front of the blazing fire. As blood drained into her head, she couldn't catch her meandering mind. Her thoughts glided over the day's events. Nicolas offering a shoulder to cry on. Nicolas wrapping his arms around her. Nicolas laughing. Nicolas kissing her . . . oh my! Now that had been the high point of her day. His kisses had been mind-blowing.

Snapping her head upright, Elizabeth hissed out her breath. It couldn't be! Surely not? There was no way around it . . . she was in love with her husband!

28

Nicolas rushed back to his solar with a tray of food. He heaved a sigh of relief once he shut the door and dropped the bar in place. After his hasty exit from Isabelle's presence, Nicolas had taken a dip in the nearby stream to cool his fiery ardor. The frigid water had nearly robbed him of his breath. Afraid he might drown before finishing his wash, Nicolas had bathed swiftly.

Following his brisk attempt to remove his stench and leave a pleasing scent for his wife, Nicolas had come through the secret passageway into the kitchen to avoid detection. Thankfully, Collette had been alone awaiting his arrival. Bless her. She hadn't uttered a word, but had made sure he had all they needed for a delicious meal. He appreciated her discretion and wasted no time in sneaking to his solar.

After Nicolas arranged the food on his chess table, he straightened and wiped his cold hands on his pants before turning to see Isabelle framed in the doorway. She was a vision of loveliness in a white gown with her hair swirling around her shoulders. He couldn't quite read her expression, but it appeared to him to be seductive. The fireplace glow from her chamber made her clothing transparent—the outline of her body distinguishable. He closed his eyes on a groan as his heartbeat tripled in time. After a deep sigh, he opened his eyes and extended his hand toward his wife. "Come. Collette has prepared a feast for us to share."

As she floated across the floor, he felt certain he saw adoration in her eyes. Mentally chastising his wayward thoughts, he hurriedly snatched a blanket off the chest. He wouldn't be able to concentrate if she didn't cover up. "Here. Permit me to wrap this around your shoulders to ward off the chill," he croaked. Carefully, he positioned the blanket to conceal her form.

"Thank you," she said in a soft voice.

Her hand brushed his knuckles when she reached up to grasp the blanket—scorching him. Nicolas stumbled over the footstool as he quickly backed away from her touch. He was irritated with himself. His actions were that of an inexperienced youth with uncontrolled desires.

"Are you all right?" she asked as she drew her brows into a frown.

"'Tis nothing. I merely tripped over the stool. Why don't you begin recounting your journey while I serve up our food?"

"I'm not sure I would call it a journey; that sounds like a fun excursion. What I experienced was far from amusing." Holding up her hand, palm outward, she continued. "I realize that my unfortunate outing was due to my own prideful behavior and take full responsibility for my misfortune."

"Isabelle, we are not here to place blame. We both know when a squabble occurs that there are at least two people involved. The fault is not all of yours to bear." Nicolas watched as she studied her hands that lay in her lap. Wanting to hold onto the alluring atmosphere between them, he hoped his words had put her mind at ease over the matter.

"I appreciate your gracious words. Now, where do you want me to begin . . . with the stabbing of my knife . . . my ride into enemy territory . . . or my actual capture?"

Nonchalantly, Nicolas looked up from the table. "Why don't you tell me what happened after your capture? Jarvis and Angus gave me their account up to that point."

For a few moments only the clinking of dishes and the crackling fire intruded upon the stillness of the room. Nicolas handed Elizabeth a plate of food and a cup of water before easing into his chair. He settled back and waited for her to begin her tale.

* * *

A noisy breath escaped through Elizabeth's nostrils. She dreaded the recounting of her excursion unsure of which details to include and which to block from her memory. Some aspects of her imprisonment would only anger Nicolas and serve no good purpose—those facts would be deleted from her story. She doubted that Nicolas would converse with Daniel to corroborate her story. With that decision made, she launched into her tale.

"First, I came across William, Laird McKinnon's son. He was playing near a pond, I thought, unattended. However, that was not the case. There were about ten men hidden from my view observing young William. You know me and children; his sweet, charming smile drew me in. It wasn't long before Laird McKinnon made his presence known. He announced that I would be riding back to his castle. He brooked no argument. I never saw Jarvis or Angus again. Naturally, I was worried Laird McKinnon had harmed them in some way and that weighed heavy on my mind."

Elizabeth paused to take a bite of her cheese and bread. Nicolas sat across from her with an unreadable expression on his face. Her heart pounded loudly in her ears as she chewed her food. Was the recounting of her trial going to drive a wedge between her and Nicolas and their newfound peace? She watched as he took a sip of his ale, and with controlled motions, placed it on the table. *Oh, God. Please protect Nicolas's heart. Don't allow my words to muddle our delicate relationship.*

"Continue when you are ready," he said.

Elizabeth's insecurities caused a knot to form in her stomach. She could not choke down another bite until she had finished her story and knew how Nicolas would react toward her. "I'll finish my meal once I have completed my report. Now, let's see; where did I leave off?"

"Daniel had taken you hostage," Nicolas supplied.

"Oh, yes. Anyway, because of the approaching storm, it was dark when we arrived at his castle. I was given a guest room."

"Was your room connected to Daniel's?"

"Oh, no. It was down the hallway. He posted a guard outside of my door; so I was perfectly safe."

"Humph," Nicolas snorted.

That one word was a punch to Elizabeth. It seemed that no matter what she conveyed, Nicolas would believe what he wanted to believe. So much for trust between a husband and wife. She glossed over the remainder of the tale since it appeared Nicolas had already formed his own opinion. Elizabeth decided to downplay her frightening time spent in the McKinnon castle. No need to give Nicolas any more fuel for his anger toward Daniel. She didn't want to be the cause of a war between two countries straddling a weak peace agreement.

By the time her story had concluded, she was exhausted. Her sleepless night attending to a sick laird accompanied by her eventful day with her husband had taken a physical toll. She quickly covered a yawn that escaped at the same time her stomached growled. "Oh, my. Excuse me," she said. "I suppose I'm a tad hungry after retelling the events of the past week."

"Please, finish your meal. Thank you for the information," he said a bit too formally for her liking. Nicolas rose with hands clasped behind his back and walked to the open window. "So Daniel never accosted your person?"

Elizabeth's appetite vanished. He still didn't trust that she had told the truth. She banged her cup to the table and stood by her chair to face her husband's brawny back. Husbands could be so wearisome when their emotions were involved. She blew out her frustration through her lips. "No! I have told you the truth. I'm troubled that you have doubts about my trustworthiness. When we were together today, you indicated that things were different between us; and I thought our new relationship consisted of honesty and trust. Obviously, I was mistaken," she said.

Nicolas dropped his hands and turned to face his wife. "I desperately want to believe what you say is true, Isabelle. However, I find it difficult to understand how Daniel could resist your magnetism . . ." He moved slowly toward her rigid body. When they stood toe to toe, he continued in a soft voice. ". . . when you draw me as a moth to a flame." His palm cupped her cheek. "Irresistible."

With their eyes locked together, Elizabeth reached up to stroke his face with her hand. "Oh, Nicolas . . . how can I be lured by another when 'tis you I yearn for?" she whispered.

That was all the encouragement Nicolas needed. He captured her lips in a searing kiss. A kiss that tilted her world upside down. Her body was on fire as her head spun in circles. Elizabeth wrenched her mouth away to catch a breath. She looked into Nicolas's eyes that were full of love and promise. In that moment, her life was forever changed. God had given her all that she had longed for and more.

"What say you wife? Will you be mine forevermore?"

His words vanquished her doubts. She smiled broadly. "You have given me much to pray about. Will you grant me this night to devote to prayer about our future?"

Nicolas looked intently into her eyes, but she held fast to her position. If she had gone strictly by her feelings, she would have dragged him to the bed right after that kiss. However, she wanted—no *needed*—God's direction.

Dropping his hands from her face, Nicolas said, "As you wish."

Elizabeth wanted to leave him with hope and anticipation of tomorrow. "Thank you for this short respite. Unless God surprises me tonight, I imagine we will be truly wed by tomorrow evening," she said. When she reached the open door, she looked over her shoulder as the blanket fell to the ground and gave him a come-hither grin.

Nicolas's brows shot straight to his hairline. "You had best bolt your door tonight!"

Elizabeth's laughter filtered through the door as the bar slid into place.

29

Nicolas had tossed about most of the night with thoughts of his wife and Daniel. He desperately wanted to believe Isabelle that nothing had transpired between her and Daniel. What if she were playing him false? What if she planned a secret rendezvous with Daniel at some future point? His pillow had been torn asunder from his brutal attack born of frustration—feathers scattered all around.

The echo of the rooster was actually a relief from his torturous thoughts. His eyes were gritty and his body weary as if from battle. He had slept a couple of hours in a fireside chair but now splashed cold water in his face. What would the day bring—contentment or misery? There had to be some type of resolution to his dilemma for the sake of his sanity. All depended upon a sprite of a woman in the next room who had caused disorder in his orderly life. His once peaceful heart was now in constant turmoil—not wanting her love but needing it beyond reason. A warrior and leader should be in control of his emotions and his surroundings because lives depended upon him; yet over the last months, weakened by desire, he had managed neither.

The creaking door brought his wandering mind back to the present. He looked down to see a bare foot peep around the door's edge. His eyes popped wide open. What the devil? Was she trying to kill him with her taunting behavior? Ever so slowly, her toe was followed by a fully clothed, yet tousled woman. Nicolas closed his tired eyes and let loose the breath he had been holding.

"Goodmorrow, my husband," Elizabeth said softly.

Straightening up and wiping his hands on a towel, Nicolas returned her greeting. "Goodmorrow, my wife."

"Did you sleep well?"

"Yes." How pathetic could he get? Reduced to lying in order to salvage his pride.

"I must admit, my night was restless. I spent most of the nighttime in prayer and listening for God."

"And did God answer you, Isabelle?"

She sauntered up to his frozen form and placed her hand on his chest. Peeping at him through her messy hair, she said, "W-e-l-l . . . tonight I will be a true wife to you."

With nostrils flaring, Nicolas breathed in the sweet smell of Isabelle and breathed out his pent up emotions. At long last, she was his for the taking. "'Tis good to hear." Before she could form a reply, Nicolas wrapped her in a firm embrace and fastened their lips together in a fiery kiss. The fervent kiss continued with intensity and passion. He was sure they would both burst into flames. When Nicolas would have withdrawn, Elizabeth held him fast. He then rained kisses over her face, down her cheeks and ended with a light peck to her upturned nose.

"We must cease this line of affection unless you are prepared to be thrown into that four poster bed this morning," Nicolas half-heartedly said. *Maybe she won't wait until evening.*

"Oh, me. I will need the full day to prepare for our night together. This morning is much too soon for my total submission," she said sheepishly.

Nicolas watched her blush spread to her hairline. Their foreheads touched as he closed his eyes in agony. "Isabelle," he breathed. "Your announcement is most pleasing, but waiting for nightfall will be pure torment for me." He took hold of her upper arms and stepped back from their tight embrace. Still holding her at arm's length, he said, "I will busy myself with castle duties and sword training in the lists to keep my mind occupied. Hopefully, I won't be distracted by thoughts of my wife and get cut to shreds by one of my men," he said with a laugh.

On a quick intake of air, she said, "I certainly pray not. Now that we are in one accord, there is much living to do."

Nicolas dropped his arms and whirled around on his heel. With rapid, jerky motions, he buckled on his sword and yanked on his boots. When he stood, he noticed that his wife was just as he had left her—mouth open and eyes wide. Without touching her body, he leaned down for a final peck of affection. "Until sundown, my lady . . . have a care." With that he disappeared through the open portal.

Elizabeth lightly touched her lips that still held evidence of his kisses. "Oh . . . my."

*** * * ***

After Elizabeth had eaten a light breakfast, she went outside to see a child's wooden wagon at the bottom of the steps. Racing down the stairs, she wasted no time in rounding up the children to try out their new toy. Once Henry had seen the small wagon, he had run through the castle grounds to find Pierce and Patrick. Merry and Gwendolyn had heard his shouts and came to see what the excitement was about. A few other children tagged along out of curiosity.

"Henry, run and find Angus and Jarvis. Tell them we are going on an outing in the nearby meadow. We are in need of their protection," Elizabeth directed.

"Yeah!" Henry shouted.

"Where are we going today, Lady Isabelle?" Merry asked.

"Well, for certain, we will stay away from the water. That trip did not end well. No, today we will head up the small hill next to the castle where we will test out our new wagon."

"Oo, thet should be fun," Merry squealed as she and Gwendolyn clapped their hands.

"You children wait here while I go get one more thing we need," Elizabeth instructed. Holding her dress up, she took off at a run back up the steps and all the way to the room she would share with Nicolas. Just one glance at the huge bed made her stomach jittery—in a good way. She skittered away from the bed as if it would grab her, and she headed toward the harp. She didn't think Nicolas would mind if she borrowed his mother's harp to serenade the children under the large shade tree atop the hill. The harp was still on the stool by the fireplace where she had left it after playing for Nicolas before their disagreement almost a week ago. Wrapped in a blanket, the harp was tucked under Elizabeth's arm as she carefully picked her way down the stairs and outside where the children awaited her return.

Henry pulled the empty wagon by the rope handle as they trailed out the gate and up the grassy hill west of the castle walls. Children's laughter floated in the crisp morning air. The sound of it brought such joy to Elizabeth which caused her mind to shift to tonight. Would her intimacy with Nicolas lead to the beginning of a child—an heir for Nicolas? She certainly hoped so. The thought put a spring in her step. Joyfully, she challenged the children to race up the hill. Nicolas wasn't the only one who needed a distraction from their upcoming tryst.

Elizabeth collapsed under the tree out of breath as she declared Patrick the winner of the race. After all the children had reached the top of the small rise, Elizabeth volunteered to show the children how the wagon could be steered by the one riding inside of it. After putting the harp in a safe place, she tucked her dress inside the wagon and let her long legs hang over the sides. With her feet held off the ground, Henry gave her a shove as she held tight to the rope. Away she bumped and rumbled all the way to the road at the bottom of the grassy knoll. Once the ground leveled out, Elizabeth put down her heels to slow down the wagon. When she attempted to get out of the wagon, it tipped over and dumped her in the dirt at the feet of Thomas's horse.

"Lady Isabelle, are you hurt?" Thomas asked as he jumped to the ground.

Elizabeth parted her hair hanging in her face and laughed. "No, Thomas. I am fine. Really. But you may help me up."

Thomas grabbed her hands as she reached upward. "You took quite a tumble. Nicolas would be most displeased if I allowed you to get injured," Thomas said seriously.

"Nicolas worries too much. I am well. Come, walk me up the hill."

Thomas pulled the wagon in one hand and his horse in the other. "Would you care to ride up the hill?"

"Oh, no, thank you. I need the exercise."

"I think it would be best if you just watched the children play with the new wagon. 'Tis safer."

"Thomas. You are just like your brother, fretting so."

"Please, Lady Isabelle. I do not wish to be on the receiving end of my brother's wrath."

"All right, Thomas. I'll sit under the tree and strum the harp . . . and maybe do a bit of singing. What think you of that?"

Sigh. "That is much more to my liking. I will remain close at hand for your protection."

"I'm in such a joyful mood, not even the threat of an evil adversary can dampen my spirits."

The children were jumping with excitement. Each wanted to be the first to try out the new wagon and fly down the hill. Elizabeth determined that drawing straws, or in this case sticks, was the fairest way to determine the order of riders. Gwendolyn, along with several younger children, were too afraid to ride; so they sat under the tree with Elizabeth. Patrick and Pierce were first and decided to ride down together and see if their combined weight would increase their speed. Elizabeth encouraged the riders by clapping and yelling praises when they successfully completed their run without falling out of the wagon.

Jarvis sat with Elizabeth and the young ones while Angus stood off to one side watching the wooded area for any signs of danger. Thomas sat proudly on his horse scanning in all directions while he also kept an eye on the wagon riders and Elizabeth. All was right in Elizabeth's world. She was surrounded by children that brought her great pleasure, and she had a husband that showed signs of caring deeply for her—maybe even falling in love with her. A soft sigh escaped as she strummed the harp in total contentment.

Following many trips up and down the hill, the wagon riders gathered under the shade tree with the other children. Some were sitting and some sprawled out in utter exhaustion. "Shall I sing you a song?" Elizabeth asked the children.

"Oh, yea!" several children yelled.

Propped up against the tree trunk with her legs outstretched, Elizabeth laid the harp in her lap for easy access. She didn't know all the chords for the songs she wanted to sing to the children, but she knew enough to keep her on key. After a few fast-paced songs, Elizabeth tried her hand at a lullaby drawn from the recesses of her mind. From what she could see, her soft voice had lulled a few of them to sleep. Even Jarvis was dozing in the peaceful atmosphere. Angus stood off to one side with his head tilted toward the tree. Thomas was a few hundred feet away with his eyes roaming the countryside.

Elizabeth was thinking of her next song when out of nowhere an arrow whizzed over the heads of the children and skewered Elizabeth's shoulder, pinning her to the trunk of the tree. She screamed out in agony as her hand fell limp by her side.

Angus spun around from his position to see the arrow protruding out of her shoulder. At the ear-splitting scream, Jarvis erupted up from his resting place near Elizabeth; children cried in terror as some ran for the castle. Thomas raced to the tree and jumped to her side.

"Lady Isabelle? Can you hear me?" Thomas asked in alarm.

Her head lolled to one side before her eyes fluttered open. "Thomas," she whispered.

"Don't move. You are gravely injured." Fear gripped Thomas when he comprehended the seriousness of her wound. He realized he was not equipped to remove the arrow without help; thankfully, his warrior training overrode his fear as he barked orders to the others. "Angus, help hold Lady Isabelle in place and press this cloth to stem the blood flow. Jarvis ride my horse for Nicolas, and send someone for Agnes!"

"Thomas," Elizabeth groaned. "You are scaring the children."

"Forgive me, my lady. There is much to do. Please don't talk." Looking around at the petrified faces, he ordered the children to run to the safety of the castle. The bawling and shouting faded as the wee ones disappeared down the hill. However, Henry, Patrick, and Pierce stayed behind.

"What would ye have us do?" Henry asked.

"Stand watch over Lady Isabelle. I know not if the attacker is close at hand."

"I saw 'im," Henry offered.

Thomas wrenched around to look Henry in the face. "What did you say?"

"I saw the attacker. He came from that clump of trees, yonder," Henry said as he pointed not fifty feet away.

Thomas knelt down and grabbed Henry's arms. "Do you know who it was? Was it one of our own or a Scotsman?"

"'e looked familiar, but I can't be certain."

Thomas released Henry and stooped down near Elizabeth. "My lady, I must leave you in Angus's care. Nicolas will be here post haste . . ."

"I'll survive," Elizabeth squeaked out. "Go get him."

After only a moment's hesitation, Thomas picked up his quiver and bow and struck out in the direction Henry had pointed out. The attacker already had a five-minute head start. Time was crucial if he wanted to apprehend the assailant.

Nicolas heard screams before he saw Jarvis ride in on Thomas's horse. If Thomas were not on his horse, something dreadful had happened. Jarvis waved his arms frantically as he repeatedly hollered Nicolas's name. Something was wrong, desperately wrong. Nicolas took off at a dead run to meet Jarvis half way.

"Lord Nicolas, Lord Nicolas . . . Lady Isabelle . . ."

"Slow down, Jarvis," Nicolas demanded. "What has happened?"

"Archer . . . shot Lady Isabelle . . . in 'er shoulder," he cried as tears formed in his eyes. "She's alive, but in grave peril. Robert is getting Agnes. Please, hurry."

"Where is she? And where is Thomas?"

"Top of the hill west of the castle wall. Thomas has gone after the man. Hurry, my lord, hurry!"

Nicolas wasted no time. He pulled Jarvis down and swung up on Thomas's horse. Several of his men had already mounted up and followed him out the gate and galloped up the hill. His insides twisted with the thought of revenge. Even though he was angry that Thomas had left Isabelle's side, he prayed Thomas would catch the vermin. From a distance Nicolas could see his wife leaning against the tree trunk and Angus hovering over her. Henry, Patrick, and Pierce stood guard around the tree.

Upon arrival, Nicolas kicked his feet free and jumped from the horse before it had time to stop. There before him was his wife impaled by an arrow. Blood had soaked the front of her dress with fresh blood still draining down her arm and dripping off her hand that lay by her side.

Kneeling down, he looked at Angus, who only shook his head. Nicolas saw that removal of the arrow was necessary before his wife could be freed. "Isabelle," he called softly.

Her drooping eyes flickered open—they spoke of pain and agony. "Nicolas," she murmured.

"I am here."

"Someone didn't like my singing." She attempted a smile.

Her effort at humor fell flat with Nicolas. "Sit quietly while I decide our best options." Nicolas knew he couldn't stall long. What he had to do would cause more damage to her shoulder and great pain. "Isabelle, you must stay motionless. I need to grasp the arrow protruding from the front of your shoulder and slice it off with my short knife." The whoosh of the knife leaving its place inside his boot echoed loudly in his ears. "Angus will assist me by holding you tightly against the tree trunk. You will experience excruciating pain, but you mustn't move. Do you understand?" As her mournful eyes met his, they tore a hole in his heart.

"That's my husband . . . straight to the point . . . no sugarcoating the problem." She grimaced as she huffed out each phrase.

As Nicolas took hold of the arrow, Elizabeth cried out. He couldn't allow her suffering to stop him. The faster he completed the appalling task, the better for his wife. She had lost much blood and needed Agnes as quickly as possible. While Angus anchored her to the tree, Nicolas made one quick downward thrust with his razor sharp knife. Even though he had a tight hold on the shaft, the action shifted the arrow which caused Elizabeth to faint from the unbearable pain.

"She has swooned. This is a blessing. Angus, hold the arrow at the back of Isabelle." Nicolas tenderly pulled his wife's body straight toward him as she slid off the arrow shaft. Of course, once her body was free of the shaft, blood flowed liberally.

"Angus, hand me the blanket. I must wrap her shoulder to slow down her bleeding." The men worked quickly, yet efficiently, to ready her for transport. Henry had caught Nicolas's horse and was holding him nearby. Five of Nicolas's warriors had ridden off in pursuit of the enemy while the others stood guard around the area. Once Nicolas mounted with his wife cradled in his arms, he dashed toward the castle.

Oh, God, please spare Isabelle. I need her. He hadn't realized until that moment, he was in love with his wife!

30

Nicolas and Phillip found themselves once again pacing Nicolas's solar. Remembering the cries of his wife as Nicolas had cauterized her wound was horrifying. When the bleeding would not stop, she had pleaded for him to let her die right before he touched her shoulder with the scorching blade. The ghastly sound and smell of her sizzling flesh had caused his stomach to rebel. He barely made it to the chamber pot before he lost his breakfast.

Nicolas pounded his fist against the stone wall by the open window. "I grow concerned that Thomas and the men have not returned. What if Isabelle's would-be assassin escapes capture?" Nicolas growled. He moved back and plopped down in the chair across from Phillip.

A tapping on the door to the hallway brought both men to their feet. Phillip opened the door while Nicolas stood tight fisted—waiting. There stood wee Henry with eyes as large as walnuts. "I need to speak to Lord Fairwick," he said. Phillip stepped aside and allowed Henry to enter the room. With head hanging low, Henry walked to stand directly in front of Nicolas.

"What do you here, young Henry?"

"I came for me punishment."

For a brief moment, Nicolas's fury at the situation faded to the background as he viewed the small child weighed down by guilt.

Nicolas sat down so he would be closer to Henry's eye level before speaking. "What punishment would that be, Henry?"

Henry raised his tear stained face. "Me punishment for not protecting Lady Isabelle," he said through trembling lips.

Nicolas could contain his misery no longer as he pulled Henry into an embrace while they both wept silently. "'Tis not your fault," Nicolas said hoarsely as he peered over Henry's head into Phillip's anguished eyes. "No one could have prevented the arrow from finding its target. Ye did ye're best and that is all I expect from any of my warriors."

Henry looked into Nicolas's face and asked, "Is she going to die?"

"Only God knows the answer to that question. The best we can do is pray for God to heal her. Can you do that?"

"Yea. I'll go tell the others to pray for 'er, too."

Nicolas released Henry and stood to his feet. He placed his hand on Henry's shoulder. "Lady Isabelle speaks highly of you as her protector. She would not want ye to worry. So, off with ye and spread the word to pray for her."

Henry left the room with his head held high as he went to carry out Lord Fairwick's command. No sooner had Henry departed when there arose a noisy cry from down the hallway. It grew louder the closer it got to the room. Both men looked at each other and said, "Brigette."

Brigette burst through the door with wild eyes roaming the room. "Where is Isabelle?" she asked hysterically. "I need to talk to her immediately!"

Nicolas grabbed Brigette and placed his hand over her mouth. "Brigette, cease this deafening noise. You cannot see her. She is in Mother's room and has suffered a severe injury."

When Nicolas let her go, she slumped to the floor covering her face with both hands. "Oh, no. 'Tis all my fault . . . oh, no," she moaned while rocking back and forth.

Nicolas couldn't stop the rolling of his eyes as his temper flared. He was in no mood to endure one of Brigette's performances. He seized her arm and tugged her to her feet. "What gibberish do you speak?" he asked as he snatched her hands from her face. "Answer me!"

"I didn't mean to cause this! Truly I didn't," she cried, "But I think I know who shot the arrow."

"How are you privy to such information?" he demanded.

Twisting to pull her hands free, she said, "Stop. You're hurting me."

"Answer me, I say!"

When Nicolas failed to loosen his grip, Brigette screamed, "I think it was Eugene!"

Nicolas flung her away from him. "How could you possibly know this, Brigette?" he asked through clinched teeth. He stood over her with every muscle taut from strain.

"I can't tell you. I can only tell Lady Isabelle," she sobbed.

"Phillip, escort our *sister*," he hissed, "to her room and put her under guard while I get to the bottom of this debacle." Brigette's sobs bounced off the stone walls as Phillip half dragged her away from Nicolas and toward her room. Nicolas rubbed his brow with a trembling hand. The thought that his sister could be partially responsible for Isabelle's accident was not to be borne. "Hurry, Thomas, before I lose my mind," he spoke to an empty room.

After Phillip and Brigette were out of range, silence reigned once again. As he took up his pacing, Nicolas got a glimpse of Jarvis and Angus sitting outside his door. Jarvis hugged the harp to his chest. Oh, how he wished he could blame someone for this outrage; but deep down in his soul—he knew—he could only blame himself. With visions of Isabelle coming to his bed, he had thought of nothing else all morning long. His mind had been engaged in fanciful notions. Nicolas knew he had committed the unpardonable offense—he had dropped his guard—leaving Isabelle wide open for attack. *God, forgive me. You entrusted me to protect Isabelle, and I have failed. Please, God, please spare my wife!* A lone tear eased down his cheek as his head drooped under the heaviness of his botched duty.

At the sound of angry voices filtering through his door, Nicolas's head jerked up. Was that Thomas's voice? Nicolas strode to the open door just as Thomas came into view. The blood on his face and clothing spoke of a heated exchange.

"I have him!" Thomas announced. "'Twas Eugene. A man we trusted!" Thomas spit out.

Nicolas stepped into the hallway and pulled the door shut as quietly as his tense muscles would allow. "Where is he?"

"In the dungeon."

"Did he offer an explanation?"

"He kept repeating that he did it for the love of his woman. What do you think he means with such nonsense?"

Nicolas couldn't believe what he was hearing. Had Brigette conspired with Eugene to kill Isabelle? Surely not! While Nicolas contemplated the meaning of Eugene's actions and words, he noticed the muscles in Thomas's neck were bulging—he was about to split wide open from rage. "You have done well, Thomas. Leave Eugene in the dungeon with only water until I say otherwise. He can stew and wonder about his fate while we figure out this mess. You may wish to clean up to be more presentable when Isabelle awakens."

At the mention of Isabelle's name, Thomas's face softened. "How is she faring?"

"I had to cauterize her wound to stop the bleeding. Afterwards, Agnes thoroughly cleaned the gash and bandaged it up. With the aid of some sleeping herbs, Isabelle is resting at the moment under the watchful eye of Agnes. Now, we pray that she will remain fever free. We have done all we can; we must wait for God to bring about her healing." Nicolas hoped his words would bring some comfort to Thomas since they weren't helping Nicolas one bit. His insides were like a knotted seaman's rope.

Nicolas watched as Thomas lumbered down the passageway. Thomas's shoulders slouched from the gravity of the situation. Life was just cruel. Nicolas looked toward the closed door adjoining his room and remembered. He had seen his mother suffer unto death in that very room. Would he now have to watch his wife die, too? And what would he do with Brigette if she was indeed involved in the attack? The only bright spot today had been when he received word that the King was delayed due to muddy roads and was remaining at Lord Sherwood's castle.

"She's awake," Agnes stated, "and asking for you."

Nicolas snapped out of his melancholy and made a brisk, direct path to his wife's side. She was deathly pale from her loss of blood. Kneeling down, Nicolas took her left hand and covered it with both of his. It was so cold. "Isabelle," he whispered. "I am here."

Her lashes flickered open and she gazed up at him through anguished eyes. With a tiny smile she mumbled, "My right shoulder burns . . . like fire . . . put it out."

"Oh, Isabelle, if only I could take your wound and make it my own."

"Did you catch . . . the devil?"

"Yes, Thomas brought him back."

"W-e-l-l, don't make . . . me beg," she huffed.

"'Twas Eugene."

A frown creased her brow. "Eugene?"

"Yes."

"Odd . . . I don't think . . . he liked me."

Nicolas's lips twitched with a half-smile at that remark. "No. Obviously, he did not."

"What . . . aren't . . . you telling me?" she pressured.

"I don't have all the facts, yet. I will not leave you unaware, but for now, you must rest." He was very much aware of her labored breathing. She could barely get her thoughts out and grimaced with each word spoken.

"Not a good beginning . . . to our first night . . . together, is it?"

"There will be others for us to share," he forced out as he ran a finger across her forehead.

"I don't think so . . . not this time . . . I'm not going to make it."

"Cease your prattle. I will not accept your defeat. You will survive. Young Henry and the children are praying for it. God wouldn't disappoint the wee ones," he said heatedly.

"Of course . . . you are right . . . I was just testing you," she murmured. "I think I will rest now . . . kiss me."

Nicolas choked up at her request. Would this be their final kiss? "As you wish, my love. I'm here to please you, but do not grab me and pull me off balance," he said teasingly. He leaned in for a light kiss. "You are so bossy when you are hurt."

"Stay . . . with me?"

"Of course. I have nowhere else I want to be."

"You are . . . my . . . most . . . valiant warrior," she struggled to say.

His unshed tears clouded his vision as he watched her close her tortured eyes praying they would open again for him. "Sweet dreams, my beloved." He eased down and leaned against the wall by her bed with her hand still encased by his.

Nicolas had fallen asleep propped against the wall when a noise startled him awake. There in the doorway between his room and Elizabeth's room stood Phillip. Nicolas raised one finger, and Phillip moved back into Nicolas's room. Bones creaked and snapped as Nicolas rose from the stone floor. He felt like an old man; the emotional upheaval today had taken a toll on him physically, as well as mentally. He carefully extracted his hand from Elizabeth's hand. As he stood over her still form, she appeared to be resting peacefully even though her breaths were shallow. He scanned the room and found Agnes watching him from the chair in the corner of the room. Agnes nodded her head toward Nicolas reminding him that she was ever watchful of her patient. Nicolas tip-toed from the room and eased the door closed.

"What news have you?" he asked Phillip.

"I practically beat the information out of Brigette. I wasn't leaving her room until she told all. It is worse than I thought. You had best sit down to hear it."

Nicolas heaved a disgusted sigh as he trudged to the chair. Phillip seemed to be gathering his thoughts when Nicolas erupted. "Don't leave me in suspense! Get on with the telling."

"Brigette was extremely jealous of Lady Isabelle when you brought her to our home."

"Jealous? Jealous of what?" Nicolas demanded.

"Of your affections."

"Preposterous!"

"I would call it disgraceful," Phillip remarked. "Brigette had loved you in an unhealthy way. Not as a brother and sister. Somewhere in her growing up years, a maid had told her she was only a half-sister-the result of one of our father's indiscretions. She planned to be the next lady of the castle."

Some reckless words flew from Nicolas's mouth before he pounded his fist on the arm of the chair. "This gets worse by the minute. Carry on," he fumed.

"When you refused to force Isabelle to leave and, in fact, decided to marry Isabelle, Brigette took matters into her own hands. She decided since Eugene favored her that she would use him to do away with Isabelle. He was left to his own devises on how and when that would occur. Of course, this was contrived before she developed an affection for Isabelle. By the time Isabelle had won Brigette's heart, Brigette had stopped speaking with Eugene and forgot their agreement."

"How could Brigette forget planning someone's demise?" he bellowed. He jumped to his feet and would have dashed out the door to her room if Phillip hadn't grabbed his arm.

"You will regret if you act in haste. There has been enough of that surrounding this tragedy. Why not let Brigette and Eugene stew in their guilt for a while? A few days in confinement will be at least some type of punishment while you tend to Isabelle and plan your assault. Brigette already shows remorse about her part in this catastrophe. You have to ask yourself; what would please Isabelle? She is the fragile character in this drama."

Nicolas stood seething as he listened to Phillip. He just wanted to run his sword through someone—Eugene could be first. But when Phillip had mentioned Isabelle, Nicolas's rage was averted. She would be most displeased if he tortured and killed Eugene and gave Brigette the whip. Females! They could bring a seasoned warrior to his knees. "I will think on what you have said. Punish the two offenders anyway you see fit until I make a decision as to their fate." Phillip released Nicolas's arm and strode out the door leaving Nicolas to brood over his next confrontation.

Lord, God, the Almighty, please give me the Wisdom of Solomon. Even as he prayed for insight into the tangled mess called 'his life', he knew there was one piece of unfinished business he had to see through.

31

Nicolas rode hard to get to the pond that bordered his land and the McKinnon land. Five of his most trusted men rode with him. Earlier he had sent a message to Daniel to meet him in their usual place at sundown. Even though Daniel would still be spitting mad at Nicolas for sickening all at the McKinnon castle, he knew Daniel's anger wouldn't last. It never did—ever since they were tots.

Seeing the boulder at the top of the hill, Nicolas halted the men. His men spread out their guard at the bottom of the hill as was their usual custom when Nicolas and Daniel met. The friendship between Nicolas and Daniel had been forged through the innocence of youngsters. Even when their fathers were in skirmishes as they defended their borders, Daniel and Nicolas found it great fun to conduct their own covert operations—playing at the pond hidden from their fathers. If only this were such a mischievous meeting instead of a dreadful reunion.

Nicolas left his horse with Braden and continued the rest of the way on foot. With the stealth of an owl in flight, Nicolas made little sound as he picked his way through the thick underbrush. He could see Daniel perched on their favorite rock near the pond. Prior to stepping into the open, Nicolas scanned the area and was relieved to observe Daniel was alone.

"Come on out in the open. I hear you," Daniel said.

"You might have sensed my presence, but you did not hear me," Nicolas boasted.

Daniel threw a stone into the pond and watched the ripple effect before standing to his feet. He wasted no time in addressing the message that he had received from Nicolas. "What mean you that Isabelle is near death? How can that be?"

Nicolas approached Daniel so his voice would not be carried by the breeze. "I have an enemy from within who shot the arrow."

"That's the worst kind of enemy. Do you know who it is?"

"Yes. Thomas tracked him down, and Eugene now resides in my dungeon. He thought he was doing a service for my sister if he disposed of Isabelle. 'Tis a most convoluted tale. Suffice it to say, I have some difficult decisions to make concerning all who are involved. My instinct tells me to run Eugene through with a sword and leave him with a gut injury so he will suffer before dying. However, that would displease Isabelle, and that is not a consequence I want to see come to fruition." Rubbing the back of his neck, he said, "Banishment is a painless result that does not suit me, so I am in a quandary."

"Bring him here," Daniel suggested.

"Here? At our pond?" Nicolas asked confused.

"No. Here to Scotland. Drop him off over the border without any defense and let my men take care of him for you. Isabelle need not know the outcome."

"I don't know. Somehow she finds out everything."

"It's the least you can do after wreaking such havoc at my castle. I will feel vindicated for your poisoning of my people, and you can be rid of your attacker without upsetting Isabelle." Daniel began to rub his hands together the more he warmed to the idea. "We all can be victorious. Well, everyone except Eugene."

"The idea has merit. I will take it under advisement," Nicolas said. "But for now, I must be on my way. I don't want to leave Isabelle overlong. Did you bring her?"

"Need you ask? She is tied over here. I covered her in a dark blanket so she wouldn't be a beacon in the night." Taking hold of

Nicolas's forearm, Daniel added, "I did it for Isabelle—not for you."

"Thank you . . . old friend."

Daniel pushed back a hanging tree branch to reveal Midnight. In addition to the blanket, her white face and legs had been rubbed down with mud—disguised for her ride home.

Daniel held onto the bridle for a brief moment as he said, "Take care of Isabelle. I will pray for her recovery . . . old friend."

Nicolas nodded his head not trusting his voice to speak due to his volatile emotions. He wasted no time in hurrying to his men with Midnight trotting behind him. They gathered near him as he mounted his steed. No words were exchanged as they headed back to Fairwick Castle with their prize in tow.

It was long past the dinner hour when they rode over the bridge. Once inside the gate, the portcullis dropped into place for the night. Nicolas gave Robert instructions to wash and brush Midnight so her coat would gleam white. He then hurried to wash and change his clothes before going to see Elizabeth. He didn't want her to wonder where he had been for so long. Maybe she had slept through most of his absence and wouldn't question him.

He practically ran over Agnes as she was leaving Elizabeth's room with a bowl of bloody bandages. Nicolas's eyes grew wide when he saw the blood was still bright red.

"She was restless," Agnes said, "and reopened her wound."

"I will sit with her now. Will you ask the cook to send me some dinner?"

"Yea. Abigail is in thar now," she said as she walked away.

"Abigail?" Nicolas shook his head in bewilderment. He eased open the door to see Abigail sitting by the bed reading to Isabelle. Abigail failed to hear his approach and jumped when he spoke.

"Ye frightened me," she whispered.

"Why are you reading to Isabelle when she is asleep?" he asked in a hushed voice.

"It seems to soothe her and keep her from being as restless. Agnes suggested it. I will take my leave now that you have arrived." She laid the Bible on the table and rose to her feet.

"Thank you, Abigail," he said with a hand on her shoulder.

Abigail's eyes became misty. "I have grown quite fond of her. She has been most helpful in Phillip's recovery. Of that, I am most grateful." Her sniffles trailed after her as she left the room.

Nicolas eased into the chair Abigail had vacated and stretched out his long legs. Leaning his head back against the chair, he viewed Isabelle through hooded eyes. She had a fresh bandage wrapped around her arm that anchored it to her stomach. No doubt, Agnes had found a way to keep Isabelle from moving her shoulder too much. She was still quite pale, but her breathing seemed less difficult—or was that his wishful thinking?

Shuffling feet brought his attention toward the open doorway. There stood Collette with a tray of food. "Place it on the table near the fireplace. I will eat it later."

"How is she, my lord?" Collette asked as she arranged the food on the table.

"I have just arrived from an errand, but she appears to be more comfortable than when I last saw her."

"All of the castle's folk are praying for her. She is greatly loved," Collette said in a low voice.

"Thank you, Collette. Prayers are much appreciated and greatly needed. Tell everyone to keep God busy tonight listening to their petitions on Isabelle's behalf."

"Yes, my lord." Collette curtsied and drifted from the room soundlessly.

When Elizabeth shifted in the bed and moaned, Nicolas's eyes darted toward her. She didn't awaken but a frown creased her forehead. She was in pain even while asleep. He leaned up and rested his arms on his knees. With clasped hands dangling between his legs, he offered up his own prayer.

"Lord, my soul is sorely troubled. Isabelle is in great need because of my negligence. I've read in Your Word that You are our strength and our shield, our refuge in times of trouble. I proclaim those words for Isabelle. Father, have mercy on her and save her from her affliction."

"That was sweet," Isabelle mumbled.

Nicolas's head jerked up. Gazing back at him was his wife. "How long have you been listening?" Nicolas asked red-faced.

"I've been awake . . . since you first . . . walked in the room."

"You could have made your awakening known," he reprimanded.

She smiled. "I think not. I would . . . have missed . . . the sweet exchanges."

"Isabelle, you are a mischievous nymph. How fare you?"

"Some better. When will . . . this . . . wretched burning . . . cease?"

"I know not. Have you had any broth, yet? It will help strengthen you."

"Not hungry."

"Well, you will not get your surprise until you have drunk some broth."

"What surprise?"

"I will not tell you. Sip some broth, and I might be persuaded to give you a hint." Nicolas got up and went to the food table. Sitting near the fire was a warm bowl of broth. No doubt Agnes had also tried to get Isabelle to take some nourishment. "I will spoon feed you if you wish," he offered.

"Ugh."

He grinned. He had won this skirmish—for now. "'Tis a wonderful surprise," he taunted. He put some broth in a cup and brought it to her bedside. She was glaring at him out of mere slits. "I have cooled the broth so it will go down easy," he said conversationally. "Now 'tis time to prop you up. This will be a bit uncomfortable, but I know you will rise to the challenge." Nicolas hoped his words irritated her. If so, she would tolerate the pain by shear will to prove she could do it. For he knew excruciating pain was sure to come when he repositioned her body.

He sat softly on the edge of the bed. "I will be as gentle as possible so as not to cause you extra misery." He leaned in and kissed her head. "Are you ready?"

"Yes. Just do it," she said through gritted teeth.

Nicolas reached across the bed and got the extra pillow to put behind her shoulders once he raised her forward. He situated his hands under her back and shoulders. "Here we go."

"Ahh!" she hollered.

Nicolas worked quickly. "There. Take a moment to recover," he encouraged. He watched his wife take short, quick breaths as she tried to regain her composure. Each painful breath caused him to grimace inwardly.

"Whew! That . . . was . . . awful," she huffed out.

"You are a courageous woman, Isabelle. I am proud to call you my wife."

She gave him a weak smile. "Thanks." She squirmed a moment longer before saying, "I think . . . I'm ready."

Nicolas laid a cloth across her chest and arm to catch any drips that might fall. "I have put the broth in a cup. I hope that will make it easier." He held the cup to her dry lips and tipped it for her to drink. She slurped her first swallow.

"Mm. 'Tis good."

Nicolas repeatedly held the cup for her to sip until she had taken over half of the broth. When it dribbled on her chin, Nicolas dabbed it dry. Their eyes locked together making the simple task an intimate one. At one point, Nicolas wiped her chin and mouth before stealing a sweet kiss.

"Mm. Now that 'twas good," Nicolas rumbled.

"I agree," Elizabeth sighed. She placed her left hand on his chest, twisted his shirt with her finger and pulled him down. "How about another one?" she breathed against his lips.

Naturally, Nicolas granted her desire. He carried out a slow, tender caress of her lips leaving both of them breathless.

"What is . . . my surprise?" she panted.

"Oh, you are a wicked woman, Isabelle—trying to trick me into revealing your surprise. I will tell you that it is something you adore."

"Oh," she huffed. "I adore many things . . . that doesn't . . . help me a bit."

"Tomorrow, I will show you your present. So don't ask any more questions." Nicolas tapped her nose and stood to his feet. "I'll clear away your meal and then settle you down for the night."

"Will you . . . sleep . . . with me?" she asked.

Her pitiful plea tore at his heart strings. "As you wish."

32

Seeing her prize had to wait several days. Nicolas had insisted Agnes keep his wife sedated so she wouldn't reopen her wound.

"I'm not staying in this bed . . . another minute," Elizabeth fumed.

"Movement could reopen your wound, Isabelle," Nicolas said with a clinched jaw.

"If you don't take me downstairs to eat with the family, I will . . . I will do something rash," she challenged.

Nicolas stood over Elizabeth's bed like an avenger for the helpless. He rubbed his whiskered face and then glared at his wife. "I will consent if you agree to rest when I say to rest."

His snippy comments didn't bother Elizabeth—they showed her he cared. "I will *consent* to your demand if you won't be unreasonable in the amount of time I can have . . . between rests," she dared to add.

"Isabelle," he snapped, "you can be a most troubling woman."

"I know." She then turned on her sweetest smile to soften her reply. "Isn't that the trait that made you choose me for your wife?" she asked nicely.

"I think not!" he sputtered as he sat down on her bedside. "There were many facets of your character that I found fascinating, my lamb," he said softly. His eyes held her spellbound as he stroked her hair. “I will be happy to describe each one in detail when I am able to act upon my desire that thunders from within. For now, I will have to be content to assist you to the great hall for a brief meal.”

“Thank you,” she whispered. His words had stirred a longing deep within her soul for her husband. She hoped she didn’t die before finding out all the secrets of the marital bed. Whew! She needed a gust of wind to cool her heated face.

“I will call Agnes to secure your bandage and prepare you for transport. I’ll brook no argument when I say ’tis time to rest,” he said as he stalked toward the door.

“Ah, always the warrior in command of the situation. You make me sound like . . . like a shipment leaving the harbor,” she said with a grin. She really didn’t care how he referred to her as long as he allowed her freedom from this dreary room.

Nicolas continued on with a shake of his head as he left the room. His loud, demanding voice filtered back to her as he strode down the hallway calling for Agnes. Elizabeth smiled to herself. Her husband was a fierce warrior but could be kindhearted and gentle when it came to his loved ones. Just the thought of being one of his loved ones filled her with wonder. One day she was close to death and left to die at Nicolas’s doorstep; soon afterwards she became the Lady of Fairwick Castle and in love with the powerful Lord of the Castle. What a whirlwind of events in such a short time span. She conveniently didn’t think on her additional near death experiences—pointless. Today was a happy day. She was still alive.

* * *

“This is most embarrassing,” Elizabeth complained. “It’s my shoulder that is wounded, not my legs. I’m capable of walking,” she added with a disgruntled frown. She was thankful that today she could talk without gasping from excruciating pain.

Nicolas ignored Elizabeth’s grumbling and continued on toward the great hall with her snug in his arms. He slowed at the bottom of the stairs outside the main room and kissed the tip of her nose. "I'm relieved that you have the energy to cross swords with me this fine morning, lady wife."

Elizabeth had to smile at him. "You're right. I'll probably be in a debate when I'm ready to breathe my last."

When Nicolas and Elizabeth entered the main hall, all heads turned their way. Conversations died away. Servants came to a standstill. Someone in the corner began a slow clap and soon everyone in the room joined in. The men and women came to their feet out of respect for their beloved lady.

It thrilled Elizabeth to see the cheery faces of the castle folk. Oh, how she had grown to love these people. She was even happy to see Abigail seated beside Phillip. The only one missing from the scene was Brigette.

"Lady Isabelle," Thomas exclaimed. "'Tis delightful to see you up and about. You amaze me how you seem to cheat death at every turn."

"Thomas!" Nicolas bellowed. When Nicolas drew near, he gave a swift kick to Thomas's foot. "You have much to learn about deportment."

Nicolas set Elizabeth in her usual place on the dais beside Thomas. There was extra padding in her chair to accommodate her arm which made her grateful for her husband's thoughtfulness. Elizabeth fidgeted until she was comfortable before responding. "Oh, Thomas, I do appreciate how you speak your mind instead of dancing around the obvious. I'm like a cat with nine lives." Those within hearing chuckled at her comparison.

The applauding roar of the people diminished as they began to take their seats once again. Nicolas prepared Elizabeth's morning gruel with butter and honey while Thomas made sure she could reach the goblet of water. Abigail came up behind Elizabeth's chair and leaned in close to her ear. She spoke a word of encouragement and offered her assistance when needed. Elizabeth glowed with pleasure from all the well-wishers, especially from Abigail since their acquaintance started off less than amicable.

"Where is Brigette?" Elizabeth asked.

"She is confined to her room," Thomas snarled.

Elizabeth turned her face toward Nicolas for an explanation. "Why is that, my husband?"

"We will discuss it in private. Now, we will break our fast together. Father," Nicolas boomed, "lead us in a prayer of thanksgiving for the food and for Lady Isabelle's recovery."

Elizabeth tried to focus on the eloquent prayer, but her mind was whirling as to why Brigette was in trouble. What could she have possibly done this time to invite her brother's ire? She didn't linger over much on that question as she felt the warmth of her husband's leg press against her own. His closeness alone filled her with such peace and contentment . . . and excitement. Then there was his scent. Ahh—the smell of earth and his unique masculine aroma which made her lose all concentration as thoughts of him filled her mind.

"Amen."

When Elizabeth failed to raise her head at the end of the blessing, Nicolas wrapped his arm around her waist and with his lips touching her ear asked, "Isabelle, are you in pain?"

Her eyes peeped open to be face-to-face with her handsome man whose hand was now making a slow caress on her back. Goose bumps covered her body as her mind wandered to their early morning kiss. "I'm fine," she squeaked. "No pain."

"You are acting most peculiar." His hand came to her forehead to feel for a fever. "Your face is flushed as if you have a fever."

With her free hand, Elizabeth removed his left hand from her face. "Trust me. There is nothing wrong with me that a little cuddling with my husband won't fix," she whispered. She added a wink for good measure.

The wink must have flustered Nicolas for now his face glowed red. Without a word, he looked straight ahead and began inhaling his meal. Elizabeth let out a giggle. It was rare that her husband was ever caught speechless.

Before long the brothers were bantering back and forth with one another. Each tried to one-up the other with a tale of adventure. It was great entertainment for Elizabeth to hear their amusing stories. It gave her a better glimpse into their personalities and their lives at Fairwick Castle before she came on the scene.

Many of the peasants came by the head table to speak a word to Elizabeth. They offered words of support, as well as reminding her of their prayers for healing. She took the time to really look at the people who spoke to her. Some of their clothes were tattered and worn but their clothing didn't matter to them. They were happy and displayed how appearances have little to do with the heart. She relished each man, woman, and child that took the time to talk with her. It wasn't long, though, before she grew fatigued and slumped against Nicolas.

Nicolas acted immediately upon contact. "Thomas, go fetch Isabelle's surprise. We will meet you outside," Nicolas instructed. Draping his arm around her, Nicolas spoke softly, "If you can prevail a few extra moments, I will have you resting in our bed shortly."

Mustering up her best smile, Elizabeth nodded her head in agreement. "I can withstand almost anything if I get a prize in the end."

"Bear up. I will be as gentle as possible; but undoubtedly, there will be pain when I lift you in my arms."

Elizabeth bit her lip to keep from crying out when Nicolas gathered her close. The ache in her shoulder had been manageable during the meal but had returned with a vengeance. She laid her head against his chest as they made their way out the door of the keep. Crisp, cold air momentarily took her breath away when it struck her face as they emerged onto the portico.

"Midnight!" Elizabeth cried. There pawing at the ground and shaking her head in welcome was her beautiful white horse. Elizabeth looked up at Nicolas with tears in her eyes. "You kept your promise."

"Yes, my wife," Nicolas said as he rubbed noses with her. He moved down the steps at a slow pace and brought her next to Midnight.

Thomas had a tight hold on the bridle so Midnight wouldn't jostle Elizabeth. She reached her hand out and stroked Midnight's silky nose and forehead. Questions raced through her mind. When had Nicolas achieved this great deed and how had he come back unscathed? Had he seen Daniel? Had Nicolas made some type of trade to get Midnight; and if so, what?

"Were you surprised?" Thomas asked with a lopsided grin.

"Oh, yes. 'Twas a grand and glorious surprise, Thomas." As she gazed into her husband's eyes, she tried to give him her most loving expression. "Thank you, Nicolas. Just knowing she is once again safely within these walls will allow me to rest peacefully. I don't know how you managed it, but I am overjoyed with her return." Nicolas seemed to stand a little taller after her words of gratitude.

"Now 'tis time for your rest. Thomas, you may return Midnight to her stall . . ."

". . . while Nicolas returns me to my stall," Elizabeth interrupted.

Thomas laughed as he pulled a reluctant horse toward the barn. "It would seem Midnight doesn't wish to be separated from you again," Thomas threw over his shoulder in parting.

Nicolas carried Elizabeth back inside and straight toward their room. A few individuals tried to speak to Elizabeth when Nicolas walked past, but he would not allow any delay in his mission. "Nicolas, you were almost rude," Elizabeth reprimanded after they were alone in the hallway.

"When you have recovered, you may talk as much as you wish. However, now is not that time."

Once Agnes had adjusted the bandage and given Elizabeth some herbs for her pain, she left the room to allow Nicolas some privacy with his wife. Nicolas sat on the edge of the bed and took Elizabeth's hand into his own. As he stroked her knuckles with his thumb, he realized he needed to reveal his heart while there was still time.

"Isabelle," he said softly. "There is something I must tell you."

"Oh my, that sounds ominous. I must be dying."

"Isabelle!" he said in exasperation.

"Forgive me. Please . . . continue," she said sheepishly.

"I never imagined having a wife, yet here you are; but what's more astonishing is how you have captivated my heart." He blinked away tears that wanted to flood his eyes. After clearing his throat, he persisted. "You have truly taken up residence in this cold heart of mine, warming it with your presence. I love you, Isabelle Emma Fairwick, with all of my being." He closed his eyes and shuddered. "You must survive this ordeal, for I can't bare the thoughts of life without you," he said quietly.

Elizabeth pulled her hand free from his hold and placed it on his cheek. "Oh, Nicolas, you are truly my brave warrior. As long as I'm still breathing, God is not finished with me. But if God calls me home, you will survive without me; although, if God allows it, I hope to hear those precious words for years to come. My heart bursts with happiness knowing I'm not in love alone." She tugged him closer to share a tender kiss. "Now, come join me in this huge bed and whisper sweet words in my ear while I rest. 'Twill make for a most delightful afternoon."

* * *

Nicolas came out of Elizabeth's room with his face a thundercloud. He had remained by her side while she slept—watching and praying for her healing. When she awoke, she had asked to see Brigette—Brigette of all people! Pointing out all the reasons she should not talk with Brigette had only created more distress for his wife. What was a husband to do under the circumstances? He came into his room to find Philip, Abigail, and Thomas waiting anxiously.

"Phillip, please fetch our sister and bring her to speak with Isabelle," Nicolas announced. Abigail gasped as Phillip jumped to his feet. Thomas twirled around from his place by the window.

"What?" Phillip and Thomas asked in unison.

"You heard me aright. I lost this skirmish with Isabelle. She would not surrender to my requests. Make sure you inform Brigette that she is not to upset Isabelle or cause her more anguish than she already suffers or I will beat Brigette myself. I want you to use my exact words. Understood?"

"Yes. I do not like it, but I will return post haste," Phillip said.

"Thomas, I need you to fetch Eugene; she wants to see him, too. Make sure he washes so his stench won't offend Isabelle. Keep him at the end of the passageway near the back kitchen stairs until I tell you otherwise. I don't want him and Brigette to cross paths."

"This is outrageous!" Thomas fumed as he kicked the footstool and pounded his fist in his palm.

"I couldn't agree more, Thomas. However, at this time, I will do all in my power to grant Isabelle her desires." His last statement hung in the air like dense smoke—oppressive. No one in the room would dare say it; but in all probability, each person entertained thoughts of Isabelle's impending death. Nicolas could not allow his mind to wander in that direction. He needed Isabelle. Nicolas watched Thomas stomp out the door before he went back to pacing the room while Abigail remained silent, deep in her own thoughts.

After a short time Nicolas heard Brigett before he saw her—her sniffles preceded her into the room. Phillip pulled her into Nicolas's solar and then promptly dropped her arm. He stalked away from her and stood behind Abigail's chair. Brigette's head hung low as she stood there trembling and whimpering. Her white-knuckled hands were clasped in front of her. Nicolas might have had compassion for his sister if she weren't the one responsible for this atrocity.

"You may have a few moments with Isabelle, but you mustn't overtax her with your theatrics. I will not suffer it," Nicolas forced through clenched teeth.

"Thank you," Brigette said softly.

Nicolas wouldn't have heard Brigette's answer if he hadn't been looking directly at her face. He waved his hand for Brigette to proceed him into Elizabeth's room. He was afraid of what he might do if he touched his sister. Brigette's tread was light as she shuffled into the next room. When Nicolas looked down, he saw that Brigette was barefoot. Phillip must have caught her unaware when he hauled her out of her room.

Elizabeth opened her eyes when Brigette stood just inside the doorway. She held out her hand toward Brigette. "Come, sweet girl." That was all the encouragement Brigette needed. She hurried to Elizabeth's side and fell to her knees with her forehead on the bed.

"I'm so sorry. Please, please forgive me! The fault is all mine," she wailed.

"I do forgive you," Elizabeth said compassionately. She stroked Brigette's hair as she tried to reassure Brigette of her love. "We all make mistakes, Brigette."

"But mine was a most grievous error in judgment. I know I am destined for eternal torment," she cried.

"Did you confess your sin to God and ask for His forgiveness?" Elizabeth asked delicately.

Brigette lifted her tear stained face to look directly at Elizabeth. "Oh, yes—many times over I have begged for God's forgiveness, and that He would allow me a chance to speak to you before my punishment is final."

"There's no need to keep asking God to forgive you for the same sin. When you ask with a repentant heart, He hears you the first time and puts that sin as far from Him as the East is from the West. The hard part is for us to forgive ourselves—that will come in time. Is there anyone else from whom you need to ask forgiveness?"

With her head bowed, Brigette twisted slightly to glance back at Nicolas. "Nicolas," she confessed. Her eyes swung swiftly back to Elizabeth.

"Nicolas, did you hear Brigette?" Elizabeth asked.

"I am not ready to discuss it," Nicolas stated from his rigid stance in the corner of the room.

"Nicolas?" Elizabeth asked more forcefully.

"I will talk with Brigette further about this matter. I'm sure in time we will reach some type of settlement. Please let that be enough for now, Isabelle," he pleaded.

"All right. For now." Glancing back at Brigette, she asked, "Is there anyone else?"

"Phillip, Thomas . . . I guess everyone in our realm," she sobbed. "All the people love you—I have sinned against them all," she bawled in earnest.

"Once the people know that I hold no animosity toward you, they, too, will absolve you of guilt. Now, dry those tears. I want you to bath, eat your midday meal, and pray for God's help in forgiving yourself. All will be as it should be . . . you will see."

Brigette grabbed and kissed Elizabeth's free hand. "Thank you, Isabelle. I don't deserve your forgiveness, yet you have offered it. I am most grateful," Brigette said as fresh tears began to fall.

"Go and do likewise, Brigette. Treat people the way you want to be treated. Allow God's love to take up residence in your heart so much that His love will spill out onto others from your abundance. God has a special plan for your life, Brigette. You must read His word and obey His commands. Now, off with you."

Standing at the door to Nicolas's room, Brigette turned and said, "Isabelle, I love you like a mother." With a loud sob, Brigette flew from the room.

Tears gathered in Elizabeth's eyes. "Well, I think that went well."

From the darkened corner where he had been watching, Nicolas said, "Isabelle, you handled Brigette with a mother's touch. You knew the words that would calm her and bring about her healing."

"Thank you, husband. I love her as if she were my own; but enough of this mushy stuff. I would appreciate having my midday meal in my room. I need fortification before I see my assailant."

33

Collette had just left the room with the remainder of Isabelle's meal when Nicolas erupted. "Isabelle, you have done enough for one day. You must cease your activities or risk reopening your wound. I've known of others who came down with a detrimental fever when they didn't rest adequately."

Elizabeth acted as if he hadn't spoken. "Please get Agnes to help me prepare to talk with Eugene. I will not allow him to see me in this bed where I look helpless. I want to be dressed, have my hair combed, and be sitting in the war room."

"What? The war room?" Nicolas sputtered. When she continued to stare at him through mere slits, he threw up his hands in defeat and dropped down in the chair at her bedside. "Isabelle, I seem to be off balance when I am in your presence and very seldom the victor when we disagree. You have the tenacity of a seasoned warrior. I am pleased we are allies for you can be a most formidable opponent."

Elizabeth reached for his hand that was upon his knee. Once their fingers laced together, she said, "You may seal our future alliance with a kiss if it pleases you."

Nicolas scooted out of the chair onto his knees positioning his head near her pillow. "As you command, my courageous wife,"

Nicolas said against her lips." He didn't linger long with his kiss for fear of overtaxing her stamina—she could be quite passionate.

"Please help me sit up on the edge of this bed. I have much to do when Agnes arrives."

Nicolas noticed how wobbly Elizabeth was once she was sitting upright. "You are unsteady."

"Hurry . . . go . . . I'll manage," Elizabeth said with effort.

"Abigail, your assistance is needed," Nicolas bellowed.

Elizabeth glared scathingly at her husband. Nicolas's raised brow was her only reply. Once Abigail was by her side, off Nicolas sprinted to do his wife's bidding. Knowing this would be an unpleasant exchange between Eugene and Isabelle, he wanted it over and done with. He gave new orders for Thomas to return Eugene to the dungeon until his wife had finished preparations. It gave Nicolas some satisfaction to know that Eugene would ponder his fate while he languished with the rats—a small recompense.

※ ※ ※

"I do not like it," Nicolas reiterated again. "You are not strong enough to withstand this confrontation."

Elizabeth sat perched on Nicolas's throne chair in the war room—a queen ready to behead her enemy. Her face flushed, from anger or exertion, Nicolas was unsure. Yet when he glanced at her hand resting on the arm of the chair, she appeared delicate . . . almost fragile. Her bandaged arm and shoulder were hidden under her overtunic so Eugene could not comprehend the extent of the injury he had inflicted.

"When he arrives, let me do the talking. Understood?" Elizabeth directed her question at Nicolas.

She sounds like me! "Yes, Isabelle, I understand. However, I will intervene if I think your strength is waning. Understood?" He didn't want to provoke her, but she needed to remember who was in charge.

Elizabeth ignored Nicolas and focused her attention straight ahead at the massive doors pushed open by Thomas. There stood

Eugene with an iron collar attached to a chain which adjoined the shackles on his wrists and ankles. He was flanked by two heavily armed guards. Thomas gave a slight tug to the chain which propelled Eugene forward to stand in front of Elizabeth. Eugene wore his disdain like a theatrical mask—easily seen by all.

"Kneel before Lady Fairwick," Thomas growled.

"Thank you for your respect, Thomas, but that is not necessary. I wish to look my attacker in the eyes," Elizabeth said. "Please know, Eugene that you are free to say what is on your heart without additional repercussion. So without further ado, why did you wish to kill me?"

That's my battle commander—straight to the heart of the matter, Nicolas thought.

Eugene's angry eyes shifted to Nicolas before he spoke. Once Nicolas had nodded his head to proceed, Eugene answered. "You were a threat to my beloved," he sneered.

"Your beloved would be Brigette?" she asked.

Eugene's eyes grew large for a brief moment before he cloaked his reaction. "I will not name her. That would put her life in danger."

"It matters not. Brigette has already confessed to her part in the scheme to end my life," Elizabeth declared.

"You are the reason her life is in peril. All would be well between us if you had died," he snarled. "You caused a rift between my beloved and me."

"Cease, you filthy dog," Thomas spit out as he kicked Eugene in his stomach. The blow brought Eugene to his knees.

"Thomas, stop at once," Elizabeth ordered. Turning her attention on Eugene, she offered him some hope. "Eugene, you know I have the power over your life as my husband and I decide your fate? Have you no remorse in your part of this plot?"

"My only regret is that I failed." His face contorted with wickedness as he glared at Elizabeth. It was apparent to all in the room that Eugene oozed evil from his defiant stance to his twisted expression.

"Eugene, just as Christ granted the thief on the cross pardon, you have the same opportunity. It is not too late to repent and seek our Savior," she replied calmly.

Eugene laughed at her appeal. "I want no part of God!"

Elizabeth didn't even flinch from Eugene's insolence. "Oh, Eugene, my heart is heavy for you. You should never pass up the chance to redeem your soul. As long as you have breath, there is hope; but if Lord Fairwick decides not to spare your life, all hope is lost. You will spend all eternity in torment."

"My life is already forfeit; I want no part of God . . . or you," he hissed. His countenance screamed of meanness and hatred.

"I deeply regret your reply. Though you reject God's love, I will continue to pray for your salvation," Elizabeth offered.

"This inquisition is concluded. Remove the prisoner to the dungeon where he will await his sentencing," Nicolas commanded.

Eugene resisted the pull on his chains as the guards hauled him toward the door. "Do you really think Lord Fairwick will allow me to live?" His laughter echoed around the room. "Then you do not know of your husband's cruelty to prisoners," Eugene spewed out with his evil tongue.

Once Eugene was out of sight, Elizabeth slumped in her seat. "I knew it," Nicolas said as he knelt in front of his wife. "This was too much of a strain on your stamina; and no, I do not torture my prisoners. He told an untruth."

"I didn't believe him. You are a noble man; of this I know." Tears filled her eyes. "Oh, Nicolas, I know he is a liar and evil in other ways; but he will spend eternity separated from God if he doesn't repent."

Holding her cold, limp hand between his two sturdy ones, he tried to comfort her. "Isabelle, you cannot save a man; he must choose to trust our Lord and Savior. You have planted a seed. Mayhap time in the dungeon will change his mind, and he will seek our Lord Jesus." As tears dripped down her chin, Nicolas lifted her into his arms and took her to their room. A respite was needed.

* * *

Elizabeth had slept the afternoon away while Nicolas, Phillip, and Thomas had discussed business and their plans for Eugene. "I say behead him in front of all our people to remind everyone that this kind of behavior will not be tolerated," Thomas said in anger.

"Thomas, that is too gruesome for children to witness. I think we should hang him from the gallows until he is dead," Phillip offered instead.

"Phillip, how is hanging any better for the children to see than a beheading?" Nicolas asked incredulously.

"There's no blood involved," Phillip said matter-of-factly.

"I will not hear of it!"

Three heads swiveled to see Elizabeth holding onto the door frame between the rooms. Nicolas had insisted that she would rest better in the quiet of her room while the three brothers talked in his solar. After recovering from the surprise, Nicolas hurried over to assist his wife.

"Isabelle, you should have called me. I would have carried you in here to be with the family," Nicolas said contritely.

"Then I would have missed your plans for Eugene, gentlemen," she said with force. Thomas hopped out of his chair to make a place for Elizabeth. Nicolas pulled the stool close to support her feet and legs. "I am comfortable, husband. Thank you." She eyed each one with a pointed look. "Now, I'm ready to speak of Eugene's punishment."

She watched as the brothers looked from one to the other. Their faces told much. They had no intention of discussing any of this with her; hence, the whispers she had heard from her bed. "Well?"

"This is not an appropriate conversation to have with you, Isabelle. We, brothers, come together to plan our battle strategies, as well as the treatment of prisoners and such," Nicolas said.

"Exactly," Thomas hurriedly added.

"I think 'tis time to get Abigail and have our evening meal," Phillip said as he made his way toward the door.

"Stop right there, Phillip. The four of us will come to an agreement over Eugene's sentence. I'm the one who was shot with the arrow; therefore, I should have a say in his judgment."

"It is nigh on the evening meal; why don't we have our meal together and then discuss his verdict?" Nicolas proposed. Thomas and Phillip nodded in one accord.

"I think not. 'Tis a dreadful ploy you have concocted to leave me out of this. If you three are so famished, then we need to hurry this little conference along." The vexation written on their faces was enough to make Elizabeth smile, but she refrained. No need letting them know that she found amusement in foiling their plans. "He is not to be killed or left to rot in the dungeon," Elizabeth announced.

All three of them exploded and were talking and sputtering at the same time. Watching their facial expressions and body language was almost comical for Elizabeth if she hadn't realized the gravity of the situation.

"Isabelle, you leave us no other recourse for Eugene's transgression. If we can't hang him or leave him in the dungeon, what are we to do?" Nicolas stammered.

"You can banish him from our realm," she answered with a calm voice. "Let God do with him as He sees fit. If you end Eugene's life, then he has no chance of trusting Christ our Lord." She saw the three brothers were crestfallen. "I'm sorry if you are disappointed that death will not be involved, but that is my ruling on the matter," she said with authority, "one I think will please our Savior." She had sealed the decision with her final words. How could any of them argue against allowing God to exact vengeance? "Might I remind you that the Bible says, 'Vengeance is Mine, thus saith the Lord?'" she added for good measure.

"Isabelle," Nicolas groaned. "How long have you been planning this conclusion?"

"Since I saw the evil in his face. I cannot be at peace with any other ruling, Nicolas," she said quietly.

The necks of Thomas and Phillip were sure to break from rotating back and forth between Nicolas and Elizabeth. They were wise not to intrude on the conversation. Best to let Nicolas control his own wife.

"As you decree," Nicolas conceded.

"As you . . ." Thomas began before being cut off by a compelling glance from Nicolas. The three of them were stunned by the turn of events. One moment they had been in charge, and the next Elizabeth had taken over the debate.

"I am most appreciative of your consent, my husband. God will take care of the details. Shall we eat?" She decided a quick change in the topic would be best. Let them stew on her decision over a meal. "Nicolas, will you carry me to the grand hall? I'm feeling a wee bit weak."

Snapping out of his bewilderment, Nicolas readily agreed. He lifted her gently and held her close to his heart. With her hand wrapped around his neck and playing with his hair, Nicolas had eyes for her only. Thomas and Phillip watched them parade out the door without a by-your-leave.

"Did you see that? Nicolas agreed to Isabelle's plea for Eugene's miserable life! What is happening to our brother?" Thomas asked befuddled.

"Ah, Thomas. One day you will experience this illness of the heart. It can be a most painful, yet an exhilarating condition. This state of the heart causes one to act in a way absolutely opposite of one's customary behavior. Love . . . Nicolas is undeniably in love with his wife," Phillip said with a grin spread across his face.

Thomas stood completely still while he absorbed all that Phillip had said. Shaking his head he concluded, "I don't think I want that sickness. It seems quite dangerous."

"One day you will think differently. Come. Let us go break our bread together," Phillip said as he clapped Thomas on the back.

34

The great hall was buzzing with activity. Nicolas had sent word to Collette that Elizabeth would be joining them for the evening meal. Cloths and the silver candlestick holders adorned all the tables. The room smelled sweet from the fresh rushes on the floor while the fireplace blazed bright. All dogs had been returned to the kennels for the duration of the meal. Elizabeth had made her preferences clear about nasty, smelly dogs in the dining hall. Therefore, the wishes of their lady were to be carried out to please her. Fresh greenery and peacock feathers garnished the tables in honor of Elizabeth's attendance.

Nicolas stood in the archway allowing his wife to gaze upon the finery in the room. "Oh, my!" Elizabeth exclaimed. "The room is so grand. 'Tis as beautiful as the day of our wedding feast. Did you arrange this?" she asked looking back at Nicolas.

"After the drama of the day, I thought some festivities were in order."

"What a wonderful idea, husband. I must admit, I'm thankful to see only peacock feathers this time," she said with a mischievous smile.

Nicolas strolled onward and stopped in the middle of the room. He made a slow turn so Elizabeth could see all of the embellishments. "This is all for you, Isabelle. The mercy you extended to Brigette and Eugene has run rampant through the castle and the village. From the scullery maid to the cobbler in the village, your compassion for others is renowned. Without ceasing, the villagers have asked how they might be of assistance in your care; and this was my lone plan. There will be music as well."

"It's just perfect," she sighed.

Nicolas continued to the high table and placed Elizabeth in her chair decked with colorful ribbons and satin. "Your throne, my lady." Elizabeth slid from his arms into her chair without a hitch. Abigail and Phillip were already in their places next to Nicolas's seat.

Thomas stood and bowed toward Elizabeth before she was seated. "I am delighted we are seated side by side. Mayhap my brother will allow us to converse during the meal," he said playfully.

"Thomas, you never cease to try to annoy your brother. Remember, he is older and . . . larger than you," she said with a grin.

As she turned back toward the room, much to her surprise and delight, the guards had escorted Brigette up to the doorway. Elizabeth saw how the servants were eyeing Brigette as if unsure how to treat her since they knew of her part in the assassination attempt. Some began whispering among themselves. Elizabeth wasn't going to tolerate Brigette's being snubbed; she struggled to stand to her feet and called out, "Brigette, I'm so glad you could join the festivities. Please, come and join me at the table." Elizabeth extended her hand toward Brigette which caused her to wobble on her feet. Nicolas quickly grabbed Elizabeth by the waist to give her support. With her head down, Brigette weaved her way through the men and women until she reached Elizabeth's hand.

Brigette stood on the other side of the table and curtsied low to Elizabeth and then kissed her outstretched hand. "My lady, 'tis an honor to be at your table."

"Brigette, come and sit beside me. Thomas, please move down one place to make room for your sister." Thomas scowled at Brigette, but obeyed Elizabeth—even if he did so resentfully.

The room had gone deathly quiet as all watched the scene unfold. Thomas made his displeasure apparent with his huffing, not to mention the loud scraping of his stool. Brigette quietly took his place on the stool and rested her tightly clasped hands in her lap. When Nicolas eased Elizabeth into her seat, she whispered into his ear, "Do something."

At first Nicolas gave her a bewildered look until he saw her eyes cut to the open room. She added a slight nod of her head to make sure he comprehended the problem. He gave her an annoyed frown before he stood to his full height and clapped his hands. "Where is Father Bryan? 'Tis time for the blessing."

Father Bryan walked into the middle of the room where he would easily be heard by all. "Please, let us stand and join hands in one accord on this special evening. We are grateful for God's mercy He has extended to Lady Isabelle and wish to unite our prayers as we seek God's forgiveness of our sins and blessings for good health by all."

The men removed their hats, and then every man, woman, and child stood with their hands linked together. Elizabeth remained seated but couldn't help but smile. Joy filled her heart at the affectionate scene before her. She let her eyes roam the room until she saw precious Henry holding the hand of his sister. Overcome with emotion, she bowed her head in praise to God for all His provisions for her.

"Dear Lord God Almighty and Father Everlasting Who hast safely brought us to the beginning of this day by Thy holy power, grant that we keep Thy holy laws and do Thy holy will. Lord deliver us from all evil, from all sins and from all the temptations of the Devil and keep us safe from all perils. Sweet Lord Jesus defend us, give us strength and good health, the will to do what is right, and the courage to live justly in this world and not to fail. Lord, save us that we may sleep in peace and awake with Thee in the glory of paradise . . ." Nicolas stomped his foot and loudly cleared his throat. Father Bryan's head snapped up to see Lord Fairwick staring at him. The prayer came to an immediate close. "And our Great and Mighty Father in Heaven, bless this meal and the loving hands that prepared it for our partaking. In Christ's Holy and Precious name I ask it, Amen."

"Thank you, Father," Nicolas said. "Let us begin our feast . . . musicians, please."

Shuffling noises filled the room as everyone took their places at the tables heavy with food. "You will need to assist Isabelle; try not to poison her," Thomas said under his breath to his sister. Brigette let out a shocked gasp as her head whipped around to look at Thomas.

Elizabeth observed Brigette's rigid posture and heard her quick intake of air. She tilted her head toward the siblings and asked, "Brigette, what is amiss between you and Thomas?"

With both elbows on the table, Nicolas leaned around Elizabeth and jumped in the conversation before Brigette could respond. "I will not abide theatrics betwixt you two. Your strife must be set aside while we dine this evening. Is that understood, Thomas? . . . Brigette?" Nicolas asked with a formidable frown.

Brigette once again lowered her head as a lone tear slipped down her cheek. "Yes, my lord." Thomas was not as penitent. In answer, he gave a slight jerk of his head when words failed.

The mood at the family table had been set. Tense. Nerve-racking. How could anyone at the high board possibly enjoy the festivities when there was such animosity amongst family members? Thankfully, the gathering in the room was too engrossed in their merrymaking to notice discord among the Fairwicks. Music from the stringed instruments floated on the air mingled with laughter and lighthearted banter.

Even though the quarrel had been slight, Elizabeth's body had tensed during the altercation causing pain to radiate from her wound. Along with the pain, Elizabeth felt certain she was running a fever—alternating between shivers and sweats. Not wanting to alert Nicolas to her condition, Elizabeth pasted on her smile determined to make polite conversation.

With a choppy sigh Brigette whispered, "I should not have come."

"Nonsense. I wanted you here," Elizabeth soothed. "It will make me happy if you will eat and act as if you are having a grand time of it. Can you do that for me?"

"As you wish, my lady." Brigette said one thing but her anguished eyes told a different story. "I will attempt to do all that you ask." A weak smile followed her remark.

"Thank you, my sweet. I do love you, and your presence alone puts me in high spirits." Elizabeth watched as her words worked magic on Brigette's wounded soul. Her countenance brightened, and she sat up straighter.

Elizabeth attempted to eat enough so Nicolas wouldn't fret over her. However, her appetite had not returned since being pierced with the arrow. The dinner time passed in slow motion for Elizabeth as she watched the tables being cleared and moved for some lively dancing by the peasants. None of the family ventured out on the floor, but no one seemed to notice or care. Even Jarvis took a twirl around the room during one of the dances. It was quite a scene to witness, bringing a smile to Elizabeth's face. Nevertheless, she wilted more with each passing hour.

Nicolas had ventured into a debate with Phillip when Elizabeth had been talking with Brigette. Every once in a while she would hear a derisive snort emerge from her husband, but it didn't concern her. She knew the brothers could discuss controversial topics for hours with yelling, as well as pounding fists, and still emerge unscathed—even surface with laughter. On the other hand, females caught in a dispute might scream, kick, pull hair, and leave madder than when they started. Women could learn much from their men on resolving arguments.

When Elizabeth lightly touched Nicolas's arm, the look on his face would have alarmed her if she didn't already feel like a woman with one foot in the grave. Shaking her head, she said, "Nicolas, if I didn't know you better, you could have made me swoon from that fierce expression. I must look a fright."

"You are the most beautiful of women, my beloved. But I must apologize for overlooking your needs and not returning you to our bedchamber long ago. Your face manifests your fatigue.

Come. We will bid our guests good eventide." He stood and lifted her into his arms.

Elizabeth wrapped her free arm around Nicolas's neck. As had become her custom, she threaded her fingers through his collar-length hair and nestled her head on his shoulder. Without a word, they made their way out of the room. The dancers parted, leaving a wide pathway for Nicolas and Elizabeth to traverse. With her eyes closed, Elizabeth didn't see the troubled features on their faces. It was plain to see they feared for their lady's life—some with tear-filled eyes.

* * *

All was quiet as Nicolas walked down the passageway to their room except for his clicking boots on the stone floor. Burning torches lit the hall so Nicolas had no fear of tripping while carrying his precious wife. Standing outside of Nicolas's solar door was Angus who had guarded the room while Nicolas and Elizabeth were downstairs in the main hall. He nodded to Nicolas that all was well before Nicolas entered the room. The solar had a roaring fire in the hearth to ward off the chill in the air, as well as burning candles to provide light. Nicolas decided that his wife would sleep with him tonight. He knew not the number of days Elizabeth had left; therefore, no more separation would be permitted.

"We are here," he said softly.

"I'll sit in your lap near the fireplace. Does that please you?"

"Yes. Holding you close to my heart always pleases me." Nicolas eased into a chair with his bundle as Elizabeth pulled her arm into her lap. Her touch was frail; in his judgment her weight was too light. How would she ever heal if she kept losing weight? He breathed deeply of her hair close to his nose; her softness and scent enveloped him.

"Stop sniffing my hair," she whispered. "I probably smell like smoke from the great hearth downstairs."

"Nay. You are delightful." With a slight reprimand, he said, "I had hoped you would go to sleep."

"I want to talk."

"Isabelle, you are beyond exhaustion."

"I don't wish to waste another minute of my time with you. We both know I'm getting weaker instead of stronger."

"Stop speaking as if you will not survive. I won't hear of it," he said with anguish.

"My apologies."

She remained quiet for a few moments. He hoped the drumming of his heartbeat in her ear along with the crackling fire would lull her to sleep. She felt hot to his touch which was not a good sign. Feeling helpless, he knew he would need to have Agnes in their room for the night. She would know what to do for his wife's delicate condition. Thankfully, Elizabeth's breathing became more even as she dozed monetarily. Nicolas closed his eyes in a silent prayer. *Oh, gracious God and Father, please spare my wife. She is most precious to me . . . I need her . . .* Before he could finish his prayer, Elizabeth let out a deep sigh. Realizing there was no hope for it, he gave up trying to get her to rest; she was quite stubborn.

"I have something to say, and I don't want to be interrupted. Understand?" Elizabeth spoke quietly.

She has learned well; she sounds like me when I give orders. "Yes, my wife." Nicolas couldn't help but smile at his little commander.

"Now, remember. Hold your tongue until I'm finished." She placed her hand on his cheek and brought his attention to her eyes that were fixed on him. "You are a courageous and noble husband. I couldn't have picked a more honorable man to be my mate. You are valiant in the face of danger, and you love as fiercely as you do battle. My distrust in you at the beginning has given way to my devotion," she smiled. "God was gracious to me when he dropped me on your doorstep. I know not how long I will tarry, but I want you to know that I have no regrets in marrying you. It has been a glorious adventure."

Nicolas sat spellbound by her words while his chest burned from within. At no other time had he ever felt such deep anguish of his soul; the thought of his wife's death was crushing. It far outweighed his own mother's passing. Elizabeth had crawled in and taken up residence in his very moral fiber. Gazing into her eyes, he wondered how he was ever to carry on without her. "Oh, my Isabelle." Nicolas leaned his head against hers. "You are as necessary to me as my next breath. I do not wish to look into the future and not find you there. I love you." He gave her a light kiss with trembling lips. "I have prayed diligently for your recovery and for the Lord's help through this darkness. He will hold you safe in His bosom. So until our Lord and Savior separates us, we will speak of this no more. Understand?" he asked with a wink trying to dispel his own torment.

"Of course, my husband. You are in command, after all," she added sweetly.

Nicolas threw back his head and roared with laughter. "Surely you jest? Since setting foot inside this castle, you have ceased to let me be in command. Why, every person in this castle bows to your wishes and desires. Of this, I know for a fact." He watched her give him a mischievous smile in return.

Elizabeth cocked her head. "Did you hear that?" she asked. "I think I heard thunder. Let's go peer out the window and see what God is doing, shall we?"

Nicolas just shook his head. Here she was giving orders again, but he didn't mind. She could command him for all eternity if she would just stay by his side. "Certainly, my precious." After reaching the window, Nicolas stood Elizabeth on her feet and wrapped his arm around her tiny waist. They surveyed God's handiwork as lightning flashed across the sky illuminating the castle grounds. The wind and rain slashed through the air as nearby trees bent in tandem with the force of the storm.

"Do you realize that I haven't had a memory flash in quite some time? I suppose God wants me to forget my past and press on toward my future He has planned for me. What think you of that, husband?"

"I'm not sure, Isabelle, but I like your reasoning." They continued to observe the thunderstorm in silence—each lost in their own thoughts—until Nicolas felt her shiver. "Come, let's rest on the bed together."

"No. I think not. I would like to go back down to the main hall and sit by the hearth. Hopefully, the hall is devoid of other people, each having returned home. The night is young; maybe we could have the family join us. I so enjoy our family discussions. May we do that?" she asked with pleading eyes.

Weariness was etched across her face; nonetheless, he couldn't deny her. "I will agree but only for a short time. You need some rest and . . . "

"And what?"

"If you must know . . . I like having you all to myself."

"Fair enough," she grinned. "Don't forget to send for Brigette and Thomas and, of course, Phillip and Abigail. I want everyone in attendance."

※ ※ ※

Elizabeth was wrapped in a blanket with her chair scooted close to the fireside. Thomas sat on the hearth and leaned against the stone wall whittling a piece of wood. Nicolas had sent for Brigette, and she had arrived with her guard as an escort. Elizabeth wasn't happy that Brigette was being treated like a prisoner, but she would take that up with her husband in private. Now was not the time to bring him to task.

Phillip walked into the room alone. "Abigail sends her regrets, but she has retired for the evening."

"What?" Thomas asked in surprise. "'Tis early."

"I had wanted to declare our news together, but I will not delay any further. Abigail is with child," Phillip announced.

Nicolas smacked Phillip on the shoulder. "Ah, so that's what ye've been about these long nights," Nicolas exclaimed with mirth. Phillip's face flushed from embarrassment.

"Nicolas," Elizabeth reprimanded as she shook her head, "that is a delicate issue, not to be discussed in mixed company."

"I beg your pardon, Isabelle," Nicolas said sheepishly while shifting his laughing eyes toward Phillip.

Elizabeth knew Nicolas wouldn't let Phillip rest over the next eight months, for he would tease Phillip without end. As she contemplated the excitement surrounding Abigail's pregnancy, she just hoped she would still be around to help Agnes deliver the baby. However, based on the dreadful way she was feeling, it was doubtful.

She noticed that Brigette was off to the side of the group as if she didn't belong. Elizabeth yearned to bridge the chasm between Brigette and her brothers. Phillip seemed to accept Brigette's presence without being troubled, but Thomas and Nicolas had yet to even look her way. "Brigette, bring your chair close to mine," Elizabeth encouraged. "Women need to stick together when there are so many brawny men about."

"You have that aright. I almost took down Braden in our recent sword practice," Thomas boasted. Elizabeth could have sworn Thomas's chest inflated after his bold statement.

"Thomas, you have yet to best me," Nicolas added.

Thomas was not deterred. "I will one day, brother mine. Be on your guard," he said with a silly grin directed at Elizabeth.

So began the bantering among the brothers which was a harmonious tune to Elizabeth. As the men talked of swords, knives, and killing enemies, Elizabeth tried to draw Brigette out of her tightly woven cocoon. "Brigette, have you worked on your needlepoint lately?"

Brigette barely looked at Elizabeth before dropping her head down again. "No, my lady. I have been distracted."

Elizabeth reached out her free hand and touched Brigette's chin. "You may call me Isabelle. Now, hold your head up and look me in the eye when you are speaking to me. I have forgiven you, and I wish our former relationship to return. No more shamefaced behavior. Please?"

"I will do my best . . . Isabelle," Brigette said and followed her statement with a tentative smile.

As the family discussed various topics, the storm continued to rage and beat hard upon the glass panes. At one point, Phillip and Nicolas walked over and made sure the shutters were fastened shut. While they were on the other side of the room, Braden bolted into the room with a frantic expression. "Fire! The barn is on fire!" he exclaimed.

Thomas and Phillip ran from the room while Nicolas ran toward Elizabeth. He pointed his finger at Brigette. "You, to your room." Then he pointed at his wife. "You, stay put. I will return post haste. You will be safe here." As Elizabeth drew breath to speak, he was gone.

Brigette's eyes were wide with fear, but she didn't offer any resistance to her brother's command. Her guard dragged her out of the room with speed born from alarm. Guards and servants rushed past the room; some carried buckets while others carried cloths to beat at the fire. Elizabeth could hear the shouts of orders being given and screams from those most likely paralyzed by fear.

"Stay in this room, indeed," Elizabeth spoke to the empty room. She pushed herself up onto wobbly legs. After pausing for a moment, her balance was more secure. Having her arm bound to her body was certainly an inconvenience. With her free hand, she grabbed the broom propped on the hearth to help keep her upright. Her steps were slow and deliberate but determined as she made her way toward the outside door. The only sound in the grand hallway was her shuffling feet against the background of the raging storm. Thankfully, the massive door stood ajar as the people scurried out to fight the blaze; at least she wouldn't have to struggle to get outside.

The moment Elizabeth stepped outside, the rain pelted her face. She rapidly blinked away the water to clear her vision and see what was happening. People whizzed past her as she picked her way down the steps. Once on solid ground, she gazed at the frenzied activity surrounding the castle—guards had formed a human wall to direct the horses toward the back of the castle as they bounded out the barn door. The barn that housed Midnight was fully ablaze. As Elizabeth looked on in distress, a pain raced across her forehead causing her to stumble. *Cinnamon!* Shaking her head, another ache skittered over her eyes. *Garrett! He's trying to escape on Cinnamon. Oh, no! He sees me. He has a gun. Nana. Papaw.* Memories flooded her mind—almost too rapid to comprehend. *Liz, come back. What's the matter with you?*

Elizabeth fell to her knees as she recalled each incident that had occurred on her last day on the farm. Her name was Elizabeth and her cousin, Garrett, might have murdered her grandparents! With that realization, Elizabeth doubled over in agony and let loose a blood-chilling scream that rent the air.

* * *

All of the horses in the barn had been turned loose to run free of the burning stable except Midnight. Nicolas had a halter on Midnight so he could protect her from the other horses and pull her to safety. Her eyes rolled back as she yanked against his hold. She was terrified of the blaze and smoke that swirled around them. As she screamed from fright, she tried to rear up and break away. With all his might, Nicolas held fast as they made their way to the entrance of the barn and freedom. Just as horse and warrior emerged from the blackened, smoke-filled barn, Elizabeth's scream ripped through the storm and reached Nicolas. He immediately recognized that cry—Isabelle. Surely not! He had left her safely ensconced by the hearth—or so he thought.

With Nicolas slightly distracted, Midnight broke free and took off at a run. Midnight's head was down as she crashed through the barrier of men with her sights on Elizabeth. Bedlam ensued. With the break in the hedge of men, horses ran and kicked in all directions. Nicolas yelled out but to no avail. There was no stopping Midnight. The guards had their hands full trying to divert the stampeding horses. *Isabelle will be trampled!* Nicolas took off at a run. He had to reach his wife!

Nicolas saw Elizabeth slouched at the bottom of the keep steps. She must have fallen down the stairs and landed on her injured shoulder. She rocked back and forth as her tortured cries filled the air. Nicolas kept running but knew he wouldn't reach her before Midnight. He stopped midway to the keep and watched in horror as Midnight skidded to a halt and straddled Elizabeth. He could barely keep his eyes focused on the scene knowing his wife would be torn to shreds by Midnight's hooves. However, to his astonishment, it appeared that Midnight was protecting Elizabeth from the other charging horses. Midnight nipped and struck out with her hooves at any horse or person that came near; yet she never touched Elizabeth.

"Isabelle, don't move," Nicolas yelled.

Thomas, Braden, Robert, and Hastings had redirected the horses closest to Elizabeth in an attempt to save her. When Nicolas reached the men, he slowed his pace. He quickly devised a plan with Thomas to rescue Elizabeth. Midnight was still quite excitable; not wanting to further endanger Elizabeth's life, Nicolas held out his hand to gentle the horse. The worst of the storm had moved on and left a steady rainfall in its wake. Nicolas spoke soft words to Midnight in hopes of settling her enough for Thomas to capture the halter while Nicolas grabbed Elizabeth. He might cause additional harm to her wound, but it couldn't be helped.

When the time was right, Nicolas gave the signal; quicker than an arrow leaving the bow, Nicolas snatched his wife into the safety of his embrace. She quivered uncontrollably while Nicolas trembled from fear for his wife. He rushed inside barking out orders and calling for Agnes with each step. A flurry of activity took place in preparation of drying and warming up Elizabeth. She was already weak; this incident could take her to the grave.

"I remembered . . . I remembered!" Elizabeth exclaimed as she turned tormented eyes his way. "And it's not good," she cried in anguish.

"Hush, my love. I will make it right—of this I pledge," Nicolas said with reassurance.

"No, you can't fix it. You can't fix it," she whimpered.

Nicolas was thankful when Elizabeth ceased her disturbing remarks. By now, he was afraid. He was afraid she might have another husband. What if she had another family that would demand her return? She might even be a princess from another country, and her father would seek revenge on Nicolas over the forced marriage. His stomach churned with uncertainty while his mind reeled with unanswered questions.

Take therefore no thought for the morrow: for the morrow shall take thought for the things of itself. Sufficient unto the day is the evil thereof. God had spoken to Nicolas through His Word in Matthew 6. Nicolas had to remember that God was in control of his life, as well as Isabelle's. Nothing depended upon Nicolas except his obedience to his Lord and Savior, Jesus Christ. May God have mercy on them all.

35

All three brothers found themselves in Nicolas's chamber with a monumental problem to solve. Elizabeth had revealed all of her memories to Nicolas and now he wondered about her sanity—from the future, indeed. That was impossible . . . wasn't it? How much should he tell his brothers? If they knew all, would they fear Isabelle . . . or rather Elizabeth? Nicolas rubbed his aching head. He glanced over at his wife's sleeping form that was all but lost in their huge bed. Agnes had given her a sleeping potion; she would finally receive the rest her body had craved all day. Elizabeth was fitful. Her abundance of tears had left her body racked with hiccupping sobs even in her sleep.

Each brother had taken the opportunity to wash the soot from his arms, hands, and faces; but their clothes still reeked of smoke. There had been no time to change clothes. Braden had taken over command of the men left to battle the remainder of the fire when Elizabeth had needed help. There had been no saving the barn; fortunately, only one horse had received burns from a falling beam. The torrential downpour had helped to extinguish the blaze. If only the raging storm within Nicolas could be so easily doused.

Nicolas studied his brothers as he thought over the latest catastrophe. Normally, Thomas would be pacing the room and spouting out his idea of how to remedy the problem. Not tonight.

He was unusually quiet in the wake of the recent events. Phillip was tense, but calm on the outside. That was an attribute of a great leader—controlled emotion. Rubbing his gritty eyes, Nicolas stood near the fireplace.

"Isabelle has recalled her past," he said reluctantly.

"Is she wed to another?" Thomas blurted out as he leaned forward.

"No."

Phillip remained stoic while Thomas released a deep sigh of relief. Thomas's immaturity was glaringly evident to Nicolas. It made him appreciate Phillip's wisdom and calm in the face of danger, or in this case, in the face of the unknown.

"Her family is not our enemy . . . 'tis where she hails from 'twill be our challenge."

"If 'tis far, then we can wait until spring . . ." Thomas began before Nicolas held up his hand for silence.

"Cease your interruptions, Thomas, or you will not be included in this discussion. 'Tis a grave matter I must present . . . a grave matter, to be sure." Nicolas sat down on the hearth; with his elbows resting on his knees, his head hung low. "What I am about to reveal must not leave this room." Peering up at Phillip, he said, "No one, not even Abigail, must know this information. It could produce severe consequences for Isabelle."

"As you request," Phillip said in all seriousness. Thomas nodded his head in agreement with eyes wide.

"Isabelle's given name is Elizabeth. That name is foreign on my lips; therefore, I will continue to refer to her as Isabelle. There is another suitor in her past, but they were not betrothed. Isabelle said she had gone to visit her grandparents on their farm. She was at that farm when her injuries occurred as she fled from her evil cousin. She is convinced that her cousin, Garrett, attempted to murder her grandparents—and might have succeeded. Of that, Isabelle is unsure."

Phillip steeped his fingers under his chin. "What is her request of you, brother?"

"Isabelle wishes to return to her grandparent's farm to see what has become of them."

"Do you find this an unusual request?" Phillip asked with a tilt of his head.

There was a long pause while Nicolas massaged his temples. He looked at his brothers with sorrow-filled eyes. "She claims to be from a future time."

"A future time?" Thomas asked. "What mean you?"

"A time in history that is still to come. Over three hundred years in the future, according to Isabelle," Nicolas said softly.

"Preposterous!" Thomas said in a loud whisper as his head swiveled around to look at the bed where Elizabeth stirred.

Phillip sat very still while shaking his head. "Not another word of this. Not even in this room. I shudder to think what could happen to Isabelle if she were tried as a witch," he whispered.

"I have to agree with you, brother. However, I will grant her this one request—to return to the place where we found her. She insists that if she climbs into the tree, somehow she will be returned to her location in time. I have agreed to take her on the morrow. I will climb to the first limb of the tree and hold Isabelle there until she disappears from my arms, or until I deem the quest ended. Thomas, I want you to accompany me, along with Braden, Hastings, and Robert. Phillip, you will remain here. If I do not return, you will resume your place as lord of the castle."

"Do not return!" Phillip sputtered. For the first time during the discussion, Phillip was flustered.

"Isabelle believes that I will travel forward in time with her if she remains in my embrace. No matter; I will not leave her to face the waiting alone. At this point, I do not know what to believe or expect. Nevertheless, before dawn I will send two messengers to Laird McKinnon asking him to hold back his border guards. I do not wish to be questioned about our motives for sitting in a tree at the edge of our two countries."

"Do you think it wise for Isabelle to travel in her condition?" Phillip asked with concern.

Nicolas's shoulders slumped. As he rested his elbow on his thigh, he placed his forehead in his hand. "No . . . no 'tis not wise. She will probably not survive the trip." With watery eyes, he looked at Phillip. "I must grant this request—it could well be her last."

* * *

The morning greeted the travelers with a heavy mist and a thick fog covering the area. Poor visibility coupled with Elizabeth's weakened condition would probably extend their ride to well over two hours . . . much too long for Elizabeth to endure. She had insisted that she wear the bloodied gown Nicolas had found her in. He then wrapped Elizabeth in a hooded animal fur to keep her warm and to protect her from the elements; not to mention, he wanted to hide her ghastly gown. As he prepared her for their journey, Agnes had changed Elizabeth's bandage. Nicolas couldn't help but notice that her wound looked like a red spider web. Of course, it was pointless to bring it to Elizabeth's attention; he knew she would not surrender to his desire of postponing the trip until she was stronger.

During the preparation for their excursion, Elizabeth had remained quiet. Each time Nicolas had looked at her, silent tears had slipped down her cheeks. Her face was ravaged with grief; it pained him to look upon her sadness. How was he ever to make things right when she held fast to her belief that she was from the future? Nicolas had stayed awake all night pondering that question along with the knowledge that Elizabeth might not survive another day. The love he felt for his wife was deep. Having her ripped away from him would leave him to bleed to death from the damage.

A somber group rode across the drawbridge. All in their small party were privy to the seriousness of Elizabeth's condition; hence, the going would be slow. Nicolas didn't want to create a more uncomfortable journey for his wife with excessive jarring from riding too fast. For now she was nestled against his chest with her legs across his lap. His body would cushion her from the impact of riding but not from all of it. Nicolas had left off his chainmail opting to wear only his leather jerkin so he could provide Elizabeth with an easier ride, as well as feel the soft curves of his wife's body. Of course, he was not without protection; he had his sword strapped to his back and his dagger in his boot. More than likely, he would only encounter Daniel at the border who would want to see that Nicolas was not mistreating Isabelle.

With a heavy heart, Nicolas and his company trudged onward. Elizabeth dozed off and on and only spoke when Nicolas directed a question her way. She was withdrawing from him which displeased him greatly. In fact, he would not allow it.

"Isabelle? . . . Isabelle?" She squirmed and moaned when he called her name a second time. He felt some remorse for waking her when he knew she desired a reprieve from her troubles; but he needed her companionship more than his next breath. "Isabelle, are you awake?" he persisted.

"I am now," she said disgruntled.

"Ah, there is my beloved. I have missed your sweet words that drip from your lips like honey from a comb," he said tongue-in-cheek.

She peeked up at him with a crooked grin. "You should have written poetry instead of being the lord of a castle." Not giving him a chance for a rebuttal, she forged ahead. "What is it you want of me?"

"I desire not for you to withdraw from me. You have barely spoken a word to me since your memory returned. No matter what facts you have recalled, we are still husband and wife. For me, nothing has changed. I yearn for us to remain wed, and I am willing to negotiate with your family if they desire a bride price; but I need to know if you feel the same?" He had dared to leave himself vulnerable before his wife. Her next words could close the hole in his heart or split it wide open with no hope for his survival.

After a long pause, she said, "I have pledged my love to you for all time and long to remain by your side forever. I do not fear that my family will require a bride price or that they will denounce our marriage. What concerns me is that you will not wish to follow me to the future and leave all that you know. I panic at the thought of going home and not being able to come back to this time and place . . . and to you," she ended on a whisper. Elizabeth inhaled a shuddering breath as tears threatened to spill down her face while she waited on his reaction.

With tenderness, Nicolas stroked his finger down Elizabeth's cheek. "Ah, my sweet Isabelle, how I do love you." He glanced away and drew in a deep breath. Looking back at his wife, he said, "I am willing to go with you." He quickly held up his hand for silence when she would have interrupted his declaration. "Before embarking on this journey, I spoke with Phillip. He is prepared to resume his position as the Lord of Fairwick Castle if I do not return."

Elizabeth's eyes went wide with surprise. "You would do that for me even if we were never able to get back here?"

"Yea, my beloved. You have ensnared my heart. It will refuse to beat without you."

Braden called a halt just as Elizabeth started to speak. Braden and Thomas had taken the lead for their entourage. Nicolas and Elizabeth were sandwiched between their guards with Robert and Hastings bringing up the rear. When Nicolas looked up the small rise, there sitting proudly on his steed, was Laird McKinnon blocking the road. Nicolas nudged his horse forward separating Braden and Thomas.

"Wait for us here, but stay alert," Nicolas commanded his men. Elizabeth twisted around to see what had captured everyone's attention.

"Oh, my. I had hoped to avoid being seen by anyone."

"Fear not. I sent word to Daniel. There will be no other guards to confront us." Never taking his eyes off Daniel, he continued. "Let me do the talking for once, and no buts." Nicolas smiled inwardly when Elizabeth let out a snort. She did like to be in charge . . . little vixen. Once they were close enough for Daniel to hear them easily, Nicolas stopped his horse.

"Weel, Marion, hou fair ye?" Daniel inquired.

Elizabeth smiled. She had forgotten using Marion as her given name. "I think I'm dying, but Nicolas won't allow it."

Daniel quirked one brow up while his eyes stayed focused on Nicolas. "Ah sairy ta haur it. Wee William misses ye. 'e sends his loue."

"Ah . . . I do miss that sweet boy," she said longingly.

"Enough," Nicolas announced. "We have little time to keep our appointment. I thank you, laird, for withholding your men. At my wife's request, we will be checking out the area around the tree where we first found her." He flicked his head toward the bottom of the hill. "Until we meet again . . ."

"God speed to ye."

Nicolas knew Daniel watched as they descended the hill. Once Nicolas reached his men, he noticed all four of them wore scowls. "All is well. We will proceed as planned."

It had been no easy feat to get Elizabeth into the tree without further harm. She now sat on a tree limb seven feet from the ground encircled by Nicolas's arms and legs. There was no danger she would fall from the tree with Nicolas holding tight. Braden, Thomas, Hastings, and Robert were on guard in the surrounding area. Now to wait . . .

Nicolas was thankful that once Elizabeth was situated on the limb she dozed off leaning against his chest. He imagined the long ride had worn her out, not to mention the horrible ordeal of hoisting her into the tree. Nicolas leaned his head back on the tree trunk and gazed heavenward.

Almighty God, please rescue Isabelle. Whether we remain together is no longer my greatest concern. I pray You will save her. Grant her favor in Your sight and bless her frail body with Your healing. Forgive me my failings and do not hold my sins against Isabelle. I love her with my whole heart, but am willing to give her up if that's what You require. Help Your servant to endure Your decision, Christ my Lord. Amen.

After pouring his heart out to God in prayer and coming to the place where he could honestly say he would relinquish his hold over his wife, Nicolas relaxed. All was in the Lord God Almighty's hands. Nicolas dared to close his eyes and prayed he would not be alone when he awoke.

36

Beep . . . Beep . . . Beep . . .

With closed eyes, Elizabeth lay very still as she tried to place the strange sound. What was it? She flared her nostrils. And what was that smell? Her ears perked up with each unusual sound as her eyes darted back and forth under closed lids. Did she hear shuffling feet? She dared to crack open her eyes—only a slit. Bright sunshine filtered through a window and sliced through an unfamiliar room leaving a haze around each object. Scanning the room left her disoriented. She was, however, able to discern two shadowed forms present in the room . . . *friend or foe* . . . she knew not. Fear of the unknown had caused her heart to double in time. There was no help for it; she would have to open her eyes fully if she wanted answers.

As she weighed her options, pain radiated from her shoulder down her arm. It felt like someone was using her sore shoulder as a kettle drum . . . pounding . . . pounding . . . pounding! Why was the pain so excruciating . . . ? *Beep . . . Beep . . .* The arrow! Of course! She had been shot by Eugene! Events rapidly raced through her mind as she recalled her last few days with more clarity. Her eyes popped open.

"Nicolas?" she croaked.

"Elizabeth? Are you awake?" The whispered words floated across the room. One of the shadowed forms pushed up out of a chair and moved over to Elizabeth. She grabbed Elizabeth's lifeless hand that lay on the bed; unfortunately, with the light behind her, the person's face was a mere silhouette—undistinguishable.

"Who are you?" Elizabeth asked in a low voice.

"It's Nana, dear. Don't you know me?"

Once the woman leaned in closer, Elizabeth's eyes focused more clearly. "Nana?" she whispered.

"Yes, sweetheart, Nana." The woman stroked Elizabeth's hand while a frown formed between her eyes.

"Nana!" she exclaimed coming to full realization. "You're alive!"

"Well, of course I am." Nana's head swiveled away from Elizabeth as she called out, "Papaw. Wake up. Elizabeth has come back to us." Nana released Elizabeth's hand only long enough to pull her chair next to the bedside. "We have been so worried about you," Nana said as she sat down and pulled Elizabeth's hand between her two gnarled ones.

"Papaw's alive, too?" Elizabeth asked as she watched him hobble over to the bed.

"Yes, Lizzy," he said. Elizabeth observed a worried look pass between her grandparents before her Papaw continued. "You're the one who was injured during the storm."

"Storm?" Elizabeth asked. She shook her head as memories rolled around like loose marbles. "But I heard gunshots. Then I saw blood in the kitchen." The more she talked, the more clearly she began to think. The face of her cousin, Garrett, swam before her eyes. He had been at the farm that night! He had fired those shots! "When I couldn't find you, I just knew Garrett had killed you!" Elizabeth said in a rush.

"Whoa, honey. Maybe we had better start at the beginning. You seem to have your facts all twisted. It must have been from the blow to your head," Papaw said a bit too gruffly.

"I know what I heard. You and Garrett were in a heated argument, and then there were three gunshots. When I got to the kitchen, you and Nana were gone and blood was on the table and the floor." Elizabeth squirmed in the bed as she made her point. She couldn't believe her grandparents were discounting the whole episode to her imagination. Unfortunately, each movement only brought stabbing pain in her shoulder.

Nana silenced Papaw with a *look* before taking over the conversation. "Sweetheart," Nana started, "calm down before you cause yourself more harm. You've been through quite an ordeal the last few days, and we don't want a setback. Please . . . for me?" Nana pleaded.

Elizabeth reached up to rub between her eyes as her head began to pound. "Okay, Nana, please start at the beginning and tell me your side of this muddled mess," she groaned.

"Papaw, would you please tell the nurse that Elizabeth is awake. I'm sure she'll want to alert the doctor." Turning back toward Elizabeth, Nana began. "If you remember, you and Garrett were both at the farm that night. You went to bed early since you were tuckered out after traveling back from Guatemala. Papaw and Garrett were at the kitchen table discussing the needed repairs on the farm when it began to storm outside. Even though Papaw's knee hurt, he staggered out to secure the horses in the barn while Garrett yelled for him not to go. Anyway, Garrett ran out to help your Papaw, but didn't reach him in time before the barn door slammed against Papaw's head and knocked him to the ground. It took both of us to get him up and back inside the house. Papaw had a gash across his left eye. Every time his heart beat, blood spurted out. He was a mess," she said. She turned love-filled eyes on her husband of fifty-five years as he entered the room followed by a nurse and the doctor.

"Well, it's good to see you awake," the doctor said with a smile. He grabbed her chart and walked over to the bedside. "You gave your Nana and Papaw a scare when you didn't want to wake up. Let's get a few vital signs, and then I'm sure we'll be able to order you some food. I bet you're hungry," he said.

Nana and Papaw moved to the foot of the bed while the nurse and the doctor checked Elizabeth over. After asking Elizabeth some pointed questions about how she felt, the doctor told her she would stay one more night. He was pleased with her progress but felt another night of observation was in order since she had been unconscious for several days; if all went well, he might release her the following afternoon to go home with her grandparents. Upon leaving, the nurse assured Elizabeth she would get her a juice and some applesauce until dinner arrived.

After the room had cleared, Elizabeth picked up the conversation right where they had left off. She was anxious to hear all the details of her fateful night.

"Papaw, I'm so sorry you got walloped in the head. I hope you haven't had any ill effects."

"I'm fine. You're the one we've been worried about," he said with tear-filled eyes.

"I'll be alright, Papaw," she said with a smile. "Getting back to what you said, though, I'm sure I heard gunshots while in my room," Elizabeth insisted.

"Oh, that must have been the thunder and lightning strikes," Nana said, as if that settled it. "Garrett was applying pressure to Papaw's cut while I gathered my medical kit. But before I got my kit opened, lightning had struck the tree by the barn causing it to splinter. Garrett and I ran back outside to see the tree on fire and part of it on the roof of the barn. Your Papaw was not about to stay inside with all of the excitement happening outside. So out he came."

Elizabeth's head started to hammer in earnest. She closed her eyes as she tried to visualize all that her Nana was telling. How could she have mistaken lightning and thunder as gunshots? . . . or maybe her grandmother wasn't telling the whole truth. Maybe she was smoothing over the real facts to protect Garrett.

"By the time you ran outside—in my white gown I might add—the barn was engulfed in flames, and Garrett was trying to pull Cinnamon to safety," Nana said.

Not to be outdone, Papaw picked up the story as Nana took a much needed breath. "Honestly, I don't know what possessed you that night, Lizzy. You ran full speed toward Garrett waving your ball bat as if you might knock him in the head. But right before you were within striking distance, you stopped. Then you did the oddest thing—you turned and ran into the darkness. Garrett yelled after you, but you never slowed down. "

Nana took over the tale while Papaw shook his head in bewilderment. "We had our hands full trying to empty the barn before it was totally overtaken by the fire. Papaw drove the tractor and four-wheeler out the backside of the barn while Garrett and I secured the horses safely in the corral. I was worried about you, dear, when you took off like that," Nana said while she stroked Elizabeth's hand.

All Elizabeth could do was stare wide-eyed at her Nana. Their story didn't match what Elizabeth remembered. "Where did I go? Who found me? And how did I end up here in the hospital?" she challenged.

"Slow down, sweetheart. I'm getting to that," Nana added. "When I went inside to call 911, your papaw and Garrett went to look for you."

"That's right," Papaw jumped in. "We split up and went searching for you. I yelled until I was hoarse but couldn't find you. Of course, the noisy storm hindered my search," Papaw lamented. "Garrett, however, had better luck. He found you under the tree where I built your tree house. You had a cut on your knee, and your feet were all bloodied from running barefoot through the underbrush. Not to mention, you had a goose egg on your head. Garrett covered you with his jacket and stayed by your side until the paramedics arrived."

"The paramedics never did figure out what caused the puncture wound in your shoulder," Nana added. "So they recorded that you were skewered by a tree limb even though the doctor said it was unlikely since the wound was perfectly round—almost as if an arrow pierced your skin," she said as an afterthought.

The mention of the arrow jolted Elizabeth's memory. "Where's Nicolas? Did he come with me?" Elizabeth asked anxiously.

"Who, dear?" Nana asked

"Nicolas! Where is he?" Elizabeth asked as she struggled to sit up. "He's my husb. . . my friend."

"No . . . no one by that name has been to see you, but Jonathan has called every day to check on you. He met us at the hospital the night we brought you in, but he said he couldn't stand to see you in such pain. He will return when you are better. Naturally, he wanted us to call him once you woke up."

"I never liked that boy," Papaw grumbled.

"Now, Papaw. He's practically family," Nana said tightlipped.

"Jonathan said he would come back when I was better?" Elizabeth asked with a raised brow. "More likely he would come back when I was more pleasing to the eye," she scoffed. Elizabeth realized that she had been settling in her relationships instead of reaching for the best God had planned for her—Nicolas. With Nicolas, Elizabeth had a man who put others' welfare in front of his own desires . . . a man who would die for her . . . not a politically correct man looking for a "trophy" wife like Jonathan. God had answered the question that had haunted her thoughts for two years—marry Jonathan or not? Not!

"Now, Liz, try not to become distressed over Jonathan's absence. I was relieved not to have him under foot," Papaw said. "That boy doesn't set well with me."

"Papaw!" Nana exclaimed. "That's enough talk."

"Nana, you and Papaw look worn down from this ordeal. Why don't you two go on home and get some rest? The nurses will take good care of me, and I promise not to give them trouble. I'll even stay in the bed and rest up, too." Not to mention she had some issues to resolve in her own mind.

"Are you sure?" Papaw asked.

Elizabeth's face softened at her Papaw's concerned voice. "Yes," she said softly. "I'm sure. I really appreciate both of you sticking close to me. I know I can always count on you two." What she didn't say, hung in the air—her own parents were unreliable.

"I don't think we should leave you. You just woke up. You might need us," Nana said.

"Please? I'll rest better knowing that you are at home in your own beds."

"Well, if you insist," Nana said. "Only if you promise to call us if you need us . . . no matter what time of night it might be."

"I promise." Elizabeth watched her aged grandparents gather up their belongings. From the vastness of all their possessions, it looked as if they had been sleeping in her room the past few days. What precious people God had blessed her with in her life. She was actually relieved when they walked out the door. Elizabeth had much to think about and a plan to form—how to get back to Nicolas!

37

During her second week of recovery, Elizabeth's grandparents had gone to the grocery store and left her to bask in the sunshine. She relaxed in the lawn chair when Garrett came for a visit.

"Hello, cousin," Garrett said tentatively. "May I join you?"

"Sure," Elizabeth said as she pointed to the vacant chair across from her. "I was wondering when you would show up." She gave Garrett a tiny smile to help soften her words. She no longer had ill feelings toward Garrett—in fact, she needed him.

Garrett sat down and smoothed his hands down his pant leg before crossing his feet at the ankles. Looking directly into Elizabeth's eyes, he said, "You scared us, Elizabeth."

"You know, Garrett, I didn't plan any of this. It was merely an accident that God helped me survive." Giggling slightly, she added, "No hard feelings for the bat thing?"

Garrett visibly relaxed. "Nah, no hard feelings. But I must say you looked like a crazy woman when you waved that ball bat at me. What was going through your head? " he asked. Elizabeth briefly closed her eyes before looking back at Garrett. "Garrett, I have something unusual to tell you. Now, I don't want you to make any snap judgments until you hear the whole story. Okay?"

Garrett never lost eye contact as he steepled his fingers under his chin. Tilting his head one way and then another, Garrett contemplated a moment before responding. "I'll do my best, but I can't guarantee it," he said with a grin. "What's up?"

Elizabeth began by restating all that her Nana and Papaw had said transpired the night of the storm and her accident. She watched as Garrett shook his head in agreement at certain key facts as she plodded through the tale. She even explained that she thought he was trying to kill her grandparents—hence the ball bat episode. However, when she got to the part where she ran to her tree house, Elizabeth decided to tell Garrett her side of the story.

"When I reached the swinging rope, I clawed my way up to the first limb and secured the rope so you wouldn't see it."

"What? No, that's not how it happened. I found you lying in the grass," he said.

Elizabeth held up her hand to stop him from further comment. "Please, let me finish. It's quite a tale, and I need you to be an attentive listener. You mustn't miss any details. It's very important."

"Fine. I'll try to be quiet," he agreed.

"Once I climbed to the center of my tree house, I curled up and kept praying for God to protect Nana and Papaw and help us all out of this predicament. I eventually fell asleep. Now this is where it gets a bit . . . shall we say . . . bizarre? Anyway, when I woke up, I was lying face down in the grass; but I was in Medieval England." Before she could continue, Garrett exploded.

"That's crazy!" Garrett jumped up from his chair and began pacing around the chairs. "That knock on your head has really addled your brain!"

Elizabeth allowed a sigh to escape her parted lips. "Garrett, you said you would listen."

After several minutes of stomping around, he plopped back down into his chair. "Let me hear the rest of your story . . . not that I'm going to believe it, but I'll listen," he said disgruntled.

"Thank you," she whispered. Elizabeth took a deep breath and released it slowly while her mind raced. She didn't want Garrett to write her off as completely screwy . . . so, how much to tell?

Elizabeth decided to tell the highlights of her adventure and leave out the details. She wanted to give Garrett just enough information for him to agree to aid her in her plan—she wouldn't succeed without his help.

By the time Garrett had heard Elizabeth's saga, he voiced his concern for her mental stability but had agreed to help execute her future plan. She had appealed to his love of the farm to get him to check on Nana and Papaw several times a week now that Papaw was frailer. Both Elizabeth and Garrett decided to convince Nana to allow them to have four meals a week brought in so she would rarely have to cook or go grocery shopping. Garrett even expressed an interest in moving to the farm and commuting to his law office three days a week. Since he wasn't married, moving in with his grandparents wouldn't be a hardship for him—temporarily anyway.

Naturally, Garrett wanted to talk with his parents before implementing any of their ideas. Garrett's mother, Sylvia, was the daughter of Nana and Papaw. Sylvia loved her parents and would want to be in on the process of seeing to their care. Elizabeth's father, Kyle, was their son. However, Elizabeth had no intention of contacting her parents since they were self-absorbed, and they didn't even check on Elizabeth's grandparents.

After much debate on the upcoming plans, Garrett finally left. Elizabeth was comforted knowing that Garrett would watch over her sweet Nana and Papaw in her absence. Now . . . on with her preparations for her future.

* * *

Elizabeth had wasted no time in making arrangements to sublease her apartment to her friend, Lacy. Unfortunately, Lacy kept questioning Elizabeth's odd behavior; so Elizabeth had explained that she was in love with a man from England and hoped to join him there. Since Lacy was in love with Alex, she totally understood Elizabeth's need to be close to her man. By the time of Lacy's marriage, the lease would be up; and Lacy agreed to move the furniture out. What items Lacy didn't want to keep were to be sold or given away. Elizabeth had no intention of returning to claim anything. Elizabeth decided to leave no forwarding address for her mail since she didn't want anything going to the farm and upsetting her grandparents in case she had vanished.

Shopping for her trip was exciting, as well as terrifying. First on her list was a dark green or brown hiking backpack. It couldn't have any snaps or zippers or Velcro—only buckles. The first item she bought to fill her new backpack was chocolate candy bars. A girl always needed her chocolate. Then she went on to purchase a first aid kit, a book on natural remedies with herbs, a few toothbrushes, floss, and a mirage of other items that couldn't be found in Medieval England. As she went about gathering her items, her mind would begin to wander. What if her plan didn't work? What if she was never able to return to Nicolas? When those questions intruded on her thoughts, she quickly dismissed them. No need worrying over what she couldn't control. Right?

Elizabeth wasted no time in contacting old friends and arranging luncheons. She had great fun laughing and reminiscing—not wanting it to end. Of course, Elizabeth made sure to capture each of their smiles with a snapshot that would have to last her a lifetime. The majority of her time, however, was spent on the farm. She cooked with her Nana, fed the animals with her Papaw and rode Cinnamon around the ranch hoping to memorize every aspect of her life. She soaked up the love of her grandparents like water on parched soil.

All too soon Elizabeth's preparations were complete. If she made a successful trip back in time, Garrett had the information needed to look her up in the history book. Elizabeth had refused to look for herself . . . she was afraid her name might be missing . . . that Nicolas might have another wife listed in the book. She held out hope that her name would appear as the wife to Nicolas—well Isabelle, at least. Garrett was then to explain everything to Nana and Papaw; and of course, to her own parents if they came looking for her. In any event, she wrote a personal letter to each family member that she would leave on her bed at the farm. She certainly didn't want anyone grieving over her disappearance. Now the hard part—to say her good-byes.

What she hoped would be her last night at the farm, Elizabeth bounded down the stairs to her grandparents' den. Naturally, both Nana and Papaw were sitting in their respective chairs. With her arthritic hands, Nana was knitting a new scarf for Papaw to wear during the winter. Papaw was stretched out in his easy chair watching an old comedy movie. There was a small fire in the fireplace to ward off the autumn chill in the air. The fire was a reminder to Elizabeth that many weeks had passed in the present time making her wonder how much time had elapsed for Nicolas. Would he still be waiting for her? Had another woman taken her place? Shaking her head to dispel any negative thoughts, she sat down at her Nana's feet.

Nana reached over and brushed her hand down Elizabeth's hair—smoothing her wayward curls. "It's so good to see you smiling after these many weeks of recovery. I feel like I can breathe a sigh of relief now that you are better."

Elizabeth laid her head in Nana's lap, basking in the affection. "Yes, Nana. I am completely healed and very happy. Did I tell you I had met a young man during my travels?"

"No, dear, I don't recall your mentioning anyone. What's his name?"

Before Elizabeth could answer, Papaw chimed in, "Good. Does that mean you're getting rid of that no-good Jonathan?"

"Papaw!" Nana exclaimed in exasperation.

"It's okay, Nana. Papaw is right. Jonathan was not the man for me."

"Humph," Papaw exhaled.

"Quiet, Papaw, let us hear about her new beau."

Elizabeth was absorbing this sweet interchange and putting every aspect of it to memory, so she could pull it out when she longed for home. "Well, his name is Nicolas. You would like him, Papaw. He's extremely muscular and strong enough to protect me which he does rather often. Nicolas also puts others' welfare before himself—he is very gallant. I hope he will pursue our relationship when he learns I'm free of Jonathan."

"He sounds quite dreamy," Nana purred.

Papaw rolled his eyes at Nana's comment which made Elizabeth smile. "We had many opportunities where I saw his good qualities in action. He is a Godly man, too, Papaw. I knew that would interest you since Jonathan is lacking in that area."

"I'm glad to hear it, Lizzy. Having a Godly man is your first priority in a husband."

"Yes, I know that to be true, too. There's only one problem?"

"What's that, honey?" Nana asked as she laid aside her knitting.

"He lives in England."

"Oh, my! England is quite far." After a moment's pause, Nana continued, "But if he's the one God has picked out for you, it will all work out. I've never been to England but would love to have a reason to visit."

"Oh, Nana, that means so much to me. I had hoped you would be happy for me."

"Of course, we're happy for you, Lizzy. Nana is right; God will work out all the details if Nicolas is the man for you," Papaw said.

Nana laid aside her knitting and walked over to the bookcase. She pulled down an old, frayed photo album and brought it over to the couch. Patting the place next to her, she said, "Come join me, Elizabeth. I want to show you some of the pictures of our courtship. Your Papaw was quite a dashing young man."

"Aww, she doesn't want to see those old pictures of us," Papaw said.

"Yes, I do, Papaw." Gazing at the way Nana ran her hand over the binder, Elizabeth knew this was very special to her grandparents. "I don't think I've ever seen this photo album before."

"Well, I try not to bore everyone with these old pictures, but you're different. I know how much old family pictures mean to you."

"Old? More like ancient," Papaw chimed in with a grin directed at Nana.

"Elizabeth has always been interested in our family history, haven't you, dear?"

"Absolutely. More than you can imagine. Please, tell me all about your dating days."

Nana and, eventually Papaw, both reminisced about days long since passed—their first date . . . their first kiss . . . the day Papaw had proposed. As Elizabeth examined each picture, Nana told the story attached to it. With each story told, Elizabeth gathered more facts about her family and her beloved grandparents. "Do you have an extra picture I could have to carry with me?" Elizabeth asked.

"Certainly, dear. Here, take this one of us on our wedding day. I have several of these."

Nana pulled the picture from the album and handed it to Elizabeth. Seeing the wedding picture made Elizabeth yearn for Nicolas, but at the same time, long to remain here with her family. Her heart squeezed inside her chest as she realized that she couldn't have both this side of heaven. Just when her eyes misted from her torment, Papaw spoke up.

"All of this talk about love has worn me out. I think it's our bedtime." Papaw eased out of his chair and held out his hand to his wife. "Come on, momma, snuggle time."

Elizabeth saw her Nana's face light up. Years washed away from her face as they regarded one another with affection. No words needed to be spoken—love radiated from their eyes. "I think I might turn in early as well. I don't feel as strong as I did before my accident," Elizabeth said. She hugged and kissed Nana and then Papaw. "Your love and support means so much to me. I adore you both to the moon and back," Elizabeth said playfully.

"Oh, honey, we love you, too. Sleep well," Nana said as she patted Elizabeth's cheek.

Elizabeth stood in the middle of the room as she watched them shuffle hand-in-hand out of sight. She breathed deeply of the aroma Nana had left behind—her favorite perfume. Her eyes roamed around the room capturing every detail like a camera. Once the lights were out, Elizabeth turned to see the low, glowing flames flickering around the room. Her eyes filled with tears as a wave of nostalgia washed over her. No matter where she ended up, she would never forget this night.

* * *

"Nicolas, how many times will you make this trip?" Phillip asked.

Nicolas continued to strap on his belt and sword. "Until my bride comes back to me," he snapped.

Phillip's loud huff echoed off the stone wall. "It has been months since she disappeared from your arms. Did you ever entertain the thought that she might not reappear?"

Nicolas spun around to face Phillip with a scowl on his face. "Don't ever . . . say that . . . to me . . . again," he growled. "She will return." Nicolas grabbed his cloak and stomped from the room. *Never return indeed! She has to come back to me or . . . or I will cease to live!*

Nicolas stormed out of the castle and mounted his horse that Thomas held at ready. Thomas, Braden, Robert, and Hastings had accompanied Nicolas on this particular journey every day since Isabelle had vanished into the night. They were the only ones who knew the true events of that fateful night. Well, Phillip was also privy to that morsel of information. Yet none of them dared to question Nicolas's judgment on making what could be considered a useless outing. Every morning they all left before sunrise and returned home after nightfall. Provisions of food were always ready for them thanks to Collette's supervision in the kitchens.

The horses snorted puffs of frosty air as they flung their heads up and down in readiness. The cold air of winter was now upon them. It wouldn't be long before snow covered the area—all the more reason for Nicolas's urgency. He couldn't endure the thought of his beloved being stranded out in the elements of England's harsh winter weather. When she had left, she had been in a weakened condition. Caught out in this weather would surely push her into the grave.

Nicolas had told the castle folk that Isabelle had gone to visit her relatives in another country. Of course, he didn't elaborate nor would he allow any probing questions. The first few weeks, Nicolas had ridden out with great expectations. Now . . . he spent his ride in silent prayer for his wife and her wellbeing. Each new day brought more uncertainty and despair. He didn't need Phillip to remind him of an undesirable outcome. He lived it each day!

As was his custom, Nicolas halted a short distance from the infamous tree while Thomas and Robert checked their surroundings. When no evidence was found of human activity, they each went to a designated spot to wait out the day. Usually, Nicolas rode up and down the road at a slow pace scanning the area. He didn't want to miss any indication that Isabelle might be close at hand.

On this day, he was feeling unusually despondent. He trotted around the bend in the road to be out of the sight of his men. Looking heavenward he called out to the only One who could help him. "God, this is your servant, Nicolas. I beseech You on behalf of my beloved, Isabelle. She has been taken from me, and I don't know where to find her. Please, Lord of the universe and creator of all things, if it be Your will, please, send my Isabelle back to me. As it says in Your Word, 'Search me, O God, and know my heart; try me, and know my anxieties . . .'" Tears of sorrow escaped their boundaries as they flowed unchecked down his cheeks. He hung his head in misery. "I am incomplete without her," he whispered. Sitting still in his saddle, he listened for God's voice.

"*. . . Let not your heart be troubled, neither let it be afraid.*" As Nicolas listened to God, a current of peace flowed through his body and calmed his soul. Nicolas could be at peace knowing that God was in control and would protect Isabelle. However, his fear was that it was not in God's will for her to return to his side. If that were the case, then living each day would truly be a struggle for him—not something he felt he could bear.

Nicolas wiped away his tears and squared up his shoulders as he rode back toward the tree. When he rounded the bend in the road, he pulled his horse up short. There . . . leaning against the tree . . . was Isabelle? The woman was like a vision—dressed in white! His heart skipped a beat—his hands trembled. Was he only seeing what he wanted to see? Was it really her? If he approached, would she disappear?

Nicolas nudged his horse forward until he was within touching distance of who he hoped was his wife; his heart now beat double time. Peering down at her, he said in a controlled voice, "You have been away overlong, wife. Are you hardy and well? What say you?"

"I have much to say, but for now I say get down here—I'm freezing!"

Upon hearing that familiar bossy voice, all control left Nicolas as he jumped from his horse and engulfed his wife in his arms. She was wrapped within his cloak in a tight embrace before she had time to draw another breath. "Oh, Isabelle, I thought you were a figment of my imagination." He reared back to look into her eyes. "But you're not!" Squeezing her close to his heart he said, "I had almost given up hope of ever seeing you again."

She laughed with delight as he kissed her all over her face and neck until she grabbed his face between her cold hands. "Stop. Let me look at you." She searched his eyes before saying, "Oh, Nicolas, I have missed you terribly . . . and have so much to tell you." He allowed her to pull him close for a slow, passionate kiss that left his head spinning. When they surfaced for air, Elizabeth whispered, "Take me home."

That's all Nicolas needed to hear. He shouted for his men as he mounted his horse and pulled Elizabeth into his arms. It took only a few minutes for his men to appear and shout joyful greetings to their lady. Elizabeth was happy to see each of the men, but she had other things on her mind. She pulled Nicolas close and whispered in his ear. No one but Nicolas was privy to her words, but they caused a stir in Nicolas. He set out for home at a gallop with his Isabelle wrapped in a snug embrace.

With her face buried under his cloak for protection, Nicolas gloried in her muffled words. She spoke with such excitement as she told that her family were all alive and well. Nicolas didn't comprehend all that she said, but he knew the details would be sorted out at a later time—like what did she carry in her pack? For now, he was just pleased to hear her voice floating into the wind—swirling all around him. The warmth of her body next to his was exhilarating and, at the same time, soothing to his soul.

He did remember to offer up his thanks to his Lord. *Oh Lord, my Lord, how majestic is Your name above the earth. You are my helper and my protector. Unto You I lifted my voice and You heard my cry. I am exceedingly and abundantly overjoyed with Your answer. Thank You for the return of my Isabelle whom I love with abandon.* Before Nicolas could finish his prayer of thanksgiving, his wife's tiny hand touched his whiskered face—drawing his attention back to her.

"When we have children, I would like to name our first son after my grandfather and our first daughter after my grandmother. Of course, only if the names will fit within your family heritage," Elizabeth murmured seductively.

Her words caused a stirring deep in his spirit. Primarily, her declaration meant she would abide with him as his wife for his lifetime. She had chosen him and this place in time over her previous existence. He was humbled; yet, the thoughts of children caused a hot flush of desire to course through his body. He was anxious to return home with his bride and snuggle her close in his bed tonight and forevermore . . . the chopping down of the tree would have to wait!

Epilogue

Garrett drove toward his grandparent's farm with dual emotions churning through him—eagerness and dread. Would Elizabeth still be there? Since there had been a terrible thunderstorm the previous night, did that mean she traveled back to her Nicolas? Garrett had found some facts similar to those he heard from Elizabeth at a historical website last night but was reluctant to believe it. It could have been a coincidence. The suspense made him speed on his way.

He pulled up beside Elizabeth's convertible parked in the circular driveway at the farm. It took all of Garrett's control to act naturally and not go barreling inside the house and up to Elizabeth's bedroom. He found Nana and Papaw having eggs and biscuits as they read their newspaper.

"Good morning," Garrett said as he entered the kitchen. "I see you both weathered that bad storm last night with no ill effects this time."

"That downpour wasn't as bad as our last one. But we do have one fatality from this tempest," Papaw said.

Garrett's brows shot straight to his hairline. "Oh, what was that, Papaw?"

"Lizzy's special tree was struck by lightning and split right down the middle. You know the one that had her tree house in it?"

"Uh, oh, what did she say about that?"

"We haven't told her yet. Actually, we were surprised that she slept through that uproar last night. She's usually a light sleeper," Papaw said.

"I think she's worn out from all her gallivanting around lately. She has been meeting with her friends for lunch and then doing a lot of shopping the last couple of weeks. It's probably been too much for her after being in the hospital and everything," Nana remarked.

"I'll go wake her for you," Garrett offered with a devilish grin.

"Now, Garrett, I'm not sure she would welcome that," Nana said.

"If she wants any breakfast, she had better get up anyway. Go ahead, Garrett. You have my permission," Papaw laughed.

"Oh, you boys. Elizabeth can be a bit grumpy when she first wakes up, especially if she's awakened by one of you!" Nana scolded.

Garrett barely heard Nana's words as he raced up the stairs. He knocked on Elizabeth's door and waited only a moment before barging in the room. It was empty! Her bed was neatly made and there were several envelopes lying on her pillows addressed to different family members. With a trembling hand, Garrett picked up the one with his name on it and began to read:

Dear Garrett,

If you're reading this letter then know that I am ecstatic—I have made it back to Nicolas! Please don't be sad because I am exactly where I want to be. My only regret is not being able to take Nana and Papaw with me, but I was afraid they were too frail to live in this time period. Remember I am counting on you to break the news to our grandparents gently. Please convey my excitement of marrying Nicolas and how much I love them. Give them their letters and do whatever it takes so they won't file a missing person's report!

I think your best defense is to get on your computer and look me up. Don't forget; my name could be any combination of: Elizabeth, Isabelle, or Emma. But my last name should be

Fairwick! Plus I hope to convince Nicolas to name some of our children after Nana and Papaw. So look for their names as well.

Watch after Nana and Papaw and take care of yourself. Thank you for being my partner in this great adventure! I love you, Elizabeth.

Garrett plopped down on the bed. It had really happened! Somehow his cousin had traveled back in history to marry Lord Nicolas Fairwick of Fairwick Castle in England. Wow! Unbelievable! A thin line of perspiration formed above his lip and along his hairline. How was he ever going to convince his grandparents of this preposterous occurrence? Why had he agreed to go along with her scatterbrained idea anyway?

His descent down the stairs was much slower than his previous ascent. He was shaking with fear and trepidation. It was not a pleasant sight when Nana got riled up about one of her *babies*. Alone, Garrett walked into the kitchen. Nana was cleaning up their dishes while Papaw continued reading the sports section of the paper.

Nana turned from the sink and asked, "Heavens, Garrett, you look like you've seen a ghost. Was Elizabeth that terrifying?"

"No, ma'am," he whispered. "Come and sit down, Nana. There is something rather important I need to discuss with both of you."

Nana dried her hands on the towel. "Is anything wrong with Elizabeth?" she asked concerned as she looked toward the stairs.

"No, there is nothing wrong with her. In fact, she is quite overjoyed with the recent events in her life." Garrett began telling Elizabeth's story as carefully as he could to keep from upsetting his grandparents. It didn't take long before they both charged up the stairs to see for themselves. While they were gone, Garrett brought his computer up to the previous site he had found with all of Elizabeth's information.

Nana and Papaw returned to the kitchen pale with each one holding an envelope in his or her hand. Garrett was worried about their health and hoped he could convey the essential details exactly as to Elizabeth's wishes. She assured him if he followed her plan, their grandparents would understand and be pleased with her journey. He certainly hoped she was right.

"Why don't you each read your letters from Elizabeth, and then we'll look at some interesting data I have on the computer." It was almost painful as Garrett watched the emotions pass across their faces. He saw shock, disbelief, joy, and then confusion. Garrett sat quietly until they both were finished reading. Papaw slowly laid his letter aside and scrubbed his face with his hands. Nana held her letter tightly in her hand as she peered up with misty eyes.

"Garrett?" Nana said softly. "What do you know about this?"

"Everything you read has already come to pass. She went to England last night during the storm."

"By way of her tree house?" Papaw asked.

"Yes. The tree house was the catalyst by which she was transported. I wasn't surprised when you told me that something happened to that tree during the recent thunderstorm. It seemed fitting. She won't be back."

"Oh, dear," Nana said with her hand covering her heart. "This is such an unbelievable tale," she uttered as she turned distressed eyes toward Papaw.

Papaw reached across the table and enclosed Nana's hand with his own. After giving her a reassuring squeeze, he turned his attention back to Garrett and asked, "Is our Lizzy happy?"

"Come close and let me show you." Garrett turned his computer around so his grandparents could see the screen that contained the family crest of the Fairwicks of England. "This is the crest of Elizabeth's family."

"Oh, my. That looks quite impressive," Nana said in awe.

"Wait until you read about your granddaughter." Garrett scrolled down until he came to the paragraph that mentioned his cousin. "Read that area right there," Garrett suggested.

"Oh! She named two of her children after me and papaw—William and Anne. It really is her!" Nana exclaimed as she looked at Garrett with eyes swimming in tears.

"I couldn't be happier for our sweet Lizzy," Papaw said as he wiped his eyes. "She always did like to be dramatic, and I would have expected no less from her," he chuckled. Papaw stood and pulled Nana to her feet. "Come here, momma." Papaw tugged her into a loving embrace. "Don't worry, sweetheart. She will be all right. All I can say is look out medieval period." Then they both laughed through their tears.

Garrett looked away to give his grandparents privacy and re-read Elizabeth's history.

Lord Nicolas Henry Fairwick of Fairwick Castle married Isabelle Elizabeth Emma Andrews of Lexington. They moved from Fairwick Castle in 1621 when Lord Fairwick agreed to revive Sanddown Castle on the coast. It was there that Lord Fairwick supervised all incoming and outgoing coastal ships. They had seven surviving children: William, Anne, Henry, George, Grace, Christopher, and Joan. Interesting tidbit: Lord Nicolas Fairwick often called his bride, Lizzy.

DISCUSSION QUESTIONS

ELIZABETH

1. How could Elizabeth improve her handling the disagreement with Jonathan?

2. In the first chapter what is Elizabeth's strongest personality trait?

    Is it positive or negative? How did this trait help her later in the book?

3. How did Elizabeth's presence at the castle affect the Fairwick family?

4. Explain how prayer and scripture sustained Elizabeth.

5. Even though this book is fiction, what is God's ultimate goal for Elizabeth?

NICOLAS

1. Can you identify characteristics that might indicate that Nicolas has a dysfunctional family?

2. In what ways did the tragic death of Nicolas's mother shape his life?

3. What are Nicolas's most redeeming qualities?

4. How did Nicolas's attitude change over the course of the book?

5. What specific events in the novel led to Nicolas's realization of God's love for him?

**Teresa Smyser** lives in Northern Alabama with her minister husband and their deaf cat, Spock. They have two married children and one grandson. She graduated from Eastern Kentucky University and now works part-time from home as an accountant and divides the rest of her time between family, friends, church activities and writing. Teresa's prayer is that not only will her novels entertain, but they will point people to the love and the hope found in her Lord and Savior, Jesus Christ.

For more information about Teresa and her books, visit her on www.facebook.com/teresasmyser

She loves hearing from her readers. Send questions or comments to authorsmys@gmail.com

If you enjoyed

THE WARRIOR
& LADY REBEL

then read:

Warrior Bride Series: **Book 2**
Find out what happens to Brigette

COMING 2016